C000109264

A
SONG
FOR
NIGHTFALL

ALEXANDER LINTON

Copyright © 2023 Alexander Linton
All rights reserved

Alexander Linton has asserted the right to be identified as the Author
of the Work in accordance with the Copyright, Designs and Patents Act
1988

All rights are reserved. No part of this publication may be reproduced, stored
in a retrieval system, or transmitted in any form or by any means without
prior written permission of the author, nor may it be otherwise circulated
in any form of binding or cover other than that in which it is published

All characters in this publication are fictional and any resemblance to real
persons, living or dead, is coincidental

www.alexander-linton.com

To Joshua, Jasmine, Sophie and Sienna

With all my love

1

...and to those who shall inevitably yearn for the forbidden; we pray you may never earn your share of the wounds we who forbade it are burdened. Heed our solemn declaration, lest you discover the forbidden to be rarely so without reason.

Excerpt from *The Birth of the Hominum*
Farro Zan Me
Village Chief of the Hominum Tribe
Generation of Farro
First Recorded Generation

P ale dusk light paved the forest floor in broken pieces. The pods on the trees were nearly full and bursting, close to blooming. Lia and Kai Ro walked among them with their best guile.

Kai savoured the joy of witnessing the pods in this state, in knowing that no other in the tribe dared see it for themselves. He and Lia often spoke of the sonnets their descendants may one day share with great cheer; sonnets of their daring to tread the forbidden, while those who cowered from it when bade to would not be mentioned in any page. But as for who would care to write tales such as siblings finding flowers *nearly* in bloom before going home with nought but blistered feet, they did not care to consider.

Their daring steps into the forbidden were often minuscule and mildly satisfying, and that was often enough for them.

They had said *one more* for hours, with assurance that each would be the last on their hunt this dayfall. Lia Ro said it once more at the sight of the chubby rabbit merrily gathering its stock for nightfall.

Their quivers were finally close to empty, with nothing to show for all their labour but calluses on their hands and groaning from their bellies. To face the elders empty-handed late to the ignition of the ignis; Kai Ro could scarcely bear the thought. A lone rabbit would offer little but a slither of conciliation in the form of a final feast of meat caught with their own hands, before what would be another long drought without.

Kai took the last of his arrows from his quiver and aimed at the rabbit. It was by no means majestic, but it was sturdy enough to last many a hunt unscathed. Kai wished it had earned its ambitious name of *Slayer*, but the bow had so far slain only wind and had punctured only dirt for all its vigour.

The rabbit was fully invested in whatever it noisily chomped on. Kai peaked up from behind the moss-ridden rock and loosed the arrow from his fingers with a wisp. It predictably missed its target. By far. By so far that the rabbit did not so much as flinch, but just frowned in their direction.

Lia howled with laughter for what must have been the tenth time this hunt. Only then did the rabbit take off startled, with all the food stock it could hold in its paws. Kai sighed and slumped onto the rock face, staring down at his sister who held her stomach in pain.

'It's not *that* funny,' Kai said with a huff.

'It is,' Lia said, with a gasp for breath. 'Oh, how hard you try, little Orphan-Star.'

'You haven't hit anything either,' Kai said.

'My arrows at least scare them a little,' she rebuked.

Kai just glared, which made her break into laughter again. He kicked her and sheathed his bow onto his back. He felt quite low with the last of his arrows spent and lamented over all that wasted labour and lost sleep spent sharpening branches into the sticks with pointed tips, which they called arrows.

'How many do you have,' Kai asked when Lia finally spent the air in her belly.

'Two, which I'd prefer to save.' She skipped along the dirt track, clearly in higher spirits than he. The hunt was fun, he supposed, but short-lived, as usual.

'And still, we didn't see any purpura,' Kai said. 'No glowing flowers. Just closed pods, as usual.'

Lia didn't respond. They walked in silence for a time. The evening crickets had grown quiet in their hibernation, as that rabbit and the other animals of the Ameyali forest soon would.

Kai couldn't help himself. 'When *will* we see them for ourselves?'

'Who knows,' Lia said. 'Ask me again when you eat a meal you kill with your own bow. At this rate, that'll be *never*.'

Kai ignored the joke. His mind's eye was already invested in the wonders of the forest he longed to see. One day, they would be strong and brave enough for the forbidden. *Soon,* Kai assured himself. *Next dayfall, we'll be hunting our dinners with our own hands.*

The shattered sunlight grew paler the further they walked. They could already see the red ignis flame dancing atop the elders' tipi in their village beyond the woods. All sure signs that dayfall was already over and that the genesis of their nightfall would be a bitter one.

'So,' Lia said. 'Flame duty? Tipi cleaning? Perhaps they'll have us dumping the waste buckets if Omaraa Zan is feeling cruel.'

'Nothing would be worse than last nightfall.'

'Omaraa Zan's mother? You had to remind me.' Lia laughed. 'Those crusty feet still haunt me in my sleep.'

Kai snorted with laughter himself. 'Watching you massage them every cycle was what got me through that nightfall.'

'*Every* cycle is right. I haven't forgotten; you were never asked, and you never offered, no matter how I begged.'

'You just have the hands for it.' Kai's laughter soon quietened. 'We maybe shouldn't laugh about her,' he said. 'She's dead now.'

'We certainly should. It's not like she cares.' Kai shook his head but couldn't help grinning with incredulity, as was often so when Lia's mood grew coarse. 'Really,' she continued. 'All that's left of her is those memories now. We should laugh at them all we want, or they'll be lost too, right?'

Kai pondered this as they left the last tree of Ameyali forest behind them and entered the dying but fragrant field of lavender. It was contrary to tribe etiquette to speak mockingly of the dead, but it brought Kai some joy to do so this time. He decided that Lia had the right of it. It was surely why she was still regarded so favourably by the elders; because, despite the misfortune that her *curious* nature unfailingly caused, she was discerning with it.

Kai had not yet earned the same respect she had, nor could he speak with the clarity that she could. That was at the core of why he always took his sister's words to heart; that others might too take his own words to heart someday.

They soon approached the village, where the gates lorded over them with sharp wood at their peak. Kai often marvelled at how these mere walls and gates were able to thwart whatever dangers the Ameyali Forest held in nightfall. It was two nightfalls ago that Ogmul told him it was instead the torchlight along the walls that protected the tribe. Kai still knew not how or why this could be true and he found that few in the village did. The elders no doubt knew best and Kai intended to ask them whenever he was next in their good graces.

Lia was still in high spirits, even as they were sighted by the gatekeeper, who looked both stern and smug leaning against the open gates.

'Really?' Charaa said. '*Really*, you stupid brats?'

Lia shot him a smile back. Kai tried to smile too, but he dreaded what awaited beyond those gates too much to do more than contort his lips.

'Are you surprised?' Lia said with a healthy bit of sass.

'That you disregarded the same tenet which you disregard every other nightfall? No. What surprises me is how you two can be so stupid so consistently.'

'We made it back, as we always do.'

'You barely did. You pushed it this time and I mean it. If I hadn't ignored the ignis myself, the gates would have been locked, with or without you. So no, you didn't make it back in time at all.'

Some well-hidden shame washed over Lia's face. 'Thank you, then.'

'Don't bother. They'll be angrier than usual, so it might be that you'd have been better off in the forest.' Charaa gave them a reassuring smile mixed with pity.

Kai felt little relief but great sadness being home again as Charaa barred the gates behind them, as a final assurance that another nightfall would soon begin, spent in the monotonous safety of the Ameyali Village walls and torchlight.

Kai gave one last longing gaze to the forest beyond the fields before the gates closed and marked the end of dayfall. *One day,* he assured himself in the same vigorous tone as every dusk.

*

Charaa was neither wrong nor exaggerating. Kai could not remember a time the elders had been quite so furious. None spoke, as they glared with vitriol toward him and Lia stood in the centre of the chamber. Lia held Kai tightly by the hand and he felt her tremble; another disconcerting rarity.

Kai was taken by the deep red shade of Miire Zin Fa's face, who tapped her stool rhythmically with her fingers. He imagined absolute silence would have been less terrifying than this.

Lia couldn't let it linger any longer. 'We're both--' she started.

'No,' an elder hissed; one whose name Kai could never remember, as he was rarely seen outside this chamber and rarer still engaged in conversation. 'You will not speak first, Lia Ro.'

'Do you not care for the pain you cause this village, children,' Miire Zin Fa said, who could barely keep from shouting. Her voice was already hoarse with strain. 'Are you so determined to endanger us?'

'No, Zin Fa,' Lia instinctively replied.

'Then why do you do so? The gates were left open after the ignis was lighted, waiting for *you*. Nightfall will be upon us at any moment and the village would have had its gates open to it, had we waited any longer.'

'It's the torches that protect the village,' Kai mumbled, too loudly and against his better judgement.

Miire Zin's face grew redder still. 'Boy, are you truly so--?'

'We were merely caught up in the hunt,' Lia hurriedly said. 'Forgive us. We never intended to endanger anyone.'

'You never do intend it,' Poruus Zin Ka said. 'But do you recall, young Lia, that you have said those very words at every other hearing, with every other dusk? Or do you simply not care for honest remorse?' Kai rarely heard Poruus Zin speak either and each time he did, he found his monotone voice just as grating as the last, like the voice of a goat trapped in a man's body.

'We pray that our words will reach you well,' the quiet elder said. 'As we seem to every dusk. But you show time and again that they never do and never will.'

'We always take your words to heart, Zin…' Lia trailed off and shot Kai a look. She almost smiled at the blank face Kai met her with, and Kai was just about tactful enough to not dare smirk.

'*Zin Or* speaks truly,' Omaraa Zan Ri said after too long a moment. 'You once again have wilfully endangered the lives of your tribe. And for what purpose? Merely to enjoy your hunt?'

Kai caught Lia's nervous eye. The elders had a right to anger, but it felt like more than that filled the air in the chamber. Kai could *feel* the bile in every one of their words.

'We truly are sorry,' Lia said again, with far more earnestness. Chief Omaraa was one of the few elders Lia truly liked. Omaraa Zan's anger on this cycle would be one that touched Lia the most. 'I know we always say this, but we won't allow this to--'

'*We* say what, Lia Ro?' Miire Zin said, her voice louder still. 'We hear these words only from *your* mouth.'

'Let us not interrupt when she is speaking,' Omaraa Zan said. 'This is a hearing for them, not for us.'

Miire Zin glared but grew a little meeker for the moment. 'Go on, Lia.'

'We won't allow this to happen again,' she said. 'We promise we'll be more mindful of the village's safety in future.'

'Of course,' Omaraa Zan said. 'Are you finished?' Lia meekly nodded. 'And do you have anything to add, Kai Ro?' He shook his head in the same defeated fashion. 'You correctly say this will not happen again, Lia. It has become something of a tradition for us to name your punishment at the end of this hearing, but we will learn well from the past this time. We know that the threat of labour does little to dissuade either of you or teach you anything of responsibility to your tribe. We have been treating you like children for too long and that was our mistake.'

Kai furrowed his brow. This was *very* different. He had grown quite fond of such treatment and had learned to capitalise on the lack of responsibility it came with. Kai sensed now, as much as Lia did, that those days were soon to prematurely end.

'So, we promise you,' the chief continued. 'Should the time *ever* come again that you are outside the village walls after the ignis has been ignited, you will not be permitted back through the village gates until nightfall passes, however long that nightfall may be.'

Lia gasped despite herself. 'Omaraa Zan?'

'And,' the chief continued, ever mild in tone. 'Seeing as we have just had your assurance that this will be the last time, we know that this will not be a problem for either of you, will it?'

Neither Kai nor Lia answered for a long moment, as they both struggled to form the word on their lips. They each knew very well what their hesitancy meant, and they hoped that the elders did not.

'No,' Lia finally said, through gritted teeth.

'I thought not,' Omaraa Zan said. 'And I am happy to hear it.'

The rest of the hearing followed the same tired pattern it always did. Poruus Zin Ka read some old quotes of old generations, then followed with a summary of *The Tale of Waya*; all of which Lia and Kai could recite word for word. They had to hear every word again until they were finally permitted to leave.

There was another unprecedented aspect to that hearing, Kai realised upon leaving their tipi into the cool dusk air; they had been given no punishment for their disobedience. Kai could not tell whether this change gave him relief or dread. He felt somewhat lost already, acquainted as he had become with the routine of harsh nightfalls and angry elders.

He, however, already knew how they would spend the nightfall after this one, just as he knew during every guilt-heavy walk home after a hearing.

The Ameyali forest was truly mesmerising at the closure of dayfall and so easily drew the two siblings into imagining the sense of freedom that would come when they finally dared cross the forbidden and set their eyes on the unknown.

Come what may, he and Lia would enjoy the taste of forbidden freedom again.

2

Smile in earnest...with your fire spent
May the dust of a life well-loved our maker lent
Feed the ones you leave from her boundless might
And be our beacon through the darkest nights

Excerpt from the *Hominum Tribe Burial Song*
by Moro Ki
Generation of Osas
Second Recorded Generation

The air was harsh enough to chill through flesh and bone on the first cycle of nightfall. The moon was fuller and brighter than Kai ever recalled. He sat staring up at the night sky, huddled with his sister at the fire beside their tipi and grumpy with hunger. They waited impatiently for the cooks to deliver what would be one of their last meals with any flavour to speak of, until next dayfall.

Boiled rabbit stew arrived steaming in the kindly lady's hands. Kai and Lia savoured the first bite with immense pleasure. The rest of the meal passed like a blur and they were soon satisfied.

They chatted at length beside the fire, imagining what meals they could soon be expecting. They would surely be the kind made up of unflavoured mushrooms or soggy lettuce.

They sat by the fire late into the evening, far later than either of them typically stayed awake. They both loved sleeps far too much stave it off their naps before their last meal of the day. This was the only exception they happily made, to watch the pods in the Ameyali forest bloom the purpura.

Their glow was a beacon in the dark when they were birthed, like purple fireflies in a black sky on the horizon. A beauty far surpassing any other.

It was not yet late enough. Kai and Lia had been blessed to witness the exact moment of blooming every nightfall so far. The purpura often waited until the first and brightest of the stars to appear in the sky until their birth; *Orphan Star*.

It grew colder through the hours they waited, and they kept the fire ablaze with wasted wood pieces from the woodworkers' yard.

A Hominum approached them about the time the fire began waning again. Kai knew the footsteps very well; the steps of a man well-fed, who lacked the zeal to lift his feet fully from the ground when he walked. Kai could not fathom how he kept so much fat on his bones in nightfall, with only vegetables and potatoes to feed on, and paltry portions at that.

Here came that booming voice again. 'Sa'ar Kaali,' it said.

'Sa'ar Kaali, Ogmul,' they said together, with almost as little vigour as he did.

'This is different,' Ogmul said. '*Duties* this time, for the two of you.'

'Duti--oh.' Lia's voice betrayed how her heart sank. She had forgotten, as Kai did, what Hominum were *supposed* to do during nightfall. Of course, they knew that the torchlight wouldn't light itself and the meals wouldn't cook themselves, but those sorts of labour rarely ever fell on their hands.

'It's not as bad as all that,' Ogmul said, waddling closer. Kai felt his shadow towering over him. Ogmul may have even gotten fatter since they last spoke. His cheeks hung lower and fuller than ever, and one chin barely hid another. 'I don't much fancy talking to the backs of your heads,' he said.

'You've seen our faces many times before,' Lia said, her gaze on the forest unbroken.

Ogmul made his distinct sigh behind them, which he saved for times of mild irritation. 'For that, you'll be starting your torch-lighting *before* supper. You can have it when it's cold and tasteless if the rats don't have it first.'

'Isn't it too late for assignments?' Lia asked.

'Not if you're a torch lighter. It's work time for you. It's late now, so, get to it.'

'In a bit,' Lia said.

'Did you hear me say *now?*'

'We're waiting for the bloom,' Kai said.

'The bloom? Well, the bloom isn't waiting for--' Ogmul let his words trail off as the forest finally began to change. Kai and Lia stood together and watched with a special tone of silence, struck with special awe.

It began with hundreds of tiny purple spots hanging in nothingness, spreading widely on the horizon and slowly brightening as the pods spread their shells. They glowed brighter and brighter still, showering the lavender fields in purple light. Then came the moment they relished the most; the pale wisps that flew gracefully above the trees, dancing about like candle lights. The forest became alive with their majesty. The Ameyali Forest of nightfall was swiftly born.

Kai and Lia watched gleefully, even as the blooming ended and the forest settled into its long night. 'It's even prettier than last nightfall,' Lia said, and Kai eagerly nodded. The wisps looked livelier and the purple shone deeper every time.

'Pretty and evil,' Ogmul said with a grunt. Kai and Lia barely heard him. 'Ten minutes. That's all you're getting, and I'll be back with your torches.' They barely heard that either.

The kindly lady returned with their supper during those ten minutes. They had no idea what it was, even after their first bites. It was nothing as luxurious as fresh meat, not nearly tender enough. It had the taste of something decrepit made only during the turn of dusk, like badger or rat meat. The greens with it were practically devoid of colour and hard to swallow.

They managed half their meal before Ogmul came waddling back, exactly ten minutes later as promised. They were forced to don their heavy furs and abandon their meal to the wind and vermin, no matter how they protested.

Ogmul handed them each a long staff, taller than any man by a good measure, and marched them to the walls. Many a Hominum eyed them as they passed. These were disapproving eyes Kai and Lia had long grown accustomed to, now as much a part of their every dusk as their hearings before the elders were.

The oldest of the Hominum always treated them with great tenderness, by stark contrast. Cook Olaf clapped Lia on the back when they passed, with the same hearty laugh that shook his lips whenever he wasn't bellowing out fables and jokes. Ogmul flicked their heads when he caught them smiling back at him.

Their mood dropped when they reached the first of the torch stands. They were taller than Kai had realised, now that *he* was the one to light it.

They dipped their staffs into the cauldron of fire at Ogmul's say so. The torches lined the entire length of the walls and bathed the village in a ring of light and a subtle scent of lavender when lit. It was to be a long hour of sore arms and rumbling bellies.

Lia lit the first torch with Ogmul's eyes on them. It glowed in dim orange and burned with a pleasant herbal essence. Kai lit the second and Ogmul left them to their work after Lia lit the third. They huddled together under their furs against the bitter cold as they made for the fourth.

It was a lonely hour of labour, with the village growing increasingly barren and with the Hominum back in their tipis for food or sleep, which they themselves longed for.

'I feel like porridge,' Lia said, cheerily. 'I think that'll be our breakfast tomorrow.'

'With what oats,' Kai said, miserably. 'We both know it'll be gruel again.'

'Dream big, Orphan-Star. There'll be enough oats left for a few bowls. It'll be warm porridge too. We'll eat at *our* tipi, and we'll warm it on our own fire.'

'Sure, and maybe Chef Olaf will make us some jam too,' Kai said, sarcastically but admittedly eager at the prospect.

Lia gave him a teasing nudge with her elbow. 'See? *That's* how you dream big.'

Lia lit the fifth torch. The fragrance from the others now filled the stagnant village air. Dusk truly felt over, with the reminiscent smell of nightfall as a final reminder.

'You can keep going,' Lia said before they made for the sixth. 'I'm heading back.'

Kai furrowed his brow. 'Why?'

'Someone has the stave off the rodents if we still want to eat tonight.'

'But why you?'

'Why not me? My hands are freezing, see? You have to take over as the man of the family.' She couldn't stay serious for long with the pout Kai shot her. She laughed and pulled Kai in for a hug.

They savoured the warmth of each other's embrace a while longer before they parted to the embrace of the winter air.

'Stay safe, Orphan-Star,' Lia said.

'Safe?'

'Yeah, safe. Your hands are already frozen stiff. Hard to hold onto that thing with a claw for a hand. Don't burn yourself.' She laughed cheerfully and left Kai pouting at her back.

He walked on as bid, shivering harder and cursing the cold air under his frosty breath. 'I didn't say *yes*,' he muttered.

He lit the next torch with some difficulty, with not much feeling left in his fingers but for the pain that shot through them as he climbed. He warmed his hands by the staff's flame for a while, until his feet suffered the cold instead.

He crossed the stream onto the grounds of the sacred burial tree to light the next, kept company by the wild birds singing their evening songs beyond the wall. The tree stood majestic and tall, shedding its purple plumage and growing them just as swiftly. Kai relished the sensation of purple petals raining on him, bidding *Kali* to Mother Earth as he did. This place emitted serenity and reeked of life, regardless of the burial rites which took place on its sacred ground. This was the sole place in the village Kai *loved*, raining petals through dayfall and nightfall alike, and ever blooming with or without the tribe's care.

It was the only place where he could forget his longing for the forest for a time and live happily in the moment.

He bitterly moved on after a time, growing weary of lighting torch after torch and dragging his feet on in the dirt. He found his thoughts being drawn again to the unknown, as he lit the next. He wondered what manner of creature could invoke such fear in his kin, yet so easily be kept at bay by mere fire along their walls. He pondered it often and hard, yet only determined that his imagination had limits until his eyes could finally see their nature for himself.

He eventually found himself back where they had started, beside the cauldron of fire. Lia had left the staff on the ground, a few strides away from the stand. He sighed, a little irritated at her laziness, but he smiled anyway.

He leaned their staffs against the cauldron and headed for the tipi, walking awkwardly with the chill deep in his toes. It was a lonely and dark walk, with only his footsteps keeping him company and their fire to guide him.

He returned to an unpleasant surprise; their cold food laid still on the trays beside their dying fire being eaten by a pair of mice, and their tipi was dark with no torchlight inside. Kai frowned, confused. He entered, where he found their bed empty and neatly made, with no sign of Lia.

He sat upright in bed and waited, sad and disappointed. Lia was often impulsive, but rarely so thoughtless to leave him alone before they slept, and on what would be the last moments of dusk no less.

He waited for several hours while enduring his belly's lamentations. Lia never came, no matter how long Kai waited. Kai surely stayed awake through the end of dusk but could not see the beginning of nightfall for himself from inside his tipi. He finally laid his head down when he grew too bored of staring into nothingness.

After a time spent staving off worry and anger, Kai slept hungry and alone on the first cycle of nightfall.

3

Sa'ar (Sah-ar):

Noun
The light of the setting sun, during the transition from dayfall to nightfall.
Marks Mother Earth's time of rest
> *A declaration of gratitude for Mother Earth's work in the dayfalls of the past*

Kali (Kah-Lee):

Noun
The light of the rising sun, during the transition from nightfall to dayfall. Marks the end of Mother Earth's time of rest.
> *A solemn request for Mother Earth's blessings on the new growth of crops in dayfall.*

Kai awoke on the second cycle of nightfall to a cold new day and a choir of birds greeting the new moon. He woke with the bedsheets all to himself, and Lia's side untouched through the night.

Kai got dressed alone for the first time in recent memory. He broke out of his tipi, past the tray of cold potatoes, berries and water-moistened oats waiting for them.

He was met by the Ameyali forest glowing every brighter amid the dark sky. He instinctively bade it *Sa'ar Kali,* but spared it no other mind, making straight for the elder's tipi. The early rising elderly Hominum greeted him with as he passed, with mouths filled with breakfast outside their tipis.

Kai soon happened upon Ogmul. 'You're up early,' he said. 'Was on my way to check on the torches, but now I'm thinking you--'

'Lia's gone,' Kai said. His mouth moved before he could filter his words. 'She didn't come home after last cycle.'

'*Gone,*' Ogmul echoed with a grunt. '*Skiving,* more like. One evening of light work and you two couldn't manage even that much.'

'She wasn't skiving. She was working, and she disappeared.'

'Yes, *disappeared.* And you'll be telling me tomorrow how she's taken ill and will be needing all the grapes and jam she can swallow before she lifts her hands again.'

'Stop. Just help me find her.'

'Fine,' Ogmul said, resigned and deeply nonchalant. 'I'll tell the elders, so you'll have to check the torches instead.'

'No, I have to tell--'

'*Yes,* actually. Check the torches. The elders will be talking to you after I'm done.'

'But--'

'That means now.' Ogmul left despite Kai's protests and waddled in the direction of the elders' tipi.

Kai ran to complete a swift check of the torches. Most Hominum were out braving the nightfall air by the time Kai finished his round. He saw his and Lia's breakfast tray still sitting by their unlit firewood as he passed their tipi, going to waste. He decided he'd suffered hunger long enough and hurriedly ate his share of the potatoes and berries.

His mouth ached for the fruit's sharp taste. It had been so very long since he had eaten anything so sweet, with berries only ever in full ripeness at dusk, and its juices brought him a new vigour for the morning. He hated experiencing this sensation alone. He wrapped Lia's portion safely in their bedsheets before he left.

Kai felt a little better after the sweetness had touched his lips until he approached the elder's tipi to find Ogmul warming his bones at the tipi's entrance, engaged in small talk around a small fire. Kai grew hot with anger.

Ogmul broke from his talks when he saw him coming. 'Ro, that was fast. You better have--' He let his words trail as Kai stormed past him into the tipi.

Gal Ni, the old herbalist, stood in the centre of the chamber of elders, addressing them on some matter regarding her stocks. Miire Zin Fa's face went its usual shade of bright red at the sight of Kai.

'Ro, have your senses--?'

'Lia's gone.' Kai said. 'She went missing last--'

'We are in the middle of a hearing,' Miire Zin continued, already shouting.

'It's about my sister missing.'

'And you can tell us about it when--'

'No, Miire Zin,' Gal Ne said, with some harshness. 'I have made the case I intended to and trust that you will consider it amongst yourselves.' She took a swift look at Kai before leaving the chamber with the echoing thud of her walking stick. She was ever stern, and her presence ever imposing.

'Well then, young Ro,' Poruus Zin Ka began. 'What's this about your sister?'

Kai spoke quickly about the events of the last cycle and the circumstances of Lia's disappearance, in very few breaths. The elders listened until he had finished.

'Strange,' Houli Zin Me eventually said. 'But it has not been long. She mentioned nothing to you about this?'

'No,' Kai said, increasingly irritated at their apparent lack of urgency.

'A long while for Lia to be out alone,' Chief Omaraa Zan said.

'She has done far stranger than this,' Miire Zin Fa said, resting her chin in her hand.

'Okay, Kai Ro,' Omaraa Zan said. 'Find Ogmul for us and tell him we must speak with him.'

Kai waited not a second longer before making for the doorway.

'Before you go,' Poruus Zin said. 'You're certain Lia said nothing to you of where she may have gone? Think hard.'

Kai's blood boiled. *They think me so foolish to forget such a thing,* Kai thought, bitterly. He waited only a short moment before responding; 'No, she didn't.'

'And you said that Lia left you to save your supper. And she didn't do so?'

'No.'

'Then we know that Lia disappeared right after she left you.'

'Was that not obvious from what the boy just told us,' Houli Zin said, sounding impatient himself.

'No,' Poruus Zin said. 'Lia surely intended to do just as she said. She would not deceive her brother, of all people, or purposefully let his food go to waste. That she did not do so makes her absence more suspicious.'

The chamber was quiet for a time. The elders shifted their weight in discomfort. Kai was the quietest among them, now lost deeply in an idea he could not shake.

'It is perhaps too soon for talk such as this,' Omaraa said, shooting Poruus Zin a very deliberate look.

'It is *not* too soon if it is true,' he said.

'She didn't bother hanging the lighting staff,' Kai finally forced from his lips. His heart felt close to bursting in his chest. He spent his breath hard and fast. It was dead silent in the chamber. The elders looked far less disinterested now. 'She's in the forest,' Kai said before the silence could linger any longer.

The chief's face was full of sympathy. 'We do not know this for certain,' she said.

'No,' Poruus Zin said. 'Though unfortunate, it is likely. Just as it is apparent that she has left the village of her own volition--'

'We do not know this,' Omaraa Zan repeated, the agitation clear in her tone. 'And we will arrange for the village to be searched *before* making conclusions.'

'And should it be that Lia Ro is no longer in the village,' Poruus Zin said, unfazed.

'We would discuss the matter *after* the search, Poruus. Do as stated, Kai. Find Ogmul and we will ensure the village is searched until she is found.'

'Stop treating me like I'm clueless,' Kai said, in his grief. 'She's in the forest. She must have climbed the gates.'

'We do not know--'

'*I* do.' Anxiety gnawed viciously at his heart, and he could do little to slow it. '*I* know she is.'

'*We* do not, Kai,' Miire Zin Fa said, coldly. 'We will search the village for Lia Ro and that is the best we can do. If she has chosen to leave the village as you say, she did so of her own accord, knowing full well the consequences.'

Kai was incredulous. 'What are you saying?'

'You were warned not one full cycle ago in this very chamber; you shan't be treated as children any longer. If she is in the village, you have no cause for concern. If she is not, you cannot expect us to risk--'

'Miire!' Chief Omaraa Zan shouted with an anger in her voice Kai rarely witnessed. It hardly sounded like her at all at that moment.

Miire Zin's manner quickly softened, and her face showed a healthy measure of shame. 'I apologise, Kai Ro,' she said. 'I will choose to believe that Lia would not be so senseless, and I hope my confidence is not misplaced.'

'But you won't help her if she has,' Kai stated. Miire Zin closed her eyes and shook her head. 'Why not?'

'You already know why,' Miire Zin hissed.

'No, I don't know.'

'Yes, you do. Tell us why.'

Kai swallowed. 'Because you're cowards. All of you. You're cowards and you only care about yourselves.' Miire Zin was hushed and joined the elders in astonishment. Kai's outburst was pure. The words had long been brewing deep in his heart and longing to burst forth. Kai let them flow still. 'You tell us, again and again, how dangerous the forest is in nightfall, but now that my sister's *there*, you do nothing? All you do is sit there, read from your stupid old scrolls, and threaten us with your stupid rules. And you keep telling us you're our shepherds. If you won't even help us when we need you, what's the point of you?'

Kai breathed a little softer, though his blood felt hotter still. He felt near elated, relieved of a pressure he had long contained within him. He was almost *happy*.

'We know you are upset,' Omaraa Zan said, back to her soft manner. 'And we know you do not mean what you say, Kai.'

'Yes, I do,' he said. He meant it with all his heart. He had long grown so very tired of suppressing what he truly felt, all for the sake of old proverbs and vague texts of warning. He and Lia had endured trepidation for their entire lives, and now that same trepidation looked far more like weakness than caution. 'Because it's true,' Kai continued. 'You're cowards, just like the rest of the tribe.'

'You do not speak of your kin this way,' Miire Zin said, as harshly as she could. Kai said nothing in response, understanding any purpose to this hearing to be spent. It was only through some sense of courtesy, however misplaced, that he stood in that chamber still.

Miire Zin Fa did not suffer the silence for long. 'And do not dare accuse us of abandoning our people. It was Lia who abandoned--'

'We do *not* know that,' the chief interjected, through gritted teeth.

'—who abandoned her village, *if* she is in the forest, as you believe. We will not endanger anyone else for her poor judgment. So no, Kai Ro, we will not be searching the forest for your sister. You may call it cowardice now, but the day will come when you truly understand what separates cowardice from wisdom.'

Kai could not help but make one last appeal, if only out of spite and self-assurance. 'If you won't go,' he said. 'I'll go to the forest myself. I won't abandon her like you.'

Omaraa Zan sighed loudly. 'Kai, don't be so--'

'No Omaraa Zan, let him own his words.' Miire Zin sat forward on her stall, piercing Kai with a look perilously close to malice from his point of view. 'If you leave the village, that will be your choice, as it was Lia Ro's. But should you do so, you will not be permitted back into the village this nightfall either, just as we promised.'

An ice-like chill ran through Kai's spine. 'You won't let Lia back in the village?'

Silence. Miire Zin quickly shrunk into shame, frozen in an expression of dismay. Omaraa Zan held her face in her hands. Kai had heard all he needed and more than he wanted. He would not suffer these people a moment longer.

He stormed out of the chamber with the sound of the elders' appeals behind him. He rushed past the Hominum still huddled around the fire and ignored their sympathetic looks.

He could imagine well how these next cycles were to go, should the tribe have their way. The Hominum would have their eyes even more intently on him than usual, ensuring his whereabouts were always known. The elders would continue to feed him their narrative of caution and their false assurances of care until his anger waned. Kai would have none of it.

He had the foresight to stop at his tipi and pack his mostly unused hunting bag, along with the remains of breakfast, to don his fur coat and to sling *Slayer* onto his back, before he was on his way.

Perhaps this was meant to be a moment in Kai's life that would be heavy with the burden of a critical choice; one that should have hounded his waking hours and obsessed his every thought. But he did not even consider this a decision so much as an acknowledgement that he had been left with only one true option.

Kai knew better than to climb the gates. He instead made for his treasured burial tree and escaped the confines of the village walls by the grace of its long arms. He left the Hominum tribe's village behind him on the first cycle of nightfall, before the morning birds had finished their song.

4

Hominum:

Noun
Given name of the Ameyali Village tribesmen residing on the border of the Ameyali Forest
    As named by the first recorded generation of Hominum elders; the Generation of Farro, eight generations prior to the Generation of Omaraa

It was a dark and gloomy path to the Ameyali forest, with nothing but its distant purple glow to light Kai's way. The cold had seeped deeply through his furs before he reached the lavender fields. He walked quickly to keep his blood flowing but shivered despite it. He raised his hood when the village walls were out of sight and the chill grew stronger still.

Kai readily admitted to himself how scared he was. It wasn't that he regretted his departure or the place he was bound for, but that he alone for the very first time. He had grown accustomed to acting on impulse through Lia's influence and care, but this time was different. He could not remember ever acting so decisively on his impulse alone, without his sister to help shoulder any consequence.

He was filled too with dread for soon having to brave the forest in the freezing air. Rubbing his arms helped little. His stomach grumbled already, but he resisted the urge to reach for his pack. It was still his intention that Lia would have her share of breakfast soon.

He could not deny his excitement despite his fear, as the forest glowed brighter the nearer he drew. It was only now that it dawned on him; he had something to thank Lia for when he found her. He would finally see the purpura up close; a full nightfall and dayfall before he imagined.

'Pearls in the snowflakes of nightfall,' Kai began to sing. *'Dayfall shines. But by the reeds by the ashes of the daring are the brightest and truest of lights.'*

Lia had told Kai a great many nightfalls ago that singing warmed the spirit as much as fire did and Kai still firmly believed it. They had made many a song together and this one was the latest. They would always sing in the most bitter of nightfall cycles; usually when snow fell, and their fire did not burn so well.

'When they tremble and stutter.
We hold our heads high.
And memories of the forgotten
Will fill the pages of time.'

And the pages turn beyond
The hand's many ages.
Until the newborns' brave hearts
Break from their cages.'

'Then we reeds will grow stronger
And taller than the weak.
And time will cheer then
For we valiant and…our cheese.'

Kai laughed, almost as loudly as he had last nightfall. Lia had slapped his head every time he sang it. They had been called to Omaraa Zan's mother that nightfall before they could finish the song properly and this was the absurd lyric Kai had settled for. Lia was adamant that he had to make the last verse himself and that it had to sound clever, like the rest of the song.

'And time will then fall in the waves of the seas.' That was Kai's better idea for the ending last nightfall, though he had not yet shared it with Lia.

He sang it once more, more heartily than the first. He did not know what his last verse was meant to mean, but every word of it was a comfort. He believed Lia would make better sense of it than he did when they could sing it together again in its entirety.

A long plane was still between Kai and the forest. He walked through the fields with a distance to go, relishing in the simple comforts of the dying lavender under his shoes and the sounds that came with every chilly breeze.

It was the sound of freedom to him, in all its stark glory. He feared it and he loved it; a sensation alien to him before this. Only during the times Lia and he would stay in the forest past the lighting of the ignis came close to this feeling, but that sensation was always short-lived and died upon their return home. Kai did not believe this feeling would die so easily this time.

The forest's glow soon forced him to squint. He stared across the field with a gormless smile. The purpura's light leaked far across the lavender and they beamed while swaying under its weight. Bright wisps danced around the forest to Mother Nature's song, like huge and graceful fireflies. It was the picture of beauty, far surpassing any that Kai's eyes had ever been bestowed with.

He broke out of his trance as he felt tears coming. He imagined how Lia had surely witnessed this very same spectacle not long ago, delighted by the thought. Yet, he was saddened for another profound experience they failed to share in the same moment. He reminded himself of where he headed; the Ameyali Forest, where there would be countless pictures such as this, some far surpassing this in inspiring awe.

The air grew heavier as Kai drew closer to the purple light and he could feel it in his lungs. The chill somehow became less and less potent; he even sweated a little under his furs. The glow was all he could before long, having left the darkness and shadows behind him. He moved with bated breath as he prepared for the Ameyali Forest to greet him with whatever laid in wait.

But he took not a step more before a wisp descended from the skies and floated before his face. Its pale light was magnificent without being blinding. It floated with such majesty that it appeared frozen in the air. It stared at him without eyes to see with. They stayed locked in this silent exchange for a time.

Kai finally made a move to pass it, but the wisp moved with him and blocked him. He moved the other way, and it blocked him again. And here they stood.

'Wow,' Kai was compelled to say, while the wisp stayed very much soundless. It was a curious and pretty thing that floated before his face; it was a ball of light with nothing in its centre he could see. He wondered whether this thing could even stop him from passing at all, as he could probably walk right through it like actual light.

Kai reached out his hand. He thought he saw it tremble a little. His fingers barely stroked the warm light and it bolted backwards, making him fall back in surprise. It took flight back to the forest and was almost out of sight before Kai found his feet. He immediately ran after it, with no reason beyond curiosity and impulse.

Kai entered the Ameyali Forest at last, drawn as he was by wonder over reason.

He immediately had to slow down to avoid falling over exposed tree roots and rocks at the forest's entrance. The wisp was already well out of sight and Kai was left alone once more to marvel at new wonders surrounding him.

Lia and he knew this part of the forest well, but it was different when bathed in purple light and covered with newly fallen leaves of a vivid tone of green. No single patch of the forest floor was wasted, packed with young flowers and stones donned with a proud glaze.

Then there were the purpura themselves. They hung on tree trunks and laid on the forest floor where the pods once were, taking the shape of immense flowers with sprawled out petals. They were yellow at their centre and their arms glowed with a steady pulse. Those highest in the trees seemed to glow the brightest and gave the forest its shower of purple light. They were beautiful, just as Kai had hoped.

Truly, they were stunning, as was everything Kai could see. He struggled to digest all the beauty which had so quickly been bestowed on his eyes. The purpura themselves were, strangely, just a small facet of the awe the forest now inspired.

That was until he saw the purpura move for the first time. No, rather than *move*, Kai saw them *breathe*. They silently clenched themselves and exhaled, spreading fine white powder-like sparkles as they did, which quickly dissipated. Kai could not take his eyes off them. He watched them do this again and again as he walked on. He didn't much care *why* this was happening or what those enchanting sparkles were. All that he saw at that moment was this; the purpura were *alive*.

He spared a few glances at immense moths on the trees and the plants that seemed to grow as he passed in a daze, but it was the purpura that kept drawing Kai's eyes. He relished being bathed in their glow. He reached out and touched the next one he passed, feeling its warmth even before his fingers touched its petals. Its light receded at Kai's touch until its warmth dissipated. Kai drew his hand back and the flower slowly birthed its glow again, even more vibrantly.

Kai felt hot, suddenly aware of the forest's humidity. He found himself drenched in sweat when he removed his furs.

The purpura's warmth made Kai comfortable here, despite nightfall. He was gleeful at the revelation, immensely relieved at another gift Mother Earth bestowed him with; a means to survive a surely harsh winter away from home. It reminded him of dayfall and the cycles spent hunting freely in this very place.

A dayfall spent within the village walls was, by contrast, boring and gloomy. The Hominum would spend that precious time preparing for nightfall and the bitter winds in place of enjoying the sunlight. *All for nothing,* Kai thought.

It was so warm that he had soon forgotten the bitter chill from not long ago. He decided his furs were no longer needed here, after little deliberation. He stuffed them into a hollow fallen trunk, assuring himself that he knew this place well enough to find them again should he need to.

Kai was awash with shame as he left the furs behind; ashamed of forgetting to bring furs for his sister, who could well have been freezing here. He told himself that he would have gladly given his own furs to her and firmly believed it. He at least would ensure the breakfast in his pouch found its way into Lia's hands.

So distant Kai was in these thoughts that he paid no heed to what occurred in the shadows beyond the trees until they made their first sound. Fallen branches snapped below a heavy thud. So heavy it was that Kai froze in motion and looked to its source. He saw nothing but the trees' arms swaying in a soft breeze. It was not a natural sound to his somewhat practised ears.

He walked on a little further, slowly and measured, listening for that thud again. It never came, but Kai instead heard a long and laboured breath that chilled his spine. It was deep and hearty, like a breath from the earth itself.

He broke into a run, hesitating for not one moment, as fast as he could with his bow in hand.

Kai suddenly *feared* again. His euphoria crumbled in an instant and he was hauled back into his dangerous reality, that he ran alone and increasingly scared in a forbidden place. He was more scared when he realised that he had a bow without his quiver, which still hung empty in his hut. He cursed at his stupidity. He cursed that he brought danger to himself so soon, for all his talk and bravado.

He tried to calm himself as he ran, in what he found to be an impossible contradiction.

Absorbed again in his thoughts as he was, Kai's feet met with something soft on the ground and he was sent falling flat onto his face, his bow flying from his hands. It didn't hurt much, but the mud in his mouth tasted something like blood.

'Ah!' cried a voice at his feet.

Kai sat up spluttering and wiped mud from his lips. Then came shock, surprise, and confusion in one simultaneous burst. A *voice!* Kai leapt away from it, startled, and looked for the source.

A rabbit. Just a rabbit, lying muddied on its back. A very large rabbit, but a rabbit nonetheless. It found its feet and glared at Kai through pale red eyes. It froze with a face shot with horror the moment their eyes met. And there they stood, sharing the moment in collective alarm.

The rabbit's cheeks quivered, and it stood upright with wide eyes. It was tall, its ears as high as Kai's chest. Kai breathed deeply and sighed. He had long known enough of fear to know how adept it was at deceiving his perceptions to absurd ends, such as hearing noises that had no sense or reason. He knew this to be another.

Then the rabbit's mouth opened.

'Oh!' it said, its face turning from shock to excitement. Its mouth made the perfect figure for the sound it produced, and its eyes were far more expressive than any rabbits' should have been. It perked its ears behind its back and hopped merrily toward Kai with a jolly smile.

'It's you,' it said. 'It's really you. You scared the life outta me. Smoothskins really do look alike. Err, no offence.'

Never had Kai's mouth hung as limply as it did at that moment.

A vacant *huh* was all that escaped his lips.

5

To disobey is to rebel. To rebel is to incite conflict. Conflict is death to unity. The ununited will inevitably disobey. Such is the cycle born of necessary oppression.

Therefore, to lead is to craft oppression itself into a source of unity through comfort, for the united and the unruly alike.

Inti Zan Mo
Generation of Inti
Fourth Recorded Generation

The rabbit spoke relentlessly for a while, as Kai gormlessly watched its mouth move. It was energetic, hopping circles around Kai as it chattered. It complimented Kai's smooth skin, called his clothes *weird*, and asked if he was cold, all in one strained breath.

'Hold on,' Kai finally said, rubbing his aching temple. 'Just wait.'

'Wait,' the rabbit echoed, with something resembling a blush. 'Sorry, I never got to speak with a smooth-skin before, you know? It's all so exciting. Especially *you*. I never thought I'd get to see *you*. Are you hungry? I'm hungry too.'

'I don't--how are you talking?'

'How am I? How can't I? I have a mouth and ears, see?' It erected its long ears. 'So, I talk, and I hear. And you can hear me too. I didn't think smoothskins could hear so well with such small ears. Err, no offence.'

'You're a rabbit though?'

'That I am,' that rabbit said with a titter. 'So, you're hungry, right?'

'I...sure,' Kai said, resigned. His head felt heavy from trying and woefully failing to process any of what was befalling him.

'Good,' the rabbit said. 'You have anything to eat?'

'Huh? *You* just asked *me* if I was hungry.'

'Yeah,' it said, eyeing the pouch in Kai's hands. 'So, I thought maybe you had something to eat in there.'

'No.'

'But I smell something. Something swee--oh, berries?'

'No. They're not mine. They're for my sister.'

'Sister,' the rabbit echoed, scratching its head. Its feet were immense, and the grass under it crackled with every hop. 'Do you think your sister will miss a couple--?'

'Yes, she would.' Kai rubbed his head again. He felt trapped in the most bizarre of dreams; the kind of outlandish and nonsensical dream one could only expect while under the influence of medicinal herbs.

The rabbit's manner suddenly changed. It perked up its ears and stared at a dark cluster of trees, dead still.

'What,' Kai said. He looked to where it looked but saw only shadows around the glowing plumage. He became entranced by the darkness, staring into it and frozen with dread.

He felt a tug at his leg. 'Huh,' he managed, as he met the eyes of the now tame rabbit.

'Climb, smoothie. Can you climb? Climb fast. Really fast. Really now. Climb a tree.'

'A tree? Why would I need--'

'Climb. Hide. Please climb?'

Kai was too disorientated to do much but obey, too deep in a daze born of absurdity for rational thought. So, Kai climbed as he was bid. He climbed a tree in the way he had done a thousand times before. The trunk felt different against his fingers; softer and somehow *fuller*, as though satisfied from a rich meal.

'Climb faster, smoothie,' the rabbit called up to him.

'It's Kai.'

'I know, but don't be scared. Go higher.'

'No, my name--' Kai stopped speaking, realising that he was practically *shouting* from his apparent hiding place. 'Ok, *higher*,' he muttered, gradually losing himself in the branches and radiant plumage.

'Keep going, smoothie,' the rabbit hissed to him.

'What about you,' Kai hissed back.

'I'm just a rabbit,' was all it offered. Kai quickly became too distracted to ponder the possible meaning of those words.

An impressive radiance graced the skies as he approached the peak of the tree; a huddle of glowing wisps flying overhead. They flew with grace and silence, like a cloud carried by the winds. They passed in perfect unison and a surreal lack of majesty. Their light soon faded into the skies as swiftly as it had arrived. Only after they passed did Kai realise that he was smiling a smile that hurt his cheeks.

He savoured the grand sight of the forest while up so high. In this moment, nothing else mattered. The forest was radiant with purple light and warm yellow mists, as far as he could see. He saw the forest's colossal tree standing in the distance, covered with bright patches of light yet glazed in shadow. The entire forest emanated splendour. Even the *smell* was bizarre and vibrant, hanging heavily in the air like sweet, fragrant nectar.

Kai learned then that the times he had once believed himself awe-struck were of child's play, spent merely looking into the distance with wonder which fell far short of the reality where true spectacle had laid in wait.

The rabbit's voice eventually called Kai back into his new reality and back to the ground.

'What was that for,' Kai said, wiping the tree sap off his hands, onto his already dirty breeches.

'The climbing,' the rabbit asked, tilting its head.

'Yes, the climbing.'

'You were hiding.'

'From what?'

'*From what.* So many questions.' The rabbit was back to bouncing in good cheer. 'You're my guest, smoothie, so don't you stress. As a guest, I must feed you. So, let's go and eat now.'

A sheepish grin crept back onto Kai's face. 'Your guest? Me?'

'Yeah, my guest. Let's eat.'

The rabbit hopped off ahead through the bushes before Kai could respond. Why he followed, beyond the overwhelming sense of elation the Ameyali Forest began to gift him, he could not fathom. Kai simply opted to follow his heart and right now, it guided him onto the tail of the rabbit bouncing merrily among the purpura lights; a companion far stranger than the depths of his imagination could ever conjure.

6

The Guardian Waya regarded the forest to which he was duty-bound and sang;

*'This is fine for me
For I've a harvest before me
Yet only my mouth to feed.'*

The heavens turned red, enraged by Waya's haughtiness, and opened with the voice of thunder.

Waya hid from the downpour, under the trees to which he was duty-bound to protect and nurture. He grew arrogant in his resourcefulness, singing;

*'This is fine for me
For here is a shelter for me
As far as I can see.'*

Excerpt from *The Tale of Waya*
By Timor Ro
Hominum Tribe Writer, Generation of Inti
Fourth Recorded Generation

The rabbit led Kai over a fallen tree slumped atop a slow flowing stream and into a small wood. Every sight was like a new world opening before Kai's eyes. It was as though the forest had morphed at the purpura's will, with every patch of it now like a vibrant painting.

Kai was soon led into a field of flowers swaying with a generous wind. They were a deep shade of crimson and glowed in the tone of the purpura's overbearing light. This field, Kai realised, was another he knew well, as he remembered the plain patch of green and dying flowers that had laid here in dayfall.

He followed the rabbit, with a touch of guilt for every step and each flower he crushed. He so enjoyed the feeling of the petals stroking his feet, in truth. Even the flowers felt warm against his skin.

The rabbit stopped where the meadow ended, at the feet of a particularly tall and fat tree, then he made a peculiar crunching sound with his head buried in the burrow at the tree's base.

He muttered something, with his head still buried and his voice muffled.

'Huh,' Kai said. He realised as he drew closer that the rabbit was chopping on a pit filled to the brim with vegetables and fruits. It was a burrow well concealed and unassuming under the tree's shadow.

He finished only part of his mouthful when he repeated; 'Hep yur elpf.'

'I still can't hear you.'

The rabbit waved to the food at its feet and planted its face again.

Kai picked out a carrot peeking from the pile. It was fat. *Extremely* fat, unlike any he had seen. He brushed the dirt off it with his shirt and bit.

The assault of flavour that burst in his mouth almost knocked him off his feet. He had to breathe deeply to regain himself. It tasted like a vegetable, of course; like a carrot, as well it should have. But it was *so much* carrot in one bite. So overwhelming it was that the sensation was neither pleasant nor awful. Kai just wanted more of it.

He reached for a green...thing at his feet and stuffed it into his face. The flavour was no less intense. He felt lightheaded as he swallowed the bite. The field of lights began to look a whole lot brighter.

'Isn't it good,' the rabbit said, his mouth still half full.

'Bis ig gasi,' Kai said with newfound energy and, strangely, an empty mouth. The flavour grappled his tongue tightly like a leech. 'Gai canck dork,' he tried to say.

'Ah?' The rabbit still had his face planted and was enjoying his meal loudly.

'Ag...ooh yu haw warpa?'

'*Warpa?*'

'Naw, *warpa.*'

'Ah.' The rabbit waved its paw away from the fields. Kai ran through the trees with his tongue practically hanging at his knees, dodging the branches and rocks and squinting for the bright lights, until he found a stream.

He dove into it and hauled water into his mouth, spat it out and hauled

31

it again. The sensation leaked from his tongue far too slowly. 'Wharder,' Kai tested. 'War-der. Warder. Ugh.' He dropped onto his back after many more mouthfuls and sighed. Even the water had more *water* to it than usual.

Kai laid in the stream and stared up into the trees, short of breath, before his eyes closed of their own accord. *The air has a taste,* Kai realised. *It tastes fresh. And thick.*

He soon grew restless of laying so still. He was met with the patched face of the wide-eyed rabbit glaring down at him when he opened his own eyes. Kai yelped in surprise, which made the rabbit jump, which startled Kai. They were both drenched in water by the end of it.

The rabbit tittered. 'There you are, smoothie,' it said while shaking itself dry.

'What did you feed me,' Kai said. The numbness in his tongue had mostly faded.

'Umm…some vegetables? I didn't see what you ate, but it was all--'

'It was *so* good,' Kai practically sung. 'But made my tongue go numb. I'm not sure if I liked it.' He was conscious of himself squinting. It was as though bright snowballs danced in the forest. Everywhere he looked layered with balls of lights.

Kai scratched his head for no real reason. 'I love this forest,' he said. 'So, so much.'

'I'm not sure we--'

'I want to see more.'

'Yeah, well--'

'Are there more flowers like in that field?'

'I think you--'

'Are there more glowing flowers?'

'Listen, smooth--'

'Are there--' The rabbit pressed his paw on Kai's mouth. He tasted dirt and mud mixed with soft fur.

'Listen, smoothie,' the rabbit said. 'You can't just go wherever you want.'

'Why?'

'Because I just said you can't.'

'But why can't I?'

'You're a smoothie.'

Kai rubbed his head and groaned. He was growing more lightheaded and could see purple lights with his eyes closed. 'You make no sense,' he muttered. 'Where can't I go?'

'You shouldn't be here at all, y'know? You should go home. I don't mind showing you the way back.'

'But you just invited me here with you. Why didn't you tell me before?'

'I was hungry.'

Kai glared at the huge rabbit, incredulous. He could think of no words and simply walked away, following the stream and just about staying on his feet.

'Wait,' the rabbit said, waddling after him. 'Maybe I can take you back to my place again. You can eat some more carrots. I might even have a pumpkin I can split with you. I don't split with just anyone, y'know? But you can have a bite.'

'No thanks.' Kai swatted branches from his face as he walked. The bright purple light was becoming a constant haze before him, like a fog blocking his way.

'Okay,' the rabbit called. 'I'll split the whole pumpkin, right down the middle. You can even have some fruit with it. I'll let you--slow down! Y-you're going the wrong way, y'know.'

'You don't know where I'm going.'

'Well, that way goes back where we came,' the rabbit huffed, already short of breath keeping up with Kai's long strides. He began hopping instead of waddling. 'So, I think you'd better go the other way.'

'I know the forest better than that.' Kai grinned to himself and walked faster still.

'No, Smoothie,' the rabbit cried. He leapt and grabbed Kai's leg. He was even heavier than he looked. 'I'm a citizen of this forest. You have to listen to me.'

Kai dragged him along for a few steps, before giving up and coming to a stop. 'A *citizen* of the forest? Where did you learn words like that? How can you even speak?'

'I already told you, Smoothie; I have a mouth.'

Kai sighed again. 'Ok, *Citizen*.' He shook the rabbit off his leg and ran.

'Smoothie,' he heard behind him, but he kept going. Running was a great effort for him right now. He grew dizzier with each step. He barely stayed on his feet, burdened by purple lights watching him pass and foliage whipping at his body.

Kai sweated profusely as he ran almost blindly. The splash at his feet and the soft chill of the water were all that told him he still followed the stream.

He spent his breath completely, faster than he should have. He felt sick to his stomach and slowed to a walk. The forest had become nought but a blur of violet and green to his eyes, dancing for him to the song of flowing water.

He gazed at it all through a rush of vertigo. Only when he tried to take another step did he realise he had fallen to his knees, and only when he huffed with exhaustion did he feel bile rising through his body.

He fell onto his hands, sweating so much that it filled his ears.

'Don't leave the Hyachin,' he heard the rabbit call from atop his back. 'Stay in the Hyachin.'

Kai heard it almost as a whisper, as he gave way to an unnatural dormancy.

7

Sa'ar Kaali
By the Mother's kindness
You're hailed from darkness
Sa'ar Kaali

Sa'ar Kaali
By the Mother's kind grace
You shall be embraced
Sa'ar Kaali

Excerpt from the *Hominum Tribe Song of Birth*
Sung Every Seventh Year During the Ritual of New Birth

I t was still dark, of course, when Kai awoke on the fourth cycle of nightfall. He was soaked in sweat and parched, his head pounding in the heat. His body felt limp and sitting upright was an effort. He realised after a moment spent gazing at the red field of flowers before him that he was back at the rabbit's food burrow. Beside him were cupped lettuce leaves holding water. He took a long mouthful. It was thick and warm, but immensely relieving.

The rabbit was chomping further into the field and Kai could hear his every bite even from where he sat. He watched him a while with a small smile on his face, before finding his way into dormancy again.

Kai next woke to a crunching sound grating his ears. The rabbit laid closely beside him, gazing at the sky and munching on a carrot in his paws.

Kai reached again for the refilled leaves of water but stopped when the absence of his bow finally dawned on him. *It's gone. When? How? Where could I have lost it?*

It didn't take long for Kai to reason that he must have lost it soon after he entered the forest; likely at the time he heard that breathing sound and ran. That breathing, he now realised, was probably another animal watching him through the bushes.

He held his hands to his face to hold the shame and the anger; anger at himself for not taking the care he should have. He lamented for his lost memento, but he too took some solace in the opportunity to soon ask Lia to craft him another. She would berate him for his clumsiness, but he knew she would happily oblige. Such thoughts helped lift his mood a little.

The rabbit pricked his ears when Kai sat upright.

'Smoothie,' the rabbit sang. 'Feeling okay? Actually, don't answer. Drink first. Drink some water.'

Kai did as bid and took another long sip. It was again warm and thick, and not as potent as the water he drank from the stream. 'Thank you,' Kai said, before taking another mouthful.

'It's no bother. I was getting a drink for myself anyway. Actually, it *was* a bother. The leaves kept breaking on my way back. I had to hold the water in my mouth and make three trips to fill it up.'

Kai spat the suddenly foul-tasting water from his mouth with a retch.

'Something wrong?' the rabbit said, wide-eyed and oblivious.

'Nothing,' Kai managed to say through his spluttering. 'The water got stuck in my throat.'

'Oh. Well, drink some more, Smoothie.'

'I've had enough.' Kai laid the leaf bowl down before the rabbit could protest. 'What happened? We were at the stream, right? How did I get back--?' Kai then saw a trail of unearthed soil and crushed flowers from the trees to the field where they sat. He himself was covered in mud and grass stains running down his body.

'You fell asleep,' the rabbit said. 'I thought you were just drinking, but then you didn't move for a long time. I thought you were drowning, so I had to pull you outta the stream. Then I thought I may as well take you back here, in case you were hungry.'

'You thought you *may as well*,' Kai echoed, with more than mild surprise.

'Yeah.'

Kai rubbed his temple. The rabbit spoke so frankly that the absurdity of its words was hardly apparent. He blinked at Kai expectantly. 'Thank you,' Kai finally said. 'But why did you do all that for me?'

'Huh? What do you mean *why?*'

'I mean; why did you take me all the way back here? I must be really heavy for you, and it would take a long time. And you even brought me food and water. Why did you go through all that just for me?'

'You're my friend, Smoothie,' the rabbit said, as though the question were idiotic. 'And I would be a shameful citizen to leave you to drown when I owe you my life.'

'You *do*,' Kai asked, taken aback once again.

'Er, did you hit your head in the water, Smoothie? Do you have memory loss? Oh, do you remember that you're in the forest? Do you remember where you--'

'Yes, yes I'm okay. Can you just tell me what you owe me for?'

'For when you were last here, Smoothie,' the rabbit said, bouncing and seemingly blushing through its patched fur. 'I was gathering food for the night when I saw you and another smoothskin together. You had a weapon in your hand and were pointing it right at me. I thought that was it for me, cos I've seen other smoothskins use them to kill us with those pointed sticks.' Kai started to sweat, riddled with crushing guilt for the words he knew were to follow. He felt sick to his stomach at the thought of the hunt he considered to be *leisure*.

'But I saw what you did,' the rabbit continued. 'You moved the stick away so it would miss me. I saw the other smoothskin laugh at you. That smoothskin wanted you to hit me, right? But you saved me. So, I owe you my life, Smoothie. Taking you out of water and feeding you was nothing compared to that.'

The rabbit mercifully did not wait for a reply for Kai, as he would not have gotten one soon. 'I'll get you a carrot,' he said and hopped happily back to his burrow.

Kai watched the rabbit scuffle in his food hole and fought the tears forming in his eyes. Horrible memories flowed back to him of deer, pigs and rabbits coming through the village slumped over the hunters' shoulders, with faces frozen in the fear they felt in their last breath. The hunters would often return from the forest smiling and laughing, just as Kai did after most hunts with that addictive adrenaline in his veins.

He remembered how he and Lia would drool as the seasoned animal carcasses were roasted. The village in dayfall sporadically stank of the aromas of the meat on fires; what they referred to as a *treat*, a time of celebration and gratefulness. Now, all that meat was churning in Kai's belly and he wanted more than anything to haul it all out.

How many of those animals were like this rabbit? How many could talk and think like he can? How many were scared while they were hunted like he was? It served no purpose to ponder such things now, Kai knew, but to waver some of his justified guilt. They were all lives that had been stolen, all for the thrill of a hunt and a pleasant taste on the tongue.

His bow's absence now felt far less like a cause for sadness.

The rabbit soon returned with a beaming smile and a half-eaten carrot in its paws, the other half in its teeth.

Its smile made Kai smile too, despite himself. 'Wasn't that carrot meant for me,' he said.

The rabbit's face froze with a smile still on it for a long moment, while he chewed and swallowed. 'I'll get you a carrot,' he finally said cheerfully.

'Can I ask you something,' Kai said. The rabbit just stared back, so Kai went ahead. 'I was wondering what you meant when you told me not to leave the Hyachin.'

'Oh, the purple light. It's called Hyachin, smoothie.'

'Why did tell me not to leave it?'

'I told you; I'm a citizen of this forest, so you have to listen to me,' the rabbit said, taking another bite from the carrot in his paws.

'Ok, *Citizen*, but can I know *why*?'

'I dunno either. The queen tells us to stay in the Hyachin, so we stay in the Hyachin.'

Kai tilted his head. 'What's a queen?'

Citizen tilted his head too. 'She's a queen of the forest. She tells us what to do.'

'Like a *chief*, then' Kai said, fully engrossed. 'What would she do to you if you ignored her?'

'Well…she's very smart and knows what she's talking about. She says to stay in the Hyachin, so…we stay in the Hyachin.'

'Yeah, but has no one ever gone anyway?'

The rabbit shuffled on its feet, looking down at the red flowers he stood on. 'There's stories.' His ears went limp and his face turned gloomy.

'Let's hear some,' Kai said, unable against his better judgment to sate his curiosity.

'Just...' the rabbit started, dropping from his feet and sitting on his rear. He left Kai waiting in silence broken only by the winds whistling through the flower field. Kai saw this topic to be a painful one. 'Just stories,' the rabbit said, finally.

Kai pressed him no further. They spent the next hours on cheerier topics. He told the rabbit about his own home and the tribe from where he came. The rabbit listened with adorable wonder on his face, stating how he long wondered what lied beyond what he called the *tree walls*. Kai found some comfort in talking about the ignis, he and Lia's disobedience every nightfall, and even the elders. He managed to talk about these things without any longing for them. He wondered if the Ameyali Village would have ever felt like home if not for Lia, for how pure of heart he felt in his absence from it.

The rabbit also spoke to Kai of his own home, though his perspective had food at the core of each story. He spoke with immeasurable enthusiasm about sweet-tasting needles, mint imbued water and spicy mushrooms. Kai learned of a place where the queen resided with her feared guards and of the wisps serving as her *eyes* all over the forest.

'I think I saw one of those wisps,' Kai said, remembering his awkward encounter with the floating orb before his first step across the forest border. 'It saw me too.'

'Oh. So, the queen knows you're here too,' the rabbit said, sounding deflated at the prospect. 'The lumen tell her whatever she needs to know.'

'Lumen?'

'Yeah, those glowing yellow flies.'

'So, the queen can see everything that they can?'

'Yup. And knows everything worth knowing.'

Just like the elders, Kai thought. They would hear of any disputes, dangers, or weather changes before anyone else in the village did. He used to think as a young child that the Mother had gifted them some strange power to know all things, even while rarely leaving their chambers. Kai *still* thought they knew too much to be dependent solely on their senses.

The elders appeared to know his and Lia's whereabouts, even during their most random impulses. They would see through their every lie and confirm their every detail during their hearings; right down to their failure to catch prey during their hunts. Kai and Lia learned quickly not to bother lying whenever questioned, lest they only add more shame to themselves.

Kai suddenly smiled. It was in this state of deep reminiscence that he earned his first epiphany for the long nightfall.

He stood up with great zeal and said; 'I need to see the queen.'

8

⎯⎯⎯~⎯⎯⎯

*...but as long as we do what is right by us, we cannot expect more of ourselves.
The inevitable sleeplessness in our shame will be but a minuscule price to pay,
and this burden need not be carried but by those of us who have earned its
weight.*

*We long chose to embrace the disgrace that shall follow, for the sake of those
who shall come long after our days are spent...*

Excerpt from *The Two-Year Wander*
Author Unknown
Text Predates First Recorded Generation

Kai grew more and more accustomed to the vivid purple light the
further he walked. The carrot he ate on his way was not as rich in
flavour as the last, and there was only a mild faintness that came
with each bite. Sweat poured down his back and brows in the relentless heat.
He had the energy to eat and walk, and little else.

It was not so for the rabbit. It sped talked in every spare second, mostly
to itself, and hopped alongside Kai the whole way. He went from a rant on
his empty stomach, to praising the taste of the figs that materialised in his
paws, to grumbling about his stomach again. Then he teased Kai for his
sweaty skin and the last of Kai's attention span was spent. He took to just
saying *yes Citizen* in response to whatever he rambled about. He had meant
to mock the rabbit with it but found that occasionally saying it kept the
rabbit happily talking, whether Kai listened or not.

They soon came across another stream, riddled with pink petals from
the blossom tree over it. Kai removed his shirt to savour its cooling touch
and had a drink of it in small mouthfuls.

'I already said this is a bad idea, didn't I,' the rabbit said in between its mouthfuls. He stood on the bank of the stream as Kai laid in it. 'I have to say it again; this is bad. This is terrible, Smoothie.'

'Yes, Citizen.'

'No, really terrible Smoothie. Just terrible. She won't like a smoothskin in her forest, and she really won't be happy if you go to her court. It's terrible for me too; the queen won't like me taking—oh, do you think she already knows we're together already?'

'Yes, Citizen.'

'Yes!?'

Kai shot up out the water. 'Wait, what did you say?'

'I said *yes.*'

'What did you say before that?'

'You just told me you think--'

Citizen stopped, pricked his ears up and stared down the bank. Kai saw nothing there, but bushes surrounded by weeds and trees donned with vines.

'Dive, Smoothie,' Citizen practically whispered. 'I'll handle this.'

'What? *Dive*? *Handle* what?'

'I'm just a rabbit.'

'You're just...no, what does that--?'

'Dive, smoothie.'

Kai found himself under the water holding his nose in his surprise before his brain could protest. The water was very pure, and Kai could clearly see a deer walking along the bank before long, through the ripples surfacing the water. It stopped in front of the rabbit and seemed to clear its throat.

'Did I hear a voice,' it said, its voice deep and gruff.

'Umm, maybe,' the rabbit said. Kai could hear them talk well enough. He could see the deer standing on its hind legs and chewing on a mess of plants hanging from its mouth. Kai felt incredibly foolish in the realisation that the dear would have about as much trouble seeing him as he did seeing it, which is to say none.

Sure enough, not a second longer passed before the deer met Kai's eyes. It started with a face of nonchalance and kept staring for so long that Kai felt his breath running low. He waited for something, anything at all, from Citizen to show him *handling it*, but Citizen just stared at him as nonchalantly as the deer did.

'What's that,' the deer eventually said.

'Umm, that?' Citizen paused to think, so hard that one could practically see his brain sweating. 'That's…a mushroom?'

Kai would have hidden his face in his hands in shame if he could. *A mushroom.* He desperately wanted to laugh and might have, had he the breath left to do so. He had almost given up his sorry hiding spot when the deer said; 'Biggest mushroom I ever saw. Looks tasty.'

Kai couldn't hold it back any longer and spluttered bubbles to the surface. The deer was already otherwise engaged and talking about something else with the rabbit.

They spoke quietly and Kai couldn't hear their words anymore. It was of clear discomfort to Citizen, whatever they spoke about, as his ears drooped low while the deer spoke.

The deer eventually took its leave. Kai took a deep breath of sweet pollinated air before Citizen had raised his head.

'A mushroom,' Kai said, now with enough breath in him to giggle. Citizen nodded vacantly in response with droopy ears. 'That's what you meant by *handling* it? I can't believe that worked.'

'I'm that rabbit.'

'Huh?'

'The deer knew too. He called me *that rabbit.*'

'You're what rabbit?'

Citizen looked down at his own paws, quietly. He shot Kai the best smile he could conjure after a time, but his eyes were placid like stone. He went on hopping down the bank, without a word. Kai just quietly followed.

Together, they moved along the stream, then away from the bank and deeper into the woods. Citizen would at times pause with his ears pricked up at noises from the trees or bushes, then he would move on again, all without a word spoken.

They soon were in another cluster of trees and were draped in shadow, with scattered purple light paving the ground through the branches. Kai recognised this part of the forest, as they passed one thick tree trunk with a messy shape notched into the trunk. The arrow Kai had used to carve this was one of many he had used to hunt. He had hit nothing with that arrow either, of course, for which he was now deeply grateful. *Thank the Mother I was a poor shot.*

He had carved this shape while waiting for Lia to finish whatever she was doing in the same woods, many dayfalls ago. He had not drawn anything in particular; just some random squiggles to kill time, which slowly took the shape of some abstract boar or deer or something. Lia had decided it looked like a monkey underwater and relentlessly teased him for it for many cycles since.

It was the same dayfall when Kai first became enamoured by the purpura and the Ameyali Forest when Omaraa Zan had told him about strange tales of the forest during one of her increasingly rare walks through the village. She spoke of a *story,* which had been passed down through wiigwaasabak texts from the first known generation, of the glowing purple flowers that gave the forest its only sustained source of light for nightfall. She could not have anticipated that the tale would captivate Kai the way it did, as he had never felt nearly the same enthusiasm for anything else prior to that.

Maybe that was why she shared it with me at all, Kai reasoned. *Maybe she thought that it would be good for me to have something nice to think about for once.*

Kai was happy reminiscing about cycles long gone, but he still had no longing for home. He enjoyed making the unknown known to himself far too much to concern himself much over the familiarity he left behind in his tiny village.

He walked quickly to catch up with Citizen. Ahead of them, beyond the last line of trees in those woods, was another field, draped in orange as though its plumage were ablaze. The flowers were large and broad, each with long pink anthers in their core and vibrant orange petals. Each gracefully bowed and flowed to make way for Citizen moving through them and did the same for Kai as he followed.

He picked one flower from its stem and it swiftly lost its, shrivelling before his eyes and losing its bright radiance to a dull shade of dark brown. A sigh of awe flowed from Kai's lips.

A strange aroma clung to this field, but not an unpleasant one. It smelled of…life. Life in its purest form. It even *tasted* of life when he breathed in. It was pleasant, almost invigorating, to just exist in that place.

'Citizen,' Kai said.

'Hmm?'

'Can we stop for a bit?'

'Why?'

'I'm tired.' Kai felt just fine, in truth. He in fact couldn't recall a time he felt so vigorous. He simply wanted to savour this place while he could, to be warmed by its aura and to breathe its air for a little longer.

'We shouldn't really rest *here*, Smoothie,' Citizen began to protest, but Kai had already sat down. Citizen pouted but soon joined him.

They sat side by side, together on a patch between the bowing flowers. The smell was intense so close to the ground and Kai wondered how Citizen was able to cope with his strong nose. But then he suspected that his nose was keen for all things edible and not for much else.

'You hungry,' Citizen asked.

Kai grinned. 'Nope.'

'Me too. I think I should have--' He didn't bother to finish before he stuffed his face with a carrot from Kai's pack. Kai fidgeted with the berries still lying at the base, turning slightly rotten in the heat. *Lia won't get these after all,* he conceded. *I'll pick her some more along the way.*

'*Sagali.*'

Kai blinked. 'Huh?'

'*Huh,*' Citizen said through a mouthful.

'What's *sagali?*'

'*Sagali?*'

'Yes, Citizen, what's sagali?'

'What's a sagali?'

They looked at each other with equal confusion. Kai laughed at the pure bafflement on Citizen's face and Citizen laughed this time with him. Kai realised it was the first time hearing the rabbit laugh beyond a slight titter. It was extremely soft, a far cry from his usual voice and his ears shook as he did.

'*Sagali,*' went the voice again. But neither Kai nor Citizen were done laughing. They looked at each other again, as baffled as they were startled.

'No,' Citizen cried out, glaring wide-eyed past Kai's shoulder. 'No, no, no!'

Kai stood and spun around. He at first saw nothing but the many orange lights of the field's flowers.

Then he saw the one yellow orb hovering before him, silent and still.

'*Sagali,*' it said.

The queen of the Ameyali Forest had her eyes upon them.

9

A male Hominum must be versed in the discipline of hunting or craftsmanship to be permitted to mate and child rear.

A female Hominum must be well versed in the discipline of herbalism, cookery or craftsmanship to be permitted to mate and child rear.

None shall be exempt from this condition in The Ritual of New Birth.

Tenet of the *Hominum's Ritual of New Birth*
Imposed by Osas Zan Ne
Generation of Osas
Second Recorded Generation

'*Sagali*.' The lumen's voice was soft, like that of a carefree child. It spoke its one word with difficulty, as though it were forced from its mouth with great strain. Its glow was intense, like the lumen that came before. So much so that Kai couldn't see whatever body must have been residing at its core.

This one neither fled nor flinched when Kai held his hand out to it. There was none of the warmth on his fingers he expected to emanate from the light. He felt nothing, as though the light were not there at all.

'Catch it, Smoothie,' Kai heard Citizen say as his hand approached its core. It was enough to startle the lumen into backing away.

'Maybe it's saying *hello*,' Kai said.

'It's *not* saying hello.'

'What's it saying then?'

'It's saying *sagali*.'

Kai let out a long, measured sigh. Citizen was apparently a master at literalism. 'And what does *Sagali* mean, Citizen?'

'You're asking me?'

'Yes.'

'I don't know. What does it mean?' Kai, distracted with incredulity as he was, did not notice how close the lumen had drawn until it spoke again.

'*Sagali.*' Citizen made a leap for it but missed by a sizable margin. '*Sagali,*' it said again.

'Come here,' Citizen cried out with another leap, missing again. It hovered before his flustered face before he found his feet.

'*Sagali.*'

'Citizen,' Kai said before he could leap again. 'What are you doing?'

'Catching the lumen.' He jumped. Missed again. He spluttered angrily with the dirt that flew in his mouth.

'*Sagali.*'

'Why are you catching it?'

'It will tell the queen on us, Smoothie.'

'So? We're going to see the queen anyway.'

'No, you don't understand.' The lumen flew behind Kai, out of Citizen's reach. He eyed it like a wholly unintimidating predator. 'You're a smoothskin in her forest,' Citizen continued. 'If we could see the queen before she found out, I could explain why you're here. But if she finds us first, she'll set her hunters on us.'

'Oh.' Kai did not want to imagine what a hunter of the forest could be, and he was afraid to ask. He watched the lumen float with a rhythmless dance. 'Do you think it understands us?'

'It's a citizen of the forest, Smoothie. It probably does.'

Kai reached his hand out to it again. It seemed unbothered. 'You want to tell the queen about us?'

'*Sagali.*'

'That means *yes,* Smoothie.'

Kai had to grin a little. 'You don't know what it means.' The lumen laid on his outstretched arm. It was delicate and tickled his skin. He felt a strange pulsation from it, like a slow and soft heartbeat. 'Maybe its *name* is Sagali. Or is that all they can say?'

'No, I've never heard a lumen talk before. The queen is the only one who can hear them. She and the vice.'

'*Vice?*'

'Yeah. Anyway, don't let it get away smoothie.'

'But it's not trying to get away.'

Citizen blinked at that logic. The lumen, in fact, appeared at leisure in their company. Its glow steadily fluctuated like a pulse. Kai saw what resembled a tail when its glow dimmed and two tiny black circles, which may have been eyes.

Then dawned on him, finally, the potential peril all around them. *Orange lights.*

'Do you think there are other's here,' Kai said in an instinctive whisper. He searched through the field of beautiful light, each glow suddenly seeming sinister. Each flower blended with the others and formed a swaying sea of orange. It was deathly quiet, but for the wind rattling the petals and trees.

Alarm struck Citizen's face in an instant. He too looked about the field, with his ears erected. 'Let's go, smoothie,' he said at last. 'We really shouldn't be here.' Kai followed him through the parting flowers. Citizen bounced hurriedly for the neighbouring woods. The flowers looked to be growing brighter with every step as if to light their path. Kai could see Citizen panting as he hopped, and he saw glimpses of his panic-stricken eyes as he kept scanning the field.

Kai now felt guilty for the risk his presence had brought up this rabbit. Citizen had more to lose than Kai did, should word of his being here have reached his queen. Kai could find Lia without the queen should he have needed to, as was his original intention. But this was Citizens home, and the residents of the forest were his family and his friends. Kai considered that perhaps, for Citizen's sake, he need not see the queen. For his sake, he need not depend on him to guide him through a forest with which Kai should have already been accustomed. For his sake, he could find Lia by himself.

But sadly, there were too many eyes on them already.

It was mesmerising and terrifying to see the entire field shifting in perfect unity. Every lumen hovered above the now dark flower stems, ascending like a sea of flames. They danced soundlessly about each other in flawless harmony.

The night sky became very bright indeed, as more lumen descended from the skies and formed a rippling sheet of light with the others.

'Run,' Kai heard in the form of a shout.

So, he did. He ran after Citizen, who left the field of naked stems behind him. The descending lumen embedded themselves into the flower stems from whence the others came. Others followed him and Citizen out of the field and through the trees.

Citizen moved like a blur, hopping frantically over tree roots along the path of fallen leaves, with lumen dancing at his ears. Plants whipped Kai's legs as he ran and stumbled over vines on his way. Citizen darted into another cluster of trees, so Kai did too, ducking beneath branches and scratching himself on bushes. The lumen shone around his feet, following him through the shadows and purpura light.

Their footsteps were all that broke what would have been tranquillity there. The lumen haunted them, silently and readily keeping pace, while gracefully dodging whatever hung in their way.

Kai glimpsed more wonders they were passing; red flowers pulsating on thick drooping stems, glowing vines binding tree trunks, disfigured shapes in the shadows beyond the purpura. They all passed by like a blur.

The adrenaline of a chase was not foreign to Kai after many a day spent playing chase with his sister in the forest and stalking prey together. His body learned long ago to cope with the long hunt, but with how easily the lumen stayed with them, this felt like a chase without an end in sight.

'We can't just keep running, Citizen.'

No answer. Citizen's eyes betrayed his state of panic. He could manage no more than to run wherever his feet led him. They ran still and kept running until they were met with a dead-end, of sorts. The ground rose in a massive and steep mound, with a tree of pink blossoms at its lofty peak.

Citizen did not slow, despite the immense obstacle before them, pacing frantically towards its base. He hopped over the last rock laid before it, then he was gone. The lumen stopped at the hole he crawled into.

Kai stumbled over the rock also and spared no thought, crawling through the hole after him. It was snug, but spacey enough to move at a pace. The lumen's light from the outside kept him from being in total darkness for a moment, but it only grew darker the further he crawled. The lumen refused to follow, and soon all Kai could see was blackness.

Kai took deep breaths of dusty air, his heart pounding and his hands shaking.

'Citizen,' he called.

The only answer was his own echo.

10

Light is a curse when the path hidden beyond darkness is tainted.
I have often been grateful for the blessing of blindness in this peculiar life of mine.

Excerpt from *Memoirs of Mora the Blind*
by Moro Ki
Second Recorded Generation

Kai crawled through the darkness. The air was heavy and hot, and dirt fell onto his face. His coughing and wheezing made their own echoes through the tunnel.

It became narrower the further he went until his hair brushed against the ceiling and he was forced to crawl on his elbows. Grime slithered down his sweat ridden back, and thick webs tickled his skin. Tiny pebbles stabbed at his knees and tore his flesh.

He moved rhythmically, one elbow over the other, dragging his limp feet through the dirt. He called again, through his raspy breath: 'Citizen?' No answer. He was no doubt far lost in the darkness with his smaller and nimbler body. Kai didn't blame him for it, as he had a right to fear the queen's eyes, but Kai could not imagine a worse time to be abandoned by his guide.

'*Pearls in the snowflakes of nightfall,*' Kai quietly sang. The echo bloomed his words into a consonance. '*Dayfall shines. But by the reeds by the ashes of the daring are the brightest and truest of lights.*' The song brought far less comfort this time, as he coughed between nearly every verse and heaved for stale air. Still, he sang; '*When they tremble and they stutter, we…we hold our heads high. And…and memories of the forgotten will fill the pages of time. And* *the pa…*urgh. *And the pages turn beyond the hand's many--*'

'Sagali.'

Kai smacked his head against the ceiling in his surprise. He saw lights through the pain and saw them still when the pain subsided. He could see now old cobwebs hanging on the walls, the dust that had been plaguing his every breath and the tunnel ahead leading into blackness. Before him was a lumen. *The* lumen. The walls dulled and brightened with the rhythm of its pulse.

'Sagali.'

Were you with me this whole time, Kai tried to say but fell into a fit of coughs at the mere attempt of putting the words to his lips. His insides ached, and what was an inconvenience to breathe had become a crushing pressure each time he inhaled.

The lumen slowly drifted away, deeper into the tunnel. Kai followed as well as he could, forcing himself through his heaving and aching lungs to crawl again, staying close to his new lone source of pulsing light.

This was how they went on together for what felt like forever. The tunnel became so cramped that he practically slithered on his belly like a snake. The unending brown walls were maddening, as it only changed so much as to don dead or dying vines on its walls between webs.

He reached into his pack and stuffed a couple of berries into his mouth, and immediately spat them out again. Barely any sweetness was left and clumped on them were the remains of stale, mushy potatoes with a rotten aroma. The texture was just as atrocious as the taste. He scraped out what he could of the potatoes from his pack before eating a couple more.

Berries were not particularly his favourite, but fruit was a treat in nightfall to savour and a welcome change from the gruel and lukewarm water he was accustomed to. He hated eating these alone and he hated the necessity for sustenance he now had.

Even now, the berries tasted like dirt in his mouth; flavourless and stale. He anticipated a sweet flow on his tongue to make his jaw ache, but it never came. He kept on chewing regardless, spitting out the seeds as he went.

Then, a noise echoed through the tunnel; one not made by himself. It came from far ahead. It was subtle but was distinctly…scuttling. Or perhaps more like *pattering*, like a legion of tiny footsteps.

He stopped where he laid, helpless to what was to come, unable to turn and unwilling to proceed.

Spiders, he imagined. *There must be spiders here to make these webs. Or maybe moles. Or ants. What lives in tunnels?*

He was scared; truly scared for the second time since entering this forest again, and still unashamed to admit to himself. *Little Orphan Star,* he teased to himself in Lia's voice, reimagining her mocking gaze and haughty grin as she said it. *Orphan Star will take you home.* Kai lamented that even this false comfort was useless while the stars were out of sight.

He bit his lip and crawled ahead on his trembling hands and knees. He assured himself of his own courage, of his ability to move on in the face of what approached. But he merely had little choice, in truth.

'Sagali.'

The sound pounding down the walls soon surrounded him, as their bearers drew ever closer.

A face burst out from the shadows.

Kai erupted into a scream; one he would later rather recall as a shout or a roar. He would plan to tell Lia the same if she ever heard of this story, which he knew she somehow would. He would not resist telling her about this or the many other stories his journey would surely bring, and this one would be among those with a less than flattering image.

'You're agitating my antennas.'

Kai heard the voice clearly, despite his own screaming. It was deep and imposing yet quiet, like an angry whisper. It birthed a shiver through his back and made his skin itch.

He pried his eyes open and was met by a thousand eyes glaring back at him through the lumen's light.

He would not be able to refer to his second scream as anything but.

'Stop your wailing at once.'

He subdued it for long enough to see that the thousand eyes were more like seven or eight, each pitch black and shiny. It was a long and hairy face that owned them, with fangs protruding from where its mouth would be, spear-like at their tips. Its long, hairy legs stood tall and its knees stroked the tunnel's ceiling.

It stood flawlessly still, not even moving as it breathed. Kai, contrarily, found his entire body shaking. So overwhelmed was he that he could not find the sagacity to describe the feeling.

'You are trespassing in my abode, smoothskin. What is your purpose here?'

'Spider,' was the only raspy reply Kai managed.

'Astute of you,' the spider said. 'I will ask this only once and advise you to comply with haste; leave my tunnel.'

'But…spiders don't dig,' Kai said, in a moment of not-quite clarity, but of uninspired impulse.

'Astute,' the spider remarked. 'For a certainty, astute.'

He in truth did not know for certain, as his experience was limited to just one spider which he had found roaming the lavender fields in dayfall and taken home. He and Lia named it *Patch* after the creamy spots on its hair and managed to keep it in secret for seven cycles until it had escaped and sent the village into an evening of crazed panic and a dayfall of more than mild spite. It was released into the forest on the very same cycle.

Kai had watched it in that short time with fascination, at how it hunted by weaving its web for prey and slowly devoured the meal. But it did little else but sleep.

'Whether or not I was the architect of this tunnel is irrelevant,' the spider continued. Its mouth never moved while it spoke. Its voice seemed to flow from its core and directly into Kai's skull. It stared into him, unblinking with its black eyes. Its rear end almost filled the tunnel behind it. 'Whether or not I was the architect of this tunnel is irrelevant. I demand still that you leave me in peace.'

'I need to pass.' Kai found words flowed easily, despite how his heart trembled in his chest.

'So that you may pass deeper still into my home? You may return from the way you came.'

'I…I really need to pass.'

'Hmph,' the spider muttered. 'Then we are at an impasse.'

'*Impasse?*'

Something like a sigh flowed from its abdomen. 'How I loathe the abandonment of knowledge. It is an awkward deadlock where we can neither proceed nor retreat. Perhaps, then, you would address my question, seeing as we shall have the time. What is your purpose here?'

The spider shifted its leg. Kai trembled as its hairs brushed against his skin. He swallowed whatever sound threatened to burst from his lips. The orange at the tip of its fangs twitched as it raised its head. *It's just a spider. Just like Patch, but bigger. So big much bigger.* 'M-my friend came in here, and I came after him. A rabbit.'

'I've not seen any rabbits, but I heard footsteps not long ago and a song shortly after. It has been a long while since anyone came through this place. Your friend must have gone where the tunnel splits.'

'Where does that go?'

'Outdoors.'

'Then please, let me go after him and I'll be leaving. I promise we won't come back in here again.'

'That's fair. However, you should be warned that you will be less than…actually, that is your concern alone. Follow and I will show you the way.'

It shifted its immense body and crawled backwards through the shadows. Kai realised that the spider was too big to turn around itself. It must have had to move this way through this tunnel all the time, loaning more credit to Kai's belief that it did not dig it itself. Nothing would build its own home too small for itself.

The tunnel was long, feeling longer still by how slowly Kai crawled. He became aware again of how short of breath he was and how thick the air had become. It was like breathing a cloud of wood fire smoke. He was soaked in the sweat pouring from his brow and nestling in his every crevice. How immensely refreshing it was when a tiny gust of wind flowed through the tunnel for a moment and licked his skin.

'Down there,' the spider said. The tunnel split into two. The spider filled one of the paths with its body, looking at Kai expectantly. The other path was similarly drenched in shadow with only its entrance lit by the lumen's light. But Kai saw a glimpse of light at the end of it; a dull orange in a tone like the fields from whence he came.

'Thank you,' he said in earnest, not only to the spider but to the light itself. Never had the gift of light and the prospect of the night air offered such joy as it did then.

'Do not burden yourself with gratitude,' it curtly said. 'I want you out of my home. Nothing more.'

Kai made his way anxiously down the tunnel again, devoid of energy for the lack of air in his lungs. Pattering feet followed him on his way, no doubt to ensure his exit. Having the spider so close behind him may well have been just as terrifying as facing it, and the thought made Kai's skin crawl no less.

It was not so much further to go, Kai knew, as the outside breeze touched his skin generously.

He persevered, awaiting the first glimpse of moonlight to greet him. But it never came; not even when he fell out onto the grass through the tunnel's exit and into the outdoors.

Only through the grace of the lumen's light and the lone patch of glowing orange flowers on the ground could he make out shapes of plumage in the darkness.

The air there was bitter.

11

The rain was spent, but the forbidden fire of Waya's forest still lived.

Waya grew infatuated with its relentless strength and slept beneath it to feel its warmth on his fur, night after night.

And night after night, the desire for the forbidden burned within his heart.

Excerpt from *The Tale of Waya*
By Timor Ro
Hominum Tribe Writer, Generation of Inti
Fourth Recorded Generation

The pitch-black air came with an array of eerie sounds. Gusts and wails came from the darkness all around him. There was a chill in the wind that felt like frost on Kai's sweaty skin.

'Sagali.'

The voice and lone light from above his head were all that kept him from being alone. All that guided his feet was a trail of paw prints in the dirt he had found near the tunnel's exit. They looked fresh to Kai's eyes, which was enough to cause him to follow.

The chill gradually became more potent along his trail. It wasn't cold in truth, but nor was it as warm as he had begun to grow accustomed. He rubbed his arms and shivered, though he could not credit it entirely to the nip in the air.

An unnerving sensation crawled up his leg again; the feeling of hair stroking his bare skin. He jumped, slapping at his shin with a feeble yelp. Nothing was there, yet again. *Vines and flowers,* he told himself. *Nothing but vines and flowers.*

'Sagali.'

'*Sagali* yourself,' Kai said miserably.

Something shifted in the shadows to their voices. He halted, heart in mouth. Nothing came but the same resonating sounds from the distance.

He walked again, faster with his face to the ground and hands over his ears. *Nothing will come for me,* he decided to assure himself. *It would have come already if it were. Anything would see me easily in this light.*

He soon came to realise that no matter how long he stayed in the dark, his eyes would refuse to adjust to it. He walked into seemingly every vine and stumbled on seemingly every unearthed root along his way. The lumen shone brightly enough only to show him his very next step.

And on that next step, his face was wrapped with what could only be webbing, thicker than it had any right to be. He clawed at it, scratching his skin and ripping the web off him. He felt it sticking to his hands the more he pulled at it.

He kept clawing away until more webbing stuck to his hands than his face; both of which itched terribly. He could not contain the groan that seeped out from his lips when he was finally done.

Kai opened his eyes to find that the paw prints on the ground had vanished. He saw only webbing glistening atop the dirt.

He turned around in a rush of panic, mercifully finding the prints there behind him. Here was where they ended, in a cluster of upheaved dirt in one messy mound. Kai looked around him and saw a web ridden tree trunk with a huge wildflower growing from its core.

A disconcerting thought dawned on him at the sight of the mess of webs. He thought about how the trail of paws ended in a cluster, as though the owner had paced about in a circle. For his run to have abruptly ended in such a state, Citizen may have doubled back on himself already.

Citizen perhaps had not even realised how far behind he had left Kai, panic-ridden as he was and deaf to his call. Perhaps it was here that he stopped with his panic spent and regained some reason.

Kai did not meet him on his way, meaning Citizen must have strayed from the trail. Kai thought he may never find him again if he had strayed into the darkness as he feared.

'Citizen!' The shout came out of impulse. He waited, but he was answered only by the wind wailing through the trees.

He leaned against the tree bark, feeling suddenly faint and short of breath. Following his guide only served to make him more lost. He had no semblance of an idea of how to proceed.

'*Sagali.*'

Should I wait here, Kai thought. *Citizen might remember this place and come back to it, knowing I'd have followed him. Or he might go back to where we first lost each other. So, I should go back to the tunnel. But maybe he wouldn't care to look for me.*

Or what if he never left the tunnel? That spider wanted me to leave badly. Did he—

'*Sagali.*'

Kai looked above him, where the lumen flew around a group of large pods wrapped in glistening white, hanging from the trees. His skin itched as he fought against imagining the fate of poor prey trapped within those webs. Another spider. Another *immense* spider, to have caught prey so large. He shivered again at the prospect of meeting another of those *things* here and quickly resolved to leave, lest he became one of those pods himself.

Then, that harrowing thought bred a new one. Kai looked up again, with much more purpose, searching each of the pods where the lumen flew, meticulously.

One was unique, with a pair of floppy ears hanging from the bottom and a pair of wide and terrified eyes glowing yellow, staring at the ground where Kai stood.

'Citizen!' Kai pounced at the tree and climbed with renewed vigour. He reached the branch Citizen hung from in what felt like an instant. He hauled him up by the web that suspended him and brought him into his arms.

The lumen's light shone on them both, showing Citizen in his entirety. His eyes were huge and bloodshot. His mouth and body were covered in intricately woven webs.

Kai scraped what he could of it from his mouth. It stuck to his fur and tore some off with it.

'S-smoothie.' Citizen's voice was husky and shaky, as though the word pained him.

'Hold on, I'll get you out.' Kai clawed at the webs on his body. His fingers only became covered themselves and stuck to Citizen's fur.

'Smoothie, we have to run. It'll--'

Kai wrapped around Citizen's body and gave him what was meant to be a brief hug until their bodies stuck together. Citizen took it in silence.

Perhaps it meant little to the citizens of this forest; perhaps they expressed affection in other ways, or perhaps not. But it mattered not. This rabbit was only the second friend Kai had ever shared this affection with. He really had found himself a friend, he realised. This short time together was enough for Kai to see him as such, and not want to lose him again.

He pried himself away from Citizen with great effort and he clawed away at him again with a new burst of urgency. But he stopped almost as soon as he started, as the lumen's light became tainted with a new shadow. Kai's skin crawled once more as fear set into his heart.

He heard scuffling close behind them, on the very same tree. The branch subtly bent with a new weight burdening it. It became darker still to Kai's eyes as the shadow loomed over him, blocking what was left of the lumen's light above them.

'Smoothie,' Citizen said after the silence that dragged a long while. Kai did not prolong the inevitable any longer. He faced again the terrible figure of legs and hair. Drool fell ungracefully from its fangs.

There was only pale hair where its eyes should have been.

It said from its core; 'What a pleasant aroma you have.'

*

Kai's head ached terribly for a time. The pressure of blood rushing to his head had been nearly unbearable, rendering him about ready to pass out. His body slowly adapted to the sensation of being the wrong way up, though the dizziness had yet to subside.

He pictured himself then as a bat sleeping, or in hibernation, or whatever it was they did when they hung from the branches of the sacred burial tree in the village. They were like small birds and blended well with the nightfall sky, but Kai had good eyes.

He imagined himself now as one of them, peacefully dormant with one of his brethren beside him. It helped to alleviate the fear a little. It helped him to imagine he *belonged* here, merely sleeping, and to ignore that he was wide awake.

'Are you hungry,' came the voice in the shadows, devoid of any of its usual zeal. It sounded thoroughly drained.

'Yes, Citizen.'

'Me too. I have a polood at my burrow too. It'll be turning bad soon. What a waste. All that sweetness and juiciness and…stuff. I found two of them, but I had to share one with another citizen, cos he was bigger than me. Probably faster too, since bears are fast. Hey, if it's still ripe when we get back, I'll share some with you. You can have a bite.'

'Yes, Citi—wait, a what?'

'Huh?'

'You said *polood?* What's a polood?'

'Oh, it's wonderful, Smoothie. It's like a flower, but it's not a flower. Or, it might be. Actually...yes, it's not a flower. But it might be one.'

'So, it just looks like a flower.'

'Yeah. A big flower. And you take off the petals to eat it. But they might not be petals. But they look like petals. Actually--'

'Citizen...'

'Yeah, I think they're petals. The polood probably *is* a flower. So, you take the petals off and take out the middle bit. Then you take all the hair off and eat it like that.'

'It grows hair? Like mine?'

'It looks like hair. Actually, it might not be hair.'

'Let's just call it hair.' Kai smiled despite it all. It may have been a smile to lift his spirits more than anything.

'What's funny, Smoothie?'

'Huh? I didn't laugh.'

'But you're smiling.'

'You can see me?'

'Of course, you're right there,' Citizen weakly tittered.

'It's not too dark for you?'

'Not really. I can see you just fine.'

'Wow. You have amazing eyes.'

'Really?' Kai could *hear* Citizen blushing in his voice. It was like he sang the word. 'You're supposed to feel blind in Susuuri, Smoothie. That's what I was told last time. So, maybe your eyes are normal.'

'Susuuri? Is that where we are?'

'Yeah, this is Susuuri. Anywhere outside the Hyachin is Susuuri.'

'Well, I do feel blind. I can't even see myself.' He saw only blackness around him, with the lumen now gone, taking Kai's sole source of light with it. It was a bizarre sensation; to be hanging from what looked like nothing at all.

'*Last time*,' Kai echoed, only now realising the significance of the words.'

'Huh?'

'You said *last time*. What last time?' Silence. Kai sensed how Citizen stared at him wide-eyed, in this heavy tone of quiet. He decided this time to press. 'It was *you* who you were talking about, when you said someone disobeyed the queen, right? You've left the Hyachin before?'

The silence lingered a while longer. Kai remembered the way Citizen's voice had grown sad and how his head hung when he spoke of those *stories*. Only now was the reason so obvious; *he* was the subject of those stories. And it was why he knew so well what came of disobeying the queen.

Citizen finally uttered a feeble yet certain; '*Yes*'.

Yes. The word was harrowing and layered in a way Kai could not truly fathom. But he understood enough; Citizen had been to this part of the forest, to *Susuuri*, against the established order of things. Citizen was a part of something here that was outrageous enough to label him as *that rabbit* and have him recognised by the other animals by sight alone, as a rabbit unique among all others. The memories of whatever took place clearly still pained him.

Kai again resolved to inquire no further, and this time, to never do so again. It was enough for Kai to know that Citizen had once seen fit to rebel and suffered for it still.

12

⁓

…but the sole gift in regret is a reminder that we are born of mere dust.

Farro Zan Me
Generation of Farro
First Recorded Generation

C itizen dragged his feet through the violet plumage and glowing flowers, slower than usual. He took another bite of the huge seed-like thing in his hands, chomping on it until it turned to sludge in his mouth. He had no inkling of what this thing was. It had fallen from the trees into his hands, as could only be done by the works of fate. It was soft with a savoury aroma. It was neither tasty nor vile, but its flavours exploded on his tongue and tasted like…tree bark. Sweet tree bark, or at least how he imagined bark would taste. Citizen decided then that tree bark would be next on his list of things to try.

The seed-like thing did help in some way. Having something to bite on and having the sensation of chewing to savour on his way; it served to distract him for a little while.

He paused, for what must have been the tenth time, looking through the fields stretching out before him, wondering how long he had to tread until they ended. Then he took another bite. Then he started walking again, briskly, knowing he would pause again before long.

The cycled repeated, again and again. He wished deeply that the field where he treaded would finally end, yet he would also be glad were they to stretch on and on indefinitely.

So tense he was that even a casual greeting from a fellow rabbit in the fields made him jump. He returned a shaky greeting when he found his feet again. She merrily chatted, as expected of a bunny, but Citizen could not keep up for a rare change. He could only return polite nods, even as the topic changed to his favourite of all while she drooled.

She noted Citizen's apparent shakiness and suggested foods with which he was already well acquainted to eat, to wane off sickness. They parted and Citizen was on his way again, sauntering through the fields with heavy trepidation.

The end of the purple field finally appeared in the form of blackness beyond tree stubs glowing from the flowers at their base.

He walked sheepishly toward the paired trees that marked the end of the Hyachin's jurisdiction, erected in the form of a natural doorway into darkness.

His first step away from the Hyachin was the hardest, as it always was. He quickly felt the chill of Susuuri on his fur and weakness seeping into his body, as he always did.

Each step thereafter was a cause to despair. Each dead leaf that crumbled under Citizen's feet was like the roar of a hunter to his ears. A mess of sounds echoed his every move; slow trickling water, scuttling from the dying trees above, distant howls resonating through the ground. Beneath it all was a subtle yet intrusive sound of what must have been laughter, untamed to the point of being maniacal. Citizen walked along the natural crevice in the ground as bid and let it guide his steps.

He very nearly found his senses as the light of the Hyachin grew distant behind him, and he fought the instinct to run back to where he came from, or to anywhere that wasn't here. But his senses were sated by the marker he soon found; a simple line carved thinly into the base of a tree. It was a blessing and a curse, for he was close now, and that realisation came in the only form of terror that was at all pleasant to him.

He followed the line, away from the dying trees and into a cold shallow stream. Various herbs dwelled in the water and blessed the air with a neat and soothing aroma. The trickling sound turned into splashing the further Citizen followed the stream until it became like thunder at its source.

The waterfall's sound was well enhanced in this place of otherwise nothingness. At its base was where Citizen found the other marker; a line like the first, carved onto a moss riddled stone, this time with a crooked smile carved beneath it. Citizen sighed at the sight of it, with a warmth rising in his gut. The dread within him only grew with it.

He followed the trail into more overgrown and dull plumage. He thanked the Mother for his fine nose, that he could be assured none of Susuuri's citizens *were close by. He sniffed the air obsessively as we walked.*

Finally, in an opening where plants had been flattened into a space of resting, there was the third mark; a simple but large cross on the ground made up of dead branches. There Citizen sat, thoroughly exhausted and with his heart thumping in his throat, his energy ever sapping away.

That awaited sensation flowed through his veins at last, the sensation he only ever felt at this very moment without exception; excitement. *Excitement accompanied by a bitter aftertaste of guilt. It was enough to keep him from dormancy in his exhaustion.*

It was a quiet spot again, as it always was. She was gifted in finding serene places that no one else treaded.

'Boo.' The softest of whispers seeped into his ear, so close that her breath tickled him. He shot up, unable as usual to suppress the howl of surprise that had become the custom for their meeting. She didn't suppress her laughter, letting it flow wild and free.

Only when she finished did Citizen see her bright, radiant eyes open. They were deeply yellow with a hint of orange, warm and effortlessly hypnotising. They trapped the words in his throat and forced them back into his gut.

'Why, hello,' she said, showing her perfectly formed teeth in her mischievous smile, and flowing her tail gracefully behind her pointed ears.

Citizen himself summoned the brightest smile he could muster with all the vigour he had left, as he always did.

13

The heavens, enraged at Waya's haughtiness, called out by way of kindness;

'Do not admire the fire
For what your desire
Shall only gift you great ire.'

But day after day, the desire still obsessed the guardian Waya's thoughts and overcame his heart, until his duty and kindness were slain by greed and ambition.

Excerpt from *The Tale of Waya*
By Timor Ro
Hominum Tribe Writer, Generation of Inti
Fourth Recorded Generation

Kai dreamed of home, of the village endowed with warmth under the radiance of dayfall. Lumen scouted the village like butterflies, glowing brighter than the sun itself. From the roofs of the huts sprung purpura from his earliest childhood fantasies, not bloomed yet still bright purple. The ground was clothed with wildly grown flowers, taller than the tallest of Hominum.

It was beautiful, in every sense and way, yet it was ugly too, in more ways still. Though Kai's eyes were overcome, his ears were not even tickled. Silence. No voices of the villagers' cheerful yet monotonous talks. None of the soft crackling of fresh prey spinning over the cooks' fires. No grinding from the woodworkers' labour. No one was here but him.

He wanted to be out there, wherever the others were, beyond those walls holding him and the beauty within them, to where the outside lurked in pitch blackness like a hole in the sky.

One lonely whisper lit the air; *Sagali*. Others followed suit. *Sagali, sagali, sagali.* More joined in a harmonious melody, like a chaotic song.

The sun beamed to awesome brightness, as though in rapturous applause, as did the field of flowers wrapping Kai in an embrace. So bright did the village become that it possessed his entire vision. He tried to lift his hand before his face but found his arms pinned at his sides through the bondage of vines. He forced his eyes shut and endured the bright yellow light that seeped through.

Silence again. A short-lived silence, before one more *sagali* was uttered, close enough to his ears to feel the lumen's warmth.

Close enough for his eyes to burst open and see the light before his face.

'Get out of it.' It was Citizen's voice and it was far from a whisper. In fact, the lumens light showed him swinging aggressively, yet pointlessly, in outrage from the fine silver silk holding him from his feet.

The lumen danced around Kai's head in a frenzy. The contrast of its light to Susuuri's darkness was agonising.

'You hear me,' Citizen said, gnashing his teeth in his helpless frustration. 'Get out.'

'Citizen, what are you doing?'

'Look, Smoothie. There's a lumen in your face.'

'Yeah, thanks. I hadn't noticed.'

'You're welcome.' And on he went, swinging from his feet and gnashing his teeth. He made noises with his mouth, something like a mix of a goat and a sick bird, with all the aggression he could. Kai had to just watch all the while, utterly fascinated.

'Help me, Smoothie,' Citizen cried out.

'I still don't know what you're doing.'

'Getting the lumen.' He was deeply out of breath already, swinging only from the momentum of his bindings. 'It's spying on us.'

'It's not spying on us. It helped me.'

'How is *this* helping?'

'I meant it helped me earlier. Before I found you.'

'It might not be the same one.'

'But it's saying *Sagali* again. It's obviously the same one.'

'Huh, I think...maybe they all say--'

'You already said they don't!'

It had gradually gotten darker in Kai's distraction, with the lumen steadily ascending until its light left them in almost total darkness again. Kai could barely make out the shape of Citizen swinging before him.

Something had changed in the air. Something lurked close by that made Kai's skin crawl. He didn't need to wonder what form it would take for long.

'See, it's getting away, Smooth--'

'Shh.'

The creature made subtle scratches against the tree branches, unmistakably drawing closer. It was heavy and Kai felt the tree straining under its weight. Dread crept into his bloodstream. He had avoided pondering over why they hung where they did, until right then. He remembered how Patch would bind its prey and return hours or cycles later to sate its hunger.

Down it came, descending the tree trunk. It was as huge as Kai recalled, even bigger than the spider in the tunnel. Its pale hair glistened with perfect clarity, like torch fire, with what remained of the lumen's light. It settled itself below the branch where they hung.

Kai heard Citizen wheezing as he finally caught sight of it himself. It sat still as stone. One passing by would not spare it a second glance. This creature's natural hunting prowess was all too apparent. Its lack of eyes made it appear even less natural than it already did.

'What do you want,' Kai finally said, with some vigour that surprised himself.

'Want,' the spider echoed. Its voice was a deep whisper that slithered into Kai's ears. 'Oh, don't mind. I'm merely deliberating. Very soft and smooth skin. Not much sustenance to speak of, but you'll easily be digested. And you've little hair on your flesh, so you won't be clogging my belly. The little ball of fur over there can be desert.' Kai could hear the *fur ball* whimper. 'But I'll have to reduce it first. And peel it before that. Fancy having all *that* stuff in me.' It broke its trance and moved, crawling up the trunk again. The sound of its feet made Kai's gut churn.

'Reduced,' Citizen echoed with his voice a mess of tremors.

'Yes, reduced.' The creature hung upside down, etching its way toward them as the branch strained to hold its weight and theirs. 'I'll peel all that hair off your flesh and spit my venom down your body. You'll slowly melt in my webs, bit by bit until all that's left of you is clogs of slime. I'll suck up all that good meat and savour every morsel of you. I'll do the same to you, hairless one, but we can dispense with the peeling.'

'No, you won't,' Kai blurted out before the fur ball whimpered again. It made the creature stop in its tracks. 'Excuse you?'

'Y-you won't eat us. Otherwise, you would have covered our faces so we would suffocate. You left our heads uncovered so that we could breathe. So, you want to keep us alive.'

The creature bellowed a harrowing laugh from his core that shook even the dying leaves on Susuuri's floor. It was hollow and lifeless, not at all born of joy or humour. Just a rough and strained expression of malice.

'Amusing. Amusing and new. Amusing that my prey could be so...audacious. Even in the face of such helplessness and a great many causes for fear. Are you so accustomed to the role of quarry for the peril you face to phase you so little?'

'W-what's a quarry,' Citizen asked.

'Intriguing,' the spider continued. 'I concede that your words carry truth. *Partial* truth. Indeed, as much as it pains me to waste such a convenient and ready meal, I will not eat you on this day. However, that furball is entirely mine to savour.'

Citizen blabbered, his voice too shaky to come out as anything but a cluster of stutters. 'B-but you left my head uncovered too,' he finally managed.

'Oh, not for any extension of mercy, I assure you. The hairless one interrupted my work and I had to abandon you to catch it. It was merely an unhappy coincidence that I hadn't the time to finish you. You would be nought but a mass of fluid about now if it weren't for that.'

'Oh, thank--'

'But, understand that I am merely postponing the inevitable. I'm hungry, and you'll still be my feast for the day.'

'Oh, I-I don't--'

'That's a lie too,' Kai said, not meaning to speak aloud. *The spider happened upon me but wanted to spare me,* he reasoned. *It won't eat Citizen because we know each other.*

The spider grunted. 'Hmph. Are you so keen to meet your demise? That can eventually be arranged. You are one of far too many words. You are not in any position to make assertions.' That haunting, hollow tone made its voice truly terrifying when it shouted as it did like the voice was born from Kai's own blood. 'Someone wishes to see you. That is all you need to know.'

'Someone? Who--'

'Stop. Stop with the questions. You either misunderstand your situation, or you are very much lacking in good judgment. Do you even know where you are? Do you see all the…what is this?'

The spider only then noticed the deep yellow glow when it descended from the skies and showed every facet of the spider in unwanted detail. It felt Sagali's heat on its hairs without the eyes to see the majesty before it.

Kai saw then a subtle orange tint to Sagali's light like a flame flickered in its core.

The spider screamed a terrible, untamed outcry of agony. Its hair was set ablaze, ripping the smell of ashes from its skin. It scuffled atop the bending branch, barely keeping from falling as it frantically rolled about.

It happened all happened so quickly; Citizen had no time to even scream before he plummeted from his cocoon to the ground below in a soft but air filling thump, followed by a soft yelp.

A pulse of heat seeped onto Kai's skin when Sagali landed on his back. Warmth ran through his spine and down his legs for only a moment, as the cocoon melted away from him. Kai watched with terror as the spider made for him, with a sudden burst of urgency. But at the next moment, Kai fell after his friend.

They had not been hung as high as Kai imagined. He fell first onto his feet, then onto his hands. It did not hurt at all, as something soft broke his fall. Citizen was outraged under him, muffled with his face in the dirt. They were in darkness again, without Sagali with them. Kai struggled to pull himself upright again, with the webbing stuck to his body and pegging him to the ground. He peeled himself off his hands and elbows and onto his knees, where Citizen stuck to him by his fur like a fat man's gut.

'Let go, Smoothie!'

'I can't!'

Kai forced himself onto his feet, his back already straining to hold Citizen's heavy body. Then that scuttling sound made for them from above, drawing close and still in a frenzy. Kai looked up and saw the cluster of legs and fire erupting down the tree trunk, still screeching in pain.

'Run, Smoothie!'

'What about Sa--'

'Run!'

And run he did, without another thought, to wherever it was his legs took him.

'I can't see,' Kai yelled. He could only make out silhouettes of the biggest trees and uprooted roots enough to avoid them, but he could not see any of whatever plumage stroked him on their way. Nor could Kai see the spider webs Citizen told him to duck for and his back ached each time he did.

He grew tired quickly, too quickly for the distance he ran. He was urged on by the mess of noises chasing them in fury and the blazing fire becoming less distant. Citizen was loosening from his belly and his fur threatened to pull his skin off with it.

So tired Kai became that he slowed to almost a walk. His back felt like it was on fire and spitting flames through his heaving lungs.

'Run, smoothie!'

'I...can't...'

Kai suddenly could see clearer. The ground where he stood was lit up by the fire the screaming spider carried with it. Kai could *feel* the heat from its back, sapping away at his remaining strength. The adrenaline could keep him on his feet no longer and he fell.

And he kept falling. Or rather, he *tumbled*. Citizen and he tumbled together, with many grunts and cries of pain, and became muddied on the slope in a rolling bundle.

Bitterly cold water met them at the base of the hill. Kai kicked about with the new weight of the lake on his body, until they found the surface together, shivering and spluttering. He heard the spider plummet down the hill after them, and he frantically kicked with all the puny strength he had to stay afloat and drift away.

Kai and Citizen swam together, their heads barely above the water, finally blessed with the light of the moon and stars. All manner of chimes and grumbles of the forest went with them. They happened across a severed log floating in the lake in a passing moment of fortune, and they clung to it in relief.

Kai looked back at the hill from whence they came. Fire softly crackled at the base of it, where the spider laid dormant and silent by the shore.

14

⁓

...I no longer have any fear of fear itself. What I fear most is a new morning when I've nothing to fear. For that will be the morning when I have seen every dark corner of the world and overcome every one of its trials. On that day, any reason for living will be spent.

I love life far too much to give up on fear so soon.

Excerpt from *Memoirs of Mora the Blind*
by Moro Ki
Generation of Osas
Second Recorded Generation

Kai hauled himself out of the water and through the mud, shivering at a harsh lick of wind with Citizen beside him. The pair pulled each other up the bank and trawled through tall plumage glazed in soft moonlight.

They ran through small fields of stark white petals laid upon their stalks like snowdrops. The flowers were soft and shed a dew that itched Kai's skin terribly. He felt stones and thorns stabbing at his feet, making most steps painful, but it was a sensation he had long since been accustomed to.

Kai saw ahead even deeper shadows than before, beyond the fields where they walked. He clutched Citizen's paw tightly.

The moonlight served as a blessing as much as a curse here. It lit their way *and* lit their own bodies. *What other creatures are in the shadows,* Kai could not help but ponder after the two monstrosities he'd already witnessed.

The spider's words hung on his mind, constantly coming to the fore and dominating his worries despite it all. *Someone wants to see you. Someone.*

In this strange part of the forest, there was someone here with influence enough to force a sadistic creature like that spider to spare him. For the spider to have known to keep him alive from the moment it saw him, there was but one explanation; this entity *sent* the spider to find him because it knew he was in Susuuri.

Kai imagined eyes on them since that reasoning took hold of him. No shadow seemed safe for hiding. Every step was like thunder to his ears.

Even the air itself seemed against them. With the wind came all the grime and essence of the ground, which burned Kai's eyes and blinded him even deeper. It clung to his wet body and moulded itself into a second skin. Sweat poured relentlessly from his body. *How can it be so hot when it's this dark?*

Kai imagined Susuuri to have a source of heat like the purpura, one that did not emit light. Perhaps one that emitted darkness itself. A part of him wished he could see as well as Citizen could here, to see what wonders may have laid just beyond his vision.

He was grateful at least for the climate. The bitter cold of the village at nightfall would be a foul adversary here to accompany the eeriness.

'Smoothie?' Citizen was wise enough to keep his voice quiet.

'Yes, Citizen?'

'Umm...nothing.' They left it at that. Kai thought he understood a little. He had wanted to hear a voice for a while too, to break the sense of isolation this place bestowed. They sadly found no more words to share and instead trudged on in silence.

It was for a long time that they walked together this way. How long, they could not guess. But somehow, they went undisturbed. The eerie sounds did not evolve beyond being disturbing. Kai and Citizen were very much alone.

But their moments of relative peace served only to allow time for their anxiety to be nurtured, before the surely inevitable happened, in whatever form it would take.

'Smoothie?' Citizen said again, his voice even meeker.

'Yes?'

'I'm not scared.'

Kai felt him tremble through his fur. He suspected Citizen spoke more to himself than to him, as a self-affirmation or simply a comforting lie. 'I believe you,' Kai said.

'Me too.'

Kai smiled again, unsure why. He himself was nearly crippled with fear, but the rabbit's trembling made him a little less conscious of his own.

'Are you scared,' Citizen whispered.

'Yes.'

'Okay.'

Something hopped from the ground with Citizen's next step. He yelped a very short but very emphatic yelp before he could cover his mouth. It landed onto a white flower with a crunch, chirping. A cricket. A *big* one, about the size of Kai's foot. It hopped on, with not so much as a regard for them.

They stood, frozen and wide-eyed. Kai looked about, not daring to breathe. Still nothing came. Somehow, they were still left alone.

'I'm a little scared too,' Citizen whispered.

'I believe you.'

*

Water. It greeted them in the form of a still stream. Kai and Citizen planted their faces into it and gulped up more than they should have. The taste was underwhelming to Kai. It was chilled and relatively subtle in flavour.

They washed the dirt off themselves with haste and moved on. Citizen affirmed their direction along the way, which was to say *no* direction and walked with almost complete aimlessness.

'How do you know which way it is,' Kai had asked.

'I *don't* know.'

That was that. Kai had no better direction to offer, so the plan remained to follow their feet and hope to eventually happen upon purple light. Admittedly, this had been their plan from the moment they met, but he was more aware now of just how helpless they were as a pair.

The field of white became a field of black on the other side of the stream. It first seemed like it was deprived of the moon's light, but the plumage there was itself a perfect shade of black. It was a field of dark flowers that offered a welcome distraction, as a dozen flowers sang the same groaning sound in perfect harmony when one was crushed under their feet. It was amusing for a while, but quickly became a nuisance for the attention they could draw. Sadly, reducing their steps to a gentle press on their toes did little to douse the sound, and the flowers sang just as heartily regardless.

Kai still felt the hairs of the spider tickling his skin. He could still see how it descended the tree trunk and hung coiled from the branches. He could still hear its bloodcurdling scream and smell its burning body turning to ash. He only grew more paranoid as his mind's eye grew more potent and became sensitive to every sensation.

'Smoothie,' Citizen whispered shakily.

Kai heard it too; the flowers they had already long passed began to sing their harmonies in the field behind them again.

It was subtle at first, quiet enough to blend in with the rest of Susuuri's natural sounds. But it was soon like the flowers were calling after them, crying out in warning. They sang closer and closer still before the furthest had finished their song.

Kai turned around, against every yearning in his blood.

It was there, right before him; the physical manifestation of his worst nightmares. He had once thought himself past the dread that this creature had long instilled in him, but that nostalgic chill through his every bone assured him otherwise.

He could not bear to feel it any longer.

He grabbed Citizen by whatever his hand touched and began to run in whichever way was away from there.

The same immense body was already ahead of them, riddled with scales. The flowers groaned from under the creature's belly.

They halted. Kai felt Citizen's paw clench in his.

'What,' Citizen whispered, his voice tremoring still. 'What...is that?' Kai didn't reply. He couldn't, enthralled as he was by the hiss in the shadows. It was all he could hear.

Another voice seeped into their ears; a voice deep and strained, yet soft and mellow. It flowed into Kai's ears clearly in the form of one long, drawn-out word in tremoring waves;

'*Star.*'

Kai froze like a stone. The voice spread flawlessly through the field, unblemished. So deeply it sunk into their minds that it was as though it were never spoken at all.

'*S-star,*' came the voice again, louder. Its scales brushed against the broken pieces of moonlight, glistening in varying shades of grey down its back. It made no sound as it moved, slithering as smoothly as a bird would fly.

Then Kai saw, beyond its shining scales, its body lifted into the skies further than he could see. He tilted his head, following its body up as far as he could, until his face was pointed to where the stars would be.

He found two glowing blue slits lording over and glaring down at him.

He could not stop himself. He released a short but fervent cry that Susuuri carried far.

The snake's head came down from the darkness. Its eyes were unblinking and its folk-tongue flickering like a flame.

'*Star*,' it said again with a cacophonous voice. Kai felt a bitter cold within him. The air he breathed felt like inhaling the very sky at its core.

There Kai stayed, beholding the mesmerising blue eyes of the now unmoving beast, betraying nothing but the flicker of its tongue. He never even felt the tears streaming down his face and was unable to summon the will to blink them away.

Kai's mouth opened. For what purpose, he did not know. Perhaps to speak, perhaps to free breath he had been holding, or perhaps only through instinct as the snake opened its own.

The sound of a delicate thud beside him was what broke Kai's trance, followed by the flowers' groaning. Citizen was laid passed out on a bed of black flowers.

His body caught the snake's gaze. It loomed over him, lashing out its tongue with a low hiss from its core.

Kai's body moved on its own, against every desire. The flowers sang a new song as he moved; a melody that was almost deaf to his ears.

On his very next step, he was stood between his friend and that which stood firmly among his worst fears.

15

Though we part, we shan't think you gone
For you'll be with us, still, with every new dawn

Excerpt from the *Hominum Burial Song*

S tepping back through the village gates was agonising, a feeling Lia had not expected. Her hands shivered with the cold biting her bare fingers. The snow was deep outside the walls, as it often was so early in dayfall. Her furs were drenched to her knees by the mounds of snow clinging to her body.

Lia followed the hunter with her head down, hugging the small bunch of leaves and flowers to her chest. Gal Ne carried the bulk of it behind her, but Lia was *helping in some way,* as she had been so insistent to do. Now, there was finally some hope to break through the gloom that had been her life for innumerable cycles, she convinced herself.

It was a hope that stemmed from Gal Ne, like so many others before. Lia had come to learn early in life that there was rarely any matter in which Gal was mistaken. She had always made this readily apparent to every Hominum and carried her reputation with a great deal of pride.

Gal had talked constantly on their way back from the forest this cycle, reciting the medicinal benefits of herbs Lia couldn't pronounce, explaining the process of healing in body parts Lia never heard of and describing post-recovery remedies that Lia could never remember.

She was immeasurably grateful for Gal's unwavering character in a time she was aware to be of significant uncertainty. She had to be a part of it, a part of this kindness, regardless of how small a part it was. She convinced herself that *this act was enough to prove she was not a horrible person for what her heart truly desired; that these herbs would not be enough.*

No one had told her such, of course. No one could have wanted to confess to a child how her future hung on a flimsy and strained thread, about ready to break apart. Every Hominum appeared ignorant to her having eyes to see and ears to hear. She was young, not stupid. She spoke their language. She could hear the trepidation in their voices when they spoke in her presence. She understood it all and she had long grown bitter for it.

Even now as they made their dreaded walk to her tipi, everyone went about their dull routine, with their usual cheerful tidings and artificial busyness. She could not stand to meet the gazes of those who smiled so unashamedly in her face. She kept her head down, looking aimlessly at the footsteps in the snow as she followed the hunter. It helped a little, in that she could spare herself the thought of...anything for a while until she was home again.

There, at her tipi's entrance, she froze. There, she finally broke her conviction and let the tears stream down her face. She pressed her lips together and glared at the open tent flaps, silently weeping.

Gal Ne's padded and plastered fingers stroked her cheek. She had a sympathetic look on her face that was aged before its time. Lia allowed the sympathy to seep in, just this once. The shame of it helped her push through the dread blocking her way.

A beautiful stench of lavender struck them with a greeting. Lia's baby brother waddled around the bedside in his small furs, occupied with chasing something invisible along the floor.

Their mother lay in the bed, exactly where she had been left the last cycle. Char Ki padded her head with a moist cloth, under which Sian Ro breathed laboriously. Her skin above the fur covers was a bright shade of pink and drenched in sweat.

Lia had spent many a cycle watching her grimace with each breath. But she laid there on this cycle with a strange peace and her breathing, though laboured, was paired with no of pain.

It was terrifying.

'The mong leaves first, please,' Char Ki said, in his usual tone deprived of any urgency or zeal. One might imagine he would be a calming influence with such an easy way about him, but he proved to have the opposite effect when he interacted with his kin. Though his social sympathy was lacking, his knowledge in herbalism and biology could never be denied. 'There, beside Sian's leg. I'll

need the coca to hand. She'll need a solution for consumption.'

'Water, then,' Gal Ne said, with sarcasm in her voice that apparently went unnoticed.

'Mixed with echinacea, if you found any. If not, lavender will suffice. Warm water, if you please.'

The doctor sent Gal Ne on her way after muttering more orders for good measure. He took his deteriorating clay pot, something Lia suspected Char Ki's family had since ancient generations, and ground a handful of leaves together within, spitting inside several times until they melded together into slush.

He pulled the bed sheet up to Sian Ro's knees. Her leg was swollen by nearly double its normal size and riddled with purple and green jagged lines. Lia felt sick from imagining the pain of such a wound. But she was determined not to look away. She believed she could not live with herself if she were to look away from her mother now, during her worst moment.

That was the kind of thinking Omaraa Zan had impressed on her. She was saddened not to see her here again this cycle, but she was no naïve little girl. She understood well that the chief looked over more than just the Ro family alone, and there were others who would need her comfort and council after so harsh a nightfall.

Only now did the doctor's eyes meet Lia's. He watched her for but a moment with an unsubtle twitch of the cheek, before returning to his paste.

Kai stood beside Lia now, glaring at his mother's leg. Char Ki applied his remedy to the bite on Sian Ro's calf. She winced and gasped as he pressed the mixture into her flesh. He wrapped the wound in a large leaf and glanced up at the two children at the foot of the bed. Lia looked back at him with blurred vision and realised that she had been crying, again.

She wished she didn't. She wished she could be as vindictive in her heart as she believed was justified for this woman.

'Perhaps it would be best if you were not here,' Char Ki said, slow and measured.

'I should be,' Lia said, wiping her cheeks. What's wrong with me, she bitterly thought. Crying before her mother and giving her the satisfaction of her tears once more even while she was unconscious; it was unbearably shameful.

'Perhaps you shouldn't,' Char Ki said unmoved, this time shooting a deliberate look at her brother.

Lia looked at Kai too and saw a face on him she never had before and would pray never to have the misfortune to see again. It was the face of *unadulterated horror, the face of a boy in deep heartbreak far beyond what his young years should allow for. His mouth was wide open, frozen in a silent wail.*

The pain which Lia was struck with far surpassed any prior and indeed was a sensation she would be tormented by for the rest of her days.

'Okay,' she managed, her voice horse and barely more than a whisper.

She took her little brother by the hand, but he would not be guided. He cried out, suddenly permitted to by the despair that had contained him. She took him in her arms and hauled him away from Sian Ro in an unsightly way.

Kai screamed outside their tipi, unabashedly. The village was ground to silence at his voice, with the Hominum's routine finally broken. It was then, when eyes filled with pity were on them, that Lia finally let go.

She screamed her heart out in perfect harmony with the boy in her arms.

16

The wolf etched ever closer to the forbidden fire, and sang;

'I feel it;
The undying flame.
It is pleasant to me,
For there is no pain.'

The heavens sang in response;

'It offers warmth
But only to deceive.
Fire is known not for pleasure,
But for a cause of grief.'

The wolf took another step, enchanted by the fire's dance, and sang;

'And what of its beauty?
I see it unmasked.
Why should such a gift
Be beyond my grasp?'

The heavens sang;

'It is beyond you,
For it is a vice.
Without its beauty,
Who could it entice?'

Excerpt from *The Tale of Waya*
By Timor Ro
Hominum Tribe Writer, Generation of Inti
Fourth Recorded Generation

Kai did not know he was screaming. He was aware of a strenuous eruption from his stomach, but he was sure it was not a scream. More of a shout, in the same vein as the Hominum hunters back home, who routinely made the same sound at the beginning of a new morning. They would shout together, then laugh together, then fight each other with blunt sticks, all before breakfast. It all seemed a bizarre and pointless custom to Kai, and one of little interest to him.

He would likely never understand the purpose of the laughter or the fight with no apparent purpose, but on this cycle, he gained some understanding of their passionate shouting. He believed that they experienced the same sensation as he now did; a kind of release of the chill building in his core, making way for an eruption of fire.

But there was no one to hear the ferocity in his voice here but his adversary, who was in no way phased. The snake stared at him with an intensity that brought the chill right back to Kai's stomach, no matter how he screamed or shouted.

He somehow stood firm and unmoveable in the face of it, like a tree with his legs rooted.

I can't, Kai thought. The same words kept meaninglessly resounding in his head. *I can't. I can't.*

Kai stepped back and nudged his friend with this foot. Citizen didn't move. It could not have been a natural slumber. His eyes were closed, and he breathed slow and deliberate breaths, as though held in a deep trance.

The snake brought its immense head lower. Kai's hand moved of its own accord, readied before his face.

A wave of pain was brought back through his mind at the sight of the snake's two bright eyes; a memory of the bite he had been forced to see on his mother's leg and the death he witnessed soon after. He could not know if it was the immense snake that truly scared him so deeply, or the past despairs it represented. He only knew that whatever fear had infected his senses, it was not strong enough to carry his body away from where he stood as his every sense begged him to.

'Star,' the snake said, in a long and calm whisper. Its tongue flickered from its fangs and smacked its mouth like a splashing waterfall.

Kai's senses abandoned him completely. He lashed out with all his puny strength at the snake's head. He struck so hard that he toppled off his own feet with the weight of his swing. But the snake never flinched, even as his fist struck its scales, nor did it break its hypnotising gaze.

It simply lowered its head again to level with Kai's eyes.

'Star,' it whispered, its expression utterly unchanged.

Kai froze again, with his hand still raised before him as a pitiful shield. Even his despairing thoughts abandoned him in the silence that ensued.

It was only broken by the softest of whispers.

'Sagali.'

Kai suddenly felt warmth on his chest, seeping through his skin into his blood. There was a faint orange glow under his linens, from where the voice came.

It was enough to tear Kai away from the snake's piercing gaze.

He took the lumen gently into his hands, where it laid with a subtle emanation of light.

Kai stared at it for a time, dumbfounded. *You've been in my clothes since you freed me?*

Then, he moved before he fully understood why. He would never know how the idea found its way into his head despite the strain it suffered, but still it came to him.

He stepped toward the now cautious snake and knelt before it. He laid the lumen onto a dry flower bed and lifted Citizen onto his shoulders.

An incredible smell swiftly arose; the stench of ash. The embers coating the black field were a spectacle. It was equally haunting as it was stunning. The fire looked to ignite the night-time itself and spread through its skies along the course the wind blew.

Purple stems and black petals were consumed by the flames as far as Kai could see. He finally moved; his fear superseded by urgency as the fire furiously spread. He took the now dormant lumen into his linens and ran with Citizen on his shoulders.

Not tiring was all that mattered. The snake was unmoved behind Kai. Its blue eyes betrayed nothing but cold, calm curtesy. It offered them no chase, nor did it flee as the fire approached. It stood firm and strong, too resolute for even the embers to consume it.

Kai ran on. His arms, his back, his legs; they all cried out in pain, but he did not stop until he fell against his will, down a slope and into a cold stream.

He quickly rose again and pulled Citizen's limp body onto the muddy bank and up the small mound neighbouring it.

Atop that peak, he saw something that should have been blissful, not far off in the distance. Purple light. *Purpura.* He was relieved but too exhausted to be happy.

He dragged Citizen on and on, through the dirt and weeds, constantly looking over his shoulder to where he awaited the creature to appear and give chase. It never came. Soon, even the vast embers were gone from the horizon and Susuuri's shadows took their place.

Kai walked on, through the last dark cluster of trees, until the Hyachin finally kissed his skin again. Before him was another field of flowers, glowing dimly in violet and swaying gently with a warm breeze.

There, he finally sat and waited for his harsh beating heart to slow. He watched the flowers flow, softly panting. He stayed this way, with Citizen at his feet, long enough that for his breath to flow easily again, yet his exhaustion remained. He could not so soon remove the snake from his mind and the beauty of this place did little to distract him.

Through it all, unwelcome memories flooded through his head. Memories of home and of his mother; memories which should have been welcome for one of his age, had his life been kinder. That which should have brought joy was overshadowed by cycles of despair and pain, delivered by his mother's own hand and exemplified even in her dying moments.

He trembled at the vivid pictures of the past, but he didn't cry. He found he couldn't but would prefer to believe he refused to.

A sudden warmth in Kai's chest brought his thoughts back to the present. His chest glowed as though lit by a dying flame.

'Sagali.'

Kai took the lumen from his garments. It flew from his hands, with all the grace of a leaf in the wind.

It fell again before long onto the flowers, with its light faded and its warmth doused. Kai took it into his hands once more.

He watched it lay docile, understanding what its ever-fading warmth meant. He could not understand what led this lumen to go so far, but from aiding their escape of the spider's webbing to their fleeing through the burning fields, the flames the lumen created had had its toll. This lumen would not fly again.

'Thank you, Sagali,' Kai managed. The words left his lips devoid of zeal in his exhaustion.

'Sagali,' the lumen said once more in response.

It then laid dormant and cold in Kai's hands.

He set Sagali down on the bed of flowers beside him, miserable and riddled with guilt, and watched it sleep with bafflement. Citizen still laid sleeping by Kai's feet. He looked to be in an unnatural dormancy, stripped of any peace or ease. He hardly breathed, and the few breaths he had were silent.

All of this for me, Kai reflected. *Why? Sagali and Citizen; I've done nothing to deserve their kindness.*

He closed his eyes and recited a part of the Hominum's burial song in his head; the only part of it which he understood well enough to recite with any conviction.

Though we part, we shan't think you gone
You'll be with us, still, with every new dawn
To our maker, we pray you bless this one's sleep
And grow well instilled with its spirit. Sa'ar Ka—

Kai's eyes shot open, hit as he was by the shock of realisation.

He knelt there before the dead lumen, frozen in his position of prayer.

He felt a smile creep onto his face. Not from joy or happiness or even relief. It was just a smile for the sake of being a smile. A smile that had surely been waiting for a moment such as this.

Sagali. Sa'ar Kali... You were trying to say Sa'ar Kali.

He shook with something like excitement. He *knew* it to be true. He had no way of knowing, but he *knew* all the same. Lia *did* come to the forest. No one could have spoken those words here in nightfall but her.

But he did not truly need this lumen to be sure of it. Kai knew Lia well without a need for something as superficial as *evidence* to know the road she took. Kai understood this instinctively.

His joy in this revelation was short-lived, however. He realised how little he had learned which he did not already know.

Lia was here. Kai was here to find her. Kai had only the queen and her eyes to guide him to where Lia may be. Kai's only hope was that the queen would be amicable and freely offer aid.

Nothing had changed.

Citizen endured his dormancy in silence atop the flowerbed.

Kai stood, looking into the hyachin past the field and back to the darkness from where he came, with longing and fear;

Fear of the unknown he would have to traverse before his purpose in this place would be fulfilled.

17

Sa'ar Kali (Sah-Ar Kah-Lee):

Exclamation
A pronouncement of rich blessings to come upon a child of Mother Earth
 A wish for one to be fed well in Mother Earth's growth through dayfall and nightfall
 An instruction to remember the generous gifts born of Mother Earth's labour

D*ifferent.* That was the aptest word that came to mind to describe the transition from the mesmerizing and stunning aura of the Ameyali Forest, to somewhere far less so; to home. It felt *different*, like waking from a dream of artificial wishes and imagery to a reality devoid of...*feel.*

From the smell of the dying rosemary fields to the icy soil morphing into a freezing shoe around her bare feet to the apathetic bugs singing somewhere within the dead trees; it was all undeniably home. And that realisation was disheartening beyond words.

She felt the trees' bitter shadows as she passed, most of which she and Kai had named and given personalities to. She passed the miserable tree, Zan Fat; inspired in part by a certain sour-faced elder. She would soon be passing Zo Fo, the brooding but kind-hearted guard of these woods and the very first tree named by Kai, somewhat under duress. It meant Lia would soon be in sight of the Ameyali village gates.

She smiled. Perhaps it was the sight of home that uplifted her or the knowledge that her long and arduous journey neared its end that invigorated so. She felt more like her whole self than she had in a long time.

Lia could see the ignis atop the elder's tipi and the torch lights dancing atop the walls as she drew nearer.

The cat she carried in her arms raised its head and yawned. 'Woah, it gets *this* cold out here,' she said.

'Yup,' Lia said. She could not stop shaking. She now deeply lamented throwing her furs away when she first entered the forest, having little choice. Furs and a warm bowl of gruel were really the only things that excited her about being on the other side of the wall again. 'So, you're back?'

'Apparently,' Candy said. 'I'm hungry.'

'Of course, you are,' Lia said, with a smile. She had *missed* hearing those words in Candy's voice for the short time she was absent. Lia's journey through Crescat was a lonely one without her. 'You're here to stay now, right,' she said.

'So long as I'm away from the Hyachin,' Candy said. 'I'm here for as long as it's dark. Such is my life.' She gave a flick of her tail and a forced sigh. 'Anyway, what are you so scared of?'

Lia didn't need to see her know she was smiling right now. The cat relished every moment of this, she knew. Ever lusting for adventure, ever searching for intrigue, in whatever form it came.

'Who said I was afraid,' Lia said, in as apathetic a voice as she could muster.

'Nobody did. I said *scared.*'

'And what's the difference?'

'You tell me,' Candy said, less playfully.

Lia wondered once again why she still found herself liking this cat, despite her ridiculous nature. But Candy also had keen instincts, understanding well the feelings of others. Lia had not yet decided whether that face was impressive or just daunting.

She just sighed and resigned. 'I'm not sure,' she admitted. 'I should be used to this feeling by now.'

'Oh? Your village dismays you so? It didn't look so bad to me.'

'It's not. It's actually okay,' she admitted, for what had to be the first time. It made her smile to say it, as though a small weight were lifted which she never knew burdened her.

Candy shuffled in her arms. 'Well, better than some dark and half-buried cell, am I right.'

Lia groaned.

'Actually,' Candy said. 'At least you'd be warm there. And quite well-fed, wouldn't you say?'

'Why am I still holding you?' Lia dropped the cat onto her back, who rolled in the lavender and tittered.

Lia kept talking because the words were pleasant to say. 'It's boring here. Always boring. And there are always eyes on you. Someone just waiting for you to step out of line because they're bored with their lives too. I only hated coming home because we were always out without permission, my brother and I.'

'Which brother's that,' Candy sighed. 'I don't think you've mentioned him.'

'Shush. We would always come back to the village right before nightfall, and the elders hated us for that. And we hated nightfall because we were always being punished.'

'Interesting,' Candy muttered, voicing her eye roll expertly.

Lia ignored the unsubtle hint, thoroughly enjoying Candy's disinterest. 'But it was never that bad. The worst we got were chores. Stuff like cleaning and cooking. The worst ones were looking after the old people. One time, one of the elder's mother--'

'So, I bet he can't wait to see you again then. This *Kai,* was it?'

It gave Lia a little pause, only somewhat taken aback. 'Who knows,' she said with a little laugh. 'Might be that he can't wait to slap me in the face. *I* would probably feel like that if I were him.'

'Oh, don't worry; he'll come around. Just sing him one of those sweet little songs again and he'll fall into your arms. How did that one go? Something about pearls?'

Her smile beamed wider still when Lia glared at her. 'You cruel little fur ball,' Lia muttered.

'*Always,*' the cat said and tittered.

Lia rubbed her sore arm again. The lumen's sting only grew more painful. The burning sensation had subsided, but the itch was almost unbearable, and the numbness persisted still. She longed to see Gal for this, hoping her immense medical knowledge extended to treatment even for a sting of this nature.

'About time,' Candy said, with the gates finally in sight at the end of the icy field. 'Any longer in this stench and I might have been sick.'

'The lavender? It does something to you,' Lia asked, genuinely intrigued.

'If you mean giving me a headache, then yes, it does a lot to me.'

'Oh, that's all?' Lia grinned. 'That's a shame.'

'It's more than a shame,' Candy said distractedly. 'It'll take about a dozen baths to get this out of my fur. I daren't clean it off either; I'd probably choke to death.'

It was quiet as they drew closer, but not silent. Lia did not know whether it was morning or evening for the village, as her perception of time had been distorted in the absence of the Hominum's routine to govern her.

The village no doubt went about its usual business like nothing were amiss, just like ever nightfall that came before, whether it was morning or evening.

'I'll say it again,' Lia said. 'Don't talk when we're inside until I tell you to. Just keep quiet for once, and act like a normal cat.'

'Don't be ridiculous.'

'I mean it. It would be too much for them. You may very well be killed.'

'Oh, do you think they'll make a nice warm coat out of me? That'd be a fine way to go, so long as it's *you* who wears me.'

Lia could only groan again. She could now effortlessly hear the facetiousness in Candy's ever playful tone. And each time she did, she could see her pearly white teeth mocking her in her mind's eye. She had a strong sense that her words were yet again falling on deaf ears, causing her to lament once more the necessity of the cat's presence here.

'Just keep your mouth shut,' she said. 'Unless it's to eat or *purr*, don't even open your mouth.'

Lia felt another wave of anxiety. She remembered what Omaraa Zan had told her on that last cycle in the elders' tipi; that she would not be able to enter the village again should she be outside its walls during nightfall. But these were far from normal circumstances, and she hoped the elders would have the good sense to grant her pardon. But after coming under the shadow of the village walls again, doubt crawled back into Lia's mind. She had little cause to believe she would be treated kindly; even were they to accept the truth as readily as they should.

Lia knocked on the gates in a pattern of three, as hard as she could with her frozen hands, and waited.

A familiar voice came through the panels.

'That you, Lia?'

Lia's heart leapt; a reaction that she did not expect. Then another smile graced her face; a reaction she expected even less. The first Hominum voice was a friendly one.

She reined her exhilaration in well, as was her nature. It was Ogmul. She could not mistake the gruff, nonchalant tone which was uniquely his.

'How could you know it's me,' she said.

'That knock of yours. You knock with so much conviction when you know there's trouble coming for you because you wanna act like you're not scared.'

His voice was even less enthused than usual. It housed a tone she scarcely heard from his lips; exhaustion. He was not a man who simply grew tired like all the rest, or he was a man remarkably skilled at hiding it. He was someone who, since the days of her youth, Lia had never seen sleep. Someone out at all hours, working at his own easy-going pace.

To hear this man talk like any other did, at a time when life was particularly burdensome...it was disconcerting. It took the smile from Lia's face.

She could feel Candy's eyes on her and sense the smug grin on her face. Candy no doubt latched onto the word *scared* and in her eyes was being proven correct. Again.

Lia did her utmost to talk as she would with an old friend, to speak as though nothing were amiss. 'I guess I'm *really* in trouble this time,' she said.

'Hmph. *I guess* we've long gone past that point.'

'I need to talk to the elders.'

She heard him lean against the gate. The chains binding them together rattled as he did. 'I'm sure you do.'

'So, will you let me in,' she asked, rubbing her freezing arms. 'You can imagine I'm keen to get on with washing Miire Zin's mother's hair again. I just hope it will only be the hair on her *head* this time.'

Silence. Ogmul did not groan as he usually would at her facetiousness. His silence was heavy. There was a cheery laugh somewhere far beyond the gates, unmistakably from Cook Olaf's lips. The nostalgia it invoked in her heart was heavy.

'I heard about your last hearing,' Ogmul eventually said, his voice starkly soft. 'I was sorry at first, as I thought they spoke harshly. I knew scare tactics would mean nothing to you or your brother. You go looking for ways to scare yourself of your own will anyway. And I was right.' He paused. Lia didn't know how to respond. It was foolish, she now realised, to approach this so casually, even to someone she would consider herself well familiar. She felt more of the shame that she had become so accustomed to in her time away from these walls.

'But,' he continued. 'I didn't imagine you would do *this*. Not so soon. Only took one damned cycle. Actually, *half* a damned cycle, and you're already outside the walls again. Unbelievable. Even for you.'

He paused again. Lia this time did not hesitate. 'I know it must be hard to believe, but I promise, it was for good reason. I had no choice.'

'You never do, it seems. Something pulls you out to that place and you let it take you every time. I'm sure it's *always* for good reason, and it always will be.'

Lia sighed, frustrated. She could not tell even Ogmul what had transpired in the Ameyali forest, of the things she had seen and the truths she had learnt. She firmly believed that what she had to share had to be for the elders' ears only. This was about the only time in her life she ever concluded as such.

'Just please let me talk to them,' was all she could say, as patiently as she could. 'After they hear me, they can decide whether I left for good reason or not.'

'No,' he said. 'It turns out they weren't just using scare tactics on you. It was meant to be a warning. A plea. A plea you ignored.'

'Ogmul, listen--'

'I argued for you, at first. You wouldn't know that. *They are only children. Let me search them out. Let me bring them home.* But *the forbidden is rarely so without cause,* as Farro Zan Me wrote. For the good of the Hominum. You...you do not act for the good of the tribe. I cannot abide the danger you place on us anymore.'

Lia almost broke tears at his words. She bit her lip. Only by the grace of the Mother did she hold her composure.

The chains rattled again as Ogmul got up from the gate. Lia heard him walk away. She became flustered, perhaps on purpose.

'You'd rather leave me to freeze to death right in front of the gates,' she called after him. 'This is my home too. I'm still part of the Hominum. You're abandoning one of your own to die out--'

91

She managed not another word before she was hit with heavy furs tossed over the wall. Ogmul's coat. She held it in her hands, with no more words to offer. It was warm to touch.

Candy sat on the snow, licking her paws, badly feigning indifference. She showed her pearly white teeth again when their eyes met, with pure intrigue filling her gaze.

Lia looked again at the coat in her hands, undefeated but heartbroken, refusing to cry even as the dread she so desperately wanted to be unfounded had suddenly become a likelihood.

Let me bring them *home…*

18

Only a fool would remove a toe for the pain of a splinter.

Ailen Zan Mo
Generation of Ailen the Kind
Sixth Recorded Generation

The furs had harnessed the stench of Ogmul's unwashed sweat over the years. They were snug and large enough for Lia to wrap herself within. She would have had to join Candy for her *ten baths* to get the smell off her skin had she worn them, but the impurities in them might have even kept her warmer still.

She somewhat regretted throwing them back over the village walls so impulsively. She hugged her knees and shivered, looking bitterly at them impaled atop the gates, fluttering in the same wind coursing through her flesh. She had overestimated her throwing arm, but the furs at least were high up now for many Hominum to see, making her act of defiance more effective than intended.

Candy sat with her, typically enamoured and playing with what the Hominum had opted to call a Blush; a pale-pink petalled flower on a bed of green leaves. It was about the only flower within sight of the village that prospered exclusively in nightfall, but it appeared to lack any utility to accompany its beauty, with its only apparent purpose to make an otherwise grim nightfall a little brighter.

'Are you sure you don't want to borrow my coat,' Candy said, holding back a titter with it. 'I don't mind sharing with you, my dear friend.'

'Candy…'

'I'm just saying, you're gonna freeze. You're playing with fire here if you'll excuse the pun.'

'You mean you're just saying it for the fourth time,' Lia said. 'Or is it the fifth? Either way, thanks for your concern. You're too sweet to me.' Candy's face turned sour so quickly, Lia giggled herself.

She kept rubbing her arms with her equally cold hands. Her head and frosty hair were left very much exposed to the elements. The torches beneath which she laid huddled were too tall to grace her with any more than puny heat.

'Any moment now,' Lia muttered to herself.

'Don't count on it,' Candy said, cleaning her already clean paws a little more.

'I already am.' She despised being dependent on the whims of others, particularly on those whose whims had long proven contrary to her own interests.

But she continued to wait and continued to shiver, suffering her companion's cruel wit and her occasional snoring. It was long enough to grow hungry to the point of discomfort, and for Lia's body to become mostly numb. She made sure to occasionally call out *Ogmul* and knock, just to ensure her kin knew she still waited.

She tried fighting the cold in several ways. She tied large leaves to her feet and ran along the village walls until her hunger grew too strong. She even resorted, half in jest, to hugging against Candy's fur and got a scratch on her chest for her effort.

Relieving herself in the field was the worst of it, as she felt her legs might have frozen off from the moment she lowered her breeches.

Foul doubt ate away at her all the while. This was too different.

Lia prided herself on several things; her intelligence which she was often reminded surpassed her years, her maturity for growing to fill a role she was not meant for through her ruptured childhood, and her adventurous spirit staying ablaze despite the efforts of many a nightfall to douse it.

But her greatest pride had been her comprehension of the feelings of those around her, especially of those who cared only to comprehend their own.

That's what she hoped, at least. But now that perceived ability had been tested in a large way. True, she now froze and starved for a time, but what stood to be lost was far greater than herself and that was what hung heavy on her. It all hung on one ideal that had been nested in her brain since the cycle she was conceived; the village would never leave one of their own to die.

She had once thought that to be a lie when she was younger and maybe a little stupid. She had known death before, though little of it. The village had seen death many a time, but she learned through maturity that her kin had not *allowed* those ones to pass. The shadow of death was simply not to be tamed. She now understood death to rarely be the fault of the living but for death itself to be solely to blame.

However, were she to die outside the gates of her home, alone, cold and hungry, it would be her kin to blame. Had she died in the Ameyali forest, abandoned to dangers they themselves feared, it would have been the fault of her kin. And her own too, as she well knew. That was why she would not die there now, so close to home, no matter how close she felt to it.

That was Lia's resolve and it was strong, at first. It dwindled the longer she spent knocking the gates and calling out, never hearing a voice back and soon wondering if she ever would, before finding the vigour to call again.

She could not feel any of the skin on her body anymore. She eyed the furs she had audaciously thrown on the walls, now feeling incredibly foolish for it. But they hung far out of her reach, rendering her remorse meaningless.

'Ogmul,' she said, once again. It was meant to come out loudly and authoritatively, but it just leaked from her lips frailly so she could hardly hear it herself.

Candy pricked her ears up in her feigned slumber and looked Lia in the face. 'I dunno if I've told you this already, but--'

'You probably have, Candy.'

'...but you're gonna freeze out here.'

Lia groaned as heartily as she could. 'Yes, I'm sure you've said that.'

'So, let's go back to the forest already, back to where it's warm. Just leave these smooth idiots alone.'

'*Smooth idiots.*' Lia had to grin at that, despite it all. Even that proved painful through her cracked and pale lips.

'You could be sleeping under a Horan tree right now,' Candy said. 'Or maybe chewing on some of that sweet tree candy. All while you're lying on a soft bed of Kuro flowers and smelling all sweet. Yet, look what you have us doing instead; sitting out here in the snow like idiots, and you saying *Ogmul* whenever you catch your breath. If they don't wanna hear you, just leave them to their fate, right?' Candy smiled while she said this. She had an ability of empathy far beyond what was reasonable, bordering supernatural. She had so far used it exclusively to derive pleasure from baiting out Lia's pain and baring it proudly. Her inexplicable endearment despite this cruelty was torturous.

'Why do you want to go back to the forest so badly,' Lia said, trying to match the playfulness in Candy's voice.

'I'm bored. As if that weren't obvious enough. How could I not be?'

'I doubt that. You care, don't you? You're worried about--'

'Shut up.'

'You're worried me freezing out--'

'I'm cold too.'

'Oh? *You're* cold with all that *pretty* fur on your body? It's okay to admit it, you know. You're worried about me. You care about me. I bet you'll feel a lot better if you say it out loud. Try it.' Lia smiled at her again and it was worth another crack on her lips.

Candy rolled onto her back, hid her face from Lia and prepared to feign sleep again. 'Go ahead and freeze.'

19

Oh, graceful Mother
You ever kill my joy in slumber
By holding the night with lights
To halt my only whiles in wonder

Honi Ro
Hominum Tribe Poet, Generation of Gouyen
Fifth Recorded Generation

Kai transcended a state of mere exhaustion. Bathing in the glow of the purpura was a pleasant relief until he realised that even here, they had to stay unseen. He had to haul the sleeping rabbit onto his shoulders and find a safer place for respite.

He found one; a cave-like hole in a hill, happily beside a small stream, not far from Susuuri's border. There, he laid Citizen down to rest.

He went *hunting* for food, for anything that grew from the ground and could be picked. He found a cluster of short trees, donned with many ripe gomuls. They were one of the many fruits Citizen happily described in detail while he and Kai hung from the webs, from their round shape to their vivid colour, to their *sweet but not too sweet* flavour. He had called them *candy* at first but quickly corrected himself.

Kai only remembered their name because it sounded a bit like Ogmul, the village's carer. It had made him smile to imagine the fruit sitting on Ogmul's shoulders instead of his round face. *No one would tell the difference.*

Kai brought all the gomuls he could carry back to where Citizen lay. He had forgotten the potent flavour of the forest's fruits until he took the first bite. He washed out the first mouthful in the stream but forced himself to persevere with the next in his hunger. He soon grew accustomed to the taste, even enjoying the sweetness after the dizziness subsided, enough so to have three of them for that meal.

He was restless after he finished, unable to shed the unease from his mind. He was as unwelcome here in the light as in the dark, unable to even return home again, and was becoming familiar with the pain of isolation. He feared more for his sister, having been here for so many cycles now, alone. *How scared must she be, in a place like this with no one to guide her?*

He could not bear to lose himself in such thoughts. He rested his feet in the stream and relished the chill on his skin. He tried to lose himself in the sounds of water splashing against rocks on their passage and the wind's gentle whistle in the trees overhead, with limited success.

The melody of nature was still a novelty to him. He would happen upon streams during his hunts, but as Lia and he would so often remind each other, *predators never stayed in one place for long.* And so, they never took much time to revel in the forest's ambience. Now that Kai did, he could not help feeling that it was ultimately just a bunch of sounds. Sounds that forced some measure of serenity into him, but little else.

The serenity was accompanied suddenly by the sound of greedy munching that was not his own.

'Gomuls,' Citizen exclaimed. 'How I have missed you.' His face was already stuffed with the fruit and his cheeks furiously wobbled.

'You're awake,' Kai said.

'I'm awake. And I'm *me*.'

'You're *you*?'

'As far as I know,' he tittered through his stuffed face.

'But who else would you--'

'Oh, what happened to the snake?'

'The snake? Sagali saved us, again.'

'Huh,' Citizen said, tilting his head. 'Where is it now, that lumen?'

'I...think it died.' Kai realised now that he had no inkling of what had really happened to Sagali. To die seemingly through over-exertion alone was bizarre and terrifying, in hindsight.

Kai believed Citizen needed to know everything if only so he could lessen his evident fear of the lumen. So, he told him all; from the moment Citizen passed out, to the fire made by Sagali's glow, to the snake watching as they fled Susuuri.

'Oh,' Citizen simply said. 'That's…weird.' He took another bite of his gomul, chewing with vacant eyes.

Kai could not long bear the silence that followed. 'Why would you not be you,' he asked.

'Huh? When?'

'You said that you're back and you're you.'

'Yeah, I'm back. And I *am* me.'

'But who else would you be?'

'Depends on where I am,' he said, matter-of-fact like. 'We're in Crescat, so I'm me.'

Kai rubbed his temple. 'I don't understand. What's Crescat?'

'A place. Where we are now, where the hyachin is. If we're in Crescat, we're ourselves. If we're in Susuuri, we're someone else. Haven't you noticed?'

'*We?* You mean the other citizens? Who do you become?'

'Why so many questions, Smoothie? You've already met me while I was someone else, away from the hyachin.'

It didn't take long for Kai to realise his meaning. *The first time we met, at the end of dayfall when we were out hunting.* The time when Citizen was a small and innocent rabbit, a ball of fur down the sights of an arrow Kai was blessed to be so unskilled with. It was different then. There were no purpura to warm the forest and no wonders to see which Kai hadn't seen a hundred times. 'Why does that happen to you when you leave Crescat,' he asked.

'I'm not sure,' Citizen said, his ears drooping. 'But I'm never this big and I can't talk like this until the forest goes dark and the Hyachin appears. But that's why I love nightfall when it comes; I can talk and think and finally come out of hibernation. Didn't I tell you all of this already?'

'Never.' Kai felt himself smile inside, as another mystery of the forest slowly reignited his sense of wonder for this place. The road here seemed to grow ever longer. 'Wait,' he said, his curiosity peaked again. 'So, you can't leave Crescat without turning back into a normal rabbit?'

'Umm, what do you mean *normal* rabbit?'

'So, why did you run into Susuuri?'

Citizen blinked with wide eyes. 'Huh?'

'You ran into Susuuri by yourself. You knew where you were going when you ran through that tunnel, right? So, why did you go there if you knew what would happen to you?'

'Oh. Well…I just needed to hide.' That confession, through a dull, sad voice and a face sapped of pride, touched Kai well. Citizen had become *prey* in that moment, realising that the queen's eyes were upon him. He fled to the place he knew she could not see, even knowing that it meant losing his senses.

Kai felt now that it may have been a mistake not to press Citizen further when he last discussed his past, while they hung as the spider's prey. He was left now with more questions than before.

Citizen quietly went back to his feast. He looked as exhausted as Kai felt. His eyes lacked the brightness Kai had grown accustomed to, now glazed over.

Guilt weighed on Kai, seeing his friend in such a state. *He only ran to Susuuri because I was with him,* he knew. *He was caught and almost killed, because of me. Now, he must hide in his own home, because of me. All I've done is make his life worse.*

Kai took a long breath. He had thought about this moment a lot during Citizen's dormancy but had been uncertain in his resolve. Now, though, he was as certain as he ever could be that this would be a kindness.

'Citizen,' he said. 'I have to go.'

'Oh. Where are we going,' Citizen said, with no hesitation.

That sudden eagerness was heart-breaking. Kai bit his lip. '*I* don't really know,' he said.

'You don't? Then, why should we go anywhere? There's plenty of food and water, and the queen hasn't seen us here.'

'My sister's still here somewhere.'

'Erm, your what?'

'She's the reason I'm here. She disappeared from my village and came to the forest. I came to bring her…' Kai had to pause. *I came to do what? I cannot bring her home and we cannot stay here.* Kai felt a chill in his blood, at this new revelation of just how aimless his journey was. 'I came to find her,' he settled on.

'Oh,' Citizen said, blinking. 'So…but are you sure she's here? I haven't smelt any smoothskins here but you.'

'I'm sure. Sagali proved it to me.'

'Sagali did?'

'It's hard to explain, but I'm certain she's here and she met Sagali in Crescat. So, I have to keep looking.'

'But,' Citizen said, his ears drooping. 'She might not still be *here*, Smoothie.'

'Yeah.' Kai had considered this possibility too. Perhaps she was no longer in the forest after so long, or perhaps she was in Susuuri. Kai truly hoped the former to be true. For her to either be here, where a queen appears to hate their kind or in that dark place for all this time, was far more terrifying a prospect than his search being in vain. 'I still have to look,' he said.

'Sure,' Citizen said with curious energy, laying the remnants of his meal down. 'Don't worry, my nose can find anything. Especially if it's edible. *Mostly* if it's edible. Actually, maybe *only* if it's--'

'Citizen.' Kai's head ached with dread for his next words. 'You can't come.'

Citizen was quiet. His face went very slowly from confusion to realisation. It was painful to witness.

'Yes,' he eventually said. 'I can.'

'No, you can't.'

'Yes, I can.'

'No.'

'Yes, I can.'

'Citizen...'

'Yes, I can.'

'Look, if you came--'

'Yes, I...go on.'

'If you came with me, you'd keep running and hiding, like we are now. You said that the queen's eyes are everywhere, so what do you think will happen when she finds out that we're still together?'

'The queen already knows I'm with you,' Citizen said, not softly. 'And she hated me long before I met you. This won't change anything.'

'But you can at least try. You can go to the queen and ask her to forgive you before this gets any worse. The lumen only saw you running away, right? Tell her you were running from *me*. Tell her that you abandoned me and that you don't know--'

'What are you saying, Smoothie,' Citizen said, with such firmness that Kai was silenced. 'Abandon you? Lie to the queen? For what? To her, I'm nothing but *that rabbit*. To all my citizens, I'm just a rabbit who can't be trusted. I'm *that rabbit*, who everyone hates to see and who has hardly even gotten to speak with anyone since the last time the Hyachin appeared. You're the only one I can talk with, and I'm free from that when I'm with you. You're the only one who doesn't hate me, who hasn't thrown me away, like some...mouldy cabbage. So why would I abandon you away now for the queen, who doesn't care about me?'

His words pulled Kai from uncertainty into anguish for his conviction. But he could not falter now, else what he believed so strongly to be kindness would mean nothing at all. 'I don't deserve your loyalty, Citizen,' he said, finding the honesty easy to voice.

'You...yes you do. We're friends. You fed me, you carried me out from Susuuri, you...you fed me. You saved me even before we were friends and showed me mercy.'

It was time, Kai knew. Time for Kai to *prove* himself a friend, with the truth that could only break the friendship they had built and leave it beyond repair. *For you, Citizen.*

'I didn't save you,' Kai said, looking Citizen dead in his already teary eyes. 'I was out hunting. I missed you by accident, not on purpose.' The words lingered in the air for far too long. Watching Citizen's face regress back to confusion only made this more agonising. 'I was trying to hit you. To kill you. That was our intention; to take you home to eat for supper. I'm just bad at hunting, and I've never been able to kill anything. I didn't kill you, but I didn't show you mercy, Citizen.'

And here it was; the expression plastered on his friend's face that Kai dreaded, the one that would be implanted on his mind's eye for all his days. A face of despair.

They said nothing, only looking at one another. The air around them reeked of pain. The stream of water whispered to them on its way, like the sound of an outcry.

Citizen's face didn't change from his expression of horror. Kai used up all his emotional powers to hold his own tears back, and even then, felt himself losing.

It's for the best, he told himself. *It's for the best.* But even then, he could not completely believe it.

Citizen finally opened his mouth and left it open, as though the words gripped onto his throat.

But something stopped him before he could voice any.

It was the sound of rustles and steps fast approaching, so quickly that they could barely react before its owner was in sight.

It stood atop the cave where they had rested, lording above them with an imposing presence on its long, powerful legs. Its fur coat flowed gently with the strong gust of wind on its back.

Kai had read of such a creature before, sometime in the distant past. Or perhaps it was mentioned in one of Ogmul's stories he was subjected to around a fire. Whichever it was, it had been described in such vivid detail that Kai recognised it now, even as the first time seeing it.

'A hunter,' Citizen said with cold indifference, lacking even a hint of the fear one would expect.

The creature leapt down from what was a significant height, landing firmly yet gracefully before them. Lumen descended along with it and surrounded the three of them in a circle of light. Kai was frozen in place as it approached, in fear and reverence. It was bigger than Kai imagined. Far bigger.

The jaguar's beautiful coat rippled with the lumens' yellow glow. With a frightening smile painted on its face, it said, with unmistakable hatred; 'and here you are.'

20

Death be heaped on our heads. Death!
    That is the only blessing we should dare pray for. To accept any other would be to brand ourselves forever malevolent.

Destroyed Excerpt from *The Two-Year Wander*
Author Unknown
Text Predates First Recorded Generation

E very part of Lia's skin ached from the harsh frost. It hardly felt like her own anymore, now pale and dry like ash. She feared her sight was deserting her when she awoke again, dazed as she was with her vision filled with darkness and flashing lights.

It was only snow. *Only* snow. Little else brought her as much joy as the snowstorms in nightfall which came all too rarely through her village. It was well worth the sleepless nights spent shivering beneath her old bed furs for that novelty. She and Kai always preferred to be out building in it and fighting in it than wasting those magical cycles with dormancy.

Most of the Hominum spent their cycles in their tipis and huddled around fires during those storms. Even the most interesting among them were too engaged in the mundaneness of routine to dare enjoy such a distraction. Only Omaraa Zan would embrace that spontaneity, often playing or building along with Lia and Kai in whatever time she could spare, particularly in the nightfalls following their mother's passing. Those carefree moments they shared stood as some of Lia's happiest memories.

She felt anything but carefree now, laying in that same snow utterly miserable. Every little flake falling on her was like a needle piercing her flesh.

Feelings of uncertainty had passed and left regret in its wake. Not regret for having laid frozen outside her home's walls through such absurd circumstances but trusting in her kin's sense of loyalty and for putting herself into their hands only to be thrown aside. This was indeed abandonment.

She doubted that they would see this the same way she did. *Show no mercy to weeds, lest your harvest dies for your kindness.* That was one of the many philosophies of Inti Zan Mo which were etched into the Hominum's minds from the day they were old enough to speak. The Hominum had no cause for guilt in abandonment with such reasoning, as they merely removed what they discerned to be a weed in their midst. But Lia couldn't care much for their reasons. She just wanted out, to be free of the agony.

She began drifting again into sleep. Never had a harsh cold made her so drowsy.

A shroud of warmth covered her before dormancy found her again, along with the smell of Ogmul's coat as it enveloped her, dragged by Candy's teeth.

Lia managed to smile through her cracked lips.

*

Kai had spent all his years imagining the world which awaited him in the dancing lights of the Ameyali forest at nightfall. It was a vivid imagining that he and his sister had shared. They knew where many of the forest's paths led, named many of its growths, and acquainted themselves with the residents through failed violence. They had cause to believe that they knew the makeup of the forest well.

Kai recognised much of where he and Citizen now walked, even under the shroud of nightfall. The immense unearthed roots, the beaten paths littered with moss-covered rocks, the trees with drooping arms; it was all familiar yet different. He was grateful for these passing moments that permitted him to marvel at the dreamscape to which he had risked becoming accustomed.

The time was spent walking with no named destination, following the tail of the jaguar and its lumen comrades. Monkeys watched from the trees they passed, appearing physically unchanged by the night, unlike the other creatures Kai had thus far seen. They were still small and nimble, some swinging overhead and others walking on their hind legs. Two of them rode on the irritated looking jaguar's back, fighting playfully atop it.

Kai felt the gaze of more and more eyes the further they went, looking curiously at the alien in their midst. He understood their interest, as he felt the very same way. Some of these animals were familiar, while there were some he had never seen in the flesh, but he knew most from the Hominum's books and stories. One lizard-like creature laid on a tree branch with beautiful vibrant scales, immense in size, watching with protruding eyes. A *chameleon*. There were several of them when Kai looked hard enough.

The forest subtly changed the deeper they went on their shadowy path. It was *neater,* more uniform. The trail they walked on was cleaner and the purpura shone freely on it. Kai had never noticed how trees stood with near-perfect uniformity here, as though crafted by hand. It was all desperately pretty, and the reason was soon presented.

Their walk ended in an opening that greeted them with a chorus of tapping and rattling sounds. Little birds with long-sharp beaks went about their work, crafting art into the trees with their heads as tools. It was a gallery of circles here, even engraved into the dust on the ground.

There were many citizens feasting and conversing together. Some washed and drank from the stream which split the court in two, others lounged by the tree bridging across it. Kai recognised this stream, and indeed this court, as a place close where the forest's most immense tree resided.

There were never such patterns in the past however, covered as the trees had been in moss and the dirt on the ground long being renewed. It had appeared no more remarkable than the rest of the forest. But on in that nightfall, with all its art and liveliness, it was magical.

It all stopped when Kai and Citizen were guided into the open to be seen and all eyes were on them.

One citizen rose from its slumber and met the jaguar leading them, who dwarfed in comparison to it. It was another creature Kai recognised by sight, as it was one his tribe had long taught each other to avoid by all possible means. He felt a new tinge of fear.

'*This* smoothskin,' the bear asked, its voice low and gruff. 'It's rather puny.'

'Sure,' the jaguar said.

The bear approached Kai and lorded over him, offering Citizen only a brief glance. Its black fur was blemished by a pale scar atop its head and another long one trailing its back. The expression on its face was a picture of tranquillity, in stark contrast to its powerful and imposing body.

'Not bad,' it said.

'I would say I did better than *not bad*,' the jaguar said.

'Naturally.' The bear backed up a little, eyes still on Kai. It took him a moment to realise that it was bowing its head. 'Well met,' it said. 'Though meaningless now, I bid you welcome to Crescat.'

Kai was taken aback. The bear eyed him expectantly and he managed a meek nod of his head in return.

'What're you playing at,' the jaguar snarled.

'This smoothskin is a stranger. I am offering it a welcome it to our court, as is courtesy.'

'Manners,' the jaguar spat. 'You would waste *manners* on one such as this?'

'Courtesies are never a waste.'

'It *is* a waste on this smoothskin.'

'As I have told you, we do not yet know--'

'Yes, we do,' the jaguar growled, its voice shaking the ground and forcing Kai's heart into his throat. 'I won't let you dignify this thing.'

Kai felt himself sweat and his blood ripple. *I've done something to these citizens*, he thought. *What have I done?* He dared not ask, of course, nor make any sound but to breathe.

'You have no choice,' the bear said, slow and measured. Its eyes narrowed. 'The creature has been dignified, and I have proven us greater than it.'

The jaguar took a long breath. 'She was my friend.'

'And mine too,' the bear said, not gently. 'She was a friend to us all. That's what you meant to say, correct? Or, have you now forgotten what it means to be a citizen?'

The two stared each other down with piercing eyes and snarling teeth. The citizens appeared as on edge as Kai, silently looking at one another with bated breath.

But the jaguar simply sighed another long breath and softened his face. 'Guard it then,' it said. 'From me. Then you can be as mannered as you want with it.'

'*Polite*. I'll be as *polite* as I *wish*. Not mannered, ignoramus.' Then something strange happened; they smiled at each other, for no apparent reason. Any animosity seemed to fade in an instant, and they appeared as comrades again.

'Alright,' the bear said. Its voice was soft and welcoming again. 'Come with me, smoothskin. Rabbit, you will follow the jaguar.'

Kai and Citizen followed as bid, both far more terrified than before. Kai watched Citizen fade away into the trees, walking with his face to the ground. He was once more burdened with loneliness and fear, as he faded into new woods himself.

They walked down their own beaten paths, each drenched in darker and darker shadows on their ways.

21

But Waya, the forest Guardian, could not long sate the hunger his desires cursed him with.

And so, on the night now known as "the Night for the Endless Winter", Waya took a branch from the forest's grandest tree and lit it with the undying fire.

Waya the Guardian spent that night in great cheer, dancing with a fire to call his own and bathing in its warmth at his leisure.

The voice from the heavens called down to Waya with unbridled anger;

'Wicked creature!
You taint my forest with greed,
And made it abhorrent to me.
Now I shall gift you with fire
As far as you can see.'

Excerpt from *The Tale of Waya*
By Timor Ro
Hominum Tribe Writer, Generation of Inti
Fourth Recorded Generation

Lia woke up with the sensation of sweet warmth on her skin, candlelight in her eyes and a thick scent of lavender in her nose. The dimly lit room spun with the first breath she heaved into her lungs.

She slowly sat up under her soft fur sheet, shivering but painless. She felt heavy and her limbs felt limp, as though they weren't her own. She made out the inside of an old square tipi through her drowsy eyes. It became familiar as she grew somewhat cognisant. *Gal Ne's tipi.* Lia had passed the gates and been brought into Gal's care during her harsh sleep. *I wasn't completely abandoned.*

She would have been relieved but for the stretched buffalo skins forming the tipi making her feel sick.

Candy slept in the corner. Lia was astonished that Candy could rest so well in such a monstrosity, in a hut crafted out of her own dead citizens. She wondered if there was truly any semblance of empathy or conscience within that creature, not for the first time.

Gal Ne stood hunched over her tattered old table, grinding something in her ancient stone mortar over a small flame. It contained the lavender which stunk out the tipi. As the closest and most abundant herb to the village, Lia had long grown accustomed to the smell and taste. From medicine to teas, to meals, the herb was everywhere. Particularly in Gal Ne's tipi, which she stank out with lavender either while making new medicine or to repel the spiders she deeply hated.

Gal raised her head. 'Ahh,' she exclaimed, reaching for her cane and waddling to Lia's bed with a steaming cup in hand. 'Foolish girl. Had you not been so young and your skin so healthy, the cold may well have stolen your lungs and some fingers. Don't talk. Just cough for me.'

Lia did so, coarsely and not without pain.

'Hmph,' Gal grunted. 'Not terrible. The wonders of youth, I tell you. Drink this, all at once. Don't sip it. It's cool enough to swallow straight.'

Lia did so, in three full gulps. It tasted dreadful, as all of Gal's medicine did. Her predecessor, Char Ki, used to say that a body only accepted medicine if it tasted foul enough. Lia was always inclined to believe him in her youth and still to date.

'Now, lay down,' Gal said. 'Stay under the sheets until you're told otherwise. I'll have Zanuus start another fire. I'll have him replace that bandage too. Whatever bit you out there left quite the mark. Looks more like a burn than a bite. I'll have to ensure you're not infected.'

Lia's arm had been wrapped with clean linens. It ached to move, and the bite stung terribly. She now regretted swatting at that lumen when it saw her in Crescat. It was well justified in fighting her back and biting her as it did. She no doubt only deepened the queen's hatred of *smoothskins* when the lumen informed her. The queen had had her eyes on Lia regardless, and she achieved nothing but a wound for her defiance.

'Gal,' Lia started, feeling dizzy again.

'Are those words leaving your lips? After I told you not to talk?'

'The elders. I have to--'

'They have seen you, child. And they have bid me to tend you to full recovery, which I intend to do.'

Lia grew increasingly docile, her thoughts becoming lost in a haze. 'Where is Kai,' she vacantly said.

'Questions will wait,' Gal said. 'Now, either lay down of your own accord, or I'll have to treat you for concussion.'

Lia did so. She knew Gal well enough to know that her threats were rarely baseless, as did the vast majority who had taken ill in the village.

Gal laid a warm, moist cloth on Lia's forehead. A chill entered the tipi as a young boy stumbled inside with plants and herbs trickling from his arms.

'Oh, so you made it back this cycle,' Gal Ne said, returning to her table without the courtesy of a glance. 'You need not have inconvenienced yourself by *walking* back here, young master. You may as well have crawled on your belly like a snake.'

Gal stopped grinding when the word left her lips. She looked to Lia with rare sympathy, but Lia was fine. She really was. The word *snake* alone held no fear for her anymore, not after what she recently witnessed in the flesh.

Something like a smile crept onto Gal's face before she returned to her work.

'Sorry, Gal,' Zanuus Ka said. 'The ones by the warehouse were overripe and there was no--'

'Yes, yes,' Gal said. 'Hush now. Aloe on her toes, fingers and ears. Four times a cycle. *Only* aloe. Leave the chamomile here and you can take the other stuff back to wherever you found it.' Zanuus looked over at Lia laying on the ground, nervously. 'That means *now*,' Gal said, her back still turned.

He tepidly made his way to the foot of Lia's bed. He had not long been under Gal's tutelage and couldn't have been accustomed to treating Hominum, particularly females. But he did as he was bid and lifted the furs from Lia's feet. Her skin was pale and withered, Lia saw, as though starved of blood. Zanuus softly rubbed the gel of the aloe plant onto her toes. She felt a slight chill and tickle.

'How long was I outside,' Lia asked, if only to break the awkward quiet.

She felt Gal's gaze and expected to be chastised, but she only sighed. 'About a quarter of the cycle,' she said. 'Not long enough for the snow to do permanent damage.'

Lia would have sat up in her surprise, had she the strength. 'How...it felt longer,' she said.

'Mm. A second becomes an hour with pain, child.'

The gel started to feel pleasant on Lia's feet. It was like it relieved a pain which she wasn't aware of.

'Now I shan't suffer any more talk,' Gal said. 'You--'

'I should shut up, or you'll shut me up,' Lia said, allowing herself a smirk under the fur sheet.

Gal Ne probably smiled herself, as her voice became softer. 'Quite so.'

*

Lia did not recall falling asleep again. Yet, she was woken by the winter chill entering the tipi along with Poruus Zin Ka, dressed in his usual tattered leathers and furs. His greying hair and beard were infested with fresh frost.

He glanced at Candy, still sleeping in the corner beside a half-empty bowl of gruel. He eyed the filled bottles on the tables, taking in some of their scents, and wandered the tipi rather aimlessly.

'I was not sure you would be awake,' he said before Lia could talk. 'My son has been out a while. Out picking ivy, I imagine. He will return soon, so we do not have long alone.'

Lia was stunned already, as she often when she endured conversation with Poruus Zin. 'How do you know,' she said.

'By paying attention, as usual,' he said, nonchalantly. 'Miire Zin Fa's medication is missing grounded ivy, which I assume he and Gal Ne are now picking. Hm, not only has he left it open, but he has not mixed in nearly enough olive oil. Gal will be displeased. But I digress. I came to talk to you.'

Lia sat upright in her bed and found her body to be aching more than before. She looked over herself, seeing the golden-brown tone returning to her arms. Her fingers and toes now tingled with the aloe working still.

'You were foolish,' Poruus Zin continued. 'I want to emphasise that, in case Gal had not done so enough. Really, all you have done this nightfall has been absurd beyond reason, even by your already lofty standards. Now, to so carelessly endanger yourself out in the cold, just to enter the village you left of your own accord; the reason must be important. So, let me hear it.'

'Poruus Zin, where is Kai,' Lia said. 'Gal wouldn't speak of him.'

Poruus' stern expression didn't change. 'Be assured that we will discuss

Kai later,' he said. 'For now, if you please, explain yourself.'

So, Lia told him almost everything she knew, had seen and had experienced, while Poruus Zin listened intently with little reaction. She omitted certain details of the citizens' nature, like their ability to talk as the Hominum did and to feel as they felt. She believed it better for the elders to learn the full truth together than to tell the story fragmented. That, and she did not want to risk some perceived absurdity making her story less likely to be believed.

Poruus Zin Ka seemed to accept what she said with some ease, unphased and unchanged until he said; '*how* did you come to know all this? You surely didn't learn so much about the forest's makeup with only your eyes.'

Lia could think of no possible answer but the truth and was finding herself resigned to Poruus attentiveness. However, they were interrupted by Gal Ne and Zanuus Ka entering the tipi before she could speak again.

'—kiwi, and only with exception to *extreme* oxidation, keep it for dayfall. Otherwise, they'll be drinking berry juices and thank us for it.' Gal budged Poruus Zin aside with a grunt of a greeting and shrugged off her furs to hunch over her table. '*You* can tell them as much, boy. And inform the elders after you finish Miire Zin's medication.'

Zanuus' face brightened at the sight of his father. 'Father,' he said, as calmly as he could manage but with clear relief. 'Am I needed?'

'Right here, you are,' Gal said. 'So, you needn't bother asking.'

Zanuus watched his father, who stared into space while holding his chin. 'Father?'

'Hm?'

Zanuus frowned. 'Is everything okay?'

'Yes. Yes, as far as I know.' Poruus Zin gave Lia an intense look, which she somehow comprehended. She was glad she had opted not to share her story with the other Hominum just yet. She assumed the elders would wish to prevent panic among them and to keep this knowledge to themselves. Poruus Zin apparently agreed.

'And no, you are not needed,' he continued. 'Finish Miire Zin's medication, as Gal Ne instructed.' Then Poruus muttered into his son's ear; 'more olive oil and add ginger. Cover it next time.'

Zanuus' eyes widened with realisation, and he timidly did as he was bid.

'I assume you came by to check on our little rebel,' Gal said, busy mixing another solution and stinking the air out with more lavender.

'Partially,' Poruus Zin said. 'Actually, we have need of her at the elder's chambers.'

That grabbed Gal's full attention. 'Then you lot can come here for her,' she said, turning from her table. 'She isn't to move until I say so.'

'Unfortunately, this matter is of too great an impor--'

'Look at her, Poruus. You tell me how foolish it would be to let her out in the cold again in this state.'

Poruus Zin didn't bother looking at Lia again. 'She appears clear of frostbite and has no risk of hypothermia,' he said. 'And she has no broken skin. She's fortunate and has evidently been well treated.'

Gal's lips twitched, stuck between a smile and a snarl. 'Do you now propose to be better versed in my craft than I, *child*?'

'I would never dare.'

'Her body is not yet producing enough heat without the sheets and fire. The signs are there to see, for any trained eye. An eye I thought I had taught you well enough.' Gal Ne spoke harshly, even more so than usual. Poruus Zin's face stayed stone-like and undeterred.

Lia was surprised. She had never known that Poruus Zin was trained in herbalism, as all she had ever known of his life were his duties as an elder, just like the others. Only now did she consider that each of them may have been shepherds of the tribe for reasons aside from their age and sternness.

'And that aside,' Gal continued. 'That wound on her arm is too strange to ignore. She stays. Until her body fully rejects our agents and I deem her clear, she will not be leaving this bed, let alone this tipi. Do you hear me?'

'I hear you,' Poruus Zin said, undefeated. 'But this is not up--'

A hearty scream from outside silenced them, one that was followed by a herd of screeches and the sound of many stamping feet.

Poruus Zin ran out of the tipi without hesitation. Lia hauled herself from bed and followed, ignoring whatever Gal yelled after her, lost as she was in her heart-wrenching dread. *Not yet,* she silently begged. *Not so soon.*

Outside was rife with pandemonium, with Hominum running away from the village gates and screaming.

Lia soon saw the source of their panic and subdued her own scream only through shock.

There were two colossal spiders of the like that had terrified her in the depths of Susuuri. One laid motionless at Ogmul's feet, who lugged out the axe he buried in its torso. The other flailed its legs and scuttled for the top of the wall, with two village hunters pulling it down by its back legs.

Two swings of Ogmul's axe brought it down to the ground spurting pale blue blood.

The spider screamed agony and fury, as heartily and wildly as a Hominum would.

The hunters backed away from it, their mouths gaping open and their weapons falling from their hands. Its scream spread through the Ameyali village, for all its healthy ears to hear.

It was finally ended by one more swing of Ogmul's axe and another spray of blue.

Silence rang loudly through the village.

The silence marked the beginning of the Hominum's new reality and of the trials that would prove to test their very being.

Lia saw before her the beginning of the trauma soon to come to her and her kin.

It was a truth she could scarcely believe, but she could not deny all that her eyes had already been cursed with this nightfall, nor the sight she was now cursed with.

It's happening.

22

The single greatest failing my predecessors share is an unwillingness to learn to follow in order to properly lead.

Blood, age, name; none of these surpass the wisdom which can solely be gained as a willing follower.

Ailen Zan Mo
Generation of Ailen the Kind
Sixth Recorded Generation

Citizen knew this walk all too well.

He followed in the shadow of the jaguar down the path of perfectly maintained nature, among the roots of trees blooming with the sweetest of fruits. These grounds were fully covered and never felt a drop of rain. It was known as the queen's walk, for she could walk freely there without getting her paws dirty.

Citizen's every move gave birth to a new drop of sweat in his fur, as he suffered the spiteful gazes of his kin. He knew all the faces he passed and remembered happier times when he was just another face among them. He hadn't seen many of them since the last time he made this walk when they had mostly looked the other way, but they did not bother with that subtlety this time and instead glared with deliberate disgust.

Citizen engrossed himself with the jaguar's tail, lazily swaying to and fro. He found the motion soothing, to the point of growing sleepy. He then recalled how hungry he was. Then he remembered the sweet fruits hanging all around him. Then he had to force the thought from his mind. And the walk continued just so.

Soon, the paving was bathed fully in a multitude of vibrant colours from flowers and the trail widened into a renowned open field. A soft glow rained down from the long arms of the Genus tree and her sprigs as an endless shower of weightless sparkles.

This place summoned Citizen's deepest nostalgia. It summoned his deepest euphoria and most unyielding dread, where his most painful choices and admissions had been made. Memories of those trials still flowed through his brain in fine detail.

And here he stood again, at the base of the radiant Genus tree.

The queen's vice sat beside a glossy rock perched in the tree's colossal roots, which was the queen's throne. He watched Citizen and the jaguar approach.

The queen was not there. Citizen was immensely grateful for that.

'Is she hunting,' the cougar asked.

'Yes. Hunting.' The vice stood up on all fours, leapt down from his lofty place and greeted the pair to their faces with his renowned and unnerving half-smile.

Citizen's skin tingled. 'Can I--?'

'No, rabbit,' the vice said. 'You will not speak first.'

*

Kai had suffered many a jeer as he walked behind the bear. The beaten path only became darker, with the plumage in the trees' glowing less vibrantly. He had become engrossed in the moon and party of stars in the night sky. He had realised how long it had been since he could see them, with the trees in the forest so dense and overbearing.

In that somewhat unsheltered path, he could be comforted again by one of the few constants in his life. *Orphan Star.* The name alone made him smile in his heart. *So long as I have the eyes to see, Orphan star will greet me. I need not endure sorrow alone, for Orphan Star will take me home.* Yet, seeing that star again only made *home* feel further than ever.

And soon the star was gone, as they walked beneath the trees again, and the only light for his eyes became the hyachin.

One bird had called down from its branch, saying; 'enjoy the hole.'

Kai meekly asked the bear what it meant when they passed, but it had just muttered back; 'it meant what it said.'

Kai then soon saw *the hole* for himself; an actual hole in the ground covered clumsily with a heavy-looking mess of broken tree parts.

Beneath those pieces was now where he was trapped and confined. They refused to budge, no matter how he strained and persisted. He had since resigned himself to his bondage.

Every second in that hole stretched on, agonisingly. He sat in near darkness, hunched over his knees and hot, with nought but his own distraught thoughts to engage him.

He was grateful for the cracks in the hole's lid, as it allowed a little of the nightfall air and the hyachin's violet light on his skin to comfort him. He could also see some of that same moonlight and a few unnamed stars from where he sat.

He realised once more how much he had missed that bright night sky, and the freedom to see its beauty at his leisure. The forest was beautiful, always and forever, but with it came…confinement. Barriers. It was like a cave, full of wonders and majesty, but unable to disguise its walls forever.

It was lively in this part of the *cave*. Kai wished he could see the animals talking amongst themselves. The novelty of their being had not remotely diminished.

The bear laid outside Kai's cage on his belly, yawning once again.

Kai found it was not so easy to voice his many questions to it, still shaken by the argument it had had with the jaguar. He could not settle after they talked about him like an enemy, with clear disdain. And the conflict his presence had created between them was outright baffling.

'Have I done something to you,' Kai finally had to ask, unable to contain himself any longer.

He heard the bear sit up. 'To *me*,' it asked.

'I mean to the citizens. The way you were talking earlier, you sound like you hate me.'

'Obliviousness,' the bear chuckled, in a hollow way devoid of joy and rich in spite. Kai sensed the bitterness in its laughter and thought better than to press the matter much further. 'It's not my place to say,' the bear said, not kindly. 'Ask those sorts of questions when you're summoned to do so.'

Kai said nothing more. He tried to consider any possible wrongs he had committed, any reason he could to be hated by these creatures who were still a novelty to him and got nowhere. He *knew* he had done nothing to them. He *thought* he knew. Perhaps a smoothskin being in the queen's forest had simply caused outrage as Citizen had alluded to. If so, Kai needed only to explain *why* he had to come, and they would surely sympathise.

That's what he wanted to believe, but he could not shake the dread. He couldn't put the words between the bear and jaguar out of his head. He had *done* something in their eyes, and he could not ignore this fact, as much as he tried.

'Are you thirsty,' the bear asked after a time.

Its voice made Kai's heart jump a little in his vacant state. 'A little,' he sheepishly said.

'I'll have some water brought here,' the bear said.

'Thank yo--umm, how will it be brought here?'

'*How?* A citizen will bring it over and spit it in the hollow rock here. You can drink it through a bamboo shoot.'

Kai felt his stomach turn. 'No, don't bother,' he said.

'Problem?'

'No, it's just...it's not customary for us...*smoothskins?* We don't carry water like that.'

'Oh,' the bear grunted. 'And you would put custom over a kindness offered by your captor? Intriguing.'

Kai could think of nothing to say, lamenting his stupidity. *I insulted him again. This will only give him more cause to hate me.*

'Admirable,' the bear continued. 'I am glad to see that there exist smoothskins able to hold to their principles, even in dire straits. There is no need to spoil it with hesitation when it is brought into question.'

Kai was thrown even deeper into confusion. He managed only a meek and unseen nod. He slowly learned to find comfort in his unrelenting ignorance, as the only constant in his journey.

He spent much of his bondage in deliberate silence from then on, drinking water brought to him in a hollow rock and watching stars flicker in the night sky.

Searched though he did, he could not see Orphan Star from where he sat.

23

So, know this; peace in life is a flawed ideal and peace in death is forced upon the living.

Therefore, one who strives for peace is doomed forever to chase the wind.

Farro Zan Me
Generation of Farro
First Recorded Generation

Candy knew that this place could never have lived up to the expectations her kin had set upon it with their fables. For too long, she had let her imagination flow with thoughts of what awaited beyond the forbidden wooden walls and fire.

She had known tales of sadistic monsters residing beyond the fire, who slept in the skins of the slain and wielded weapons which killed in one stroke. The land beyond the walls had promised to be one of turmoil and anarchy, and it was meant to be a delight for Candy's eyes.

She instead tasted bitter and crushing disappointment, when she saw the reality of this place. It was made up of a bunch of smoothskins with hides softer than aloe jelly, who used fire only to warm their tired bodies and decorate their fences. About the only truth in Susuuri's stories were the sleeping shelters made up of citizen skin. Even Candy found those structures profoundly disturbing. Susuuri had little to fear from these creatures while the sun was down. Boring. Abhorrent. Pathetic.

But *this*...this was fun, bearing witness to the pulse of panic and fear spreading like a ripple through the herd. This *village* had become a whole lot emptier, with most of its residents cowering in their houses of skin at the mere sight of Susuuri's scouts.

This reaction was fascinating to Candy. For those who were among the weakest of Susuuri to spread such fear among the smoothskins, these creatures were evidently ill-prepared for what would soon befall them. Candy felt some pity, much to her surprise.

She felt great fortune that it was *Lia* who had found her on the wall back then and engaged her. Had it been any of these other cowards, she would have lost interest and turned her back on this place forever. But Lia was just too fascinating. The way she soaked up Candy's words with attentive ears, her acceptance of a new truth far beyond her established reality, her recognition of a significant choice and her ability to make it with little hesitation; it was alluring. Their short exchange gave Candy hope for new intrigue if she stuck with this girl for a while. *I've been right, so far. She's too precious to be wasted with these creatures.*

The herbalist nagged Lia now, insisting that she stay in her bed still, against her protests, while the bite on her arm was treated. Lia looked fine to Candy. All this sleep seemed like a waste of time. *One little lumen bite has them so frantic. How fragile these smoothskins are.*

Candy was perched up beside the tipi wall, honouring Lia's wish of keeping her mouth shut. That proved to be a little bit challenging. Staying meek and quiet was boring.

She held her breath again as the lavender-drenched smoothskin sauntered past her and left the tipi. The smell lingered behind her, like a thick cloud of smog. Candy had grown somewhat accustomed to this horrid place which stunk of herbs and flowers, but that woman had a mess of stenches clinging to her skin that refused to subside, and it made Candy's eyes water.

She approached Lia's bed, after savouring what she could of the fresh air upon that smoothskin's exit. Lia sat up under her sheets, fidgeting with a white wooden tube she drank from.

'Why the low tail,' Candy asked.

Lia looked up. 'Why the what?'

'Low tail.'

'What's that meant to mean?'

'Why do you look like you've been sucking on a sour citrum?'

Lia smiled a little. 'You mean I look like *you*?'

'Oh, aren't you cute? Dropping in a little banter before you take your little medicine.'

'Is this you trying to cheer me up,' Lia said, sipping from the foul-smelling tube.

'Not really,' Candy said.

'Then get lost.'

Candy jumped onto her bedsheets, which also smelt of lavender and old skin, and grinned brightly. 'So? Aren't you gonna talk to your elderly?'

'Elders,' Lia said, dropping the empty tube on the sheets. 'They're called *elders*.'

'Same thing, no?'

Lia wiped a bead of sweat from her forehead with a deep breath. 'I will,' she said. 'When I feel better and they let me leave this bed.'

Candy sniffed over Lia's body. She groaned for the rich aroma of herbs that filled her nostrils along with Lia's scent. 'You smell fine to me.'

'Good to know,' Lia tittered. 'But I don't *feel* so fine.'

'Weren't you just telling that old hag that you had to go right now?'

'...yes,' Lia muttered, twirling the bed sheet around her fingers. Candy shot a grin to herself. *Such a stubborn girl.* 'At least the elders have seen those spiders now,' Lia continued. 'So, they'll have to believe me when I tell them about Susuuri. I might not even need you to speak anymore.'

'Huh. What a waste of time and effort. Told you we should've just gone back to Susuuri. We're not even needed here.'

'*You're* not needed,' Lia said, with a smirk. 'Obviously, I would have come back anyway.'

'What other reason could you possibly have to be here though,' Candy said slowly. Lia eyed her, obviously understanding her tease. 'I'm sure he's fine,' Candy continued, cleaning her paws. 'Don't worry that he hasn't come to visit you yet. Maybe he's just finishing that sweet song for you first.'

'He's in the forest, Candy,' Lia said. 'He's out there looking for me.'

That made Candy pause. She met Lia's face, which had turned stern. 'Oh?'

'No one has dared say his name to me since we got here and they just change the subject whenever I ask about him. Even Gal refuses to answer me, and she never shies away from anything. They would have said something if he had been hurt, or if he just didn't want to see me. So, all I can think of is that he left the village and that they won't want to let him back in either.'

'Huh,' is all Candy said back. Lia's attentiveness and sensitivity to others only grew more impressive in her eyes. It was like watching a cub slowly grow into an adult before her eyes.

'So,' Lia said. 'You knew too, didn't you?'

Candy was taken aback once more, and she did not hide it. 'Huh? *I* knew?'

'I *know* you knew,' Lia said, her stare unbroken and wearing a smile. 'You wouldn't have missed any of those signs either. Actually, I think you knew Kai was in the forest before we got here. The way you kept telling me he would be okay with my leaving, and that he would be glad to see me. You wouldn't say those things to comfort me. Telling me all that, while knowing that he wasn't here, is just cruel enough for you. You knew. One of the tenebee must have told you.'

They were quiet for a while. Candy was, strangely enough, shocked. She eyed Lia thoughtfully. '*Tebirii*,' was what she settled on saying, keeping a semblance of her light-heartedness alive. She decided there was no use in denying it. 'They're called tebirii. And why would they tell me anything? I told you, they only talk to the ruler.'

Lia's smile was gone. She seemed neither angry nor sad, but stared blankly, unreadable.

Candy was not accustomed to witnessing much in the way of observation and deduction after a lifetime spent with the airheads of Susuuri. She wondered how many of the smoothskins possessed talent like this. *There could be some hope for these creatures after all if enough possess wits like this.*

'Just tell me he's okay,' she heard Lia say.

'He's fine. Last I heard, he was fine.' In truth, *fine* was an exaggeration. Or perhaps not. To be hung in webs as a spider's feast may have been fine from some point of view, and it was from Candy's too. Someone who would be consumed by a single citizen of Susuuri, and not even a hunter at that, would be too helpless to be worth concerning one's self over. Candy had confidence, being Lia's brother, that he was fine and wouldn't die so easily.

She only wished she could say the same about that foolish rabbit that hung with him. *That* creature had earned no measure of confidence in all his days but in his relentless naivety.

'You really kept it from me all this time,' Lia huffed. 'You really are a cruel fur ball.'

Candy returned her smile. 'Cruel or benevolent?'

Lia blinked. 'Huh?'

'*Huh* yourself.'

They were cut off by the tent flap opening and the lavender drenched herbalist sauntering in with a sour face, followed by a shorter and younger smoothskin.

'Alright, no more time for rest,' Gal said. 'Our witless elders need you.'

24

A leader's duty is to ensure those he serves shall prosper at the cost of all else, be it benevolence, joy, or the love of his kin.

A worthy leader seeks not the understanding of his subjects, but the ignorance of those who prosper under his labour.

Inti Zan Mo
Generation of Inti
Fourth Recorded Generation

Citizen was miserable. Utterly miserable. For once, the sweet polood juices on his tongue did nothing to elate him.

He was at least free from the hole he had resigned himself to from the moment he stepped back into the queen's court. He instead sat under a bland tree with a dull purpura on a dull patch of flowers, looking over a particularly dull view of the woods around the queen's dull court.

Citizen groaned. A mess of lumen danced zealously above him. They were the only beacons of light spoiling his wonderfully drab stage.

'Go away,' Citizen said, so quietly that it may as well have been a thought. 'Stop watching me.'

He rolled over in a huff and crushed what was left of his polood under his fur. He yelped under his breath and leapt right up again. 'Argh,' he groaned. *This will take a dozen baths to get out.*

He rolled over again onto his belly, fidgeting with another fresh polood in his paws. He didn't even feel like eating it.

Citizen spent the time contemplating nothings, feeling the lumens' eyes raining down on him still.

'Don't feel bad, rabbit,' he said to himself, with his eyes closed. 'You didn't start this, *he* did. He started it when he tried to kill you. Don't feel bad.' He sighed deeply, feeling only a little better.

'You didn't want this to happen. You never wanted to be here again. You should…we should've been back at the hole sharing this polood together. I would've let him have a whole one. As many as he wanted.'

Citizen bit on his lip, fighting against a tear he didn't understand. *I don't feel guilty,* he assuredly thought. *I don't deserve this.*

Citizen peeled open his eyes. The lumen blended well with the distant starlight in the skies.

Citizen soon slept miserably but soundly in the dull light of the hyachin.

*

The air had only grown more bitter, and the sky ever darker. Lia walked feebly, with her arm over Zanuus' shoulders, on the familiar way from Gal's tipi to the elders'.

The village was busy but deathly quiet. The lingering dread in the air was almost tangible. Word of the spider incident had surely spread through all the tribe like wildfire by now and had left its mark on them.

They would now know how limited the protection of their walls and wards were. Lia supposed this was the sensation of having one's sanctuary stripped away; the feeling of exposure and paranoia which she could now feel among her kin, without a word shared.

'Sorry about this,' Zanuus whispered.

'Huh,' Lia vacantly said. 'About what?'

'They shouldn't stare like this.'

Lia looked up. She hadn't noticed how many eyes were on her, and that the tension in the air had a mix of spite nested within. *They may think I'm to blame for this,* she reasoned. *That I brought the threat back with me.*

Lia caught herself wondering for a moment whether this were true herself. It was surely no coincidence that such an omen had befallen the village so soon after her return, yet she could not fathom any correlation. *I'm here to save my kin,* she reminded herself. *It would be worse for them if I weren't here, and the spiders would have come regardless.*

Lia kept her eyes to the ground for the rest of their slow walk and forced doubt out of her mind before an inevitably critical hearing.

*

The elders' chamber was lively, for a change, when Lia was permitted entry. The elders saw her but still spoke loudly with undisguised urgency. They looked tired, practically slumped on their stalls. Or perhaps they were merely afraid, just as she was.

They quietened a little by the time Lia sat on the stool prepared for her at the centre of the chamber, with Candy sitting by her feet. She was bestowed with greater anxiety than she had ever felt in this place, now that she was before them again. She could not imagine how any of her stories would be received, whether they would be grateful or spiteful for it. And she could not imagine how the elders would react to such an insane notion as an animal who could talk as they did.

And it just had to be Candy. Of all the citizens, this *is the one I must show to them.*

Candy, since the moment Lia first heard her speak from atop the village walls, she had shown no morsel of dependability, but to be unpredictable.

For all that was at stake, Lia was *scared* for how this hearing may have gone.

Poruus Zin Ka eyed Candy intently, even more so than when he had seen her in Gal's tipi. Lia thought she understood his trepidation of her. After the scream he witnessed from those spiders' mouths, he no doubt was baffled and suspicious of the animals' nature.

The other elders were deep in debate. Miire Zan was especially flustered, as usual. Her eyes were red and heavy, and her face was blemished with spots and wrinkles. She looked like she had aged terribly in the few cycles Lia was away.

'Do you agree with this, Poruus Zin,' the chief continued.

'For now,' Poruus Zin said, prying his eyes away from Candy for the moment. 'Keeping in mind the small amount wood gathered last dayfall--'

'At the fault of no one,' Houli Zin snapped.

'Indeed not. But the fact remains that we have limited resources still. Defence on the gate side should naturally take precedence.'

'Agreed,' Houli Zin said. Lia rarely ever heard Houli Zin Me's voice, though she saw him around the village more often than the other elders. He was usually marching purposefully about the place and was less shy in body than voice. His mild tone matched his manner perfectly. 'But I suggest we consider how to prevent the gate being bypassed at all. We should start by doubling the torchlight and making the Ignis burn brighter.'

'Heh.' The titter came from Candy, who Lia knew was smirking. She shot Candy a glare, which she didn't care for. The elders did not appear to notice, by some miracle.

'I do not believe that to be practical,' Fanwei Zin Or said. His eyes were often closed on the rare occasions he spoke, as though he were in meditation.

'So, the village's ward since ancient times is impractical now, Fanwei,' Houli Zin snapped. 'How, exactly?'

'The fire has proven ineffective,' Fanwei Zin said. He didn't elaborate.

'The torchlight has evidently failed as a ward,' Poruus Zin Ka said. 'The spiders broke into the village by climbing the gates, which is where the torchlight burns brightest. Whatever those spiders are born of, whatever they are, the fire did not repel them.'

Lia was in some awe that they concluded this on their own. She was grateful to have one less revelation to expose them to.

'Maybe it is now time to have Lia's account,' Miire Zin Fa finally said. She even *sounded* like she had aged. Her voice was raspy and lacking in conviction. It dawned on Lia then that this was the longest she had been in Miire Zin's vicinity without hearing her talk. Her silence was louder than her rebuke.

'Agreed,' Omaraa Zan said. 'Lia Ro. Firstly, it is good to see you. How do you feel?'

The room became deathly quiet, as the Lia finally held the elders' full attention. It felt like a hearing again.

'I'm fine,' Lia said, half truthfully. She felt weak and short of breath, and her head ached, but she was coherent enough to talk with conviction.

'We are happy to hear it,' Omaraa Zan said. 'There is much to discuss, and we have a great many questions. Please answer honestly and fully. Hold nothing back. Understand?'

'Yes.'

'Then, firstly,' Poruus Zin said. 'We have an admission to make, regarding the creature at your feet.'

'Ogmul said it wouldn't be a problem for us both to be here,' Lia said hurriedly.

'Yes,' Poruus Zin said, unbothered. 'An interesting choice of word. *Us.* You would refer to this creature as you would to your own kind?' Lia found nothing to respond with. Poruus Zin Ka's perception at times scared her, as it often appeared almost supernatural. 'Ogmul permitted the creature entry at our request,' Poruus Zin continued. 'Our questions will be for the both of you.'

Lia swallowed. She was genuinely confused. 'I-I don't understand.'

'Listen and you will. We Hominum know little about the creatures of the forest or of what happens there during nightfall. All that we know is only that which has been passed down through generations of elders. We have parchments recorded in the generation of Inti, and some we believe that predate him. However, little has been recorded about the forest itself, neither in dayfall nor nightfall. This has long been of great interest to me, as it is a rather glaring omission, to not even speak of the place deemed to be forbidden, despite our founders building our home beside it. How much they really knew, we don't know.

'But we believe that the earliest generations of Hominum knew more about the village and its connection to the forest than they have written. Our predecessors may have believed this omission to be for our sakes, and that any knowledge of forest's nature would be to our detriment. We have therefore endeavoured to keep the Hominum ignorant of whatever our predecessors tried to protect us from, just as they have bid us do.

'However, there is one entry in a parchment from the generation of Farro which has long stood out as bizarre and abstract. But considering the recent incident with those spiders, this entry is now one of great importance and interest. Farro stated that much of what his generation knew of the forest was learned from the forest's creatures themselves.'

Poruus Zin's long breath echoed through the chamber. Lia still did not truly understand, but his words unnerved her still. It had long been assumed among the tribe that the elders knew more than they shared, with their insistence on keeping the Ameyali Forest forbidden and them so avidly adhering to the ancient rites of new birth and the ignis lighting. To now learn about their ignorance astounded her.

'We had assumed this to be metaphorical,' Poruus Zin continued. 'That Farro's generation learned much, as we do, by observing. It would not be beyond possibility that the forest became forbidden as a result of what they *saw*. But, that choice of wording always stood apart from anything else Farro wrote. He was otherwise literal, writing for practicality rather than for eloquence. I, among others, believed that there was more to the creatures of the Ameyali forest than we know, but have never had the means to research them outside of dayfall, nor the desire to temper with the forbidden.

'Now, it appears that one of these very creatures is in our village and sitting before us, for the first time in our recorded history. We can confirm their nature, and a great many other things, for ourselves. And I believe we can hear it from its own mouth, should it choose to accommodate us.'

No-one spoke. All eyes, including Lia's, were on Candy. Candy shifted on her feet, a grin on her face slowly emerging again.

She finally said, after an uncomfortably long time; '*creatures.*'

Lia only realised she had been holding her breath when she quietly gasped.

Candy's smile quickly dissipated, after another bout of silence. '*Creatures,*' she echoed. '*Creature* is a meaningless word. You're all creatures too. Strange creatures with smooth skin and empty heads.'

Finally, the elders broke their calmness with shocked and baffled faces. They each exchanged looks, speechless.

Poruus Zin was about the only one with composure in the chamber. 'Though none of you were present,' he said. 'I described to you in detail the man-like scream the spiders made in their last moments. And I reminded you of the likelihood of this creature's ability to speak. No doubt that that is the reason you brought it before us, Lia. You must have seen some remarkable things in the forest and had you merely *told* us what you needed to without evidence, we would have doubted you. However, time is short, so the elders need to put aside their inhibitions and save their surprise.'

Candy's eyes narrowed on Poruus. 'Still you call me *creature?*'

'Apologies,' Poruus said. 'What would you prefer?'

'I would prefer nothing at all, smoothskin,' Candy said, with clear spite.

Poruus was unperturbed. 'How do your kin refer to you?'

'They *don't.*'

'Then, no name will suffice. As I said, time is short.' He now addressed Lia, who stood awe-inspired at Poruus' every word, at his calm engagement with such a fantastical entity. Lia had finally found a reason to have some faith in her elders.

'Please tell the others what you have told me already,' Poruus said. 'But this time, spare no detail.'

25

...and I make no apologies for my worthy sacrifices, nor do I lament the absence my kin's love. Such is the price of those who live and toil for the sake of others.

Inti Zan Mo
Generation of Inti
Fourth Recorded Generation

Kai crawled out of his hole and enjoyed the most blissful stretch of his life. The feel of the hyachin's warmth on his skin again was euphoric, as it felt like many hours since he last felt the sensation.

'Don't you worry,' the big black and yellow bird said, with obvious glee, from the tree that had lorded over his prison. 'You'll be back before long, after the summons.'

Summon. It was the same word Kai associated with the elders, the word that told him he had done something worth chastisement; for being out of the village during sunset, for eating weekly reserves too quickly, or for arriving late to morning duties. This summon, of course, felt significantly more severe.

The bird took off and vanished over the trees, leaving Kai in the bear's company. He followed it through the tidy and lush walk again, mostly in silence.

The bear only spoke to order Kai to adhere to their greeting for the queen; *core mine.*

'What does that mean,' Kai asked.

'That she is in your heart. While you're in our forest, the queen's authority must be in your heart. Ensure you do not forget to greet her so.'

Kai repeated the words in his head while he walked until he grew bored of doing so and instead pondered over this *queen*. Citizen never told him what she looked like or what kind of animal she was, but to be capable of leading powerful and headstrong citizens like this bear and the panther, he figured her to be even bigger and even stronger than they. He couldn't think of any such creature in all the pages he had read, or from the stories he had been told, or from the drawings he had seen in parchments. He was excited, for that reason alone. Yet, for that same reason, he was more than a little frightened.

Kai was soon taken in by a change of ambience, with the rocks on the ground now lit with innumerable colours and the trees holding lantern-like fruits, leaking bright droplets like a rain of fire. The starry sky could hardly be seen through the branches of the colossal tree above him and the moon gifted its own pale light atop them.

It was amazing, even in comparison to all the wonders of the forest Kai had thus far witnessed. Nothing had ever compared to this.

He took in all the splendour he could manage, but the walk was over far too quickly. They approached the colossal tree that Kai had long been familiar with. It was a pale shade of brown and stood further into the skies than he could see. It was the tree the Hominum referred to as the oldest, and the one which spent its dayfalls dying, only producing half-dead leaves and living its life alone in the skies, impossible to climb.

At its base was an open and clean space. It was a busy, but quiet place, with citizens watching as Kai approached the great tree.

At the roots was a familiar structure made of huge rocks, built high and drenched in hyachin light from the purpura hanging above it.

And sitting on the smallest rock at the centre of it was...a cat.

It was bigger than a cat usually would be, but not as striking a difference as with the citizens Kai had grown accustomed to seeing. The cat's normality was the most bizarre thing about it. The rock it sat upon was tiny compared to the others, which made the cat appear even smaller. It watched Kai approach with lush green eyes.

The bear respectfully bowed its head.

'Core mine, my queen.'

It was all Kai could do to stop himself from bursting out laughing. It wasn't funny; just wholly shocking.

He understood the concept of a queen, thanks mostly to the stories of *this* queen Citizen has spoken of. Those stories were all Kai had to help imagine what this ruler would be been like. He imagined a formidable figure, imposing in stature, grand in voice and egotistical enough to inspire obedience.

But this queen far surpassed, or more likely had fallen well short of, his wildest imaginings.

The bear deliberately coughed. It was enough to remind Kai of the custom.

'Gore mine,' he said and tipped his head as the bear had; an action he was happy for, as it helped him hide his grin.

'*Core* mine,' the bear growled.

'Forget it,' the queen said. 'It's all the same to him. *Core. Gore. Bore.* Whatever-*ore*. Just words. Fleeting words born from our lips solely to die when they reach our ears.' She donned a toothy smile, which glinted in the purple light drenching her.

Her voice was smooth, and her natural aura was relaxed, to the point of being suffocating. Kai's smile quickly dissipated. *She's terrifying*, he thought.

'*All the same*,' the bear echoed to her. 'This is a tradition that has been passed down through our citizens--'

'Yes,' the queen said. 'Passed down through *our* citizens. How much a citizen does the smoothskin look to you? I've no doubt it has its own greetings and traditions and whatever-*ore* words which we haven't said either.'

The bear kept quiet, though looking distraught. Kai was enchanted with the queen's aura, with the air of strength that flowed from her, to even make the bear submit with words alone.

'So, smoothskin,' she said. 'Why are you in my forest while the sun is down?'

'Huh?' Kai immediately regretted his crass and vacant response.

'Huh, who,' the queen mocked and smiled brighter still, apparently unbothered. 'You. I'm talking to you. Why are you in my forest? You trespass plenty in the day, yet we never see you at night. So, why are you here *now*?'

'My sister came here,' Kai said, this time unhesitant. 'I'm here to find her and take her back home.'

The queen appeared unsurprised. 'And what is *she* doing in my forest?'

'I…I don't know yet.'

'You don't? That means you don't know why you're in my forest either, do you?' She said it as a statement more than a question and it was one Kai could not deny. So, he said nothing at all. 'You're where you shouldn't be,' the queen pressed. 'For someone else who shouldn't be here, and you can't tell me why either of you are where you shouldn't be. Isn't that something?'

Kai nodded and blushed with his face to the ground.

'Well then,' the queen said, still unperturbed. 'I'll just ask you about *that* instead.'

Kai looked behind him to where she nodded. Blood rushed to his head when he saw *it* and his mouth hung open.

He recognised it at once, of course. It was the same garment he would see every cycle when he woke, and the same one he donned every cycle of nightfall to fight the bitter cold air.

There, on a long branch of a nearly trimmed tree and guarded by the queen's cougar, were Kai's furs. The sight of it alone almost brought Kai to tears. Not from fear, though that he had in abundance, but from of guilt it forced onto him.

He finally understood the citizen's outrage. He understood just how deeply their hatred of him surely ran. There hung what remained of a citizen; one of *their* citizens. One whose coat had kept him warm through many a cycle. One whose dead corpse was no doubt feasted on in the same cycle it died with great glee.

Kai felt nauseous. He wanted to vomit out of his body all the citizens he had ever eaten. There had been at least a dozen he'd feasted on in his life, each of which he had savoured as a break from the stale and bland food that otherwise sustained them.

'We don't forget the scent of one of our own,' the queen said, her smile now. 'And it stays on our bodies for life and long after. There was another distinct stench nesting in that one's fur. Many of my citizens recognised it but couldn't place it, which meant that they smelt it while their senses were dulled in their primitive states, while the sun was up. So, it was not hard to figure where this stench came from; it had to be the smell of a smoothskin. And soon after, my lumen told me of a smoothskin that happened to be in my forest.

'The jaguar who found you already told me your smell was the very same as the stench in those furs. We have seen the way smoothskins wear the fur of our dead and warm their own hairless bodies with them. *You* wore this citizen in the same way, didn't you?'

Kai's head went empty. His mouth shook too much to form words. Every eye was intently on him, each showing unbridled anger and blame. Pure hatred. He understood their anger, truly. He understood more than he wanted to. He could do nothing but be overcome by crippling shame. He back fought the tears welling up in his eyes.

'Still,' the queen continued. 'I know you didn't kill our citizen yourself. Such a puny and weak creature as you couldn't manage the murder of even the weakest among us. Not that I'm one to talk.' She smiled again; a nasty smile which allowed no reciprocation. 'You have *tried* to kill though, haven't you? Only, it wasn't a fearsome elk, but a little rabbit gathering food to hibernate.'

Kai felt a chill deep in his heart. 'He...told you,' he feebly said. He should not have been surprised. Citizen had a right to tell his kin the truth and Kai had no right to any manner of bitterness. Yet, Kai felt he had a right to misery. *I've really lost my friend*, he grieved. He was miserable in his own selfishness.

'Do not interrupt our queen,' the bear growled.

'You didn't kill our elk,' the queen said. 'But you instead wore him as a utility. That might even be worse. That tells me you're cowardly *and* lacking in sympathy; a woeful combination. The thought of two smoothskins in my forest at night in quick succession already sickens me, but when one comes wearing the corpse of our dead, it makes--'

'*One of us*,' Kai echoed with sudden zeal. 'You *did* meet Lia!'

'What did I just tell you,' the bear growled.

Kai barely heard him. 'You met my sister,' he said. He couldn't help himself. 'Or your lumen did? That's how you know she didn't have any furs.' Kai gasped with a monumental weight lifted off his shoulders. Suddenly, nothing else mattered. He smiled, even brighter than the queen did.

'Stop talking,' another citizen growled at him.

'Tell me, please. Where is she? Where's my--'

'Enough!' The word echoed through the forest as a deafening tremor, the bear's roar incredible. Kai hunched over and held his ears in pain, his head pounding. There was a barrage of complaints and outrage when the echo faded.

'Apologies,' the bear mumbled.

Kai stood up straight again. The queen eyed him, with a look of contemplation and an air of composure. She kept her silence until the chatter naturally died out and for a little while more.

'Take this creature back to its hole,' she said, at last, her piercing gaze unbroken. 'And keep it there, until I decide how it will repay us.'

26

Susuuri (Suh-suu-ri):

Noun
A whisper that goes unheard or ignored

Noun
Given name of the darkest area in the Ameyali Forest during nightfall.
Named during an unknown generation, preceding the first recorded Generation of Farro

'A *lumen*,' Houli Zin Me echoed, now practically leading the hearing. His interest visibly peaked with each fact learned, and he had become almost childlike with his inquisitiveness. 'And what of them?'

'They're the queen's eyes in the forest,' Lia said. 'They're small and can fly, so she can see everywhere. They look like big fireflies.'

Houli Zin nodded, resting his chin on his hand. He had come out of his usually reserved shell at the mention of the hyachin and had showered Lia with questions ever since. She even saw a hint of adoration in his eyes when he learned about the forest's citizens and their way of living.

'I assume they inform this queen of what they see, rather than transmit it to her somehow?'

'I don't know.'

'It would be better for young Lia to finish her story, Houli Zin,' Poruus Zin Ka finally said, though he appeared equally fascinated by all that he heard, in his own quiet way.

'After Crescat, we made it Susuuri,' Lia continued. 'It was very dark there and I had to depend on Candy…this cat, to guide me. She told me the king has eyes all over Susuuri, just like the queen did, and that he knew the moment anyone entered his territory. Candy says he uses ants-like animals called tebirii that only speak to Susuuri's ruler. She said he would send his hunters for me once he was informed.'

'And still, you kept on going,' Poruus Zin said, with a hint of incredulity.

Lia hesitated. She chose her next words very carefully. Though the elders had demanded every detail, there were some that they would do well not knowing. 'Candy said I had to see Susuuri for myself,' was what she settled on.

The elders looked to Candy again, who bared her teeth in return.

'I do not understand,' Miire Zan said. 'Why would you wilfully follow this creature in the first place? And without notifying the village. Not even Kai--' Miire Zan saw the change in Lia's face and reigned in her tongue, for a change.

Lia hadn't asked about Kai and didn't need to. The fault was hers that Kai followed her into the forest, and hers alone. Questioning the elders now on the circumstances of his leaving would be a waste of already limited time. She fought to keep her priorities on what she could impact, not on what she couldn't, and chose to trust Kai to be capable enough on his own.

'Unwise though it was,' Fanwei Zin said, saving Miire Zin from her awkward trance. 'Even foolish, I don't blame her for going to the forest under these circumstances. Were you a child still, Miire, would you be able to resist the demands of a talking cat?'

'Of course. In fact, I would run the other way.'

Fanwei Zin narrowed his eyes. '*That's* not the child I recall, Miire.'

'Please,' Omaraa Zan said before Miire Zan's face grew any redder. 'We waste time with bickering. Go on, Lia.'

'A question first,' Poruus Zin said. 'We would know more about this king's eyes. Is he able to use the lumen in the same way the Crescat queen does? Do they serve as his eyes also?'

'No,' Lia said. 'He only uses the tebirii'

Poruus held his chin, as was his habit while in thought. 'It was this cat, *Candy*, who told you this?'

'Yes,' Lia said, curiously.

'Then,' Poruus said. 'I ask you Candy; do these tebirii have the same restrictions as you do while the sun is down? Do they return to a primitive state?'

Candy perked up her ears. '*Primitive?*'

'Poruus, how relevant is this?' Miire Zan said, clearly agitated.

'Very, if we wish to know how well we can hide from this king's eyes, should the need arise.'

'What do you mean primitive,' Candy asked, seemingly engaged and serious for the first time this hearing.

'You described the effect that the hyachin has on the citizens of Susuuri,' Poruus said. 'Including yourself. So, I would surmise that these tebirii are affected by the Hyachin in the same way. Is this true?'

Candy paused for a swift moment before she shifted into what Lia recognised as a smile of deference. 'Yes,' she said. 'They are *restricted*, as you put it. They cannot enter Crescat either.'

'Meaning these *eyes* have boundaries,' Poruus Zin said. Lia found herself in awe once more at what Poruus was able to determine with so little information. Even details that others would not consider remotely important became critical with his intervention. 'Are there any who *are* immune to those effects,' he asked.

'Besides you,' Candy said, with a smile.

'Are we truly,' Poruus asked. He shot a look at Lia as he did; an intense one that made her feel uneasy. *I came through it okay,* she reflected. *I'm proof that we are immune.* That's what she wanted to say, but she wanted to hear it from Candy's mouth more than her own.

'Probably,' is what Candy said instead. 'How would I know? But, don't misunderstand our *restrictions*. So long as we avoid the hyachin, they don't at all matter to us.'

Something changed in Poruus Zin's manner at those words and it was clear to see. His slow morphing face was every bit as bizarre as disconcerting. His usual indifferent contemplation turned a blank stare with his eyes glazed over.

'Meaning we don't have much to fear from your citizens,' Houli Zin said. 'Since they *must* pass through this hyachin to get to our village.'

'But what of the two spiders who made it here,' Fanwei Zin asked. 'How did they manage to do so? And how did *you* do so?'

'Who knows,' Candy said, rolling her eyes in that special way that feigned indifference to any who knew how to read them.

'The cat surely left the forest before nightfall to make it to the village so soon after dawn.' Poruus Zin's voice was heavy in tone. 'But the spiders must have come from underground. That way, they could pass through the forest without ever touching the Hyachin. Which would mean that some citizens may already be under the village, specifically the tebirii. Perhaps they have been for some time.'

Lia now understood the grievous shift in Poruus Zin's tone, as did all the elders, judging by their reactions of badly restrained fear. Lia lamented her own ignorance. *How could I have not realised this,* she thought. *The evidence was with me all this time, yet I failed to realise something so obvious.*

She looked down at Candy, whose devious face was now an unreadable and blank mask. She stared at Poruus Zin with an intensity unbefitting her.

'Is this true, Candy,' Fanwei Zin said, holding his head in his hand.

'Yeah,' Candy said without pause. 'The tebirii have been able to get here, underneath your village, since the last time the sun was down.'

'They have just waited,' Omaraa Zan said. 'For all this time, they have been underneath us? Why?'

'Must you ask?' Candy said. There was no playfulness left in her voice. 'To *observe.*'

'But, how can they observe us from underground? What can they hope to see?'

'Not *see.* The king can use the tebirii in the Susuuri where it's dark because they don't use their eyes to see. They hear you. Smell you. They feel you move through the tremors in the ground. They can know all you do without ever using their eyes. That's why no one can enter Susuuri without the king knowing. And…and, no one goes in or out of *this* place without him knowing either.'

A sinister tone of silence invaded the chamber once more. Now the ringing of iron was clearly heard from the outside, of the blacksmith and woodworkers busying himself with the sharpening of tools and treatment of the village walls. Neither were so comforting a sound as they once were. Lia bitterly reflected on Candy's admittance. *That's why you knew that Kai was in the forest. The king knew the moment he left and knew where he was going. So, you knew he was already in the forest even while you helped me get back here. Are you really so cruel?*

'Providing this is true,' Fanwei Zan said at last. 'I cannot believe that you would inform us of this so readily. Your king surely won't take kindly to you being here and informing us of his intentions.'

'I'm *not* informing you readily,' Candy mumbled.

'Then,' Fanwei said, not fazed by her tone. 'Will you tell us why you've told us what you have?'

Candy smiled once more. She then said the words, without a hint of mischief or bitterness; the words which carried meaning that would eventually haunt Lia in every waking moment when she could fully comprehend their gravity to the extent that no one else ever could. Not even Candy herself.

Candy said; 'To let you believe you have a fighting chance.'

*

Poruus Zin Ka took only a passing interest in the remainder of the hearing, lost in thought as he was. His eyes and mind were constantly drawn to Candy, who was firmly at the centre of his deliberation.

Even as Lia and Candy left the hut together and the air of the elder's chamber hung heavy with new fears, one thought obsessed Poruus' thoughts; a question that had not been fully answered and the answer to which would surely be of the utmost importance in informing the village's best course for the cycles to come;

Why did this cat come to our village in the first place?

Several theories, each vastly different from the last, raced through Poruus' head. None had pleasant implications, but one stood out as the most logical.

He had decided against asking the question outright himself. If the answer were as sinister as he suspected, he expected Candy to lie.

Wiser, it would be, to allow the answer to unfold itself.

'Omaraa,' Poruus said, breaking the drawn-out silence in the chamber. 'A word?'

*

It had been a long while since Poruus last had any need to step foot in the back of the elder's chambers. Books were neatly lined up on the floor, in the same places he could last recall. The smell of the old wiigwaasabak paper was quite nostalgic.

Poruus had read these books enough times to recite their contents perfectly. Yet, on this cycle, he realised how little of their contents he had understood and how little of his predecessor's intent he had comprehended. *All their wisdom before now had been wasted on us. How could they have expected to impart wisdom to us when so little of their experiences were recorded, and we are forbidden from gaining that experience for ourselves? It is a bizarre contradiction.*

'What is it, Poruus,' Omaraa said. Her bluntness was unbecoming of her. She was only sounding more spent as this nightfall ran its course.

'I will try to be brief,' Poruus said. 'But there is much to say. Firstly, I will propose our next course of action, in light of all that the cat told us about Susuuri and this king.'

'Then this should be a discussion for all the elders to hear.'

'Eventually. But not what I will be proposing to you.'

Omaraa rubbed her eye and sighed. Poruus had to frown. *These revelations have already had their toll on you, Omaraa, yet they will no doubt pale compared to what awaits us.*

'Before that,' Poruus continued. 'We can deduce some important information regarding our predecessors.'

'And this is important for what we must do next,' Omaraa asked, confused.

'Very. Specifically, *your* predecessors; the chiefs of old. We have never openly questioned the rules and tenets they wrote. Adhering to their definition of the forbidden has been justified thus far, but with what we just learned, doubts are inevitable.

'We understood the forest to be dangerous to the Hominum in nightfall, but now there are several nonsensicalities in those warnings. Their words appear needlessly vague. Why be so vague in warning future generations about the nature of the forest if the truth were so simple? At the very least, why not record the truth for their successors to choose the wisest course for themselves?'

Omaraa sat on the sole stall in the chamber room. 'Those are good questions,' she said. 'Why do they matter *now?*'

'Because there are implications to their actions which could be imperative for our survival.' Poruus sat on the ground by Omaraa's feet, carefully laying out his next words. 'Farro of the first generation wrote much of what we already knew of the forest. I have long found his choice of wording curious in his texts. He is concise about his philosophies, yet incredibly abstract about the forest and our tenets, where our understanding should matter most.

'However, after what the cat told us, I have a theory on why Farro's texts, and those of the generations preceding him, were so inconsistent. I do not believe these texts were ever *intended* to be so enigmatic. Rather, they appear so because they are incomplete. If we were to read the texts with the belief that significant portions were missing, they will appear far less enigmatic.

'But texts of such importance would never be simply misplaced. They have been kept in this very room for generations for precisely that reason. Therefore, I propose that significant portions of these texts were *deliberately* destroyed, during one of the generations after Farro's passing.'

Omaraa leaned on her knees, looking utterly incredulous and tired. 'Why would anyone want to,' Omaraa said.

'That is the most important question. I can only conclude that one or more of the chiefs believed it to be in our best interests to not know the information they destroyed, to know only what we are not permitted to do. And the only reason I can surmise is that the truth would greatly impact our way of living.

Because of that, I believe something transpired in the forest before or during Farro's first generation, which would shake the villager's faith in their shepherd's guidance if it were to be revealed. Therefore, the texts were destroyed to ensure we stayed adherent to their enigmatic tenets.'

Omaraa sighed; a sigh of anguish Poruus rarely heard from her lips. 'That is...' she started. She lacked the words to finish.

'Yes,' Poruus concurred. 'Our predecessors frankly have much to answer for, particularly whoever among them saw fit to keep us in ignorance and to pass down a fear of the unknown. Providing, of course, that all of this is true.'

'And this is why you came only to me with this,' Omaraa said. 'To prevent any strife or fear?'

Poruus sighed, the irony not lost on him. 'Partially,' he admitted. 'But more to propose how we act on this. I had to share this theory with you first, so you could understand my reasoning. And so that you understand the danger that may lay ahead for us.'

Omaraa looked up at Poruus. Her eyes looked ever more like those of an old woman's. 'Dangers?'

'Necessary risks, for our survival, based on recent events.' Poruus took a blank wiigwaasabak from the stack on the ground and an old quill; tools typically reserved for texts made and preserved for future generations.

Wiigwaasabak was too arduous to create to use flippantly, but this would be anything but flippant.

'I will write my proposal,' Poruus said and tapped the ground with his fingers. 'Please pay attention. I will not say any of this aloud, for those who may be listening.'

Omaraa nodded, evidently understanding.

Poruus pricked his finger with the quill and coated its tip with his blood.

My blood, Poruus silently prayed. *My life force and being; I pray that this will not be a waste of you.*

With it, he wrote and drew a new page for Hominum's future history.

27

Each female and male are permitted to birth two children in their lifecycles.

A child must be conceived only during the Ritual New of Birth, which shall occur once every seven years.

Should a child be born outside the permitted period of the Ritual of New Birth, a further ten years must pass before the ritual may commence again.

For those who mate outside the permitted time, they may be fed, they may work for the tribe, and they may keep their own tipi to rest in.

But they shall never again be named as kin, and they shall exist outside of the Hominum's care, as their actions reveal their desire to be.

Tenet of the *Hominum's Ritual of New Birth*
Imposed by the Osas Zan Ne
Generation of Osas
Second Recorded Generation

L ia laid awake in her tipi, quite unsure what to do with herself. Now that the purpose driving her back to this place was effectively fulfilled, there was already monotony left in its wake.

She took one long, hard breath, reminding herself of her drowsiness. All that sleep that Gal Ne forced upon her had not been restful. She had spent half of it in a daze and half in a state of foggy clarity since leaving the elder's chamber.

The relative serenity of the village's impudent chatter had been imposing like a thick mist on her way. She had sauntered silently past any who greeted her, one thought resonating in her head like a thread wheel; she was back to being *useless* again. A mere observer to a peril which all her sweat and labour had been spent on attempting to prevent.

She had not seen Candy since they left the chamber together and she quietly wandered off. Lia was glad for it, as she could do well without seeing that creature right now, after what had been discussed.

She found little joy in resting here in her own tipi again, for the first time in what felt like a lifetime. She stared at the empty wooden hooks on the wall, bringing her a wave of sadness.

Her furs had belonged to her mother once and were gifted to her by the chief when she had grown tall enough to don them. For a long time, they held the scent of her mother, Sian Ro; a subtle blend of roses and sweet thorns, from a concoction Gal Ne would often make for Sian when the flowers first bloomed in dayfall.

Sian Ro was named *Sweetie* by most because of that scent which followed her wherever she went, as a stark contrast to her known abrasive manner. It gave Lia immeasurable disdain to be cloaked in what remained of that same aroma for all the cycles it lasted, even if out of necessity. Lia hardly noticed the scent fading until its complete absence.

Abandoning that coat in the forest stream one of the few kindnesses this nightfall had so far given her thus far.

She laid on her bedsheets, feeling alone for the first time in...perhaps ever. And for the first time that she could recall, the fur sheets did not hold the endearing smell of Kai's sweat.

*

Lia hardly slept deeply enough to dream for long before she woke again but had time enough to relive the memory of one of Susuuri's hunters prowling around her cage in a near nightmare. Its eyes had glowed red and it looked demented, with its eyes fixed on hers and with a grin etched into its face.

Drool had dripped from the fangs protruding from its mouth, and it breathed so hard that its body shook.

The air there had been harsh, and Lia shook in a blend of fear and reaction to the bitter winds. The world had felt so small and cruel in that cage. Even the Mother herself appeared malevolent from her shrunken perspective of bondage and hatred.

Lia was grateful to be woken to the present and was awoken by Miire Zin Fa's voice calling into her tipi.

'Are you in there,' she called. 'Lia?'

Lia sat up, rubbing her itchy arm. 'Yes,' she said. Lia's was often reminded about how heartily she snored, no matter how brief her sleep was.

Miire must have known she was in her tent already and asked only out of courtesy. It was a rarity for Miire to show, which already made Lia wary.

'Can I come in,' she said, as she stepped inside.

She was donned in her heavy white furs, with her equally pale face buried in a hood. There was a time that Lia would love to see them, beautiful as they were and rare as it was that Miire was out of the elders' chambers in nightfall. Lia had never seen or heard of such a creature with fur so white and thick, and her imagination often ran wild with all manner of creatures donning it. Her favourite idea was that the fur belonged to a beast from a land where it snowed so much that its own fur changed colour with it. But she was never able to imagine a way for the hide of such a creature to have made its way to the Ameyali village, so the fur instead became a beautiful mystery that even the elders themselves apparently did not have the answers to; only that Miire's ancestors had the coat before she did.

Miire lowered her hood and shook out her unkempt hair. The already pronounced bags under her eyes had grown heavier and she looked set in a permanent state of dejection.

She approached Lia's bed, saying; 'I did not imagine you would have gone through so much, or how unkind the forest would be to you.'

Miire eyes did not meet Lia's as she spoke, instead fidgeting with a rough patch on the bedsheets where she sat. Miire was not the type of woman to fidget often. 'I know,' Lia said.

'I confess,' Miire said. 'When I heard you had left, I thought you were acting in your own selfish interests, out of childish impulse. I'm very glad you were not.'

'You've never come here.' The words left Lia's lips more harshly than she intended in her half-awake state.

'I have,' Miire said. 'It's just…it's been a long while. It looks different. Sian never kept it this tidy.'

'Why are you here,' Lia asked, just as harshly as she intended. She could not recall a single time when Miire's words were *not* at least as harsh. So, of course, Lia knew her as a miserable woman, whose sole purpose in life was to trade fun with misery. Lia didn't resent her for it; she understood someone had to be a voice of reason and that it was the only voice Miire was capable of. It simply meant that she stayed away from her whenever she could, as Lia did not care much for Miire's nature. And Miire never let her forget it.

Having this woman who was deprived of joy in her sanctuary of senselessness was not a feeling Lia relished.

Miire Zin said nothing for a while; a short while that outstayed itself. She eyed Candy sleeping by her feet again and said; 'I must apologise.'

That made Lia sit up straight. 'For what?'

'There is much,' Miire said. 'As you may have gathered, Kai left the village shortly after you did. I first must apologise for allowing your brother to leave at all. It was...I thought the threat of banishment would dissuade him, but that was a foolish decision made in anger. I spoke far too harshly to him at a time he would have been most vulnerable, so soon after your absence. I failed in my duty as an elder to be empathetic, to him and to you.' Miire's head hung low as she spoke, with a long breath between each admission. 'I understand that this will mean little to you now, but I want you to know that I think I understand, more than ever, why the two of you detest me as you do.'

Lia felt her heart blood chill at those words. 'We never detested--'

'No,' Miire said. 'I am not blind to it. Perhaps you do not realise it, but I know it to be true. I have been harsh on you both, harsher than most, for all your lives. I make no apologies for that, but I only regret never explaining why. I had hoped to explain it to you now, with your permission.'

Lia nodded, almost against her will. Miire had been a distant entity in her life in all the memories she had of her. That had two consequences; Lia and Kai regarded her solely in the harsh manner of which she now spoke of and she was distant enough for them to not care much of her perspective of them. They were happy to indulge in their forbidden fantasies if the cost was Miire Zin's lectures once per nightfall.

So, Lia never really cared for *why* Miire acted as she did towards her, so long as their meetings never grew more frequent. Lia merely nodded now only because she could find no excuse to deny her.

'I have been strict with you,' Miire continued. 'Because I know of the adventurous spirit that is in your blood. Your father and Sian both had that same spirit. Your brother's very life is proof of that, as you well know.'

Lia found her excuse. 'I don't want to talk about them,' she heartily declared.

'Nor I,' Miire curtly said. 'But I am afraid I must. It is important that you understand this; I wept for your father with your mother when he died. I cared for Kai after his birth, while your mother was still weak. I was with your mother most cycles after she was bitten and while she laid in Char Ki's care. And it was I with her in her last moments.'

'Stop,' Lia implored.

Miire Zin hesitated for barely a heartbeat. Her eyes were glazed over, as though she were aware of nothing but her own words. 'I was an ear to her final words. She would speak of nothing but the two of you and her love for you, in her strange way. Despite her knowing--'

'Get out.'

Miire Zin blinked, her eyes shooting open with a daze of confusion. 'Lia?'

'Get out.'

'I do not--'

'Now.'

The air hung heavy and foul between them. Miire slowly found her feet and betrayed something that resembled dejection in her face, before raising her hood and dragging herself back to the bitter outdoors.

Lia had not raised her voice. She had just let her words flow freely and so foully that they tasted bitter in her mouth. But they *had* to be said to someone who would speak so kindly about a woman as foul as Sian Ro.

Lia felt good for it. Even now, her hands were steady, and her eyes were bone dry. She was...fine. She sighed out the meekest of beats in her heart and was *fine*. She had long dwelled on her mother's untimely demise and believed her lack of mourning to be justified, no matter what Miire and the other elders had told her long ago to the contrary. *Maybe that had made me bitterer than I thought.* Lia quickly realised that she was content with that bitterness too.

Lia laid down again, for what would undoubtedly have been a sweet and sound slumber.

But she was soon disturbed again by a commotion from outside. It was loud enough to take her from her bed and to watch from her tipi.

There before her was a small group of Hominum gathered around a mound in the snow; Miire Zan Fa, who had made it a slow dozen strides from Lia's tipi before falling face-first into the ground.

Any semblance of contentment was suddenly torn from Lia's being.

28

⁓

Waya, the forest guardian, grew afraid of the wrath heaven promised to him, but feigned haughtiness, saying;

'No fire will fall,
But by fire I am amused.
And what you bid me guard,
You would lament to lose.'

But the voice's anger blazed at the wolf's stubborn wickedness, saying;

'This place you have marred
And it is you who shall groan.
For what I bid you guard
Is your only home.'

Excerpt from *The Tale of Waya*
By Timor Ro
Hominum Tribe Writer, Generation of Inti
Fourth Recorded Generation

'**A**hh.' Citizen sang. *A bit grizzly.* He took another sip of the juice from the hollow wood stump. He could taste polood in it of course, as he could effortlessly detect a mere drop of polood in a mudslide, but he didn't know what else it was made of. It was sweet, thin and cool. The elk that filled the bowl must have had a very healthy mouth.

He flicked the silver flower again. '*Ahh,*' it cried with perfect melodious grace.

'Hmm. Ahgh—-ahem. *Ahh.*' *Still a bit grizzly.* Citizen took another sip.

He flicked the flower again. '*Ahh.*'

'Ahhhh.'

'*Ahh.*'

'Ahhhhhhh--!'

'Rabbit!' Citizen threw the bowl at the elk's head with a yelp, but thankfully missed by a long way.

'What,' he said, as casually as he could after a long pause of surprise.

'What was that,' the elk said.

'Err, what was what?' Citizen cunningly said, thankful that he threw that stump too hard and fast for the elk to recognise it as its own.

'You just threw something,' it said.

'I--What did I throw?'

'I...dunno.'

'Oh.'

Citizen was happy to let that silence linger and let the question just fade away with the wind.

'What happened,' the elk asked instead.

'To what?'

'You were crying for help.'

'Cryi—I wasn't crying for anything.'

'I heard you crying.'

'I was singing,' Citizen protested.

The elk raised the general area of its face where its eyebrows would be. '*Singing* what?'

'Just singing. With the voxi.' Citizen flicked the flower again for effect.

'*Ahh,*' it sang, spreading its petals and exposing the red in its core.

'See,' Citizen said. '*That's* what I was singing.'

'Not even close.'

'Okay.'

Citizen waited until the elk strode suitably out of sight, before practicing again with a meeker tone of voice.

'Pearls on a—pearls on a snowflake...snowflakes on the...argh.' Citizen rubbed his head, cursing his terrible memory. Smoothie must have sung this song half a dozen times, yet he couldn't recall even the first line, despite having tried to sing along with him. Citizen at least remembered what Smoothie said the song was about. Sort of. After mumbling something about lights and a great tree, Smoothie had admitted he didn't really know either, since he and his sister never finished it.

Citizen had pangs of warmth in his chest when he thought of his part in singing along to the song when it was finally done.

*

Kai was parched. He stared longingly at the water in the hollow rock but suppressed the urge to reach for that bamboo straw. He had grown accustomed enough to the water's bizarre and powerful taste to hardly notice it, but this lot looked suspiciously thick. Kai suspected the citizens had this time not bothered carrying it all the way in the hollow rock like before.

'I'm not thirsty,' Kai said again, his voice raspy. His being permitted to relieve himself outside not one hour ago likely didn't help much. In truth, he was hungrier than he was thirsty, but he refused to admit to that too in his bitterness.

'This front is only a burden to yourself,' the bear said.

'I'm not thirsty.'

'Suit yourself,' it said, for the third time.

Kai looked down at his aching hands. Though they were too dark to see, he imagined them riddled with cuts and invaded by splinters. The lid of his prison was far sturdier than it appeared. He could barely feel the pain while he shook and pushed and struck at it to no avail when the boredom grew unbearable, but now it took its toll. He had taken only one mouthful of the thick water to clean his hands with, and that had stung horribly.

'I need a moment,' Kai now heard outside, from an unfamiliar and authoritative voice. He saw through the lid the bear obediently walking away and a huge, majestic cat with spikes peaking its ears taking its place. Another stream of sweat ran down Kai's back as the lynx's bright eyes met his through the darkness.

'I've come on behalf of our queen,' it said. 'I'm the vice.'

'Please,' Kai said. 'I can't stay here anymore.'

'I think you can.'

'You won't tell me where Lia is, no matter how much I ask. I have to go and find her myself.'

'As I understand it, you *demanded* answers to our queen's face, in front of all her subjects, more than you *asked* for them,' the lynx said, unmoved. 'Is it any wonder you've found yourself in the position you have?'

Kai bit his lip, silently admitting the vice's words to be true. Not that it much mattered, as with Lia still out there, he was not the only one suffering for his impulses. 'That was the first I have heard of her since I got here,' Kai confessed.

'Yes. The reason you were sent back here, away from our enraged citizens, is because our queen knows that. You're here for your safety more than a punishment.'

Kai breathed a sigh and dropped his head, cursing his ignorance. He cursed his lack of empathy, thinking of himself first as always. He thought shamefully of how difficult he had been to the bear, who in hindsight had evidently been trying to take care of him with his persistence. *I'm such a child*, Kai thought bitterly. 'She must be really smart,' he said.

'That's why she's the queen,' the lynx said. 'She does the rational thinking for our citizens, and we make sure her will is done.'

Somewhere out in the distance there was a hearty laugh that spent one's breath too quickly, followed a crowd of laugher. Kai shivered despite his relentless sweating. 'What'll happen to me now,' he asked.

'Weren't you just saying that you can't stay here,' the lynx mocked. 'Giving up already?'

'No, I'm not.'

'Good. The queen has stated that you are to be freed.' The lynx knit its brow and donned a wicked smile at its own words. A purpura lording over Kai's prison shone faintly in its eyes. 'You'll need that resolve still.'

Kai shivered harder still. 'I don't understand,' he said.

'Then listen,' the lynx said. 'Most citizens will know by now that you are in our forest, and most of them will know that you disrespected our queen. And they will know about the corpse you wore when you first entered. They will of course hate you and all smoothskins like you. The queen wants none of that animosity in our forest, and so she demands that you leave and take it with you.'

A smile nearly crept onto Kai's face, but his senses quickly gripped him. 'Doesn't the queen hate me too,' he said instead.

'Not hate. She is not as senseless as the rest of us. But do not misunderstand; she in no way regards you favourably. She wishes only for us to be left alone and for your kind to stay out of our forest when the sun is down. Reasonable?'

Kai nodded, quite emphatically. He was aware that it would be painful to leave this place behind when the time came to, which would apparently be soon. But this forest had taught him one lesson that could not easily be forgotten; he and his kind did not, and never would, belong here. This was the *citizens'* forest.

'She hopes that her mercy toward you will not go unnoticed among your kind,' the lynx continued. 'And that your return to them will mark the last time our kinds share words.'

'Please tell me where my sister is and I'll never return,' Kai said in all sincerity.

'You will first do as our queen decrees.'

'But you said--'

'We do not know where the other smoothskin is right now.'

The lynx said the words so curtly that Kai didn't register them at first. He felt a tightness in his chest and a throbbing in his head when they did. 'Then...how can--'

'I am not finished.' The lynx approached Kai's cell and sat majestically with its face before him. It smelt of citrus and flowers. 'We know only that it left Crescat and entered Susuuri. The queen wanted to capture it as we have you, but it is now beyond our grasp now.'

Kai's confusion only grew. 'You wanted Lia? Why? And why is she beyond your grasp?'

The lynx's eyes narrowed. 'So, the rabbit took you into Susuuri and did not tell you this? I will answer your second question first. You should know that we change when the sun is out and the Hyachin is resting, yes? Weakened and with dulled wits. We are unable to step outside the Hyachin for long while the moon is out, before likewise becoming weak and being rendered immobile. We believe that we would eventually revert to our primal selves, should we stay away from the Hyachin for too long. The same applies to the Lumen, though we believe they can wake themselves with the Hyachin they emanate.'

Kai remembered how Citizen dove onto him when they first met, to keep him from leaving the Hyachin. He remembered how Citizen laid dormant as Kai dragged him away from that snake and Citizen's willingness to leave the Hyachin, despite knowing the consequences. *He really did go to Susuuri so the queen couldn't find him*, Kai reasoned. *Where even the lumen couldn't see him.* 'If you went after Lia,' Kai said. 'You would just pass out?'

'It is not as simple as that,' the lynx said. 'You have been to Susuuri yourself. Did you not see the citizens there?'

'Yes,' Kai said, scratching the itch on his arm at the memory of those spiders. He did his utmost to keep that snake away from his mind's eye.

'*They* are the reason that we are forbidden stray from the Hyachin,' the lynx said. 'And the reason we are forced to hibernate while the sun is up, regardless whether it is our nature to do so or not. You no doubt noticed that they live in darkness, but do not lie dormant and their wits are not dulled. They cannot reside outside the dark, just as we cannot reside outside the light. The Hyachin has served as a border to prevent…genocide, to be frank. For aeons of time.'

'*Genocide*,' Kai echoed, never hearing this vile sounding word before.

The lynx donned a wicked glare. 'Meaning the death of many.'

Kai bit his lip. 'Why,' he asked, with a trembling voice.

'Why what? Why would there be death at such a scale? It is the result of a feud that has outlasted most of us. You need not know more than that without the Hyachin, this forest would have long ago been one largely devoid of life.'

Kai swallowed. 'Then what about when the sun's up?'

'An astute question,' the lynx said. 'Susuuri is not willing to live on the forest's growth alone, so they hunt us while they can, to kill us and gather our corpses to feast upon. The citizens of Crescat gather food toward the end of the Hyachin's cycle, to survive in hiding for as long as we are able.'

Kai was not, like any Hominum, a stranger to death. It was in fact a strongly embedded aspect of the Hominum's way of living; to know always that life was born from the grace of Mother Earth and that it would be returned to her eventually with one's passing. He had been to many a burial and sung the burial song at many a ritual under the sacred burial tree. Yet, since the moment he set foot in this forest, or indeed in all the times it blessed his eyes, he had thought only of its majesty. The revelation of conflict existing even here was a tragedy in Kai's mind.

'Now then, onto terms of your release,' the lynx abruptly said. 'There are two. Firstly, you were not freed. You escaped without our knowledge. I will tell you the exact route to take to best avoid detection, but if any of our citizens find you before you reach Susuuri, you are to deal with it yourself. We will not free you if you are brought back a second time and we will be unable to protect you should they wish to harm you. Understood?'

'Yes,' Kai said.

'Secondly, when you are found by Susuuri's citizens, you are to give them a message for their king from our queen. This will be the same message we intended for the other smoothskin to deliver.'

A king? Kai was not nearly as surprised as perhaps he would have been even a cycle ago, to hear of the existence of such a being, but he remembered again sitting at Omaraa Zan's feet and having only the words of a tome to inform him of such titles. Considering how terrifying Susuuri had been for the brief time he had been within, perhaps the *king* of such a place would be closer to his imagination than the queen was.

The lynx said; 'The message is this. Crescat offers peace.'

Profound confusion hit Kai again with great impact. '*Peace?*'

'Yes,' the lynx said. '*Peace.*'

Kai could not hide his incredulity. '*How?*'

'Enough questions. You need only say the words to any citizen of Susuuri who is willing to listen. Do not forget them, as they may well save your life. Repeat them; Crescat offers peace.'

Kai obeyed. 'Crescat offers peace.'

'Fine. Should you somehow avoid contact with any citizens when you find your smoothskin, just return to your kind and tell them about the mercy we extended toward you and our demand that your kind does not disturb us again. Say it once more; Crescat offers peace.'

'Crescat offers pea--'

Kai jumped back having barely uttered the words, as the lynx bit down on the cell's lid with a jaw of protruding muscles and laid it down in the dirt with a low grunt and clear ease.

The lynx grinned down at Kai's frozen gasp and said; 'You are excused.'

29

...and know that the grace of falling is never wasted on petals that are incapable of new growth.

Maia Ki
Hominum Tribe Writer, Generation of
Ailen the Kind
Sixth Recorded Generation

Citizen was terribly out of breath. What a thrill this was. He hadn't even needed to run yet, surprised by his own guile and cunning taking him so far already. Sure, he had yet to see a single citizen on his way, but none had seen *him* either. The one clutter of lumen he had seen so far seemed too occupied with something high up in the trees to care for him.

He had reached halfway into these forbidden woods unscathed, with only Smoothie's soft scent to guide him. He only wished his chest would stop burning with the adrenaline. All this excitement was making the polood in his hands even more tempting.

Citizen skilfully dodged another patch of singing voxi flowers by walking around the border of the small field. He had learned, only recently, that the prison holes were built in these woods because of the very same voxi, which made escape difficult with the sounds to follow their steps.

Citizen wondered how one could hope to escape woods with such impenetrable security. Still, he believed he'd find a way. He had easily avoided detection thus far after all.

He planted himself against another tree root, hugging the polood for a little more courage. He saw the first hole, blended seamlessly into the hill where it had been dug and covered with slabs of tree pieces. There were only three holes now, from what he could recall, but he was sure this was the one with which he had become far too accustomed. Seeing it from this angle was far less daunting than his previous view from the inside.

Citizen approached until he could see clearly that it was empty. It probably had been unoccupied since his time spent inside, as the tree pieces had been overgrown with vines and sealed in place. Citizen smiled a little. *I thought of that myself. Clever rabbit.*

His smile didn't last on his way to the next cage, with memories of the last time he was last brought to this place. He didn't remember all that much, probably because there wasn't much to remember. He was broken in heart and body and dragged by his ears, in the teeth of the queen's lynx to be tossed inside. He had never eaten so little than during his time in that cell, haunted by his unrelenting endearment for that stupid cat. He cursed himself for allowing himself to become so infatuated with her.

Citizen became distracted by another citizen and was pulled back into the present. He pressed himself against the thick tree beside him and watched the deer stroll along the stream ahead. Between the clicking of its hooves on the rocks, he could hear it laughing with the badger sitting on its back. Citizen had seen few watchmen in the past, but they had all been far more intimidating than them. They gradually became a distant echo and Citizen pressed on through the stream and past another patch of voxi.

The second hole was also unguarded, and Citizen could examine it at his leisure. It was empty and disused like first. That was about all Citizen could deduce from it.

The third was closer, with only a few voxi and trees between him and it. The tree pieces beside the cell looked fresh and recently placed. Citizen could see bite marks in the lid, which were still damp. The hole itself had been left very open and very empty.

Citizen approached to search every bit of it, just to be sure. There was nothing inside but a bamboo straw, a barely touched bowl of juices and Smoothie's faint but distinct smell.

I'm too late. I took too long to decide and now Smoothie is gone. Smoothie escaped.

Citizen dropped the polood from his hands, drained of zeal. He preemptively mourned for his only friend, mortified at allowing the best of times to become a painful memory once more.

*

The cycle flew past as a blur, yet it felt like the longest of Lia's life. It began in Gal Ne's chamber, just as it had the cycle before. She woke up alone, to a modest breakfast of warm oats, and ate lean meat pieces with more than mild guilt, spurred on by pity from Zanuus and assurance from Gal of the necessity. *You must consume the meat and blood to recover the spirit you have spent,* she justified. Every bite made Lia nauseous.

Miire Zin didn't move much, but to shiver under her sheets. Her face was pale white under the warm green pad on her forehead. Her eyes never opened, resting red and swollen.

Lia stayed with her for as long as permitted that morning, until Gal Ne heated a concoction of foul-smelling herbs and strongly *suggested* that she leave.

Lia had a remarkably normal routine for the rest of the cycle, except to be more helpful to the tribe than usual. She offered to help Ogmul on his torch-lighting rounds, much to his astonishment and suspicion. She learned no small amount about steaming vegetables from cook Gira Fe. She even laboured a while with the carpenters after dinner, when the day began to drag. Craftsmanship never much appealed to her beyond making the bows for her and Kai's hunts. It had been a labour of the village which just happened without her caring for details, like refuse disposal and herbalism. But watching the zeal with which the men fortified the walls and refined weapons with timber and stone brought the village's peril ever closer to a reality in Lia's mind. She needed this clarity, she knew.

But even as the cycle ended and Lia ambled back toward her tipi, she felt much the same way as she had when the cycle began; burdened with guilt which she couldn't shed.

Miire Zin had contracted pneumonia mostly due to exhaustion in her ageing body, as Gal Ne had told Lia. She had given Miire Zin an herbal mix to drink each cycle to treat something in her blood and she had not been sleeping as much as she had been ordered to. But Lia was not dense; she knew the latter was in large part due to the worry and guilt that she and Kai had caused her.

Maybe the guilt Miire Zin had tried to express had been weighing heavily on her as it now weighed on Lia. *I should have just listened,* Lia kept on reminding herself. *Even if her sickness was not my fault, I should have just listened and helped her ease her guilt.*

Miire Zin's sickness was a reminder for Lia that she too would be burned under the sacred burial tree and her life would be returned to the Mother one day, like all other lives. Lia couldn't bear the thought of anyone, even someone who was so often rotten and dull as Miire Zin, carrying solely painful feelings in her last moments, of letting those be her final thoughts in this life. *Never again,* Lia promised. *I'll treat anyone like that ever again.*

Lia was reminded of her mother; the lady the Hominum called *Sweetie.* Lia still so hated that absurd and endearing nickname. She had hated suffering the name in her ears as a child after each cycle of aggression and pain only she and Kai knew well of. The few scars still embedded on her skin without fail brought those memories of her mother back, with hardly any of the fondness she wished they could bring with them. But even still, for the very first time, Lia truly hoped that Sian Ro's heart was not too heavy when she passed. *Not even she wouldn't have deserved it.*

Lia felt a little better as she neared her tipi, a little less burdened and her steps a little lighter. She thought of all the work that lay ahead of her, of how she would finally erase the animosity between her and Miire Zin.

Lia would start her work the moment Miire Zin awakened, with an earnest apology.

But at the end of the very same cycle, one that marked the premature beginning to the peak of nightfall, Lia learned the harshest of life's lessons.

There was the sound of knocking wood, deep into the evening. It was a loud, hollow knock which unfailingly brought the Hominum away from their suppers and slumbers, to the centre of the village to hear the elders' dreaded words; a sound to announce a burial ritual for the new cycle to come.

Lia was stunned into silence, too deeply to even hear the chatter of her kin along the way.

She arrived at the centre, outside the elders' tipi. Her chest thumped with anger and tears streamed down her face.

Even after Omaraa Zan announced Miire Zin Fa's name, few cried or despaired as Lia did.

30

To those who have wondered how I find the strength to shoulder the responsibility of generations of Hominum, of those who came before and those who will follow, know this;

True strength is born when you have no choice left but to act with conviction. None among us are born convicted, but we may live with conviction when our eyes have seen enough pain born from our idleness.

Inti Zan Mo
Generation of Inti
Fourth Recorded Generation

A relentless scraping sound gnawed at Citizen's ears. His arms ached terribly as he scrubbed the stonework, with less vigour with every motion. Other citizens, who had been assigned the same duty as he, scrubbed to the same harmonious and terrible melody of stone against stone.

For the longest time, the citizens were confused as to what the strange fur-like material was that the smoothskins wore, patches of which were often found littering the forest. It was originally thought that it was grown and dropped by some type of tree, but it was proven otherwise when the citizens found that the material never degraded as anything natural should have. They since stopped wondering, and just knew that smoothskins wore it to cover their flesh, for whatever reason.

A citizen somewhere and at sometime had found that wrapping rocks in the material made cleaning easier, so every single piece found since was then used for that purpose. The citizens found enough eventually for dozens of citizens to be cleaning the queen's court at the same time.

Citizen could hardly think with such a terrible noise. Although, it may have been a blessing to be free from his thoughts for a time. He would have been permanently rid of his guilt, had only everything gone to plan; to break Smoothie out of the hole, to take him to Susuuri and to tell him that he forgave him for trying to kill him, before parting ways. It was surely a fail-proof plan and the burden Citizen had carried would finally have been lifted. *Now what am I to do?*

For now, he simply cleaned. Then he helped bring supper for the other workers when they got hungry. Then he cleaned some more. Then he was eventually out of options and had no choice but to confront the thoughts that haunted him still. *I must tell someone,* Citizen concluded.

As was so often the case, his past mistakes were made when he was at his lowest and when the slightest flicker of joy was teased on his dark horizon. That joy had come in the form of a cat; one just as majestic and cunning as his queen. A cat with a wicked smile and an alluring way about her. And how allured Citizen had become, from the very moment he found her walking about Crescat, where she should never have been. She had greeted him with that smile now etched in his head.

Citizen had asked her; 'Why're you here,' or something similar.

He remembered, very vividly, her saying through her sharp white teeth; 'I was walking. Then I kept walking and now I'm here.'

Such a rebellious spirit was just too tantalising in the monotonous routine that Citizen's eyes were suddenly opened to.

He was hooked to her from that very moment. He would go to the same spot each cycle, to wait until she appeared again. On the cycles she wouldn't, he would return to his aimless routine of eating and sleeping and obeying his queen's whims. On the days she would, he followed her about with a dumb grin, for as long as her time away from Susuuri would permit before she became too weak and risked undergoing her change. That short time together became the sole part of Citizen's routine that he anticipated with joy, along with his food.

One time, she had found one of the fields where the lumen rested and became enthralled by the glowing plumage.

'It's like fire,' she had said. 'Like the field with all its pretty flowers is on fire and burning to ashes.'

Citizen had to drag her away before the lumen woke. They watched them fly as a flock from afar and there they stayed for a long while; for too long until the cat fell asleep in her weakness. Citizen had to carry her on his back, through every burrow and trench he knew of to avoid the queen's eyes. He dropped her in Susuuri, in what looked like a cave, and fled. That had turned into one of his happier memories, despite the terror of leaving the Hyachin behind him for the very first time.

She visited Crescat more often after that incident and Citizen would even at times go back to Susuuri with her, usually against his will and better judgement.

He eventually would go to Susuuri himself to meet her, following increasingly bizarre directions to find her in secret places. She may have enjoyed showing him the darkest and grittiest parts of Susuuri more than she enjoyed exploring Crescat herself.

Citizen understood that those times could only last so long before they would be found out, but it happened in a way he never expected.

One of the last times they met was on the border of Crescat and Susuuri, as the moon began to set. The cat had wanted to plan something different and *fun* for the next time the moon rose.

'I'm going to see the forbidden land beyond the fire,' she had said, with her wickedest grin.

'No, you can't,' Citizen had said with the most resolute of objections.

'That's a meaningless word since I'm going anyway,' she had said.

'But you'll be away from Susuuri for too long. And what if the smoothskins see you?'

'And what if they do,' she said and smiled a smile that Citizen knew to mean her mind had been made. 'To them, I'll just be a stray cat that wandered too far. And maybe darkness will be enough to sustain me, whether in Susuuri or not. I'll find out.'

'But why--'

'I *am* going, you know. I can find my own way if I have to.'

'But the queen will see you if you go through Crescat.'

'Then I guess you should stop that from happening.' And that was it. That was enough to render Citizen helpless and to lure Citizen into absurdity once more. He would guide her to the forest's border on the next rising on the moon.

'You wanna know a secret,' she had said before they parted; a question she had never asked him before, in a tone of voice Citizen had never heard from her mouth. It for certain lacked her usual flippancy. Citizen didn't have to answer, as she spoke regardless, freely and frankly.

She told him an overabundance of truth. She told him her true reason for so abruptly wanting to see the forbidden land of fire, her reason for coming to Crescat so often, and even her reasons for bringing Citizen to Susuuri with her as she did.

It was all so calculated, all so deliberate. All so ruthless. Any words to describe Citizen's heartbreak at that moment be a terrible understatement.

All the joy and wonder of those cycles were torn away from him in one swoop. Many a revelation hit him like a rolling tree. *I've been helping Susuuri. The smoothskins are gonna be wiped out. The citizens won't be killed by the smoothskins anymore.*

And one revelation stood above all others, which would prove to haunt him the deepest; *I've been used.*

Of course, he had thought. Why else would such a beautiful and fascinating creature spend so long and risky a time with a creature of such habit and boring routine as himself, if not to use him for her own sake?

He knew not whether to laugh or cry, so he did neither. He would from that cycle, and for many cycles after, ask himself the same question and regret not getting his answer back then; *why did she tell me?*

But he didn't much mind the plans she told him Susuuri had for the smoothskins, in truth. Citizens of Crescat lived in unrelenting fear while the sun was up. Fear of being stolen away or being killed first.

Were it to be Susuuri alone who hunted Crescat's citizens, much of their fears would be abated. Citizen saw his broken heart as a worthwhile sacrifice for such a future, in a strange and perhaps absurd way.

So, Citizen kept his promise and agreed to take the cat to the forest border. He waited in another long period of boredom and anxiety in hibernation, for the sky to darken again.

They were to awaken shortly before their hibernation ended and meet close to Susuuri's border. It was on his way to this meeting that Citizen first saw Smoothie, when he had been in the forest *hunting*.

He had fled to Susuuri's border, waited there until he underwent his change, as the hyachin began to awaken.

The cat met him on the border as promised, and together they made for the forbidden land of fire, on the most terrifying journey of Citizen's life.

It had gone smoothly for a time. Citizen took all the crevices and ditches he knew of, to avoid the queen's eyes. The cat travelled for much of the time on Citizen's back, as her energy was spent in the hyachin and she fell asleep.

Citizen had grown impatient as they went and took a route more direct than it was safe, where they inevitably crossed paths with the early rising lumen.

Citizen had one more act of defiance, or perhaps of resignation, left in him for the cat's sake and all she claimed to work for. He took her by the fur and ran as directly as he could to the border, with the cause for guile lost. A myriad of orange lumen lights flew above them all the while, spurring Citizen to run beyond his limits until they finally left the hyachin behind. It was then that Candy awakened.

Citizen stopped running, but she didn't. She ran, as daringly as suited her nature, leaving him to quietly watch her go.

She spared him only a glance over her shoulder, with a look that sent as strong a shiver down his spine as when they first met, with a smile devoid of any motive or sincerity.

Then she was gone, and Citizen was left alone to face the consequences of his naivety.

He had barely crossed back into Crescat before he was bathed in lumen light and lorded over by one of the queen's hunters. The jaguar had taken him in his teeth before the vice, who spoke with a lot of words which Citizen barely heard before he was thrown into a cell where he felt like he nearly starved for the cycle from loss of appetite.

He was freed after a short time and left to his usual monotonous routine. Most citizens knew of his disobedience and how he had often been tainted by Susuuri's air. They hated him for it, and Citizen resented them back.

Citizen very quickly came to accept that his life among his kin would henceforth be one of isolation and loneliness.

That was until Smoothie fell over him while he napped, on the very same cycle he was released.

Upon reflection, Citizen found he had very little reason for the guilt in him. Smoothie had proven to be as false a friend as that damned cat had, and he had left him in no better a state than she had.

What am I to do now?

Food and sleep would have to be enough to distract him from his melancholy. And so, with a motiveless smile plastered on his face and a tear in his eye that wouldn't fall, he slept again in his lonely burrow.

His broken heart was still worthwhile.

31

What intrigue lies beyond the purple glow that eludes us so? To what did our predecessors bear witness in that place, to create this maddening law for nightfall which our generation blindly honours still?
Maddening!

Curse our ignorance of the unknown. Such oppression of free wonderment shall only end in pain. The hard-headedness of our shepherds shall one day be the cause for mass discontent, whether in a dozen or a hundred seasons from now.

Eventually, someone will surely come along to break this mould for the sake of their generation and that of their descendants.

Someone far bolder than us.

Destroyed Excerpt from the *Memoirs of Honi Ro*
Hominum Tribe Poet, Generation of Gouyen
Fifth Recorded Generation

The smoothskins appeared obsessed with fire beyond reason. Just about every patch of the village was drenched in an amber glow like that of the lumen.

But their obsessiveness rose to new heights on this cycle. A group of them stood huddled together under the sole tree in the village with purple plumage, each with a torch ablaze in hand. Candy stood atop the walls, close enough to clearly see where they stood on the *sacred ground*, as Lia had once called it. It was a mound surrounded by a small stream and held the tree, which looked well-fed for all its long life.

Candy had gathered what those loud bells not long ago had meant, from the unsubtle shift in tone among the smoothskins. One of them had surely perished, and Candy did not much care to know which. But, now watching the custom that followed, with the heavy air of grief and uniformity raining down upon it, it was all very interesting indeed.

Candy could hear them singing but couldn't differentiate the words from so far away. She crept along the wall as closely as she could while keeping unnoticed, easily enough with the smoothskins so occupied.

The song took more shape the closer she drew. The one they called *Omaraa Zan* stood highest and sang louder than the others. They all had their eyes closed.

They sounded…not terrible, with their voices united.

'Dance freely in our maker's embrace.
May the light of her peace forever be your place.
Undisturbed in your restful sleep,
We pray your slumber is sound and deep, though we weep.'

They sang in low and meek voices, partially drowned out by the crackle of torch fire and soft trickling water. There was the putrid smell of new death and burning wood emanating from where they stood.

'So, smile in earnest, at last, with your fire spent.
May the dust of a life well-loved our maker lent,
Feed the ones you leave from her boundless might,
And be our beacon through the darkest nights.

'Though we part, we shan't think you gone.
You'll be with us, still, through each new dawn.
To our maker, we pray you grow well,
Instilled with our sister's spirit.
Until we are one, farewell.'

They sang the words again. Then again. Then once more, each time louder than the last.

Candy looked on, the pretty words hitting her with the most powerful of realisations as they neared their conclusion.

It was first a type of realisation that was difficult to fathom, then it became a kind that was utterly shocking, then a kind that was incredible.

I see.

Candy believed she had just stumbled upon a piece of the greatest of mysteries, which she never realised had been missing. A truth she never thought she would care to know until it now hit her like a wave of fire.

I get it. The king's relentless hatred for these smoothskins. His determination to take the throne and to take Susuuri as his own. I understand now.

The song was spent, and the village chief used her torch to light the body and put it to true rest.

Candy laughed.

A bond stronger than being born of the same Mother Earth, indeed.

The smoothskins fell silent with their heads bowed to the dirt, and still Candy's unkempt laughter spread through the land of fire as an echo.

She couldn't have stopped, even if she wanted to. She wasn't *happy*, it was simply all too hilarious.

All this new king's planning.

All Susuuri's anticipation for chaos in the forbidden land.

All the strife which had manifested over so many generations to culminate in this very era.

All Candy's own sacrifices and labour from the shadows, which she had believed to be so significant.

It all ultimately led to one pathetic and hopeless reality;

It will all be for nothing.

32

The burden of hatred placed upon a ruler's shoulders is to be expected, by any versed in our history.

The hatred and abandonment of my kin were never enough to stop my conviction to bring prosperity to my tribe. Such conviction has proven me a worthy ruler, despite the words and the exodus of a few from the haven of our ancestors.

> Gouyen Zan Ne
> Hominum Tribe Chief of the Generation
> of Gouyen
> Fifth Recorded Generation

Lia sang heartily until her lungs were sore and her voice was coarse. She closed her eyes and pressed her hands together in prayer until they ached. Miire Zin Fa's body burned on her dry bed of wood until her ashes were embraced by the soil of the sacred tree. Those present sang once more as the embers warmed their skin and silently prayed until the fire died.

Lia was soon left there in solitude, watching the tree's glowing petals fall upon the ground where she stood. She didn't know why she waited there, sat in the embrace of the sacred tree's light, but it felt right.

There she stayed, for an unknowable time, pondering nothingness. The burial rite was to alleviate any sadness felt from loss and would replace it with contentment in the reminder of where the dead now resided. Not this time. The sadness was indeed gone, but nothing had been left in its wake but the same guilt that had plagued Lia since Miire Zin's final waking moments.

Lia was eventually joined by her shepherd.

'It is hard to let go of the sadness, even with the rite done,' Omaraa Zan said, sitting beside her. Lia knew it was her before she had even spoken. Few others would have bothered to comfort her at this time, for few would have thought that that comfort would be needed.

'I'm not sad,' Lia said, still watching the falling petals.

Omaraa eyed her. 'That's good to hear.'

'No.' Lia looked down at the dirt where all the dead had been laid to rest. It was dry and barren, as it was meant to be. 'I should be sad, because I'm never seeing her again, nor anyone who is resting here. There are Hominum here who lived long before me, and ones I barely knew. I will forget many of them in time, and others will forget me when my time comes. But I won't ever forget Miire Zin. I was the last one to see her alive and I was so cruel to her when I did. She came only to comfort me, and I didn't let her. She told me she thought I hated her, and I let her think it were true. Maybe I believed it myself.

'The last words she ever heard were from a stupid child, who she thought hated her all her life. And now, I'll never be able to tell her that she was wrong. I was just scared of her because she was what Kai and I needed. She was sensible and strict with us, to keep us safe from our own impulses. And I didn't realise that until she was already gone.

'Yet, I'm not sad. It's because I'm thinking only of my own guilty feelings. Despite all I did to make Miire Zin suffer, I've learnt nothing. It's like no matter what, I can't stop being a selfish child.'

Lia spoke mostly to herself. All these thoughts had long been resonating in her head, but they felt far realer when they were voiced aloud. The words came so easily that there could be no doubt of their sincerity.

Lia had forgotten she was with company until Omaraa Zan's large hand was on her shoulder.

'Do you remember the stories I told you,' she asked. 'The stories of my childhood in Gouyen Zan's generation? What sort of a child would you say I was?'

Lia looked at her for the first time since they sat together. 'You liked having fun.'

Omaraa Zan smiled. 'To put it mildly, yes. I lived for fun and nothing else mattered. And so, I am sure you can imagine the heartache it caused me to live in *Goyen Zan's* generation, of all Hominum. She was the embodiment of routine and order, at the cost of all else. Especially at the cost of *fun*. It was all so maddening. But, what do you suppose Miire Zin was like back then?'

Lia didn't find it difficult to guess. Miire Zin had the air of someone who was always old at heart. 'I guess she liked Goyen Zan's generation more than you did.'

'That she did,' Omaraa Zan said. 'She was the opposite of me back then. Really, she never much changed. She had a reputation for being grumpy and adverse to fun, even as a child. Too much a stickler for the rules to be liked by many, including myself for a long time.

'We were practically enemies when we were about your age. She would tell me day after day to take more responsibility in my life, and I would tell her she needed to stop taking life so seriously. In fact, I thought for a while that I *hated* her, but I just did not like seeing people around me live so miserable a life. There was enough sadness and strife in Gouyen Zan's generation without someone like Miire Zin preventing the fleeting moments of joy we had. We just could not get on.

'But once, when we were a little older in Ailen Zan's generation, the two of us were sent together into the forest to gather herbs for Char Ki. I was to find awa' herbs and Miire Zin was to find lotus flowers. The moment I stepped out of the gates, I walked the forest at my leisure, for hours upon hours until the cycle nearly ended.

'I did not realise that Char Ki needed those herbs for one of our hunters, who had been injured. Miire Zin had found plenty of lotus flowers, and so Char Ki could treat his wounds. But I returned almost empty-handed, with barely enough awa' to numb the pain for half a cycle. I still now remember the look that hunter gave me when he was told how quickly the pain would return.

'I believe that was the first time I ever despised myself. My sense of worth felt shattered. The ignis was lighted and the gates were closed after we returned. I moped around in my guilt, avoiding anyone I saw. But Miire did not leave me alone for long. She found me, took me by the hand, hauled me over the walls with her and escorted me to the forest to pick as much awa' as we could carry.'

Lia was equal parts incredulous, fascinated and shocked. '*You* went to the forest at nightfall? With *Miire Zin*?'

Omaraa gave her a knowing smile. 'Almost. The forest had not yet begun blooming, but the ignis had certainly been ignited. We picked the awa', ran out of the forest, and climbed back over the walls, all before nightfall had started.

'I of course realised that the elders would know I had been away from of the village when I gave Char Ki the awa' and that I would be in even more trouble than before. But when I told Miire that, she said; *then you will be in trouble again, but you have this time earned your trouble for doing the right thing.*

'She was correct. I was punished more severely than I ever had been. The disappointment of my parents touched me deeply and even kept me awake through some cycles, as did my sore backside. But I had no doubt in my mind that I had done right by my kin. It is fair to say that Miire's words...Her words had a profound effect on my life, even while I disliked her. And they often guide my steps still.'

Omaraa Zan rubbed the beads around her neck. Her hand was still on Lia's shoulder, but she was barely there in mind.

Lia looked down at her feet, where Miire Zin rested. 'I can't imagine her doing that.'

Omaraa blinked and smiled. 'You did not know her well. Neither did most of our kin or perhaps more would have attended the resting rite. She was serious, stern, strict, and often miserable. But she was all those things because someone must be. She helped teach me what it meant to shepherd this village, long before I became an elder, by living the way she believed she had to. She knew how her kin spoke of her when she could not hear them, and sometimes when she could, but she never let that dissuade her. Do you know why?'

Lia managed a sad but wholly sincere smile. 'Because she was doing the right thing,' she said. She had always known, surely, but had never acknowledged it. She had always respected Miire Zin deep down, though she could never like her.

'Miire Zin always had a way of making me feel guilty with her council,' Omaraa Zan said. 'She asked for adoration or gratitude. Yet, she tirelessly worked to ensure we were happier than she was. I loved her for that. She always seemed more suited to shepherd this village than I, even after I was chosen. I often felt inadequate for leaning so much on her council, and that of the other elders too.

'But that feeling taught me responsibility and helped me grow into who you see now; from a formerly silly young girl who thought only of her own pleasure, to a shepherd whose greatest joy comes from helping her tribe prosper. And you are far from selfish, Lia Ro. Not many could have cared for your brother for all those years as tirelessly as you did. Not many could have endured the pain Sian Ro quietly subjected you to and persevered for your brother's sake. Your perseverance inspired me too, to never allow any Hominum to cause the pain Sian Ro managed to cause ever again. You have inspired us elders, more than you know.

'So, I have no doubt that you will grow to embrace the guilt you are feeling now too. Just do not tear yourself down before you can persevere again, okay?'

Lia smiled.

She didn't remember the moment Omaraa left her alone under the sacred tree. She pondered herself there for longer than she had ever had cause to. That weight of sadness and guilt felt better suited with time and contemplation.

'Lia,' said the familiar voice of a young man, riddled with nerves. Zanuus Ka, the young herbalist, called to her as he crossed onto the sacred ground. 'Are you okay?'

Lia eyed him thoughtfully. She wondered how many times she had heard that question from his lips. It was a great many. Always caring, yet never overbearing. Always kind, yet never overstated. That was the Zanuus Ka that Lia had enjoyed for far too long, with little gratitude.

'Thank you,' she said.

'Huh? What for?'

Lia smiled again. 'For asking.'

33

The second greatest failing of my predecessors was to appoint shepherds, not by merit, but by right of blood.

No blood exists great enough to impart wisdom in place of learning to shepherd through tribulation.

Ailen Zan Mo
Generation of Ailen the Kind
Sixth Recorded Generation

The moonlight was all that guided Kai's steps for a time after he finally left the hyachin behind him and passed Susuuri's border. He saw silhouettes of half-dead trees swaying ungracefully, with the wind flowing through each of their fingers. Wails from beyond the darkness and laughter beyond those saved Kai from maddening solitude, as he crept from tree to tree.

Dying leaves under Kai's feet echoed in the air. He soon found a crimson light far ahead of him, as a lone beacon. He made for it, hidden in the shadow of each tree he passed and cautious to not allow the crimson to expose him for long.

Kai could see the source of light as he approached; a small field filled with ominous red and black flowers. They each emitted furious red in the pocket of shadows, as though each petal bled bright blood.

They glowed darker still as Kai lorded over them, as he was drawn to abandon reason in favour of intrigue and exposed himself fully in their light.

The sounds from the darkness grew deaf to his ears and he became encapsulated by a low hum emanating from the field of red. It was terrifying and beautiful.

A cluster of the flowers cried in a strained hum, then hummed again in tranquillity. The sound snapped Kai out of his daze, and he found himself surrounded by redness, surprised by how far he had walked in his daze.

He saw a single blemish in the perfect red glow ahead; a dead beetle in a broken shell. It was abnormal, as was the forest's standard of normality. It was larger and fatter than Kai's hands combined. A chunk was missing from its abdomen in the form of a bite mark and dull-yellow blood.

Kai looked up into the trees from where the beetle had fallen. There were creatures above him in the shadows in slumber, hanging from the branches by their feet.

Kai softly stepped away by pure instinct. He kept stepping back, his eyes fixed on the sleeping bats. They rested overhead silence. There were more and more of them above him, no matter how far he crept. They were huge, with some almost as large as Kai.

Kai fought every urge in his body to run. He shuffled away with every effort to keep the flowers silent under his feet.

One bat hissed from right above him, which was carried as an echo and felt like ice water to Kai's skin.

It was all he could take. His feet carried him away, faster than they should have. The dead leaves were like thunderclaps in his ears, ringing hollow in the blackness as the bloody glow of the field was swiftly left behind.

*

It was in a field of wandering auras, in an expanse of glowing blue flowers never for a second dormant and swaying in near-perfect harmony, where the cat's mood had shifted even more profoundly than usual.

She had abruptly stopped and turned to face Citizen.

'You wanna know a secret?' she had asked. It was a question she had never asked him before, in a tone Citizen had never heard from her lips. It scared him with the lack of her usual flippancy. 'The king says we have a bond with the smoothskins, stronger than merely being born of Mother Earth, but he has never told us what that bond is. He was probably being metaphorical or philosophical or something. But I don't really care because, in the end, it won't matter.

'What matters is why I've come to Crescat so often. Do you wanna know? Wanna know why I've tolerated you and allowed this bond between us to fester? I like you, true. You've helped me fight off monotony for a while, and I like you

for that. But that's not why I have suffered you for so long or why I let you suffer me. This new king has allowed me to enter Crescat, time and again, all so I can help sow the seeds of genocide.'

*

Kai stumbled in the darkness and fell into the dirt. A muffled groan ran through his teeth, then laboured heaving through his lips.

It was another field of dully glowing flowers, this time silver and silent. Hisses rained down on him, from where more bats surely rested.

Kai closed his eyes where he lay. *She can't be okay.* A tear ran down his cheeks despite how he fought. *She can't be okay. She can't have survived here for so long, all alone.*

Infallibility, limitless cunning, endless courage; those had been the qualities that defined Lia's character for her whole life. But even one such as her could not keep those qualities alive so long in a place so dark and deprived of respite.

He sat upright, utterly miserable and defeated.

He opened his eyes.

Two blue glowing slits met his frozen gaze.

The grey scales of a colossal snake glistened with a silver ripple.

Kai found that he couldn't run. He couldn't scream. He couldn't move. His body refused to obey his head.

The silver flowers lit the snake's fluid body in harsh grace. Its face sunk to the ground to meet his.

This way they remained, with their gaze unbroken and Kai's blood turning cold.

The snake's forked tongue hung from its mouth like blood trickling from its lips. Its mouth opened and, with a quiet but piercing voice, one word filled the air.

'Star.'

The flowers petals shot open, exposing the vivid red in the heart of their stalks.

'Star,' they echoed, in perfect and beautiful unity. The snake's scales rippled to a fresh tone of red.

A thousand eyes shot open from the heights of the trees. They were purple and bright.

The bats released a terrible screech, as they spread their wings and fell.

*

'I had to know about Crescat to know how to get through it,' the cat had said. 'So that a citizen of Susuuri can finally break out of this forest and into the land of fire, and we can learn how their land affects us. That's me. I'm to be used as an experiment, it seems. A test to see how Susuuri's citizens will be affected when we break into their land. Isn't that an honour *for me?*

'If I don't return, I guess the king will have to reconsider. If I do, then we'll know we can survive away from Susuuri, and we'll have a gauge of the strength the smoothskins possess. Then we will end their oppression in the way the false king--oops, I mean the way the new *king desires. All will end in their death.'*

*

The screeching which descended from the heavens was deafening. Kai covered his ears, as he sat in the field of flowers that echoed the bats' terrible voices.

Kai may have been screaming, but he couldn't hear himself. The screeching only grew more excruciating, as more bats joined to sing from above and the flowers at his feet sung louder.

Kai finally found his feet, through sheer will and terror, and moved. He ran as fast as his feet were able, away from the snake and flowers, with his hands to his ears and his eyes weeping for the bright red glare.

He left the field behind, but the bats followed with even more terrible an outcry.

Kai took only a dozen steps more before the ground vanished from under his feet. It wasn't a long fall, but he landed hard into the base of a large hollowed-out tree.

He quickly tried to stand, but toppled over and clutched his foot, clenching his teeth. He tried, and tried again, but could not find his feet.

He opened his eyes to find a green light floating before his face, emanating from the tree. The trunk was filled with slimy, fat creatures clinging to its walls. Worms, or grubs. They were like mice in size and their hearts beat as a rhythmic green pulse within their bodies.

'Guy.'

Kai felt the snake's whisper down his neck, from the top of the hill from which he fell. Its two blue eyes floated in the darkness above him.

Beside it stood more of Susuuri's creatures, baring their fangs with their eyes glowing purple and their dark fur rippling in the pale moonlight.

*

Citizen, despairing in the truth which had been forced upon him, managed to force from his lips the words; 'Why? Why would you tell me all this?'

Candy smiled, her wickedest and nastiest smile, and said in her playful way; 'What are you gonna do?'

*

Wolves approached Kai and silently stared him in the eyes with his back pressed to the tree.

Kai, despairing in his hopelessness, managed to force from his lips the words; 'Crescat offers peace.'

The silence was brief but profound.

Vicious laughter followed, for what felt like forever.

Rain fell from the skies.

34

One will always be beholden to the choices of those who precede them. Such is how the Mother has made us.

We have happily been beholden to our ancestor's choices. My duty is to ensure my descendants will be happy to be beholden to ours.

Mother Earth guide my steps.

Excerpt from *The Birth of the Hominum*
By Farro Zan Me
Generation of Farro
First Recorded Generation

The village had a dour vibe about it, despite the snowfall and dire murmurings spreading through the Hominum like an infection.

The workers of every discipline were strained to their limits. The herbalists, the hunters, and the craftsmen had worked through an evening, maintaining weapons and producing medicine.

Lia was hungry. She and everyone else had been subjected to hunger from restricted resources. Every bite was to be taken only during the designated time after waking, and only those assigned work in the evenings were permitted a small meal before sleep.

It had only been one cycle since that rule had been declared, but the strain was already plain to see in the Hominum's declining morale and energy.

Cook Gira Fe, more than anyone, looked peaked.

'My tummy grumbles just like yours,' was all he said whenever his stringent portions were protested. The Hominum had learned to collect their meals quietly on the next cycle, with the occasional grumble in thanks.

Candy took great joy in ranting at anything which had the ears to hear. She had been using her gift of speech to the fullest again since her gift was widely known, and she no longer had cause to hide it. She became a novelty to most and had become even more vindictive in the wake of Miire Zin's burial, even mocking the Hominum's death rituals and their state of mourning at every opportunity.

Lia had seen little of her since the rite and couldn't bear to share any word with her. The peace of her absence was deafening in a way, but she hated dwelling on that damn cat for any longer than she needed.

Lia made for Gal Ne's hut after a breakfast of stale bread and uncooked vegetables. She still felt a little weak and the cold still felt harsh on her skin, but this check-up seemed to her like a waste of Gal's time, with everything else happening.

Lia had not been called upon for anything else, as the elders surely knew all they needed to from her account, and she felt wasted. Just when her impetus was at an all-time high, she had nothing to use it for. It was maddening.

Gal Ne was slumped over her stool, as usual, concocting something in her old bowl, as Lia entered her tipi. It reeked of lavender again.

'Zanuus will check you,' she muttered after Lia removed her furs. She despised wearing those things, even if out of necessity. She had told Candy as much while she had laid outside the village gates, perhaps out of guilt or to assure her of her objection to this insult to her kind.

But Candy had laughed and said; 'The citizen is already dead. Why would it care about your guilt?' It was enough to have Lia reconsider her thinking and to consider that it may be more an insult to let her furs go wasted for the sake of her own conscience. She was undecided but chose to wear them until she would be.

Zanuus bade Lia *sa'ar kali* and helped her to lay down. He went about the check-up silently, holding her wrist, checking her eyes, laying sweet-smelling leaves on her forehead and taking a sample of her saliva, blushing all the while.

He then gave her a cup of foul-smelling sludge to drink, which would make her vomit if her body was healing as expected. She did vomit.

'Sorry about that,' Zanuus said, after dumping the filled bowl outside. Lia just smiled in return. Her stomach ached a little, as she had had little food in there to be thrown up.

'I think she's stable,' Zanuus said to Gal Ne.

She stayed hunched over, grinding her mortar with her pedal. 'You *think*, do you?'

Zanuus bit his lip. 'She *is* stable now.'

'Then she's excused, isn't she?'

Lia drank the tea Zanuus offered to her. It, of course, had the aroma and taste of lavender. 'Gal,' she said. 'Have you seen Candy?'

'*Candy,*' Gal muttered. 'Why you named that creature is beyond me, and *Candy* no less. There's nothing sweet about that thing. Should have named it *Headache.*'

Lia smiled. *I guess that's a no.* She had only named her *Candy* as an ironic joke at her sour attitude. She wholeheartedly agreed with Gal's sentiment.

'Can I help you with anything,' Lia instead said.

Gal looked up with a snarl. 'Help here? And for how many years have you studied herbalism? I think not.'

Lia stood with a dumb look on her face, taken aback. Gal was usually harsh, but not so unfairly.

'She's stressed,' Zanuus said, reading Lia's face well. 'We're to make batches of medicine for hypothermia and large amounts of fluid imbued with lavender without healing properties. We're having to--'

'And with what herbs do they expect this miracle?' Gal turned away from her stool and ranted. 'We're already running low of the paltry supplies our hunters brought for us last dayfall, and they order me to use yet more lavender, with no incoming supply. And all for what? We're to work ourselves thin and starve, yet there's not even been--'

'Gal Ne,' Zanuus said, to both Lia and Gal's surprise. Few dared to interrupt Gal mid-rant, but for Gal herself. 'Shall we get back to work?'

Gal grunted. 'Shall I get back to watching *you* mix up this lavender, while I rest my old bones for a moment? Yes, I shall.'

Zanuus shot Lia a proud smirk as she left. She was impressed and surprised at once. *He's changed too,* she realised. *We're all slowly changing.*

Lia left the tipi, her stomach already groaning. Houli Zin Me marched about the place, stern-faced and purposeful as usual, as befitting the chief hunter and overseer of the craftsmen. Lia imagined he had been subjected to more stress than most after her account, as it burden of preparing the village would chiefly be his. She had never spoken directly to him, as his manner was so standoffish. But she too was making changes.

'Zin Me,' she called to him before he passed. 'Can I help you with anything?'

Houli Zin didn't hesitate and gave her the wooden utensils he was carrying. 'Summon everyone to our tipi for us.'

*

Poruus Zin Ka addressed the Hominum from the centre of the village, from atop the speaking stone outside the elders' tipi. Most of the kin were gathered, shivering in a huddle with mist flowing from their lips.

All the elders were present, save for Fanwei Zin Or. The tribe had been kept in ignorance of the threat to the best of the elders' ability, but the incident of the screaming spiders had stayed very much on their minds and tongues, which was surely the cause for this emergency call.

Candy was still nowhere to be seen. Lia could not much longer deny her concern and would need to go hunting for her after this address was done. *There's always something with that damn cat.*

'I must first warn you all that what I have to share with you will not be well received,' Poruus Zin started, in his usual measured manner. He had an impressive ability to be heard, no matter how quietly he spoke. 'You will know by now about the spiders at the gates six cycles ago. We have cause to believe that we face imminent danger from the ones who sent them. We also believe that those spiders may have been sent here to test our wards. If so, it is likely that that incident merely precedes a worse one to come.

'As I said, what I have to say will not be well received, but we would not bring this to your attention unless we were certain. That is why you have heard so little from the elders on this matter, until now. We must prepare for the likelihood that the village will soon be endangered again and, if those spiders are any indication of the nature of the threat, we will not have the resources to do much about it.

'Therefore, attempting to make any sort of defence here would be nonsensical. We all know how poorly our walls and wards protected us against those creatures, so they would only serve to trap *us* here as their prey.'

Lia noted how quiet the other elders were as Poruus Zin spoke, including Omaraa Zan, practically hiding in the shadow of their tipi. Lia herself was usually only so quiet when she knew she was either in trouble or about to be.

'We have discussed the best course of action,' Poruus Zin continued. 'The *only* course of action left to us. We cannot fight back and we cannot defend ourselves, so all that is left for us to do is flee.'

Lia could hear the incredulity in the silence. Her heart thumped in her ears. The words were too absurd to digest.

She suddenly and fully understood the elders' unease. Omaraa Zan had her head bowed to the ground, in a rare show of what looked like shame.

'To go where,' someone dared ask.

'This deep into nightfall,' Poruus Zin replied, with as little hesitation as ever. 'And with so harsh a winter wind, the only place which may be safe is the forest.'

Lia couldn't hold back a gasp, and hers was lost in a choir of many others. There was much outcry, which grew until Poruus Zin voice could no longer be heard. Outrage and offence spewed from the Hominum's mouths in revolt.

But Lia was quiet, with the wisdom in Poruus Zin's words dawning on her well, as her first lesson in strategy.

We're to stay in Crescat, she reasoned. *Susuuri is the danger. Rather than fight and risk losing, we're to stay where they can't go.*

Lia knew of no animosity in Crescat toward them, so there was more wisdom in appealing to them than in fighting Susuuri. Poruus Zin had omitted the detail that the source of the danger also came from the forest itself, no doubt to avoid even more trepidation of this move. Their kin was not to know about the citizens in Crescat until they were already safely there. It made sense.

But Lia could not contain her worry any longer. *Kai. He won't have a home to come back to. What if he comes back like I did? How can we allow him to return to an abandoned home?*

Poruus Zin beat the sticks that were handed to him, gradually bringing back the quiet among the tribe. 'I understand your trepidation,' he said, having to shout to be heard. 'I do not relish the thought of leaving my home behind, nor of seeking refuge in a place which has for so long been forbidden. I do not wish to abandon generations of our predecessors' labour. But our only options are retreat and death.

'You have all worked tirelessly to prepare the resources needed to support the journey. We have food, medicine, and weapons, so there is little sense in waiting much longer. I propose that we leave in exactly four cycles from now.' Poruus had to knock the sticks again to stop the outcry. 'If anyone has any valid reasons for why this cannot proceed, come to us in the chamber as usual and we will hear you. If not, I for one will abandon the village in favour of my life, in four cycles from now. You have the freedom to come along with me or to stay here and await the Mother's embrace. I suggest that you all use that time to think carefully and to pack what you can comfortably carry.'

Poruus walked off the speaking rock to the sound of outrage, fear and bafflement. The elders retreated to their chamber and the tribe was left in a state of emotional turmoil.

Lia bit her lip. She was guided by the benefit of perspective, though it felt more like a burden. She understood well that her brother alone would not be a valid cause for waiting and for endangering her kin once more, in the blind hope of him returning of his own volition. She decided quickly that she would not approach the elders with this and would instead suffer her dismay in silence. *What a lousy sister I am,* she lamented. *To have to leave him to fend for himself, now of all times...*

She would pray that the Mother would keep Kai in the forest, by whatever possible means. *I'll find him,* she resolved. *Wherever he is, I'll find him. And I'll never leave him alone again.*

But in the chaos that would soon unfold, Lia understood her immediate purpose, and the significance of her purpose in the coming cycles; to finally put her trust in the Hominum's shepherds.

35

Indeed, deciduousness is not indicative of a final passing. Petals shed only to blossom anew, again and again, until their hour of final passing is chosen.

Maia Ki
Hominum Tribe Writer, Generation of
Ailen the Kind
Sixth Recorded Generation

Citizen longed for the time he could for once make this walk along the beaten path of the forest's prettiest plumage, without the accompaniment of dread. To walk in this beautiful place with the comfort of innocence to guide his step.

Citizen actually quite liked his queen. She was playful, chaotic, wise, and wickedly smart, all in one majestic bundle. She reminded him a lot of that other cat, in fact, but a little *less* chaotic. He wished he could simply enjoy the queen the way she was meant to be enjoyed; as a wise and loving ruler.

But not like this. He followed in the shadow of the bear hunter to the court, for what must have been the...who knows what time. They approached the throne where the queen was sat, dry and sheltered from the pouring rain.

Her vice sat at her right side, with a look of disgust fixed upon Citizen. But he was too accustomed to those eyes now to be more than mildly shaken.

'Look who it is,' the queen said, with a face as hard as stone. '*Core mine*, rabbit. How may this humble cat help you this time?'

Citizen swallowed the air in his mouth and breathed out a hiccup. It did nothing to soothe his nerves. His paws trembled, but he spoke with all the puny conviction he could muster. All his quiet deliberations led him to this moment.

'I have something to tell you,' Citizen started. He had imagined how this moment would feel. He imagined relief at standing before his queen, to unload the burden which he had so long shouldered. He imagined how the words would leave his lips like an unbounded gazelle when called upon.

It was not to be. Reality was not as glamourous as Citizen expected, as usual. Ultimately, he was just reminded that he was a weak and insignificant rabbit, stumbling into mess after mess.

This realisation, harsh and sudden as it was, dazed Citizen into silence. He stood before his queen, with his mouth open and unable to relieve anything but one long sigh. *What am I doing,* Citizen wondered, not for the first time this cycle.

'Oh, are we playing this game,' the queen said, forming her first smile. 'Allow me to take a guess then. I'd say that you're here to tell me about Susuuri's plan to kill the smoothskins. The same plan you failed to tell me about the last time you were summoned here. Am I right?'

Citizen looked straight into the eyes of his haughty queen. His heart thumped harder. 'Y-you--'

'Do you take me for some fool, to not know about such a plan before my subjects do?'

It hardly felt real. It was like the queen's words were coated in a sour sap and couldn't be easily digested. 'How,' Citizen managed to say.

'By thinking about it, rabbit. Why else would they send that cat, their outcast queen, to the land of fire and bring one of the smoothskins that they so hate much back to Susuuri? The king must have wanted to see how his subjects would change in the land of fire, and how the smoothskins would change while in Susuuri. So, for what reason would they possibly need to do that?'

She knows everything, Citizen realised, in awe at her flawless reasoning. *She knows, without even needing to hear for herself. She's amazing.*

'That wasn't a rhetorical question, rabbit,' the queen said.

'Umm, r-rhet…rhetor--?'

'It means I'm expecting an answer.'

'…what was the question?'

The queen smiled, nastily. 'Why would the king need to know how the smoothskins would change while in Susuuri?'

Citizen looked at his feet. They hadn't been cleaned in a while. 'To attack them,' he guessed.

'One thing at a time, rabbit. He wanted to test their weaknesses. That could be for one of two reasons. Either to defend Susuuri while the sun is up and the smoothskins return to the forest or to fight them while the sun is down. Tell me which plan it is.'

'He plans to att--'

'No. I'm telling you to tell me which plan it is, based on the information we have, and why.'

'I don't know,' Citizen quickly and shamelessly admitted. He had long grown so accustomed to those words that they no longer inspired the self-loathing that they once did.

'Then think about it until you do.'

Citizen tried. He came to his conclusion faster than he would have believed. So quickly that he distrusted his own logic.

He nevertheless said; 'He'll attack while the sun's down because he wanted to see how the smoothie was affected without sun.'

'Yup,' the queen said, without a hint of surprise. The vice beside her didn't hide his astonishment, as his stare turned wide-eyed. 'And so,' the queen continued. 'What other reason would there be to fight the smoothskins with the sun down, while they're still hiding beyond their walls and fire, if not to kill them?'

'I--'

'That one *was* rhetorical. There's no other reason. That leaves one more question; what did the king learn from the smoothskin they took to Susuuri? What do you think, rabbit? Do tell.'

Citizen frowned, feeling himself sweat. This was surely the most horrible hearing yet. 'I don't--'

'And if you're about to say *I don't know*, you should reconsider.'

Citizen did reconsider. He took precious time to ponder. *The king took the smoothie to see how it changed in the forest. The king will attack the smoothies.* His *precious time* was wasted pondering those same two statements stuck in a vicious circle in his head.

'Nothing?' That's what Citizen ultimately said, unable to hide the inquisitive tone of his voice.

'That was a guess, wasn't it?'

'Yes.'

'A lucky guess, rabbit.'

Citizen beamed with a smile. *A lucky guess.* It was the closest thing to a compliment he had ever heard from the queen's lips. *I'm a lucky rabbit.* His newfound sense of worth was very pleasing indeed.

'So, the king plans to risk attacking the smoothskins in their own territory, despite holding one of their own for the very purpose of creating an advantage in his own land,' she continued. 'So, either the Hominum showed no change in that time, or the Hominum escaped before they could see it change. Of course, I already know the smoothskin escaped and came back through Crescat.

'I also know he sent spiders to the land of fire not long ago, probably to further test how his subjects would change. He would only act this quickly if he were desperate, and he would only be this desperate if the smoothskin that escaped could deliver information back to its own kind that would be detrimental to him. So, obviously, he plans to attack the land of fire soon, before the smoothskins can act.'

Citizen blinked. 'Okay.'

The queen laughed. 'You're not stupid, rabbit. You're reckless, and absurdly impressionable, but not stupid.'

Citizen was at a loss. *That was a compliment. A real compliment.* His very first. He had never been gifted with words that made him feel this way; warm in his heart and lifted. He could find no words himself to respond with.

'If you were kind or smart enough to come out of concern for Crescat after this plan is done, you needn't have,' the queen continued. 'We've already sent some insurance for the king, which will make it clear who we favour in this fight. And should favour turn against Susuuri in the coming cycles, they'll at least have a hostage as leverage.'

It took Citizen no time at all to comprehend the queen's meaning. The harshest of chills ran through his body. 'Did you send the smoothie--?'

'But,' the queen interrupted. 'You didn't come here out of any sort of nobility and you didn't come to tell me anything for Crescat's sake. I can see it all over your filthy face. You only came here because you feel guilty, for trying to keep this from us. Not only did you put my subjects in danger with your witlessness, but now you have the shamelessness to try using *me* to rid yourself of guilt.

'You almost disgust me, rabbit. The fact that you are still one of my subjects is your only redeeming quality. Get out of my face, now. And the next time you show it before my throne, I'll have it torn off.'

There was no further room for clarity. Citizen was taken out from the queen's grounds by the scruff of the neck, dejected as he had been all the times before, yet more elated than ever. He was utterly conflicted.

Though her harshest words rang the truest, her kindest words rang the loudest and the most shocking revelation resonated the deepest. He clung, for now, to the kindest. *I'm not stupid.*

*

The queen let out a long sigh and slumped on her throne. She was exhausted whenever that rabbit was in her presence, yet toying with his innocence and ignorance was like an addiction.

'So,' she said, turning to her vice. 'What do you say *now*; stupid, or utterly brain dead?'

'I still say you waste time with that one,' the vice said. 'He proves time and again to have no regard for your headship, yet he goes almost unpunished. Why?'

The queen smiled. 'He's fun, so he's never a waste of time. And leaving him to his own devices is punishment enough.'

The queen left her throne and court, alone, to wander into the trees along the familiar and lonely walk. She found her favourite quiet patch and sat under the trees, which bore rich and vibrant plums on their fingers. There she rested, pondering her *own* guilt, which only seemed to grow as the night went on.

Guilt was not a sensation that she was accustomed to, nor the feeling of doubt in her choices and sadness at their consequences. It was that damned rabbit. She truly despised his predictableness. Him so zealously guiding that cat to the land of fire felt even more her doing that his, predictable as it was.

She could not help but feel worse for having to outcast the rabbit, who may have unknowingly done the greatest duty to Crescat to date and served as a key contribution to the smoothskins' extinction. And to have to reprimand the rabbit for feeling guilt he should not have been burdened with; it was hypocritical, and the queen so despised a hypocrite.

This was the sole place she could still be at peace, free to imagine the new forest, where the smoothskins' presence would be firmly and forever in the past. *Not long now.*

For that future, her heavy heart and the rabbit's self-hatred would be worthy prices to pay.

36

For how long have we aimlessly traversed these lands, through winters and scorching heat? We have starved, we have frozen, and we have grown sick. We have allowed kin to die, in peaceful respite and vehement bloodshed alike.

We sought peace and found only madness in lands rendered desolate but for creatures hungry for blood. We are filled up by food with the taste of ash and water with all the refreshment of dirt.

These lands have long been abandoned by the Mother. We were fools to have ever abandoned her care.

Excerpt from *The Two-Year Wander*
Author Unknown
Text Predates First Recorded Generation

L ia woke to face a new cycle. It was a dark one, but not so dark for the heart of nightfall.

It snowed still. Lia could see a tone of orange in the blackness of the sky when she stepped out of her tipi.

She spent most of her breakfast of hard oats admiring that beautiful orange tone and relishing the cool flakes falling on her mostly healed skin.

She then sat huddled in her furs, still with some guilt in her heart. She recalled Candy's mocking words when she had sought to burn her furs, back when she had first escaped from Susurii;

I doubt burning their empty corpses would revive them, but feel free to try.

Candy had laughed, but she had of course been right. What purpose would be served in Lia burning the remains of a long-dead corpse, but to ease her own conscience?

Lia assured herself once more that it was better to use the remnants of those poor creatures for the sake of her kin, but that reasoning still made her feel sick.

Candy was still missing and no one who Lia asked had seen her. Candy was not the sort to stay in one place for long, nor to give much regard to the worry of others. Lia didn't put it past her to be gone for good, as was more than a likelihood now, to who knows where. She would surely not be welcome back in Susuuri again and Crescat remained impossible for her to reside in.

The village would likely be the only place Candy could seek refuge, which Lia knew she would not relish. Her disgust for the Hominum had hardly been hidden, despite her incomprehensible, but invaluable, assistance to them.

Lia believed that all that would be left for her would be to chance the unknown lands. She had stepped into the forbidden many a time, so there was little to dissuade her from stepping into the greatest unknown of all, with no home to return to.

There was still the other, more worrying, possibility that she indeed had returned to Susuuri to share all the information on the Hominum she had now gained. But Lia wondered whether there was cause for concern. Candy had already been missing when the elders announced the plan to leave the village, so she should not have been aware of it. *But the elders still have a right to know,* Lia decided. *To know of anything that might endanger us.*

Lia returned to her tipi. She and Kai never had much to call their own, so she had very little to pack for the journey. She ended up with a sack of trinkets she couldn't bear to leave behind, but were otherwise useless, namely the few wooden toys she and Kai had crafted together, most of which had hardly been used.

She couldn't help but look through the sack of toys again, with thoughts of Kai resonating in her head. She wanted to think of him more often than she did, to think of the unbridled joy it would bring to hold him in her arms again. She wanted *that* to be what would fuel her through all the inevitable tribulations ahead.

But it wasn't to be. She was instead riddled with guilt at every thought of him. She was beyond the time she spent in the forest weeping for her loneliness, for her absence from the village, for yearning to get back the boring routine she had taken for granted, even if she never outwardly cried. She too had to be done with stressing over that which she could not control.

Kai was gone from her, and she from him. Lia firmly believed in the wits of her brother and that they would carry him through whatever trials he faced, just as it did her. That unwavering believe would have to suffice until they met again.

She took in a deep breath, inhaling the subtle but persistent aroma of the dead citizens which formed her life-long home, for what may have been one of the last times. She was soon to leave her home and the memories of the woman who raised them here with it.

Her resentment of that vile woman had never lessened. All the time spent remembering her youth showed Lia that she was just as bitter toward Sian Ro as she had always been.

She hoped, with all her being, that this exodus would be enough to finally expel the odious feelings which haunted her.

*

Candy could feel it in her bones; the ever-persistent sensation that taunted her from the moment she touched Crescat's light. The change was seeping into her, hard and fast, like the teeth of a rabid hunter.

It was a difficult feeling to express, the feeling of one's self being torn from their very fibre. Her blood cried to be freed from her prison of a body, yet there was no pain. Candy recalled dreams where she was conscious that she slept, or where she saw herself through another's eyes. This perhaps was the best comparison.

It was still the early stages of the change, early enough for Candy to remain in control of her thinking faculties. She used them to revel in the glee of the unknown that lay ahead. She leapt from tree branch to tree branch, with unwarranted conviction.

It was a wonderful life, finally. She *earned* this after countless cycles spent clinging onto an aimless and melancholic life in the shadows, all for the sake of an equally pointless tomorrow. Suffering pointless adulation, then pointless hatred from her kin, all for the sake of the blood she shared with their undeserving rulers, was so painfully dull.

Uncertainty, pressures, bondage; they were almost behind her at last, and her arbitrary purpose with them. Purpose in *freedom* and *intrigue* would prove stronger than that of *duty*, Candy was convinced.

And plenty of intrigue surely laid ahead still. Intrigue that would be manifested in the form of despair for some and liberty for others. Candy longed to see which of the two sides she herself would fall onto, with some glee.

Her imagination took a firmer hold of her than her sense did, as had become her norm, free as she was to be guided by her impulses and to be led to the path that would bring the least melancholy.

It was a wonderful, wonderful life. *So many possibilities, so many branching paths. I can hardly contain myself.*

One of the many possibilities wandered beneath the scattered branches which Candy leapt upon. This happening was, of course, not at all coincidental. It was just one more little seed to sow on her path defined by impulse itself.

But, this one turn of fate would set into course a chain of actions that would come to define a nightfall already filled with its share of defilements as *turbulent.*

Candy watched the patchy rabbit gormlessly sauntering in the flowers beneath her, looking as distraught as the first cycle they had met. The rabbit had not been difficult to find, as she had become familiar enough with his scent, and his negligence of bathing made it an easy scent to follow. It was probably thanks to that scent that Candy was able to enter Crescat as often as she did and remain undetected by the other citizens' noses. She had the rabbit to thank for the idea of her fur now being drenched in foul-smelling mud, for the very same purpose.

Candy let leapt down into the rabbit's path. It was, predictably, too stunned to talk, as their eyes met. Its mouth went limp, as was his habit when his tiny brain was overwhelmed.

Candy smiled. She felt her body growing weaker, with her change fast approaching.

'Hey rabbit,' she said. 'Do you wanna know a secret?'

37

Waya fled deep into the forest he called home, abandoning the fire he had long admired to the elements.

The wolf looked up through the trees that were his shelter with great fear. He watched as the heavens turned from a gentle tone of blue to a rage infused crimson.

Excerpt from *The Tale of Waya*
By Timor Ro
Hominum Tribe writer, Generation of Inti
Fourth Recorded Generation

Kai was grateful for the darkness. He wore a leaf as a blindfold, which had been donned on him as he was taken to wherever he now sat in waiting. He hadn't seen what it was that pulled it over his eyes but had felt the creature crawling up his back and onto his neck to do so. Another had crawled onto his arms to bind his hands in itchy vines.

Kai's foot ached terribly, and even standing was an effort. The trip from atop the creature's back had left Kai exhausted and stiff. He shivered for the rain which had fallen on his back on the way.

Kai knelt in wet mud, surrounded by Susuuri's natural and unnerving sounds. There was the pattering of rain, the thuds of wet footsteps, and the wind's voice flowing through the trees.

Here, alone in the dark and deeply terrified, Kai was forced into contemplation, to reflect on his seemingly endless stupidity and naivety.

Crescat offers peace.

Kai could only be angry at himself. The lynx hadn't lied. Kai simply couldn't fathom how peace could possibly be offered and he had foolishly let the question go unanswered. Even a miniscule dose of doubt may have at least given him some hesitancy.

It was Susuuri's creatures, who laughed so heartily when they found him, that finally caused Kai to have the realisation that he was a fool who willingly brought himself into captivity. Worse, he still couldn't fathom how his bondage could be an offering of peace, rendering his bondage utterly pointless in his eyes.

Kai was truly terrified. Not for his own safety, which he had forfeited since he first climbed the village walls. He was terrified at the returning thought of his sister being left alone in this for all this time. *How* can *she be okay? It's been so long.*

Kai had only one morsel of hope which he clung to in his nearing acceptance of his sister's likely fate; he himself was still alive. Though the citizens of Susuuri held him in their hands, still he lived. Kai could take some measure of comfort in knowing that these citizens were not creatures completely lacking in control or solely guided by primal rage. *Please Mother Earth,* Kai prayed again. *Please let her be okay. Please keep her safe until I can take her home.*

Kai trembled again, as he felt another tickle on his skin. Something thick and hairy stroked his back, as though trying to peel the flesh from his bones. He shivered at the sensation, the same one as the stroke of that spider in that tunnel.

It did not last long, and Kai heard the soft patter of its eight legs in the wet mud drifting away. He sighed.

Kai had found another cause to be grateful. That was now the fifth citizen to touch his skin since he had been bound there. He must have been in a cage of some kind, to prevent them from doing more than touching him. Without it, he didn't want to imagine what would have become of him. He remembered the taunting words the spider had told Citizen, while they hung from the branch as its prey;

'I'll peel all that hair off your flesh and spit my venom down your body. I'll suck out all that good meat and savour every single morsel of you.' Kai shivered again at the memory, feeling nauseous.

His stomach grumbled, not for the first time there. He could not remember the last time he ate. So much had recently transpired that he forgot to feel hunger until now. Perhaps the contorted smell of dampness and herbs and flowers waned his appetite somewhat. It was so strong a smell that he could picture Susuuri in his head.

He remembered seeing immense roots and plants through the moonlight when he last fled this place. He imagined how beautiful it might have looked, had it been blessed with the purpura's light as Crescat was.

Such thoughts were enough to distract him from his bindings and persistent peril for a little while until whatever awaited him was to be made manifest.

*

It was a restless slept which led Lia into another cycle of her lifelong routine. With the growing spread of orange in the dark sky, it was a beautiful new day to birth Lia's conviction; to stop dwelling on her heartaches.

The hour was early, but she was not first out of her tipi. Hominum tepidly ate from what must have been the last batch of stale oats.

Lia made for the sacred tree, crisp steps atop the settling snow. Its petals glowed proudly and danced with each gust of wind.

It was quiet there, as it had been every morning. She lost herself in the happiest memories she could, of those who had returned to the Mother in that very place. She found the memories easy to come by, with a little effort.

She stayed for a short time but left feeling ready to face a new day and all its trials. She soon joined others to eat her own share of breakfast.

The air was heavy with a strong stench around the village, one that was familiar but too overpowering to place. It had been subtler a couple of cycles before, but it now made her lungs feel heavy, though it wasn't an unpleasant smell. It was like she laid face down in a field of a great many flowers. *Lavender.* Gal Ne and Zanuus must have produced a significant amount indeed, for its scent to spread so far.

'Lia,' she heard. It was the voice of Omaraa Zan, who sat with a group in their early feast.

'You're not in your chamber,' Lia said, and immediately regretted it. She could not remember Omaraa Zan ever breakfasting with others, but she needed not make her curiosity so verbal. Lia had much to learn of tact, she admitted.

Omaraa Zan smiled. 'We shan't have chambers or tipis soon,' she said. 'Better to become accustomed now to what will soon be the norm. How do you feel?'

'Okay,' Lia honestly said. Omaraa Zan nodded and took another bite.

Lia sat beside Ogmul and Charaa and laid her pack in the middle of the circle which they formed, along with the others.

'That's all,' Ogmul scoffed when she saw Lia's pack.

'I don't need much,' Lia said, blushing. 'I'm only little.'

Something like a snigger left Ogmul's lips. Lia was taken aback. *Ogmul can laugh,* she remarked. *This is a profound moment indeed.*

'That's a good trait,' Ogmul said.

'Being little,' Lia asked.

'Not needing much. Being little can't hurt either. You can save some meals for the rest of us to have our fill.' Lia smiled sadly. Ogmul had been worked half to death since that spider incident and it showed on his face. He never did have the softest features, but he had now grown wrinkles and creases in places she never knew possible.

'Our *fill,*' Charaa echoed, screwing up his face for effect. 'Of *this* stuff? Is that even possible? Even dirt might be easier to swallow.'

Omaraa Zan raised an eyebrow. 'I would be glad to have your fill for you if it pains you so much?'

Charaa grinned. 'I didn't say I *wouldn't* swallow it.'

Omaraa Zan smiled again. 'Then swallow it quickly. We will be off soon after everyone has had their fill.'

Lia looked up at her, confused. '*Off?*'

'What do you mean *off,*' Ogmul echoed.

'We are leaving for the forest this cycle,' Omaraa Zan said.

They all almost coughed up her oats. '*Today?*' Ogmul remarked. 'But it's only the second cycle since--'

'Indeed, it is. We announced the cycle of our departure often and loudly enough, I would say. But, things change.'

Loud and often. The words carried with them a wonderful awe-inducing realisation. Lia was elated. *They said all that for the king to hear. He will think we're leaving in two cycles from now, if he heard it at all.*

It was an overwhelming thought, to leave her tipi and village behind before she had fully made her peace. But how incredible the elders were to create such a strategy when called upon for action. And to do so, even while having to keep the village in ignorance of the reason; Lia couldn't help but feel her confidence in her shepherds growing.

'We appreciate it is a significant change,' Omaraa Zan continued. 'But it is out of necessity. We will announce this to the village shortly after we have all eaten.'

Ogmul frowned, an expression far more natural on his hardened face. 'I doubt many will take kindly to this.'

'As do I,' Omaraa Zan admitted. 'But, we will be no more ready than we are now by waiting any longer.'

'So, we leave this morning,' Charaa echoed. 'While the snow is still fresh?'

'It won't matter if the forest's as warm as the girl and the cat claim,' Ogmul said. 'If not, that's what our furs are for.'

Lia and Omaraa shared a knowing look. Lia had told the elders how she had been forced to abandon her own furs on the way to the forest, and how their nature was rightfully abhorrent to the citizens. They could not hope for any refuge in Crescat, were they to enter donned in them. That was yet another revelation that would not be well received.

Many, like Lia and Kai themselves, would have a sentimental connection to their furs, deeper than their practicality. Lia did not envy the elder who would need to tell her kin that they must be abandoned.

'What do you mean *if* it's as warm,' Charaa said.

'I mean *if*. A flower producing heat, and in nightfall no less. Don't tell me it doesn't sound absurd.'

'*Absurd* is it, Ogmul,' Charaa laughed. 'I bet the talking cat would disagree.'

Ogmul grunted. 'Shut it. I could see the cat myself and I don't deny my own eyes. Where is that cat anyway? I thought you two were joined at the hip.'

Lia felt a sudden chill in her stomach. It would not be right to withhold the truth now of all times, but the truth would surely bring worry. Even if she herself were somewhat confident in where Candy's path now took her, Lia could not expect the same confidence from anyone else. She found she didn't know how to respond.

A shadow had been cast over Omaraa Zan's face, and her manner suddenly changed. 'Actually,' she said. 'I need to discuss something with you, Lia. A moment?' Lia nodded, gratefully and emphatically as she stood. 'You'll want to bring your oats.'

They left Ogmul and Charaa to their breakfast and banter. Lia followed Omaraa Zan towards the elder's chambers, feeling more and more nervous.

'I assume the cat is missing, then,' Omaraa Zan said on the way. Lia meekly nodded. 'You should have told us sooner, Lia.' Lia could not deny it. It was selfish and foolish, in hindsight, for her to presume to keep this to herself for so long, regardless of her own thoughts of it.

The chamber was empty, save for Houli Zin Me. He sat cross-legged on the floor and ate his oats, evidently lost in thought, as he barely acknowledged them entering.

'Houli,' Omaraa Zan said. Her stern voice tore him out from whatever thought he was lost in. 'You will need to hear this.'

38

The process of growth must never be painless, not in the hearts of the masses nor in our own. Pain to us is like water to flowers.

Let us embrace the pain of the past. Let us embrace inevitable pain lying in wait. Let us embrace it all in good cheer.

Mayara Zan Fa
Generation of Mayara the Bold
Seventh Recorded Generation

Kai's stomach growled. *Fifty-seven.* The novelty of his counting game wore off somewhere around thirty, but it was still more novel than the boring darkness.

It groaned again. *Fifty-eight.* He couldn't ignore his hunger much longer. The sounds his belly made were as though it ate *itself*, and it felt just as painful as it sounded.

'Food, please,' Kai finally said into the void. The words were lost so quickly in the natural symphony of Susuuri that it may as well have been a whisper.

'Food, please,' he said again, louder.

'Open up, then,' said a gruff voice in his ear. Only then did he feel something perched on his shoulder and wondered for how long it had been there.

He opened his mouth as bid. Something slimy touched his tongue. It was big, soft, and exploded into sludge when bitten. It slithered down Kai's throat before he could wretch.

'Open up,' the creature on his shoulder said again, the taunt clear in its gruff and pitchy voice. Kai relented, and did so again, fighting the urge to haul as the thing tarnished his belly.

They were quite filling after half a dozen, but his stomach grumbled still, louder and several octaves lower.

His mouth watered in outrage. It was so foul that his tongue went dumb.

'More,' the creature asked, with a titter that only a bird could make.

Kai groaned and finally asked for what he had been dreading;

'Water, please?'

*

Houli Zin sat stone-faced, wearing an expression somewhere between grievous and incredulous.

'That…changes things,' he said after Lia had finished speaking.

'Indeed,' Omaraa Zan said, with atypical grimness. 'But if Candy left the village three cycles ago, as Lia implies, she should not know of our intentions to leave this morning.'

'*If* being the important word,' Houli Zin said. 'It is quite a risk to take, to proceed with this kind of uncertainty.'

'Not if we have no choice in the matter. Whether we stay or leave, the risk shall be great. It is surely better to leave now, while we are still able.'

Houli Zin sighed, shaking his head. 'This cat's disappearance is far too coincidental. I do not like it, not at all. But I wonder why the cat would come this far, to warn us about Susuuri, if only to put us in further peril now.'

'*To let you believe you have a fighting chance,*' Omaraa Zan recounted. 'Was that not Candy's explanation? I suppose that may have been a lie.'

'I doubt it,' Lia said, as little more than a mumble under her breath.

It was loud enough to give the elders pause. 'Lia,' Houli Zin said. 'Be honest; did the cat give you any indication of what she was planning?'

'No,' Lia said, feeling her heart drop a little, insulted at the implication. *So, this is how much you distrust me now.*

'Then,' Houli Zin said. 'From your perspective, how much danger is the cat likely to cause us?'

Lia thought for a moment how best to word her perspective of that creature. Nothing could be easily translated into words when it came to that cat. 'She could cause as much or as little as she wanted,' she said. 'But I don't think Susuuri would have her back after all this. She could tell them anything, but she did not seem to be on good terms with them when we last left. I don't know what makes her do the things she does, but she...she's just unpredictable. Reason doesn't apply to her and I think it's a waste of time to try to work out what she's thinking.'

'What do you mean by *unpredictable*,' Omaraa asked. 'How unpredictable are we talking?'

'She was the one who took me to Susuuri and gave me to the citizens to be locked up. But she was also the one who took freed me and helped me get back home.' Lia hadn't reflected on this absurd sequence of events for a while. Candy had said nothing when pressed about her motives, only smiling in her unreadable fashion. Lia had since convinced herself that her motives would not be worth knowing, so long as she got home and warned her kin of what she had learned. Now, she regretted her acceptance of Candy's dismissal.

'I can't think of any reason she would go through all that,' Lia said. 'Least of all because she has every reason to hate us.'

'In short, she is untrustworthy because she is unpredictable,' Houli Zin said. 'So, we must assume the worst-case scenario to be the most likely; when she left the village three cycles ago, it was to inform Susuuri of our plan to leave the village this cycle.'

Omaraa Zan frowned. 'But Candy could not have--'

'In fact, are we certain it left at all? If the cat could infiltrate our village to take one of us away, without our knowing, are we to assume it couldn't remain in or around the village undetected for a cycle or two?'

Omaraa Zan sighed. 'That may be true, but the plan was deliberately written down by Poruus so that the tebirii would not hear it. We never said it aloud, until this morning.'

'That would make it unlikely for the cat to have learned our plan,' Houli Zin said. 'But not *impossible*. Assuming it was still in the village, it could have known that we had a plan, but not the details of it. That alone may be enough to move the king into premature action.'

Lia knew the truth in Houli Zin's words and she herself didn't for a moment doubt Candy to be capable of it all, particularly with the tebirii evidently being at her disposal, for whatever reason. She bit her lip.

'Then we must consider carefully to proceed,' Omaraa said. 'Whatever we do from here on, we will be at risk.'

'Indeed,' Houli Zin said, 'But, at the very least, Susuuri can't possibly know that we suspect the cat to have informed them yet. That may be the only advantage we have.'

Omaraa rubbed her temple and sighed.

'I know,' Houli said. 'But this is the reality. I advise that we still leave this cycle. Whatever may come of it would be better than waiting any longer.'

Anxiety crawled back into Lia's blood. She had feared what awaited the Hominum in the forest, from the moment she first heard of this plan.

She had only found comfort in the elder's certainty in action, despite the danger they faced, and so she could have hope that they could overcome whatever trial they face.

But now, upon hearing their plan becoming weaker by their own admission, that comfort just seemed to fade away. All because of her *own* uncertainty and inaction.

Lia's heartache simply refused to fade with it.

*

Poruus Zin Fa stood atop the speaking rock before his kin. They watched him with anxiety and anticipation painted all over their faces.

He looked down at them, huddled together, shivering for the bitter cold and the snow at their feet. He saw red eyes and pale skin, greying hairs and new wrinkles.

He himself stood on the stone with weak legs. *There is hardly any strength here when it is most needed. This is what has become of us for living too long with contentment and comfort. We are ill-prepared for tribulation.*

Poruus breathed deeply. He would soon force himself to speak of more promises of comfort, of more reassurances to the tribe before him, who were unable to keep themselves assured. His role as a guide, as a shepherd, had never felt so heavy, and he was disgusted for that. *This is what Aileen and Mayara had warned us against,* he reflected. *We have had no cause to grow because we have done nothing to risk the failure from which we would learn. This may be our very first test of will and shall surely be far too much for most of us to endure.*

This was the sole cycle since Zanuus' birth in which Poruus had cause for excitement and the only one in which he ever had cause for such deep lamentation. His kin were about to grow by force, but it would undoubtedly be excruciating.

'Firstly,' Poruus started, to a silent and attentive audience. 'I must assure you that what I am about to say--'

It was a delicate sensation that gave Poruus pause, alien and bizarre in nature. The ground beneath the settled snow softly shook. A tremor flowed up the speaking rock and into Poruus body, like a chill on his flesh.

Poruus instantly understood its nature. *Tribulation.*

He jumped down from the rock. 'Make for the gates,' he shouted, as loudly and authoritatively as he could. 'Now.'

But *now* was evidently too late for his kin, who were not so readily prepared to act. They looked about, each as vacantly as the other. There was no sense of urgency among them, no comprehension of the significance in a subtle change. There was nothing, but hesitancy and purposeless fear.

Only when the ground beneath their feet began to open, in the most literal of senses, did the first Hominum scream and did the others follow suit.

Dark holes swallowed patches of snow around them, emitting hollow and hungry howls from within.

Chaos ensued, as the first of the creatures crawled out from a dark pit.

39

Unity. Trust. Cooperation.

These shall forever be the Hominum's greatest treasures. It is upon this unwavering belief that the tribe of Hominum is now founded.

Excerpt from *The Birth of the Hominum*
By Farro Zan Me
Generation of Farro
First Recorded Generation

A new voice seeped into Kai's ears, forcing him to awaken. Deep sleep alluded him still, as bondage in darkness had a way of distorting his perception of time and place. It may have been a mere few hours or many cycles, but it was too long a time spent powerless and trapped in self-pity.

'*What* brought you here,' said the voice. It sounded quite dignified, after the barrage of wails and wordless outcries Kai had been subjected to in that cell. It was the kind of voice he felt in his blood more than he heard in his ears.

Its owner was close, just outside Kai's cage. He thought he could feel cool breath on his face as it spoke. This citizen might even have been in the cage with him right then. That would mean that the cage door was currently open, and Kai was no longer protected. Kai swallowed.

'Is the blindfold deafening you,' the voice said.

Kai swallowed again and let the words flow as freely as they could through his tight, parched throat. 'Crescat…offers peace.'

Vile laughter rained down on Kai from all sides. *There are many others here with us,* Kai realised, feeling their breath on his wet skin. He bit his lip, trying with little success to stop himself from trembling.

'So,' the voice said, killing the laughter as quickly as it had begun. 'It truly wasn't the smoothskins that sent you. How foolish you are, to come here so willingly.'

'Vice,' said another voice, far quieter and raspier. 'As I said, there is no chance of one so puny and defenceless coming here of its own desire. Not without considerable gain for itself or its kind. It wouldn't tell us its purpose so freely. It can only be here to spy on us.'

'I doubt that,' the vice said. 'It said *Crescat offers peace.* Crescat must have sent it here, maybe with deception or blackmail.'

'That would mean this creature came at its own peril for *Crescat's* sake? I fail to see how they managed that.'

'Nevertheless, it appears to be true. How do the smoothskins gain anything by willingly sending us a captive, even as a spy? A spy who cannot share what it learns is useless.'

Kai bit his lip again. He had little left to lose, but perhaps something to gain; hope through honesty. 'I came to find my sister.'

Kai could feel the eyes on him, the cold and heavy stares. He waited and waited, for far too long, for an answer in the silence.

*

It slithered among the trees and uproots, with irresistible purpose; a purpose it couldn't comprehend, intertwined with its very being as an instinct more than a desire.

But it obeyed that instinct with great pleasure, as a welcome relief from the nothingness riddled with insanity, which had long cursed its mind.

The forest was scarcer than it had ever been, no doubt for some significant reason it should have cared about. It was free to scale through Susuuri with far less of those disgusted eyes upon it, labelling it an abomination.

It was neither a good nor an unpleasant label, in a place that felt neither foreign nor like home.

It was only the embodiment of a nightmare.

*

'You're referring to the other smoothskin with long hair,' the vice finally said, as a self-assured statement of fact. 'Your *sister?* That would explain your motivations.'

'Only if he's being truthful,' said another voice.

'One would only take so great a risk as he has for some selfish gain,' the vice said. 'This would qualify as such.'

Kai swallowed again and shivered. The rain seemed to fall harder still. 'Where is she,' he asked, as boldly as he could.

'Who can say,' the vice said. 'Perhaps she is lying in a ditch somewhere. Or perhaps floating along a steam. Or perhaps already torn to shreds and melting in a citizen's belly. I know one thing for sure; you've wasted your time looking for that one and have needlessly brought yourself to us. For that, we thank you.'

It took Kai no time at all to digest the vice's words and to comprehend the admission hidden within them.

He smiled, shamelessly and brightly, in unfiltered relief. 'You're lying.'

*

It drew close. It could feel it. The warmth of their bodies and a strong scent cried out to it in powerful beckoning. It rushed on harder still, in a state of bloodlust and desperation. It was maddening, even with its dulled wits.

Not far now. It followed its flickering tongue through the darkness until it would find the salvation its blood screamed for.

*

Kai didn't care for the laughter that followed. He *knew* he was right. He smiled still, as the proud instigator of the words they mocked.

'On what basis do you say we lie,' the vice said, demanding quiet again even from the heartiest laughs through the intensity of his voice alone.

Kai spoke freely, imbued with a fresh confirmation of purpose. 'You thought I came to spy on you because I came to Susuuri by myself. But my sister did the same thing, so you would have thought that she was spying too. You wouldn't let her go to tell my kin what she found out. And, since you don't know where she is, and you haven't tried to find out, she must have escaped Susuuri. My sister's safe.'

His smile diminished a little in the quiet the followed, as he was hit with another epiphany. *Lia had to go back into Crescat if she were going back to the village,* he reasoned. *And the queen's eyes are everywhere in Crescat...*

The implications were unpleasant, as was the confirmation of his naivety in so openly believing the words of Crescat's vice. But, even so, he did not regret his actions anymore. The truth he had just learned was more than worthy of his despair.

'Are you old by Hominum years,' the vice said.

'No.'

'Impressive, then, that you deduced that so efficiently. But it is a talent that shall go to waste, now that we have you here.'

*

It was finally in sight; a small smoothskin, which it instinctively knew as its salvation, locked and bound in its cage. That fearsome thumping resonated in its heart again. It inexplicably was infatuated with this creature, addicted to the sensation it suffered whenever it saw it.

It had become accustomed to many an alien sensation plaguing it, even through what had once been pleasurable endeavours, ever since it had bitten that smoothskin and drank its blood, so long ago.

Feasts, hunts, guile, even sleep; it all now came with the unbearable weight of another voice in its head, born solely to inflict doubt and guilt upon it, as it lived through its natural course.

But this sensation was a little different. It was certainly not guilt *that it felt at the sight of this smoothskin. Not* solely *guilt.*

'Kai,' it tried to scream, as loudly as it could.

It knew not why that word was so strongly etched into its mind, but voicing it was the one instinct it had left which its other voice did not condemn.

*

'*Guy.*'

It was that same voice again, which harshly slithered through Kai's bones. The snake's bright blue eyes shone before his mind's eye and his blood turned ice-like.

'Snake,' the vice exclaimed. 'Why are you here? You've not yet been relieved from Crescat's border.'

'It must've smelt the smoothskin,' another voice said. 'It's probably hungry. Wait, it can *talk* now?'

'*Guy,*' the snake whispered again.

'*Guy?* What does it mean by *guy?*'

'It matters not,' the vice said, growing impatient. 'As you can see, snake, the smoothskin is alive and it is not to be harmed. You will have your feast after--'

'*Oh-phar!*'

Finally, for the first time since that fateful feast of smoothskin blood, pure unfiltered instinct drove the snake once more. Two words constantly echoed in its mind as a deafening scream made by both of its inner voices.

It was a scream it couldn't subdue and a scream that demanded obedience.

'Orphan Star!'

The symphony that followed was utterly inexplicable in its nature, intensity and vileness.

It was a song that harboured every conceivable despairing sound, sung with unhindered agony.

Screams and outcries shook the very ground. Kai's cage cracked against the skirmish. He cried out in terror, still bound where he knelt.

The symphony proceeded for an immeasurable time. Kai heard every nuance of it as it slowly faded, the voices each dying out.

A sole roar marked its finale, bellowed heartily into the skies before being violently snuffed out.

Silence was the aftermath. Susuuri was fraught with the stench of blood.

The voice proudly whispered a desolate encore.

'Guy.'

40

But it is all they are; helpers. An asset to their ruler's will. A queen they did not elect, yet they are bound to obey her. What bound them to such a torturous state of melancholy? And who can guess what drove the Mother to birth them with mouths unable to speak?

Whatever the cause, we who neighbour the Ameyali Forest should and must be eternally grateful for the lumen's bindings to their queen's land.

> Destroyed excerpt from *Creatures of the Ameyali Forest*
> by Moro Ki
> Hominum tribe writer, Generation of Farro
> First Recorded Generation

Lia watched from the elder's chamber, as Houli Zin Me ran out into the snow.

Anything resembling the order which had guided the Hominum through their relative turmoil dissipated before her eyes, in an instant.

The village was filled with the despairing voices of Lia's kin, fleeing in vain from colossal spiders rising from holes in the ground.

Hominum, young and old, were dragged to the ground by the creatures gnawing at their limbs. Some fought with futile resistance, with whatever they laid their hands on. Some fled for the gates, hauling their feet through the snow, only to be stopped by more spiders crawling from the ground. Some just froze, overwhelmed by their terror.

Lia herself despaired in her powerlessness and fear. *It's too late. After all this, we're too late. They have us.*

Omaraa took her by the hand and dragged her back through the elder chamber.

'What do we do,' Lia vacantly said, not meaning to say it aloud.

'What we planned to.' Omaraa panted as she spoke, her hand softly shaking in Lia's. 'We make for the forest.'

'We...we didn't plan for *this*. They're here. The plan didn't work. We've--'

'Do not panic, Lia. I said we still have a plan to follow.'

'You don't understand. If they're already--' Lia paused, realising she had been taken into an unfamiliar place beyond the elder's chamber.

It was a room that had been disguised by a fur sheet. It was small and mostly empty, save for a lone wooden stall and two sacks on the floor. They were filled with books and scrolls, all well-aged and well-read.

Lia realised now in what room she stood and the importance of the documents within. She knew many of the ancient generations' quotes from these pages by heart, with the words being recited in many hearings and with a life spent singing their ritual songs.

She could think of no other scrolls that would be preserved so carefully and secretively, but those of the past village chiefs.

Lia supposed that it was in this room that the elders gained their limited insight into the nature of the citizens, passed down by the elders before them.

Omaraa Zan hauled one of the sacks over her shoulder and handed the other to Lia. It was heavy.

'We're taking *these,* 'Lia exclaimed, equal parts confused as exasperated.

'We are saving our history,' Omaraa said.

'Why? We should be saving--'

'Later, Lia,' Omaraa said, before leading Lia back through the chamber.

The screams reached Lia's ears again, as though they had been silenced then reborn in perfect unison. Lia's heart shook at the sound and felt like it bled.

'What will we do,' she said again.

'We must hope and pray, that Poruus' plan was as sound as we believe. If so, we need only make for the gates.'

Omaraa Zan soon had her answer, as they ran out from the tipi and were met with a bizarre sight.

Few of the Hominum still screamed in terror, but far more spiders made a collective cry of unadulterated agony. They scuffled over each other to crawl back into the holes in the snow, screaming as they furrowed. Some never made it, writhing in pain where they laid, like puppets on tangled strings.

Hominum hunters had weapons in hand, killing the spiders where they lay. Houli Zin barked orders at others, who rushed to the aid of the Hominum who laid injured, with torn and shredded limbs.

Red and blue blood was splattered in the snow. The spiders were swiftly gone, leaving behind the corpses of their kin.

Gal Ne laid on her side, a few paces from the elder's tipi. Lia let go of Omaraa Zan's hand and ran over to her.

Gal Ne raised her hand without looking at her. 'I can manage well enough,' she said. She appeared unharmed but spoke as would be expected from an elderly frightened woman; feebly and with a tremor. She found her feet and looked at Lia with bloodshot eyes.

'What...happened,' Lia dumbly asked.

'Are you blind,' Gal snapped. 'Those things just crawled from the ground and damn near slaughtered us. That's what.'

'But why did they leave?'

'*Why?*' Something changed in Gal's face, as she echoed the question. She sighed and formed as close to a smile on her lips as she was able in such a state. 'I suppose I did teach him well,' she said.

'To the gate, now.' A shout was bellowed through the village. It was Poruus Zin's voice. 'Everyone,' he said. 'Must make for the forest. Now.'

Momentary quiet followed. The tribe exchanged the same look of exasperation. *It is too soon. We are ill-prepared.* Such doubts were so clear on their faces that Lia could practically hear them. Even the hunters were frozen at Poruus' words.

'*Now,*' Houli Zin echoed. 'Everyone make for--'

Another shudder resounded through the village, and the ground beneath the snow seemed to tremble. Lia's legs shook with it, against their will. The sound grew more intense the longer she listened and the ground tremored harder the longer they waited.

'Now,' Poruus screamed, finally inciting his kin into a frenzy. All who could run ran with all their might, while those who couldn't were left to stumble behind. The orchestra of Hominum footsteps in the snow created a rumble of their own.

Lia took Gal Ne's hand by embedded instinct. 'Come,' she said.

Gal gasped in surprise. 'I told that I can--'

'Come.' Lia pulled her as fast as her legs could go. Some Hominum far ahead of them were already through the gates and in the lavender fields.

Lia felt a new ambience around her, through the panic and turmoil. Her warnings had come to fruition and her kin finally moved with some sense of purpose. Finally, there was an end to this ever-looming dread in sight. The abandonment of their home had been a terrifying prospect, yet it was now all that mattered.

But it was all too late.

Lia was quite sure only she had noticed the holes in snow growing larger at first.

From a fresh pit by the gates ascended two wolves with black fur, like dark holes in the air. More of Susuuri's citizens then rose with them, in every direction.

The remaining Hominum were encircled and backed into one another, grouped together with only a few remaining hunters standing between the tribe and the creatures. There was a panther, hyenas, wolves, huge lizards; all keeping them huddled in the village's centre.

The creatures glared at them, drool dripping from their bared teeth. Their eyes were so red, that they appeared to glow in their rage.

'Hold,' the panther said. It hardly needed to raise its voice to be heard, with the Hominum's silent terror now burying the outcry from moments ago. The Hominum hunters raised their spears at its word but dared to do no more.

'Who speaks for you,' the panther said.

Omaraa Zan did not hesitate to step out from the crowd.

'Omaraa,' Houli cried out.

She raised her hand to him. 'They gave us a chance to speak. I will take it.'

'Silence,' the panther growled, with a low and imposing voice. It stepped before Omaraa Zan and stared her dead in the face. If she were at all, she didn't show it. She stared right back into the panther's cold eyes.

'Yes,' it said. 'I believe you speak for these smoothskins and lead them. What did you do to our spiders?'

'Who do *you* speak for,' Omaraa demanded, with a rare deliberate authority.

The panther grunted. 'No one.'

Another remarkable sight appeared at its words. Two more citizens rose from another hole in the snow, bizarre in their ordinariness. They were no larger than would be expected of them in dayfall, and their features were utterly normal. But it was the manner of their appearance that was outlandish.

Lia saw first a goat, shaking the dirt and snow from its soft cream coat. It regarded the spectacle around it with the most curious and innocent of smiles, with almost child-like curiosity.

It sat down with its leg bowed and there, on its back, rested a small, decrepit-looking tortoise, sighing in a deep sleep.

The panther said; 'Our king will speak for himself.'

41

What is the cause for this outrage among our tribe? I do not destroy our history by burning scrolls, but I preserve our future. Knowledge such as this serves only two purposes; to incite unease among the strong-willed and to incite fear among the weak-willed.

Any knowledge that is solely passed to one's decedents through fragile pages is not knowledge worth preserving. We will not lament the absence of such records, and nor will the generations after us. My only lamentation is that those records were ever written.

Monsters we do not know have a greater influence on us than those we do. The forbidden shall stay forbidden, with or without our ignorance of its nature.

Inti Zan Mo
Generation of Inti
Fourth Recorded Generation

Susuuri's creatures bowed their heads. The Hominum were stunned, in silent anticipation.

There was soft, rhythmic snoring from atop the goat's back.

The panther slowly raised its bowed head. 'King,' it whispered.

More snoring. With a glare from the panther, the goat softly shook its back. The king's eyes fell open more than they were opened purposefully.

It regarded the scene around it, with a long yawn. It managed half a blink and didn't bother opening its eyes again.

'King,' the panther repeated, with a louder whisper. 'We have arrived.'

The king woke a second time. 'What is it now, panther,' he asked.

'We have arrived,' the panther repeated.

'Hmm? Yes, I can see that for myself. You're my arm, not my eyes.' His voice was forceful but weak. He looked very aged, with haggard skin and a well-worn shell. 'Now, where are we exactly?'

'The land of smoothskins, king.'

'Hmm. Ah, I see. You mean to say we have arrived in the land of smoothskins?'

'Yes,' the panther sighed.

'Well, isn't that splendid? Then, the smoothskins are dead already? How did they taste?'

'Recall that you ordered us to wait for your word before we attacked, king.'

'Oh, so I did.' The skin around the king's wrinkled mouth contorted, forming what could have been either a smile or a frown. 'Well,' he said. 'Was that not my word just now?'

The panther looked upon the Hominum with its cold eyes again and frowned. 'Understood.'

The wolves and hyenas bared their teeth. The lizards flickered their tongues.

Lia felt a hand squeeze hers. She squeezed back.

A lizard lorded over her and the hunter before her, standing on its hind legs, taller than she. She was drawn in by its red eyes, donning a glare fuelled with contempt.

'Ready,' Houli Zin called out. The hunters stepped forward, with all manner of weapons in hand.

Omaraa Zan stepped out from the huddle. 'Hold,' she screamed, at the top of her lungs. She addressed the king. '*I* speak for this village. You speak for these citizens. I demand to know why you have come here and why you threaten us.'

'Omaraa Zan,' Houli Zin called, incredulous.

'Let her speak for us,' Poruus Zin said, with his usual inexplicable calmness. Even now, his voice brought some serenity to the tension, like rainfall over a raging flame.

'*Demand,*' the king echoed. 'Who said that?'

'I did,' Omaraa Zan said.

'My king,' the panther whispered. 'This one appears to lead the--'

'Yes, I gathered as much,' the king grunted. 'Bring it here.'

The king eyed her, devoid of any expression but nonchalance. He had wrinkles below his eyes forming low hanging sacks.

'What an interesting word to choose,' he said. His voice trembled with tiredness. '*Demand.* It implies that you believe you have some influence over what shall soon befall you. Oh, how I despise you creatures for it. But it is a word that is lost on me. We have indeed come here, and you failed to stop us. So, *I* will be making the...hmm? How many years does your species live?'

Omaraa Zan narrowed her eyes. 'Perhaps sixty years,' she said, with clear confusion.

'Hmm,' the king mumbled, his deadpan face never changing, even as he deliberated. 'Yes, *I* will be making the demands here. You will make appeals to my very limited graces, most of which I will probably decline.'

'Then,' Omaraa said. 'What is it you intend to demand of us?'

'That you die. That is all.'

Lia bit her lip. They were like the words she had been told in her cage in Susuuri. She too had asked the same question of her captors; what it was they wanted from her and from her kin. *We want you to die*, was the only response she ever got, no matter who she asked or how she asked it.

Lia had relayed that sentiment to Omaraa Zan several times since her return. She could not understand why Omaraa Zan would now bother to ask again what she must have already known.

Omaraa Zan did not seem so phased by the words. 'For what reason? We acknowledge that we have hunted your kin in the past. Do you seek justice for them?'

'*Justice*,' the king echoed. 'For what, I wonder? Death for death? You've killed enough of us to warrant that, no doubt. Or perhaps for building your repulsive contraptions from my subjects' dead hides in this vile place? *Justice* is so often a fine justification to abandon rationality, wouldn't you say? But no, I have not come here for that.'

'Then, why are you doing this?'

'King,' the panther growled. 'Why do you insist on wasting time talking to these things? We are here for blood, not for words.'

'Mind your business,' the king snapped. 'It's been a long time since I have gotten to talk to these things. And after today, I will never have the chance again. You'll just have to wait a while longer.'

'But King, we may never again have this--'

'What do they call you,' the king asked.

'Omaraa Zan Fa. And how shall I address you?'

'*Zan,*' the king echoed. 'Hmph. Still with the *Zan* and *Zin* and who knows what. Time has done little to change pointless Hominum tradition, I see. As for me, we have no use for names, the arbitrary labels that they are. Address me as *king*. That's a label that matters.'

'You know our tribe name and our titles,' Omaraa Zan remarked. 'You know much about our culture.'

'Of course. You say you live for sixty years? I'm close to two hundred in this cursed life, or perhaps more by now. I stopped counting long ago. The worst of them were spent with the Hominum, where I learned all about your customs.'

Omaraa Zan did not hide her surprise. 'You lived with our tribe? When? How did you come to live with Hominum?'

The king groaned. Even that was weak and shallow, more like a sigh. 'I should have known. That's one advantage of your short-lived years; it's easy for you to ignore the past and not care for the present when you won't be alive for the consequences. But your ignorance to your own history is of no consequence to me. As for what motivates us on this day...what say you, panther?'

The panther spoke, bitterly but without hesitation. It was apparently accustomed to this king's impulses.

'Hatred,' it said, with its teeth clenched so tightly that Lia could hear them grinding. It spat out the word like venom. Lia felt chills on her skin at its voice. 'With every fibre of my being.'

'*Hatred*.' The king echoed. 'Maybe so. *Hatred* might just be the best word. But not for these creatures, really. I hate that I *don't* hate them as much as I'd like to. Perhaps I hate myself more than I hate them after all that I have seen. Does that make sense?'

'No,' the panther growled. 'How can it make sense, when you refuse to tell us *why* you hate yourself so much?'

'I do. I did and I do, and I would if I didn't. You'll have to live with that.'

The panther sighed. 'It matters not. I shall enjoy the taste of their blood, regardless of your reasons, my king.'

'It makes no sense to me,' Omaraa Zan interjected, echoing the thoughts of every other Hominum listening with pure bafflement. 'I still fail to understand your motives.'

'Hmph,' the king grumbled. 'That's fine. You will die no less ignorant than you are now. You may consider that a mercy of sorts if it pleases you.'

Omaraa Zan looked back at her kin, inexplicably fearless in her demeanour. An unpleasant sensation ran up Lia's spine. She felt a different sort of fear now, of the contentment she witnessed in her shepherd.

'So then,' Omaraa Zan said, turning back to the king. 'How can--'

'You know,' the king sighed. 'I grow weary of this. It was nice to speak with your kind once more, this time as your superior. But this conversation--'

'King,' one of the wolves called out. It leapt with incredible speed and force, at a sole Hominum.

'Don't move.' Every set of eyes shot to the source of the voice shouting. Poruus Zin Ka stood on the outskirts of the huddled group of his kin, with a single lit torch in his hands.

Susuuri obeyed in sudden confusion, looking blankly at each other and their king.

A hyena laughed, once the moment of surprise passed. Others followed and rained hearty and bitter laughter on the tribe.

'Shut up,' the king said, bringing back the silence again, with a voice too loud for a creature of his age. His face, as ever, bore neither amusement nor oddity, as he glared at Poruus Zin holding his torch. 'None of you move. *You.* What are you doing with that fire?'

Poruus Zin was perhaps the only being in that village who could match the king's aura of apathy. 'We doused the ground with lavender oil,' he said. 'I imagine you smelt it when you came through the snow? Spiders hate strong scents, and lavender was the strongest scent at our disposal. We used it to keep your spiders away after we saw the first ones you sent here.

'However, lavender oil is quite flammable. We could not make enough to cover the *entire* village, but we are fortunate that the snow has set so well, as it enabled us to spread it quite well. We need only use a torch to ignite it. That makes for a fine backup plan.'

Lia looked down at the snow. It had the subtlest tint of purple. *We are to die,* she realised, in shock and awe. *So that those of us who have escaped won't be pursued.* Lia could barely breathe for how fast her heart was beating.

'Meaning you plan to burn us,' the king said, undeterred. 'Either you have admirable conviction, or you are simply a moron. Are you truly claiming that, in order to save yourselves, you would burn yourselves to death along with us? Preposterous.'

'Not at all,' Poruus Zin said. 'At worst, we can expect some burnt legs and feet. However, all of you crawled through the snow to get here. Snow with pure lavender oil in it. You can surely smell it on each other now.'

The king's eyes widened, for the first time, as wide as they were able. 'Oh,' was all he said.

'Not so preposterous,' Poruus Zin dryly said.

The creatures began to back away. They no longer bore their fangs and tongues.

'Not *completely* preposterous,' the king said, contorting his face again into a crooked snarl. 'I admit that this is quite impressive on your part. Strategic and brutal. You remind me of your predecessors; meaning you disgust me.'

Poruus Zin's face changed with an unreadable and intense expression. '*Which* predecessors,' he asked.

'I don't care to speak their names,' the king grunted. 'Now, we find ourselves in quite a predicament. You wish to negotiate, yes? Otherwise, you would have already set the fire and caught us unaware. I assume you have terms.'

'Are they not obvious,' Poruus Zin said.

'They are *apparent*. It should be *obvious* to you that it is out of the question for you to leave this place unharmed. Fire or no fire, we have you at our mercy, and I will not let all my efforts be for nothing.'

'Yes,' Poruus Zin agreed. 'I had hoped there would be no bloodshed, but as you say, we are not in any position to negotiate with one such as you.'

He stretched out his arm with the blazing torch. Lia saw what was coming to pass. She *saw* it, but she could not believe her own eyes.

Poruus Zin Ka, with coldness of heart, said; 'For that reason, there shall be no terms.'

What followed was a moment of such disorientation, born from inner strife, that it earned a place among Lia's most defining moments.

She witnessed the only possible course of action happen before her, yet found herself incredulous in the face of such unwavering conviction.

Poruus Zin's torch fell from his fingers.

Lia watched the torch fall like a blazing snowball. Of the undying white noise flowing through her brain, one revelation was cognitive and resonate; *we're killers.*

The village was ignited with screams from Hominum and citizen alike, desperate and imbued with terror at first until they instead embodied unrivalled agony.

222

42

...and the crimson sky soon bled, emitting tears of fire upon Waya's beautiful forest. The trees were set ablaze and the sweet smell of nectar and blossom was overcome by the stench of ashes.

The wolf abandoned the forest to which he was bid to guard, preserving his life against the heavens' fury.

For days, the skies rained down fire, despite Waya's protests and rage and lamentations.

Excerpt from *The Tale of Waya*
by Moro Ki
Hominum Tribe Writer, Generation of Osas
Second Recorded Generation

I t was like a storm of fire, excessive in grandeur, kindled by a swiftly born blaze.

Harsh heat made Lia's eyes water, with tears that faded away before they fell.

The blend of sounds was excruciating on her ears; the crackling of citizen hides, the blaze rising to the skies, the roars of the creatures spending their lungs in pain.

And the smell was putrid. Each of Lia's breaths burned her chest. It stank of burning hair and fresh blood.

Lia could only see silhouettes through her blurry eyes. The citizens' agony made them writhe on the snow, bordering on contortion, with their fur ablaze.

This is death, Lia reflected. *This is* real *death.*

No Hominum was ignorant to death and its preceding nuances. It rarely came without a significant measure of sadness and sorrow, yet too rarely without a light of serenity after its acceptance.

But the death Lia now witnessed brought with it a new sensation; a harsh exposure of her ignorance. It was death in an alien form, forcing itself into Lia's well-defined world, without the comfort of the Mother's embrace or a pretty song to follow it.

So cruel. This is too cruel.

'—ry up!'

A trailing of words reached Lia's ears, through the sea of pandemonium. 'Hurry up, or we'll burn!'

It's Gal. She's holding onto me. Lia's ears rang fiercely. Gal Ne must have been screaming.

'*Hurry,*' Lia echoed.

'The gate,' Gal screamed. 'The gate.' She pulled Lia as best she could, weakly but zealously. Pain shot through Lia's leg with her first step. She looked down to see her feet were burning atop the snow, turning her skin a deep tone of red.

Yes. Yes, we must make for the gate. Her eyes cleared slowly as she and Gal broke into a staggered run, hobbling along on each other's weight.

Her kin ran ahead of them. Some were hauled to the ground by the flaming creatures. They screamed the heartiest as they were mauled and bled onto the snow. Some were hunters losing their fights, others were too slow to flee. Each were overcome by the creatures' might, even as they burned.

The soft crackling of their burning tipis ran still through Lia's skull, even as she left the gates behind her. The screams were dying out, as she and Gal limped through the lavender field. The snow there soothed the burns on Lia's feet.

'Damned fire,' Gal gasped, still leading Lia by the hand. 'What a reckless idea to use something so wild to defend ourselves. Thank the Mother for the snow.

'They're dying,' Lia said, looking back at her village, bathed in smoke and crimson.

'What? Yes. Yes, they are. But we must grieve and pray after we are--'

'They're dying, Gal.'

Gal looked down at the child holding her hand. Lia's face must have been a sight of hysteria, as she felt Gal's hand shaking.

She stopped running and held Lia firmly by the shoulders, wholly out of breath.

'Look at me, child,' she said. Lia obeyed. She looked into Gal's weary, tired eyes. The fire behind her hid her face in a half shadow. She forced softness into her tone. 'It was us or them. It *had* to be them. Those of us who die on this day will die for the sake of the many and for those not yet born. Do you understand?'

Lia couldn't answer. She couldn't find the words. *It was us or them. Us or them.* She obsessed over those simple words for some hazy measure of time, unable to manage their weight.

It was a strong chill in the air that brought her back to what her eyes saw. Her fellow Hominum were fleeing before her like wounded cattle, through the vast purple plane. Each strand of lavender crushed under their feet resonated in Lia's ears.

She realised she still held Gal's hand, as her fingers were warm. She felt something rise in her stomach at her sudden awareness, resembling heavy and burning bile. Her hand shook as blood rushed to her head.

Lia tugged it away, absently but deliberately, with the warmth in her body becoming overbearing.

She looked out over the plane they had entered. The warm purple glow of the forest had lost much of its beauty on this day. She could scarcely remember why she had worn such a gormless smile at this lonely scape, on the first cycle of that nightfall.

'Lia.' Gal's weak voice was like an unrelenting itch in Lia's bones. Lia looked upon her. She lay collapsed in the snow, exhausted. The old woman appeared thoroughly vulnerable, for the very first time.

Lia moved without thinking, wrapping her arms around her and trying to haul her to her feet. She tried, but to no avail, now conscious of her own exhaustion.

'Lia,' Gal said. She didn't shout, but her voice was all Lia could hear, with all its tepidness. 'I'm old and I'm tired. Leave me be.'

Lia's mouth hung open. '*Leave you be,*' she echoed. Her head throbbed as those words sunk into it.

'Lia,' she heard again, from a deep and powerful voice. Ogmul ran at her as though crazed, with his axe in hand. 'Come,' he shouted.

Lia looked up, to where was once home. There was a cluster of lights, dancing savagely out from the gates. Lia saw the silhouettes of citizens carrying fire on their bodies and heard them screaming as they drew closer.

'Sa'ar kaali,' Ogmul said, hauling Lia to her feet. 'Rest well in the moth--'

'Yes, yes. Sa'ar kaali yourself.' Gal's voice had a tremor, but the words were said in a tone that was uniquely her own.

'Gal?' Lia looked down at Gal's withered smile. Her chest burned and her eyes spilled tears.

'We're going, Lia,' Ogmul said. He pulled her by the hand, and they ran quickly through the field once more.

Lia never heard Gal scream, as the first of the burning citizens overtook her.

Lia's feet were heavy and painful. The soft pattering steps of their pursuers gained on them until their roars were all they heard.

Lia saw the immense jaguar baring on them. She watched as it pounced at them with a feral roar.

There was a thunderous impact, as Ogmul swung his axe at the panther's body. He was sent soaring by the panther's might, with an instant and vast splatter of blood. He landed in the snow and slid atop it with a red trail.

There was an outcry from the few Hominum who bore witness, some of whom ran to their aid.

Houli ran towards Lia with a spear in hand, no doubt calling her name. She could not hear their voices or find her own, frozen by the panther that now lorded above her, drooling and heaving heavy breaths. Its legs shook under the weight of its burning torso. Its contorted face painted a permanent and haunting impression on Lia's mind's eye, gritting its teeth and glaring with bloodshot eyes.

It was the very face of hatred, with every fibre of its being, just as it had promised. Lia saw it all so clearly, as though the hatred were her very own.

Anything semblance of a fight left in Lia's heart abandoned her at the sight of it. She smelt bloodlust on its every breath. She felt the heat of its fire on her skin.

She fell to her knees.

Harsh and violent peril reached out a cold hand to her. Yet, she had never felt so empty.

She may have even smiled in her desolation.

It's finally over.

*

The Ameyali Forest was a route of purple veins and dark green flesh when observed from the skies. The silent glow of Crescat and the resonating madness in the darkness of Susuuri; their fusion was beauty itself, blended in their own unique tones and with thorough disharmony.

A little lumen flew along with its pack, riddled with artificial but undeniable zeal. The queen had need of it now, for more than just its eyes. It was a change, and enough to inspire a relatively profound shift in its sense of being.

It was a strange shared feeling that drove the lumen to their shared purpose in unison, as they left the purple glow of their beautiful home and flew into the beyond, for the very first time.

*

The panther stood tall, possessed by fire overcoming its black body and dull yellow eyes.

Lia saw the subtle shift in its face. It was a change from blind fury to clarity in every emotive feature.

The citizen's voices of unbridled rage and disgust, coupled with burning agony, formed a dreadful symphony. Lia felt as though her ears would bleed.

The field was swiftly bathed in a glorious shade of vivid orange. The panther roared under the new light's weight and fled from it.

Lia was captivated by an innumerable army of lumen in the deep dawn sky. There were many, outnumbering even the stars beyond them.

Houli's hand found hers and he pulled her to her feet.

Poruus shouted something over the pandemonium, something that she could barely hear.

They then ran together through the field of new light, in the trail of their kin who already made for the forest and its hyachin.

Lia could not stop looking at the skies, even as adrenaline coursed through her body. *Why are the lumen here? Why would Crescat ever help us?*

She and Houli caught up to Omaraa and the hunters, who carried Ogmul on their backs. There was still a long stretch of the snowy field before them. The citizens loomed outside the lumens' light encircling them, howling in their anger.

The first lumen dropped from the sky, with its light already dimmed. Then another fell. Then another. Then many more.

Lia saw the light around them quickly becoming feebler. The citizens, though burned and enraged, kept up with the Hominum's' pace with ease, waiting still beyond the diminishing light.

Some feasted on the lumen as they fell. Even the lumens' blood glowed, as it oozed from their mouths. The fire was gone from many of their backs, by the grace of the deep snow.

'We won't make it,' Lia huffed. She didn't even hear herself over the howling, but she felt it. She felt it with each step, which felt heavier than the last.

*Heavier…*Lia's heart suddenly went frantic with a new cause. She was free of a heavy burden which she should have been carrying. The books were lost, somehow.

She recalled Omaraa's words and her gut wrenched;
We're saving our history.

She realised she had lost the last reminder of what they once called home. Every morsel of home now had been taken and destroyed by fire. *What have I done?*

Another mass of creatures emerged from the forest and made for the Hominum, drenched in shadow.

Lia and her kin stopped together, wordlessly standing in the field of almost depleted light, watching their cruel fate baring down on them.

The howls of Susuuri's citizens subsided, perhaps with patience replacing their rage. For it was easier to be patient when the end was so close in sight.

Lia's hand fell from Houli's. He looked to the skies of dying lumen, with a face devoid of much but sadness.

'We were so close,' he said. Lia heard that. They all did.

'*So* close.' It was Ogmul's strained voice, who was barely conscious and slumped over a hunter's shoulder.

'We *have* come close,' Omaraa said, through laboured breathing. 'It is too soon to--'

'Omaraa,' Poruus said. 'You have taken us far and you have guided us well. It is enough.'

He said it as too matter-of-fact, too devoid of urgency or unease. The Hominum were incredulous, yet no one voiced it. No one could because truly, he was right.

Omaraa and the elders had brought the Hominum far on that cycle, further than they had any right to reach. Truly, from the moment Susuuri's citizens emerged from the ground, the Hominum lived on borrowed time. And their time was soon to be claimed.

There were only a few kin there together in that field now. The others had gotten closer to the forest than Lia realised. She could not bear to imagine how they may have met their end by the creatures that approached.

A tear streamed down her cheeks, with all the pity and sorrow she could summon in her moment of peril.

Someone weakly squeezed her hand. Omaraa looked older than she ever had in that tone of shadow. 'Close your eyes, child,' she said. 'And pray for the Mother's embrace.'

Lia didn't want to. Blinding herself to the final moments of her kin felt like a betrayal of their unity. But she could not ignore the pleading in Omaraa's voice, the struggle between fear and courage.

Lia understood. She was still a child and Omaraa was a carer, doing what carers are charged with and finding someone feebler than they to protect. It was in her nature to nurture. It always had been. And this, right now, was the only form of it she could offer.

It took me until the very end to realise this, Lia lamented. *I wasted so much time burdening those who love me the most. Omaraa. Gal. Miire. Why did I make loving me such hard work? I'm such a foolish child.*

Lia obeyed and closed her eyes through the tears.

She tried to take comfort in her silent prayer, in knowing the Mother's care awaited, but she could not stave off the fear.

It was a striking sound; that of stampeding creatures coupled with howls of bloodlust. The Hominum themselves stood silently together, united with closed eyes and silent prayers, in what were to be their final moments.

As the exodus of nightfall was filled with a song of fire and blood, Lia was grateful for the gift of darkness.

43

...bondage of a few for the sake of the many. It was undeniable. Yet still, we are never permitted even a passing moment of peace from our own benevolence...

Destroyed Excerpt from *The Two-Year Wander*
Author Unknown
Text Predates First Recorded Generation

The king peaked his charred head out of his shell. The putrid Hominum village was a glorious sight of ashes and burnt corpses. Smoothskins lay in the snow bloodied and mauled, with eternal terror painted on their faces. It was a cause for some joy, but there were far too few of their bodies for the king to feel elated, and the body count of his own kin outnumbered theirs.

A hyena laid dead before him, its body utterly burnt, and stared him in the eye. The king groaned, and even that simple act was painful. *So useless,* he bitterly thought. *All of you. I've no doubt the smoothskins got the better of you. Even in death, you give me cause to hate you. You're disgusting, yet you never even had to know it. How I envy you all.*

The king's body was paralyzed. He felt hot and cold at the same time, as though his blood were ice and his skin was fire.

He welcomed the death he felt soon coming but lamented that the occasion was so dire. Decades, perhaps centuries, of dreaming, of built-up hatred, of plotting from the shadows, of service as a mere vice, of suffering under the foolish queens who preceded him, of having the blood of his own kin on his conscience; all for this chance to bring death to those he most despised. All to spite the Mother's cruel and absolute ruling hand, forever. All, ultimately, for nothing.

The king might have laughed, had his decrepit body permitted it.

He instead laid his head down, with his spirit finally spent, and was carried slowly into dormancy by thoughts of the past.

*

The little tortoise sobbed. He watched from the hands of whichever smoothskin held him, utterly powerless and utterly terrified. He hated this place. He hated the open air of the court, he hated its neatness, and he hated seeing the queen's throne, imposing and terrifying as it was.

The tortoise's father laid before Farro Zan Me, with a battered shell and bloodied skin, dragged by the teeth of a wolf kin. He could hardly move, paralysed with pain.

'Wolf,' the queen said, with a meek and soft voice. 'Who did this?'

'This is how I found him,' the wolf said.

'Someone who hates him, clearly,' Osas Zin Ne said, from Farro Zan Ne's side. 'He has made plenty of enemies in his defiance, not only allies.'

Osas approached the old tortoise and knelt before him, looking him in the face. The citizens quietly observed. The little tortoise was the only one who dared even cry. Other smoothskins quietly watched too, with intrigue and little sorrow.

'Who did this to you,' Osas asked.

The tortoise managed a half snarl on his bloodied lips. 'You would see them tried and slaughtered,' he said. 'I would see them free to tear me limb from limb if they so choose. My lips are sealed, smoothskin.'

'For what purpose,' Osas said, taking the tortoise by the chin. 'Look around you. Look at those who have come to see you tried. Look at how your actions have divided your kin. They wish for order, not for you to force change upon them.'

The tortoise moved his head to look upon his kin, who watched on from the shadows of the trees. 'They are scared,' he said. 'Fear has defined their very way of living, all due to your order. You are scared too, smoothskin. You fear the time coming when fear no longer keeps them bound. You fear the time that my kin abandon their cowardly queen and guide themselves. That is why I am here before you, beaten and bloodied. You would kill me, in hopes that that future will die with me.'

The little tortoise heard anger in his father's voice. He had learned much of conviction and kindness from him, but never anger. His legs shook with fear.

'You are beaten and bloodied by your own doing,' Farro Zan Ne said, from beside the queen's throne. 'You presumed to lead when it was not your place. You presumed to incite your kin into an arbitrary conflict, with nothing to gain and

everything to lose. Now, your ideals have burdened your kin with unease and disunity. That is why you stand before your queen and why your death may be demanded of you.'

The tortoise glared at the cat sitting on the throne, with blood falling from his brow. She was quiet, hardly daring to meet his eyes. 'Your negligence allowed me to act,' he said, with all the spite and vitriol he could summon. 'I planted the seeds of revolt from right under your watch, yet you were ignorant to them being sowed until discontentment began blooming. You are blinded by this order you *have created, and I am glad for it. For I've no doubt that someone will eventually come along as a result of those seeds. Someone with the tenacity I have lacked, to make a change.'*

Farro looked to the meek queen who sat on her throne, his face ever plain and unreadable. 'I pray for the sake of your kin that no one will,' he said.

'Your prayers be damned,' the tortoise spat. 'Just tell me how I am to meet the Mother. Is it to be here and now, or am I to be abandoned with my kin in Susuuri as a primitive?'

'You are too--'

'I was asking my queen, smoothskin,' the tortoise said. 'Go on, my queen. Tell us all what you desire. Give an order which is solely your own.'

All eyes fell on the cat. She looked to the smoothskins around her, who too faced her expectantly. She looked to her subjects, who waited in the shadows. She looked even to the little tortoise in the smoothskin's hands, with a wide-eyed look.

The little tortoise saw fear in those eyes, belonging to a creature holding a foreign burden. It was a look so pitiful that it stopped the little tortoise's tears.

His father had spoken only of freedom and his disdain for authority of late. He spoke loudly and often about a disease on the throne which slowly killed his home, stubbornly and relentlessly. The little tortoise saw now a queen who was just as scared as her subjects. This is the disease, *the little tortoise finally understood.*

The queen faced the old tortoise before her throne, looking him tepidly in the eyes. She spoke quietly, as was always her way.

'Death, now.'

That was all she said, but those words were carried to every corner of Crescat and beyond.

Creature and smoothskin alike were silent and in waiting, watching Farro take the pointed spear from one of his kin. He lorded above the tortoise, who looked up at him with great strain and disgust. Father, *the little tortoise screamed in his heart, but his lips did not obey. He instead watched silently, just*

232

like all the others, frozen in his fright.

'Death now,' the tortoise echoed with a laboured laugh. 'Our queen does have a voice after all.'

Farro softly touched the tortoise on the head. He winced under his fingers.

'Do you have any final words,' Farro said.

The tortoise did not hesitate. 'Only this; we all share the same blood, born of the same mother, and your fate shall be to suffer under the oppression you have brought about. Remember that. And remember too that we must not be beholden to the choices of those who share our blood. Do you understand?'

Farro stood, casting a dark shadow on the tortoise's battered shell. 'We are always beholden to the choices of those who come before us,' he said. 'However, your son will not be harmed. On that, you have my word.'

The tortoise grunted. 'For all your word is worth. Core mine.'

Farro raised his hands, with the sharp stone at the tip of his spear glinting in the hyachin.

He said; 'Core mine. Find peace in the Mother's embrace.'

The spear descended onto the tortoise's head.

His red blood splattered on the dirt.

His head fell from his shell.

The citizens all watched from the comfort of their shadows and dared not even mourn.

The little tortoise saw it all from a smoothskin's hands, through his tear-stricken eyes, and did nothing but cry out with a terrible sound, for all the forest to hear.

*

The tortoise opened his eyes to the unfamiliar ambience of Susuuri stirring his blood, woken by the laughter of a passing pack of crazed kin.

His blood burned still with the oppressive foreign air in him, and his body refused to obey him without significant strain.

But he was aware of the pain now. He understood the pain to be a result of the absence of hyachin in his blood, by means of his exile. He felt his primal urges beginning to fade and astuteness taking its place.

He had grown bigger while in his primal state. He could feel the change in his body and mind. He was becoming Susuuri. He was changing, just as he did when the hyachin bloomed.

He could not know how long he had been in this dark place already. He had hazy memories of time spent crawling in the dirt, with his only care and purpose being his next meal. Time and place meant little to him while in that state.

He heard more laugher from the beyond the darkness, from the voices of his new kin. How can they laugh, *he wondered.* What cause is there for joy in this place? *He longed to find those to laughed, to see their joy and comprehend their zeal, but he hadn't the strength. He instead laid there, alone on his bed of dirt, weak and surely starving within his burning blood.*

And he was angry. He could not yet recall why, but it was vivid and unrelenting anger that obsessed him. Each coherent thought was sown by incomprehensible hatred. It was already maddening.

I hate this place. I hate this life and all the life I know. Why do I hate so much?

The answers were there, somewhere in his mind, but out of reach, like a fine fruit hanging on the branch of a colossal tree.

There were answers that he could not grasp, no matter how he longed for them.

In his mind, all he saw was death.

*

The king's final moment was spent in agony of mind and body, surrounded by the death he longed for and filled with shame in the failure he dreaded.

One sole regret took hold of his mind and carried him to his dreaded Mother's embrace; *I have lived for far too long.*

44

...now, guilt and unease haunt my every waking moment. No, not just my own. Though our shepherds smile in our company and lead our steps confidently through these cursed lands, the burden they feel in their hearts is clear to any with eyes to see.

These burdens shall rightly follow us all our days. We are lost, no matter where we try to call home. We are sad, no matter how we try to smile. We are alone, even alongside our own kin.

...there have been talks of returning home, of this long venture all being for nought. It is absurdity born from depression and fruitless labours to think that the home we abandoned could ever be replaced.

Excerpt from *The Two-Year Wander*
Author Unknown
Text Predates First Recorded Generation

Citizen wandered about the queen's woods once again, empty-handed and alone, with an even greater burden on his shoulders to relieve. *Stupid cat.*

Citizen cursed his ever-unyielding impressionability. He cursed for whatever it was about that stupid cat that always brought him back to her. He always grew weak at the feet and hazy eyed at her gaze and enchanting voice. And her unblemished, perfectly glossy fur. And her perfect teeth, through her perfectly devious grin. And her——-

'Argh.' Citizen shook his head, cursing himself again. *Stupid cat. Stupid Citizen.*

'Rabbit,' said an all too familiar voice. Citizen was too depressed to be surprised. He just dragged his feet in the direction of the voice, where the bear sat under a polood tree. 'Where did--'

'Just a walk,' Citizen said mechanically, looking down at his own feet.

'A walk,' the bear echoed, forming a familiar frown. 'You do so love your walks. It is a wonder how your belly is so round with all that walking you do. Where were you walking this time?'

Citizen stared deeper into the crevices of his feet, scrolling through his list of excuses. It would soon grow ever more extensive, with his new life of eyes permanently upon him. He felt the glare of the lumen on him still, from high above him, ever since he had stepped back into the queen's court again.

'I was hungry,' was what Citizen cunningly settled on, not for the first time.

'How surprising,' the bear said. 'Anyway, that will be the last of your walks, until the next time the moon is up. The sun will soon rise, and we will soon hibernate again. So, I hope that walk was a good one.'

I wish it was, Citizen thought, as he walked off the beaten path, away from the queen's territory and toward his burrow.

He had spent most of his time in fear and confusion, since hearing that stupid cat's words, driving himself mad in pondering what he had learnt from her. The cat had spoken with such an air of flippancy, that anyone with a sound mind would readily dismiss the madness she had claimed to be truth. Citizen supposed he *wasn't* sound in mind, as he had believed every word from her lips, in all their absurdity. Just as his queen had inexplicably believed his when he relayed them to her.

He slumped under another tree, which bore over-ripened fruit in the pending dawn, and looked over his fur in a new shade of light.

What am I? It was a strange feeling for Citizen, to question his very being. Before now, he had been but a rabbit, who was witless in the sunlight and slightly less witless in the nighttime. He was fine with that. He never had cause to question that way of things, but this transpiration brought him anything but certainty.

What are we? It was a question of many layers. If Citizen was different on the inside than a mere rabbit, what *really* was he?

What awful creatures the citizens were, to allow the smoothskins to die, for what they believed to be their own sakes.

Citizen had allowed resentment into his heart against his only friend, just because of petty outrage. Now, he was lost forever, all because of the queen acting in what she had believed to be her subjects' best interests.

Citizen was lost, more than ever, in his aimless and pointless life.

He watched the skies in attempted peace. It rained from the clouds of languid orange.

*

This sensation was unnerving. Kai moved blindly along the forest floor, hanging from the snake's teeth by the clothes on his back.

The snake slithered rhythmically and deliberately through the trees and swamps. Kai hadn't had the will to resist the snake stealing him from his cage.

His hands remained bound and his eyes covered. There was a strange elation in the state of utter powerlessness and the acceptance that what fate willed for him could not be fought.

It would seem to be a strange fate that awaited, as the snake appeared to take great care to go undetected. It moved much like Kai and Lia would move through the forest on their rarely productive search for prey; slowly and deliberately, so as not to startle. It was how they moved when they didn't want to be seen.

The snake moved the same way. Kai had enough time to ponder the reason. There were only Susuuri citizens for it to hide from, meaning the snake was taking him somewhere that it shouldn't have. But this realisation only confused Kai more. *Why am I still alive?*

He chose to embrace the acceptance that came with his inability, rather than to grow anxious with bafflement.

Kai felt his feet on the ground again, as the snake halted and lowered its head. He heard clearly this time what gave the snake pause. There was rustling in the trees, louder than the soft wind could produce.

The snake waited long enough only for the sound to pass them by, before slithering on again through the hums of nature. It too was strange, Kai thought, that he and this giant snake had gone unnoticed for so long. But perhaps it wasn't a miracle. Perhaps there were simply few Citizens around to see them.

That idea chilled Kai to the bone, through his sweat-drenched skin, as he became more aware of the silence. *No voices and no laughter like before. It's like there is no one here but us.*

It was favourable for him, but it was also bizarre. Kai, as was now his norm, expected the worst in what fate had laid ahead in waiting.

Eventually, an answer was made manifest in the form of an outcry resounding from the tree heights. A dozen others followed.

Feral roars echoed through Susuuri's dawn sky, as creatures bore down on them from above.

The snake fled along Susuuri's floor, with incredible pace, slithering with great dexterity and grace between trees. The wind was powerful on Kai's face.

But the roars raining down on them from their pursuers would not be left behind.

Kai felt the snake's cold hiss on his back.

'*Guy*,' he heard slither into his ears. The snake was undoubtedly slowing, for its exhaustion and wounds. Its breath grew heavy against Kai's flesh.

They burst through a field of screaming roses, toward glorious orange and red born from a young sun, which even pierced Kai's blindfold.

The snake suddenly halted. Kai could feel the chill of Susuuri's air strongly where they stopped.

The snake turned and faced their hunters. Kai breathed heavily, feeling panic rising in his blood once more.

'*Guy*,' he heard. The snake's voice etched into his ears and manifested like a thought from his own mind.

Kai's ears were then bestowed with the sound of tearing flesh, and his nose with aroma of fresh blood. The snake curled itself tightly and raised its head as high as it could, standing on its tail with silent agony.

Kai was terrified in a most unique way; not of the peril he could hear and not see, but of how alone he felt in the face of it. He suddenly feared dying at the hand of creatures that despised him.

I wish, he thought. *I wish I could have seen Lia first.*

The knowledge that he would soon be leaving his sister to mourn him alone brought him the deepest despair of his short life.

I've failed. I never brought Lia home, and we never saw the forest at nightfall together.

'*Guy*,' the snake said once more. Kai himself could not voice the words he wished to make to make his last. He instead made them his silent prayer.

Mother Earth, please let me see her again in your embrace.

Kai heard the creatures drawing closer, roaring from the snake's body and still piercing its flesh.

Then, adrenaline suddenly flowed through his body and his heart raced. He felt a rush in his brain, as though he flew through the sky and sharply fell.

Then came a sudden and cold impact. His lungs ached with his first breath underwater.

He floated to the surface; his body numb with shock. The restraints on his hands fell and he was free to see again.

He saw a dull tone of orange in a cloud-filled sky. It was the beginning of dawn. It had been a longer nightfall than most and dawn would surely follow in the same vein.

Rocky faces were glazed in orange and trees lorded over the river in which he landed.

The snake stood tall, drenched in shadow on the cliff far above him, overcome by creatures clawing and biting at its body.

As the waters carried Kai along with its natural current, the snake relinquished a wail of extraordinary fervour. It was a short-lived outcry, violently cut short with the screams of the predators.

The snake fell atop the cliff in a heap, its corpse ravaged by its killers as they feasted. Kai still could smell the blood.

The tide carried Kai along until the cliff faded into the darkness and was soon out of sight.

He hadn't the cognisance to fight the current. It simply carried him to wherever it willed.

Kai didn't even know why he cried this time. But he did so, loudly, with all the vigour he had left in him.

45

*The Ritual of New Birth must forever be adhered to, for all generations to come.
Its purposes are paramount to the preservation and prosperity of the Hominum.
Foremostly, the Ritual of New Birth will serve to keep the population of our
tribe fed and for our resources to be plentiful.*

Tenet of the *Hominum's Ritual of New Birth*
Imposed by Osas Zan Ne
Generation of Osas
Second Recorded Generation

Citizen woke up to a face of dirt and numb paws. He wiped drool
from his chin, wondering how long he had slept.

'You sleep as soundly as I would have expected.'

Citizen followed the sound of the voice with his sleepy eyes and saw a
beautiful pair of bright green ones looking down at him.

'Queen?!' He fumbled to his feet.

'That's me,' she said.

'Why? Why are you...why?'

'Hm. I happened to find you sleeping. It's quite fascinating. You're
livelier sleeping than when you're awake.'

Citizen grew hot with a blush.

'Come,' the queen said. 'Sit beside me.'

Citizen tepidly did so. He sat, feeling decisively out of place, and was
unable to meet her eyes. He shuddered at the thought of how the vice or the
hunters would react to seeing him so close to their queen. Then he
suppressed a smile, as his pride was stroked a little at the thought of their
outrage.

He just watched the queen's feet and her rhythmic swaying tail. Her fur was so absurdly glossy that the hyachin rippled perfectly on her like water.

Citizen couldn't take the silence for long. 'You came here to find me,' he blurted out as his first impulse, with immediate and profound regret.

The queen's cold gaze made him shudder. 'Who came to find *you*,' she said. 'Didn't I say I happened upon you? Why do ask?'

Citizen felt sweat trickle through his fur. *Stupid rabbit,* he cursed. *You just called the queen a liar to her face. Stupid Citizen.*

'O-oh,' he stuttered. 'No reason.'

'And now you're lying to your queen,' she said with a grin. 'Come on. Don't be shy, rabbit. Tell me.'

Citizen gulped, louder than intended. He spoke with a shaky voice. 'I just thought that you wouldn't come so far away from your court. Not without a reason, I mean. Not that you'd come so far for me. I mean...I don't know.'

The queen laughed, much to Citizen's relief, and heartily at that. 'You're getting better at using your head,' she said. 'A shame that you're mistaken. Indeed, I didn't come this far from my court to find *you,* rabbit, or anyone else. I'm the queen, remember? You come to me when I want you, not the other way around.'

Citizen blushed again, but not with shame. *She said I'm better at using my head.*

'So,' he started, after a pause too uncomfortable for him. He then realised that he didn't have much to follow it up with.

'Do you hear that, rabbit,' the queen asked.

Citizen pricked up his ears. 'Hear what?'

'Nothing. Nothing at all. There's no one here but us. Not even the wind comes so deep into the woods.' Citizen pricked his ears up again. She was right, of course. The rain softly pattering atop their shelter of trees was all that broke the silence.

'That's why I'm here,' the queen continued. 'And why I come every dawn before we hibernate. It's the only place I hear this silence. Hunting for herbs is nice too, but it's not like this. Nothingness is beautiful. Nothing to distract, nothing to worry over. Just for a while.' The queen paused. Her wide grin was quickly back on her face when she met Citizen's curious gaze. 'But I found something to disrupt my sweet silence this dawn; a racket of the likes that only bears and wolfs should be capable. And what do I find but my favourite little rabbit snoring and rolling about in a violent sleep.'

Citizen hung his head again. 'Sorry.'

'You say that too often and it will soon lose all meaning, rabbit. Be sorry for being sorry and stop being sorry unless you're sorry. Are you still sorry?'

Citizen blinked. 'No?'

'Great. That reminds me; I haven't thanked you yet, have I? For what you just did for us.'

He blinked again. '*Thank* me,' he echoed. In that last hearing at her throne, with the jaguar's breath bearing down his neck, it was a wonder that words ever passed his shaking lips. The queen's level-headedness, amidst the expected outrage and dismissal from her subjects, was all that had stopped Citizen from collapsing in a heap with the stress.

'What sort of queen is not thankful to her subjects for speaking the truth,' she now said. 'I won't deny that I hate the words you spoke, but that's not your problem.'

'You didn't think I lied?'

'Nope. I doubt a naive rabbit like you could create such a lie. I didn't doubt you believed in what you said. But that cat is another matter.'

Citizen felt his heart skip several beats. 'How did you know it was her,' was all he managed.

The queen looked down on him, with haughtiness painted on her face. 'Where are my eyes, rabbit?'

'Everywhere,' Citizen said, feeling idiotic for his surprise.

'*Almost*,' the queen said. 'Almost everywhere. My lumen saw her find you in Crescat, and they saw you talking with her. They saw you carry her on your back, I assume to Susuuri, but they somehow did not see how you got her there. Now tell me, rabbit; where are the shadows that even my eyes cannot see?'

Citizen smiled a knowing and submissive smile. *Now I can never go back there. I can never hide again.*

'Did I say something to amuse you,' the queen said.

'N--no, sor--I mean, no.'

'If there exists a place in Crescat that my lumen are blind to, I must know. Especially now, after all that Susuuri has done and with Susuuri's heir knowing where I'm blind to. Tell me.'

Citizen took a long breath. 'By the lumen fields.'

The queen didn't mask her surprise. 'What do you mean?'

'There's woods next to the fields where the lumen sleep. It's dark there because there's no purpura, and I just thought, since it was so close to where they slept, they wouldn't bother looking around there.'

'Huh,' was all the queen said for a while, taking Citizen in with her eyes, in all his haggard splendour. 'You know, rabbit; I can't decide whether you're dumb as a rock or a genius. More so the former, no doubt. But when it comes to matters concerning food and sleep, you turn into a scholar.'

Citizen frowned, growing wary of so many compliments aimed at himself.

'Anyway, that's all I needed to know,' the queen said. 'I'll be returning to my throne now. I'll come here again when it's as silent as it should be. I expect that this will be the last time I see you here, rabbit. Understand?'

Citizen nodded. 'What will we do,' he asked.

The queen tilted her head. 'Hm? *Do?*'

'About...us. And the smoothskins.'

The queen laughed, nastily. 'You mean to ask what *I* will do. Perhaps you seek to know my feelings on the matter and to offer me solace? We're far from my throne right now, but do not forget who you are talking to, rabbit. I need not be sat on some rocks in my court to be your queen.'

'N-no, I--'

'What can be done, rabbit? There are two choices; accept it or hate it. I'll never hate myself, nor will I allow that thinking among my citizens. So, it appears that the choice has been made for us, hasn't it?'

'So...' Citizen started, quickly regretting it again. *Stupid rabbit.*

'And still you ask questions of me,' the queen said. 'We've done all we can and all we need to. We can never make peace with Susuuri after this, but what choice is there?'

The queen's words trailed off. Or perhaps they didn't, but she became silent to Citizen's ears.

Citizen's own sorrow and guilt had been necessary, for Crescat's sake. He had built resentment in his heart and had convinced himself that his burden of loneliness was necessary, for Crescat's sake. He had convinced himself that the loss of his only friend had been a necessity, all for Crescat's sake. But now, such burdens were nothing but a waste.

Citizen didn't know what to think.

A lone ball of orange light descended from the skies, breaking his quiet contemplation, and landed on its queen's back. It hummed a soft song into her ear.

It sounded like nothingness to Citizen's ears, but its words were heard clearly by the queen.

The lumen then flew back from whence it came, after it finished its song.

The queen stood with a rare face of stone. 'Time to meet with the predators.'

46

...bright purple lights that shine so brightly, like lavenders dancing in the dayfall sun. Why must they be purple and why so bright a tone? Why does our sacred tree shine in the same tone as the forbidden forest?

These are the mysteries that have eluded my predecessors and eludes me still. May the Mother guide me and not allow them to elude us much longer.

Excerpt from *Herbalism and Poisons*
By Char Ki
Generation of Mayara the Bold
Seventh Recorded Generation

Citizen finally got his wish, in a sense. The walk to the queen's court, in the usual shadow of the hunter bear, came with not nearly the same dread as it always had. It was quite far from it, walking by the queen's side, with no small measure of baffled and jealous looks coming from his kin.

He walked this time with some purpose and genuine longing. He too wanted to come face to face with their long-time predators and to see their now dire state for himself.

Citizen squinted for the peaking dawn sun as they approached the queen's throne. The purpura pods hung firm and brightly still from the trees around the court. Many a lumen danced in the skies to observe the occasion.

Citizen saw the creatures standing in the queen's court, looking exhausted and freezing, some with splashes of blood on what they wore, barely standing on their feet. They hardly looked like Smoothie at all. They were all taller and wider, with far more hair and bigger body parts on some.

They watched the queen take her throne and quietly listened to the vice announce her status. The queen's glare was of indescribable abhorrence and set a tense tone for the entire court.

Citizen could immediately see why. The smoothskins wore the corpses of his kin on their backs, like the one found in the forest with Smoothie's scent. It was a truly horrific sight.

'We won't need those,' the queen, nodding to the vines binding the smoothskins' wrists.

Some of the creatures flinched a little, as the lumen flew to them and melted through the vines. Citizen wondered how they could fear such harmless citizens when they themselves were such predators. Smoothie had only ever been enthralled by them.

'Now,' the queen said. 'I will not suffer all of your voices. Which one of will I be addressing?'

One smoothskin stepped out from the pack. 'I lead our tribe,' it said, its voice delicate but affirmative. 'My name is Om--'

'Save your breath,' the queen said. 'We do not care for those things here. And you *led*. As I understand it, you're now the leader of little but rubble and burnt corpses.'

The queen's harsh tone gave the smoothskin pause. 'And some of us still live,' it said. 'For that, we can't thank--'

'Isn't that the sad truth,' the queen said. 'And keep those words to yourself too, or I may well be sick.'

That gave the smoothskin pause again. 'You hate us,' it said. 'Of course, you do. I understand, as the king of Susuuri hates us too. But why did you save us?'

'*I* did nothing of the sort,' the queen shouted, louder than such a small body should have been able. The words were carried well through the silent court. '*I* was sitting right here, just as you now see me. You must have forgotten who truly saved you, for you to dare to thank *me*. Go and thank the citizens who really did the saving. The ones who were torn apart and eaten by Susuuri's monsters on your behalf. Go and piece together their mauled bodies and thank them. Tell me all the good that your gratitude does then.'

Silence followed. The smoothskins barely so much as breathed in their surprise. The queen herself appeared taken aback by her own outburst.

'Here you stand,' she continued, far more measured. 'In my court, wearing the bodies of my own subjects, and you dare to offer thanks. I can assure you that no measure of gratitude will ever stop us from detesting you.'

Citizen swallowed. He sympathised entirely with her anger but remained deeply conflicted. His kin had rushed to the aid of those who had been the cause of much persecution and heartache, to defend them against the creatures Crescat knew to be their superior in strength by far.

Monkeys, foxes, and even deer; all had run against every instinct, to what they surely knew to be certain death. Even those that returned had not done so without scars and trauma.

Yet, the smoothskins too suffered the same way. They too watched their kin being killed by predators, and they too survived burdened by scars. It was infuriating that finally seeing these smoothskins for himself not only amplified Citizen's hatred tenfold but also his pity for them.

His kin did only what they knew they had to, and what the queen had to command of them, to survive. They saved Crescat itself with their lives. They were heroes.

Citizen was proud, broken and outraged, all in one bundle. He couldn't imagine the queen's own feelings, being the commander of her kin's deaths.

The smoothskin leader stroked the fur on her body with her head hung. It was the deep brown corpse of a bear that warmed her skin.

'Then, why,' it said. Its voice was softer still. 'Why would they die for us? Why not just leave us to die?'

The queen glared at the smoothskin leader. 'You don't know either,' she said. 'You truly don't. You poor fools.' Her face slowly contorted. Vile malice emanated from her expression. It made Citizen's stomach churn, knowing the revelation soon to come.

'Answer me this,' she said. 'You've killed us and taken us beyond your walls while the sun was up. For what purpose?'

The smoothskin's face subtly changed into one of sadness or guilt. Citizen saw it clench its hands.

'Does this topic make you uncomfortable,' asked the queen, with the sarcasm in which she was so proficient. 'Do take your time and answer when ready.'

The smoothskin raised its head. 'We used your fur to build our shelters,' it said. 'We made coats to warm us in nightfall. And we cooked their bodies in fire to feed on.'

Citizen pricked up his ears at that. His kin looked at each other with surprise.

The queen's face lost some of its menace. 'You *ate* us,' she said. 'I'm surprised. And almost grateful.'

The smoothskins looked thoroughly confused. '*Grateful,*' their leader echoed. 'Why?'

'I said *almost.* You did not waste their bodies and you treated them as we do. I am curious as to why.'

'You mean to say that eat your own dead?'

'Of course, we do. Why be born at all if you don't feed life after you're gone?'

They were words which citizens of the Crescat knew well and had lived by for generations. A citizen's duty was to be fed by those who came before them upon their death, whether it be by a stranger, a friend or family. Citizen hated that responsibility and dreaded ever being chosen. He always felt sick with every bite, but it was the one part of death not heavy with sadness. He was surprised by the smoothskins' apparent ignorance of this philosophy.

'How fun this is,' the queen continued. 'Seeing your incredulity right now, unaware that you've been doing the very same thing.'

The brief silence that followed was profound. The smoothskins' confusion was almost tangible.

The leader furrowed its brows. 'What do you--?'

'First,' the queen said, with a fresh fervour in her voice. 'You answered my question, so I'd be happy to educate you now. I understand that you have a ritual for your dead, that you burn them under a certain tree and sing a song for them. Is this true?'

'Yes,' the leader said, with some surprise. 'How do you know this?

'Tell us the words. I trust the memory of the one who shared them with me, but I want to be certain of every word. You too will need to hear it again.'

'Candy?' It was the voice of a small smoothskin from the middle of the pack. It was short, slim and had long muddied hair. 'Did another cat tell you about our song?'

'Why do I hear a new voice,' the queen said. 'One I was not talking to.'

'Must I *sing* the song,' the leader quickly said, with some of the queen's flavour of daring.

'I'd rather you didn't.'

The leader began its recital:

'Dance freely in our maker's embrace.
May the light of her peace forever be your place.
Undisturbed in your restful sleep,
We pray your slumber is sound and deep, though we weep.

'So, smile in earnest, at last, with your fire spent,
May the dust of a life well-loved our maker lent,
Feed the ones you leave from her boundless might,
And be our beacon through the darkest nights.

'Though we part, we shan't think you gone.
You'll be with us, still, through each new dawn.
To our maker, we pray you grow well,
Instilled with our sister's spirit.
Until we are one, farewell.'

'Hmm, I suppose the rabbit was close enough,' the queen said, with a subtle queue of surprise. '*We pray you grow well, instilled with our sister's spirit.* Did you ever consider what exactly you were praying would grow well?'

'It is as you say,' the smoothskin said. 'As your citizens feed the living, so do our dead. We pray for the Mother from which they came to imbue herself with their lives, to grow from them and to feed those left behind. That's our purpose in death.'

'How lovely,' the queen sighed. 'And how ridiculous of you to think Mother Earth cares so dearly for your prayers. Whatever purpose you think your ritual serves, whatever words you sing, it doesn't matter. Mother Earth listens to herself and no other.'

'I don't--'

'Shush, I have another question. This tree where you burn your dead and bury their ashes; what colour are its leaves while the sun is down?'

'Its *leaves*,' the leader echoed, furrowing its brows again. 'Purple. It has no petals while the sun is up.'

'Mhm. And no doubt you've noticed the colour of the hyachin, of this light all around you. Yes, purple. Bright and beautiful purple light, made by the purpura hanging from the trees. Do you think that coincidental?'

'No,' the leader said, appearing restless. 'It confirms to us that Mother

Earth does indeed use our lives to grow and thrive after we pass. That is true, whether you say she listens or not.'

'Okay. Do you know what else is confirmed?' The queen smiled wickedly at the leader beneath her throne. Citizen stomach churned again for the words soon to come. 'What else is born from the purple light, is born when the moon rises and dies when the sun does, just like how your tree grows and sheds its petals? What else is permitted to grow and thrive for a time, while the mother grows from your spent lives? Go on and tell us; what are your prayers truly for? What really happens to your kind after you're dead and buried?'

As that question sunk into the ears of the smoothskins, they showed on their faces and bodies a slow transition from confusion, to realisation, to astonishment and to disbelief, with stone-dead silence at the climax.

Citizen heard their hearts thumping. He saw the sweat fall from their skin. Their faces hid nothing of the trauma that came from one's entire comprehension of reality turning on its head.

And against his every expectation, Citizen felt nothing but *pity*. He knew too much of self-loathing to celebrate that curse spreading onto others, even to those he had every right to despise.

'That...' The leader's authoritative but gentle voice was little more than a weak whisper. '...can't be...'

The queen smiled a smile wickeder than any before it, and indeed wickeder than any that would ever again grace her face.

'Yet, it is so.'

47

Secondly; the Ritual of New Birth will serve to keep the population of the forest's creatures minimal and manageable, ensuring any future revolts may be averted. All tenets are written for the sake of the Hominum's prosperity and survival. All tenets are born from love and wisdom.

Destroyed *Tenet of the Hominum's Ritual of New Birth*
Imposed by Osas Zan Ne
Generation of Osas
Second Recorded Generation

Lia fell to her knees, shaking.

The citizens are us, she reflected, so intensely that she heard it in her ears. *The citizens are us. They're what we become after we die.*

She heard the queen's cold and distant voice, and it was like a tick crawling in her ears. She stared at the ground, lost in a circle of crumbling realities.

Mother. Father. Miire Zan. Gal. Everyone...?

She retched and emptied her stomach. She groaned and she was not alone. No kin came to Lia's aid, paralysed as they were in a similar fashion. Anyone who didn't vomit instead grew faint under the revelation.

Lia yearned for the escapism of death, for the second time in the same dawn. Yet, the Mother's embrace was no longer one of safety. She could not so soon know whether the elimination of death's finality was a blessing or a curse.

'So,' the queen said, mostly to deaf ears, unfazed by the vomit desecrating her court. 'I should imagine that answers your question. Do you see now why I had to give that damned order to my citizens, to throw their lives away for yours? Why, though I despise you in every conceivable way, I must keep you here and offer you refuge? And you now see why your thanks is an insult to us. I must keep you alive, so that my citizens may have a future.'

'How could you possibly know?' It was Poruus who was the first to apply some semblance of reason to the madness. But even his sanity was partly lost, unable as he was to stop his voice from quivering. 'What makes you so confident in all this that you would have your citizen die for it?'

'A thoughtful question,' the queen said, still beaming a bright and honest smile. 'Susuuri's king. He has unrivalled hatred of you smoothskins, even compared to me. He is the oldest among us and claimed that he was the only living citizen to have met your kind, until now. He had impressive determination to kill you, even going as far as to make a plan that endangered his own subjects. He didn't care about the cost, so long as you all died.

'I had been wondering why he would go so far, but I realise now that I've been a fool. It should have been obvious that he knew of some connection between our kind and yours. Something that would make him despise his kin, and even despise himself, to the point of being willing to welcome death to ensure yours.'

Small colourful birds flocked among the Hominum, who were mostly on their knees. They heartily drank the vomit from the queen's grounds. Lia might have been sick again at the sight of it, had she not taken near complete leave of her senses.

'Actually,' the queen continued. 'I think I feel more sympathy for you than for us. After all that time you spent in my forest, killing and pillaging as you pleased, to build your walls and to fill your bellies. Isn't it funny? You were so disgusted to hear how we eat our dead, yet you've been doing the same thing. You've even been wearing your kin's corpses on your smooth skins. But who cares? What difference does it make, whether it's our kin or your kin? Any dead is still dead. If you eat one dead body, you may as well eat them all.'

'Please,' Omaraa forced out, in a voice of unbridled anguish from her trembling mouth. 'Please just stop.'

The queen laughed. It was a gleeful and cruel one. '*Stop* she says. Stop what, smoothskin leader? Stop speaking the truth? *Stop.* How often have you yourselves heard that word? How many of my citizens...oh, do excuse me. How many of *your* citizens have *you* feasted on that made a similar plea before they were killed? Even if it were made with a primitive tongue, a cry for mercy is quite universal, wouldn't you say? Do you dare, do you have the shame, to cry for mercy yourself, smoothskin?'

Lia tore her eyes from the ground up to the animal on the throne. She saw then the nature of one who had earned a place to sit above all others, displaying a rare asset that only so formidable a leader could possess; the ability to expend nothingness.

There was nothing behind the queen's wicked smile. Nothing to plea to, nothing to reason with. She was, in Lia's eyes, just a cat sitting on rocks, spreading despair to those she hated.

And Lia knew very well that she could do nothing about it. As did Omaraa, who no longer met the queen's piercing gaze. As did Poruus, whose levelheadedness now was decisively useless. As did everyone else, who soaked up the queen's words with tears and self-disdain.

'You all cry now,' the queen continued. 'That's great. Maybe now you'll understand that we die the same way you do. Maybe we'll no longer have to hide from you or make deals with monsters to assure our survival. Maybe we'll all be one happy, and very dysfunctional, family. Maybe, one day, I'll even see fit to let you eat our dead again. Oh, excuse me. To eat *your* dead again.'

'What?' It was Poruus who finally spoke, with rare trepidation. 'What do you mean *deals with monsters?*'

'What other monsters are there, but Susuuri and its king,' the queen said. 'The monsters who hunt us almost as aggressively as you do, when the sun rises and when our wits are dulled. And what other deal could be worth making with such ones but to ensure that the lives of my kin are preserved? They are stronger and wilder than us, so we must be wiser. *I* must be smarter. But it was a deal that is now obsolete. Thankfully, the price was merely one of your own.'

Lia had never shot awake so quickly.

'What are you talking about,' she said, feeling her blood heating. There was only one Hominum this cat could be referring to. Words left Lia's lips before she could think them. 'What did you do? Tell me.'

'Lia,' someone said.

She didn't care who. 'What did you do with my brother?!'

'Lia.' Houli Zin took her by the shoulders. His face had streaks where tears had fallen. 'You will endanger us all.'

'*Brother*,' the queen echoed, undeterred. She tittered again. 'I see. So, you're the one who that creature wanted to find so badly. You should be ashamed, little smoothskin. That creature let itself be a pawn for your sake, not ours.'

Lia felt her heart in her throat. 'What...what do you mean?'

'Tell her,' Poruus said, finally with a fraction of the forcefulness for which he was known. 'What was this *deal*?'

'The little smoothskin can answer that herself,' the queen said. 'Go on; ask it what this deal could possibly be.'

Poruus looked to Lia. 'Why?'

'It has been to this forest during this nightfall, as I'm sure you know by now. It went to Susuuri and was captured by the king's hunters. Then, it was freed by a certain cat, who took it through Crescat, back to your village. All under the mistaken belief she had escaped my eyes.'

Lia was almost speechless. 'How can you know all that?'

'Surely that damned cat told you about my lumen? Didn't you yourself get bitten by one on your way through Crescat? Since I saw you carrying that cat through my forest, it's obvious now that it must have been she who freed you. I thought at the time that Susuuri had sent you home with that cat on purpose, so I foolishly let you reach your land of fire. Though, I suppose I should be thankful for that mistake, now that your filthy kin are safely in my forest. But why do you think you were held captive as you were? What do you think the king could gain from keeping a smoothskin in Susuuri?'

Lia felt her anger blooming. 'I asked you what you did to--'

'Yes,' the queen said with a cold glare. 'And I'm giving you an answer. Knowing that, how about you answer my question? Actually, don't bother. The king wanted to observe how your kind changed while in Susuuri, evidently to help plan his attack on your home. With that much preparation and care, I had every reason to believe that Susuuri would be successful in killing you.

'So, I saw an opportunity to offer them a token, to show where our support lied. I sought to prepare for the time that Susuuri would be the only predators to contend with. And after you escaped, what better token could there be than a replacement of you, for the king to observe and help plan his assault anew?'

Lia bit her lip, so hard that it nearly bled. *Kai went to Susuuri, because he wanted to save me.*

Omaraa grabbed Lia's arm. 'Don't,' she said.

'I'm going,' Lia said. 'I can find my way.'

'What will you do when you get there?'

'I'll bring him back here, obviously.'

'How do you propose--'

'I don't care,' Lia shouted, pulling her arm from Omaraa's strong hand. 'I'm going.'

'How do propose to do that alone, in such a dangerous place?'

That made Lia turn back and meet Omaraa's eyes. They were puffy and red. Lia was for that moment confused.

'I will not let you go alone a second time,' Omaraa said. 'I will go with you, as will anyone else willing.'

Several hunters grunted in agreement, now finding their feet. Lia was dumbfounded.

'A foolish proposition,' the queen said. 'You were overwhelmed by just a part of Susuuri's strength, yet you plan to go to the heart of it? Take one step there and you're dead. All of you.'

'Then,' Poruus said. 'You will send your citizens with us. I see a bear, large cats, a cougar; enough to ensure we will not perish.'

The air changed instantly to one heavy with fresh outrage, directed to where Poruus stood.

'Poruus.' Omaraa spoke carefully. 'How can you ask that they--?'

'We need not ask,' Poruus said. 'I am demanding. Our hunters will take up whatever arms we have and make for Susuuri. The queen's citizens will escort us there because they have no choice. You are transparent, queen. You choose to treat us harshly because you can do little else.

'Hate us as you may, but if you speak truly of our connection through death, your future depends on our survival. If your citizens do not escort our hunters to Susuuri, then every male in our village will perish there. That means there will be no new birth after we're gone. I assure you that no Hominum will be willing to abandon this boy, even at their own peril. You are free to do as you please, of course, but as you well know, you will perish if we perish. Your descendants will go back to being primitive, both by dayfall and nightfall. How long do you expect to survive against Susuuri, without your wits to protect you?'

The queen looked long and hard at Poruus. The lynx at her side could no longer keep its silence. 'Preposterous arrogance,' it said. 'Such incredible--'

The queen needed only to kiss her teeth to silence it. She sat up on her throne. 'You may make such a threat, but it will only matter should they follow your order.'

'Every male in our tribe is either a hunter or an elder,' Poruus said, with ever more assurance in his tone. 'And when we become either, we swear that the lives of our kin would surpass our own. We have made a mistake in forgetting this vow, twice abandoning our own to this forest. None will abandon this Hominum again.'

The queen's glare intensified. Her voice was made of pure spite and barely contained rage. 'It would all be futile. Susuuri no longer needed to observe the smoothskin from the moment they attacked your village. You're foolish if you believe for a moment that your smoothskin has not perished by now. You demand that I send my citizens to die once more, for a lost cause. For them to be vulnerable when the sun rises, and risking being unable to hibernate before Susuuri can enter my land again. You're demanding nothing more than their deaths to go along with yours.'

Poruus did not falter. 'You have my sympathy. But either way, we will go to see for ourselves what fate he has met, with or without your kin.'

Lia felt something like joy welling up in her. She could not express the love she felt for Poruus at that moment, and for all her kin. She loved them all more dearly than ever before.

Kai wasn't dead. She had no question in her heart that his beat still. *Soon, Orphan-Star.*

The queen's face slowly contorted from the brooding glare she wielded, until she laughed again, nastily.

'Mother Earth is cruel indeed, to bind us to fools like you,' she said. 'Fine. Your hunters will go, and I will send some of my hunters with them.'

'My queen--'

'Don't bother,' she hissed at the bear. 'You hate it, I hate it, everyone hates it, but it's happening. For now, we must concede. However, smoothskin, some of your males will remain here. I will not let you risk our future when I have given you your wish.'

Poruus nodded. 'I agree--'

'That was a demand, not a request, so don't bother speaking again. Make haste. My subjects must be in hibernation before dawn breaks.'

48

Waya, the so-called guardian, howled to the heavens a wordless song. One filled with anger and lamentation. For many days the song lasted until Waya's lungs burned like his home. His only reply was his own echo and the harsh winds whistling where there was once shelter.

Waya was left alone to guard the forbidden and undying fire he had long desired as his own. His ears were never again blessed with the voice of the sky.

Excerpt from *The Tale of Waya*
By Timor Ro
Hominum Tribe Writer, Generation of Inti
Fourth Recorded Generation

Kai crawled up the muddy bank of a stream, heavy with water and cold. He coughed, feeling the burn of the water in his lungs. He crawled and kept crawling, without the strength to find his feet but enough fear to move him on.

The half-risen sun shone dully on Kai's back. He shivered as the wind licked his wet skin, far as he was now from any trees to guard him. His eyes were puffy and barely open. His throat was coarse, and he groaned with every breath.

He hauled himself to his feet with the aid of the first rock he reached and staggered away from the bank, his foot hurting terribly. The sky's brightest star was his only guide.

He heard voices again, too far away to make out their words but close enough to hear the ire in them. Kai imagined they were for him, perhaps made by the very same creatures that had given him and the snake chase.

He hobbled through a field, not caring for the flowers singing at his feet on his way. He reached woods beyond it, where he stumbled from tree to tree, with his head throbbing and sweating.

Susuuri was a little brighter at dawn, yet Kai could see only shadows resembling trees and dull flowers in his hazy state. The world danced with blurry waves to his eyes.

The floor was littered with dead tree leaves. Every step on them echoed into the woods tenfold. He recognised this place for the immensity of the trees. It was the deepest part of the forest he and Lia often went to. They never went further, purely to avoid making the walk home any longer. It meant that Kai was a very long way from home now.

He muffled a sneeze into his hands and wrapped himself in his cold arms. *How long have I been here now,* he wondered. Every tree he passed, every small stream from which he drank, every monster from which he hid; it had all merged into one sensation of relentless fear. It was all so maddening.

There were more foreign noises from beyond the shadows. Kai looked at its general direction, his capacity for fear already overused. He saw nothing, of course, but the same tone of darkness he had seen a hundred times before. He sauntered onwards again, with a sigh and a sniff.

He looked to the skies again to follow the brightest start of the few that remained. It was his sole source of comfort in this place, and even that came with an undertone of despair.

His mother had created a story about that very star, which she would tell to keep Kai awake with fear during the evenings she felt especially cruel.

It was a story about a boy she had named Pahana, who was always Kai's age when she told it, no matter the season.

Pahana was weak and despised by his tribe, who saw him as nothing but a burden. They would leave him behind whenever they hunted, travelled or hiked. Yet, he would always find them again, wherever they went.

So, the tribe waited for the darkest cycle of nightfall, took Pahana to the deepest part of the forest they knew, and left him to fend for himself. The boy had neither the weapons nor the skill to hunt and slowly starved over many days.

An immense snake with red eyes and pale white scales lived where Pahana was abandoned. It found him and stole him away, to an even deeper part of the forest. He was never seen again. The village marked that very day as a festival for eternal celebration at his passing. So overjoyed they were by the boy's absence that they referred to Pahana simply as *Orphan*, to deny that he was ever born to their tribe.

Sian Ro often told Kai that *he* was secretly Pahana and that she gave him a new name to hide him from the Hominum. She often threatened to tell the elders the truth, who would surely take him back to the deep forest, where the monstrous snake waited to steal him away again.

Kai would spend many cycles sleepless and terrified, with the story resonating in his head. He would never want to step foot in the forest, even as a child who barely learned to walk.

But Lia created a new ending to the story and shared it with Kai, during an evening in which their mother hadn't yet returned from her search for mushrooms in the forest.

The snake instead told Pahana that it would help him to find his way home and to fight off the dangers in the forest on their way. So, Pahana climbed on its back and they travelled, through dayfall and nightfall, until they found Pahana's village. They arrived during the tribe's festival celebrating Pahana's passing. Enraged, the snake slew all the villagers who had abandoned Pahana and left him to die.

Pahana was home, but sad to be all alone. So, the monster made him one more offer; to turn him into a beautiful bright star, for him to make countless friends of all the other stars he could see in the sky.

Pahana from then on became the very brightest star in the sky and resided above his former village, to serve as a guide back home for all those who would be lost or abandoned in the forest, forever.

Lia gave the boy a new name befitting his new form; *Orphan Star*.

Kai eventually grew old enough to see such stories for the fantastical fables they were. But Lia took to calling Kai *Orphan Star* on occasion, as something of an endearment.

She once took him to the deep part of the forest where he now walked, to prove that such monstrous snakes were the pure fabrication of their cruel mother.

'If ever we are lost in the Ameyali Forest, we just need to find Orphan Star and follow him home.' That was what Lia had said, in these very woods.

Kai now looked up to the star that guided his tired steps and smiled the saddest smile of his life.

After all the adventure, after all the spectacle and wonder that the Ameyali forest had gifted to him, and after his slow journey to accepting his failure in saving the one whom he loved most, he finally admitted the hardest of truths to himself; *I want to go home.*

Kai was ashamed. He was bitterly heartbroken. He was angered by his very breathing, cursing the life he had not yet lived to its fullest. *Everything I've done here, everything I've seen; it's all for nothing. I've accomplished nothing. I came here only to long for home again.*

Kai was so lost in his lamentations that he almost failed to notice a soft sound from behind his back and a rustle of the dead leaves under a new creature's feet.

A chill flowed to his chest; one that spoke less of fear and more of acceptance. It would be fittingly unceremonious, Kai thought, to meet his end in a foreign place surrounded by shadows. He sighed and turned to somewhat bravely face his fate once more.

It was a cat. Slightly bigger than a cat ought to be, but still a cat nonetheless. It sat on dead leaves and swayed its tail. It glared with an intensity that turned Kai's skin to ice.

Their eyes locked. Its gaze never broke. Kai's furious beating heart never waned.

No sound there could be heard there, but for Susuuri's cold wind.

49

This cursed knowledge must be shared only with those who have sworn to the duty of elder and shepherd. For all generations to come, the Hominum's leaders shall be charged to uphold our tenets, with this knowledge to affirm their wisdom in doing so.

Among our tribe from this day on, none shall speak of the Ameyali Forest's true nature, of the creatures within, or of the connection the Mother has created between us.

Let this knowledge stay silent among you for the sakes of your unborn kin.

Destroyed *Tenet of the Hominum's Ritual of New Birth*
Imposed by Osas Zan Ne
Generation of Osas
Second Recorded Generation

'Found you,' the cat said. It walked toward Kai with her bright green eyes fixed on his. He backed away through instinct.

'Why do you all want me so much,' he asked.

'Your cage was shattered,' the cat said. 'And the citizens that guarded you were torn apart, along with even our fearsome vice. So, what happened?'

Kai shivered as memories of the screams and the putrid stench of blood that followed came back to him. He remembered the snake screaming as it died and how he had believed his own death to be nigh. He was now grateful that he had been blind for most of that trauma.

'I asked you a question,' the cat said. The intensity in its voice brought Kai back to the present, with a chill in his blood.

'A snake freed me.'

'I already know that much,' the cat said. 'What happened after that?'

'We were chased. It was killed.'

The cat smiled. It was reminiscent of the queen's smile, but with even greater malice in it. 'Meaning it died trying to get you out of Susuuri, right? Isn't that weird? A big scary monster protecting an innocent little hatchling, like a bear protecting its cub. Or like any creature would protect its spawn, willing to give even its own life for its safety. There's a term for that kind of instinct, right?'

'What do you want with me,' Kai repeated.

'*Me?* Just seeing you is enough. I wanted to see for myself the little smoothskin that would be the cause of what's to come. You're quite unimpressive, so far.'

Kai felt another chill in his veins. 'The cause of what?'

'Where are you going?'

Kai breathed deeply, growing more anxious talking with this eccentric creature. He dared not stop though, lest she brought Susuuri upon him again. 'I'm going home,' he said.

'Home,' the cat echoed. 'Where's this home?'

'My village. The place outside the forest, beyond the walls and fire.'

The cat laughed. 'I know the place. I'd say I know it better than you do if you believe it only *beyond* the fire.'

Kai's heart missed a beat. 'What...do you mean? What's happened?'

The cat smiled still. 'Well, it's a pretty long story. I can't stand long stories, so I'll skip to the best part. Your village is gone. Susuuri attacked and overwhelmed your kind. It went down in flames and has been left abandoned to a mess of bodies and ashes. It's not much of a *home* for anyone anymore unless you're a corpse or a cannibal.'

Kai looked down at his feet and clenched his fists. Perhaps it was his exhaustion, or his heart already strained beyond its limits, but he felt very little at those words. He only felt unease for the answer to his next words. 'Whose bodies?'

The cat paused, the smile fading from its lips. '*That's* the reaction you're going with?'

'Whose bodies?'

'A mixture. Not to worry though. They're mostly Susuuri's citizens. Your smoothskins got out with most of their bodies intact. My guess would be that the oldest and slowest died.'

Kai let out a long sigh. He knew in his heart this to be the case already. His kin could surely never completely perish without his=m knowing, least of all his own flesh and blood. He did not dare to wonder who *did* perish yet.

'I'm sorry about your citizens,' he said, quite honestly.

'No, you're not. Or you shouldn't be. We fought you and lost. So, we died, just the way it should be. Anyway, knowing all this, what will you do now?'

Kai felt his fist clenching again. 'I'm still going home.'

The cat groaned. 'You're a terrible listener. Can you really call a pile of burnt wood and corpses *home*? There's nothing for you there but misery and death. Why would you want to go back?'

'I don't mean the village. The other Hominum escaped, right? They will need to find somewhere else to live. So, I'll have to go wherever they've gone.'

The words left Kai's mouth with pureness. He expressed them with remarkable ease and surprised even himself with their conviction. He looked down at his still clenched fist turning red. He felt his heartbeat through his whole body. He had scarcely ever felt such tranquillity of mind, yet he presently had all the cause for despair. It was...pleasant.

The cat's ominous laughter soon spoiled his moment of self-reflection. 'I'm surprised,' it said. 'But I shouldn't be. Of course, you would be stubborn too, but you're quite interesting with it.'

'What could you know about me,' Kai asked. 'Why do you know me at all?'

'I just told you; I knew you'd be stubborn. Not much more than that.'

'But how--?'

'Questions upon questions. They get so boring after a time. Don't you agree? Hmm, that was ironic.'

Kai rubbed his aching head. 'You're not making any sense. Why did you bother finding me at all?'

'Oh yeah, *that*. More of your smoothskins might be killed soon. I just thought I'd warn you.'

The words were too lackadaisical for Kai to quickly discern. 'Huh? *Killed?*'

'Yup. Killed.'

'You...more will be killed?

'I said *might*, but it's looking quite likely, yeah.'

Kai felt his blood heating up as the words were slowly digested. 'How? Why?'

'The same reason your village was attacked down in the first place. My citizens hate yours. Just because we took your home, it doesn't mean that that hatred has gone anywhere. They hate you because you've killed so many of us. So, don't you think killing even more of us would make us hate you more?'

Kai could not get past his incredulity. The cat's eccentric tone made its words gnaw at his brain like a plague.

Kai closed his eyes, trying to calm himself. *Susuuri is going to kill us. They couldn't do it in Crescat. So, the Hominum have either gone to the unknown lands, or the only other place they could be killed is in Susuuri...*

Kai sighed again, with all sense of tranquillity dissipated. 'They've come to Susuuri to save me,' he stated more than he asked. He felt sick.

'Ooh, clever,' the cat said. 'But they're not here yet. If they were, they'd already be dead. So, if I were you, I'd stop them before they get to the border. Though, that may be a little difficult, as I'm sure my citizens will be waiting for them there already. That is, whichever ones are stupid enough not to be preparing for dayfall right now. You can thank the rising sun that you're able to walk around here as freely as you are. Most of us will be preparing for sleep right now, or maybe mating again to make up for the dead.'

Kai looked into the cat's devilishly carefree eyes, regaining the fear he thought he had lost. 'Why? If you hate us so much, why are you telling me all this?'

'Hmm, that question sounds familiar,' the cat said. 'Don't confuse me with the mindless fools I share Susuuri with. I don't hate you, or your kind for whoever you've killed. The dead are dead and will stay dead, no matter how many of you we kill in anger. Clearly, all my kin's hatred does is help you to kill even more of us. Isn't that stupid?'

'And...that's your reason for helping me?'

'*Helping* you,' the cat said, tilting its head. 'Is that what I'm doing? Maybe, maybe not. I don't know either, so it's pointless asking *me*.'

'Then, why...?'

'For fun.'

Kai blinked, looking dumbly down at the beast spouting

incomprehensible words. '*Fun*,' he echoed.

'Fun.' The cat wasn't smiling anymore. 'Fun, fun, fun. That's the opposite of boredom. Does that sound petty? Really, why does anyone ever do anything? We can create resolutions that we absolutely must live long enough to fulfil, but they're just fabrications. Delusions to fit purpose where it doesn't belong. What happens when our purpose fails, or when our desires go unfulfilled? Does Mother Earth crumble into dust? No. *Nothing* happens, because we're arrogant and our purposes are phoney. The only meaning in purpose is avoiding boredom, or worse, being boring.

'So, I guess you could say my purpose this nightfall wasn't completely pointless. All this work to keep your Hominum from dying out and having them taken to the forest. Abandoning my boring duties here to pursue my own convictions, despite being hated by my kin for it. It was ultimately fun. But everything is boring when you know how the journey will end. Still, now that I've told you all of this, I really don't know how this will end at all. It feels nice. It'll be a fun dawn too.'

No matter how the words touched his ears, Kai couldn't make them comprehendible to himself. Their nature was just too bizarre for him to cope with. 'I...don't understand.'

The cat simply tittered, the intensity fading from its eyes as quickly as it had come. 'I know. You should be glad for that, you know. I don't think this forest could stand for long with more than one of me. Crescat should be thankful that *their* queen is so tepid.'

'You're twisted.'

The cat's manner swiftly changed again at those words. '*Twisted*?'

'You...you're making us fight and kill each other, just because you're *bored*? No matter what, it's...you're twisted.'

'Oh,' the cat sighed. 'This is coming from *you*. Then tell me; why did you come to this forest in the first place?'

Ka's heart skipped another beat. It was surreal to hear the same question he himself had pondered over said out loud, with an answer now demanded of him. 'To find my sister,' he said.

'Uh-huh. And how did you know she was here? Why not in the unknown lands?'

'I...I could just feel it.' It was not the first time Kai had expressed that reasoning aloud, but it this time sounded far more ridiculous.

'I don't doubt it,' the cat said, with no hint of mockery or irony, to

Kai's surprise. 'But, don't act like it was just through your blood bond that you felt this. You *wanted* to feel it. You wanted to tread these forbidden grounds, to find a little danger and excitement, because you're bored with your life, just like me. You saw a chance to fulfil a dream, to see the forest at nightfall with your own eyes, and you took it. Admit it; you *wanted* your sister to be here badly, didn't you? You wanted it so that you could justify being here yourself.'

Kai could hardly find the words. 'Why...why do you...know so much?'

'Just admit it.'

Kai's heart raced. Suddenly, every word from this beast's mouth resonated and was easily comprehended. He was forced to reflect on himself, against his instincts. It truly had been a wonderful journey, filled with awe and wonder beyond his puny imaginings. He had been so right in following his conviction into the unknown, against the wishes of the cowardly, *purely* for the sake of the only person he had ever loved.

Perhaps Kai had believed that this would be the motivation he would forever know to be true, the story his descendants would sing about, just as he and Lia had always wanted. A song of braving the unknown for selfless love.

It was all a lie.

Kai knelt in his exhaustion. 'I did,' he told himself out loud. 'I *did* want her to be here, so I could come to the forest too.' Kai felt his heart sink at his words. It seemed he had no tears left to cry. 'I was selfish for coming here. I wanted to come here with Lia so that we could see the Ameyali Forest at night.'

'Of course,' the cat said. It walked towards him until they were face to face. 'I don't blame you, by the way. No one should. We'll do anything to not be bored, right? I don't call that selfish, I call that *living*.

'Still, if you had never come here, maybe there wouldn't have been any cause for the pending bloodshed. If you hadn't come, your Hominum would have had no cause to enter Susuuri. They would be safely hiding in Crescat until the sun rises, and you would be with them. But still, had you never come, you would have regretted abandoning your sister, right? Even though she would have gotten herself home eventually, you would have had to face her knowing you did nothing to help her. So, ask yourself; do you regret your time here for this selfish little voyage?'

Kai had no answer yet. Perhaps he never would, and perhaps the question would loom over him for the rest of his days.

'Well, I think we've spoken enough,' the cat said. 'You'll have no home left at all if you don't hurry up and get to the border. Preferably do so before the sun fully rises, since it will only be worse for you if Susuuri's citizens change back into their primitive forms and the hyachin can no longer protect help you.'

The cat leapt up into the trees to take its leave.

'Which way is Crescat,' Kai had the good sense to ask.

The cat simply shot him one last wicked smile in response and Kai watched the cat disappear into the trees against the orange sky.

The stars were becoming dimmer, but one still shone brightly, like a pale white flame.

Kai stood up and staggered again toward *Orphan Star*.

50

...and this is where our two-year wander ends; back where it began, to where we betrayed those who were our kin and abandoned the care of Mother Earth. Now we reside beside the forest where we are justly despised, beside the only place in which we can hide from the monsters in these lands. The irony is not lost on me.

Farro assures us that we act for future generations, that the citizens' hatred of us shall fade with time, and that our descendants shall be welcomed back as their peers.

I believe he is mistaken. But whether our descendants prosper or perish by our actions, we have doomed our own generation to a life of fear, as a clan with no home and nowhere to hide.

Destroyed Excerpt from *The Two-Year Wander*
Author Unknown
Text Predates First Recorded Generation

'I cannot allow this,' Omaraa said. 'And I have no doubt the other elders will also be opposed.'

'Nor do I,' Poruus said. 'But this how it must be, Omaraa. Whether we wish it or not is irrelevant.'

'Why, Poruus,' she said, her voice already breaking. 'Why must it be you?'

'Because I cannot order our hunters to go into a danger I am unwilling to face myself.'

'That is what we *must* do as shepherds. That is the burden we are sworn to bear.'

She sounded far too emotional to Poruus ears, as was common with her. She was far too desperate to cling to the only normality she knew of.

This change for our clan is imperative indeed, Poruus was assured. *Our chief has needed this harsh awakening, more than any of us.*

'Not anymore,' he said. 'Everything has changed, Omaraa. We no longer have chambers to hold hearings. We no longer have old books from our predecessors to guide us. We stand now on a blank page from which we must build anew. Our next steps will define the foundation upon which our tribe will be rebuilt. We have a chance to prove to our kin that we are willing and able to lead as well as we have claimed we can.'

Omaraa rubbed her head. The wrinkles on her head made her look older than her years. 'But shepherds need to know which risks should not be taken, and not just shoulder the risk themselves. Our tribe also needs stability, now more than ever. They need to see their shepherds acting with caution, not out of desperation.'

'They have seen nothing but caution from their shepherds for generations. Look at what has befallen us because of it. We would undoubtedly all be dead, were it not for the Ro children abandoning caution for instinct. What they did was not solely a risk, but a necessity. What I propose now is a necessary acknowledgement of change. Otherwise, we show only that our ability to shepherd should be brought into question.'

His words could not fully reach her, he knew. Poruus could see it on her tired face. What he saw was Omaraa at her very limit, a woman who now comprehended the burden of leadership and was finding herself lacking. Poruus was grateful for it. *Be afraid only of failing without your knowledge,* he recited. *Some old proverbs will still have their place with us.*

'But I must discuss something else with you before I go,' Poruus said. 'Something that I believe should govern your future as our chief. Do you recall the theory I shared with you; that something significant transpired in this forest before the first recorded generation?'

'Yes,' Omaraa said, irritated and vacant. 'Yes, Poruus, I remember.'

'That theory would explain the contents of *The Two-Year Wander*. They were surely forced to leave this forest and seek out a new home, as a result of whatever transpired. The true reason for that voyage was probably destroyed, along with the other texts outlining the forest's nature. But a question arises; why did our clan return and build our village on the Ameyali Forest's border?'

Omaraa looked up from her hands, as though suddenly awake. Some semblance of coherence returned to her eyes. 'They could not build a village in the unknown lands,' she said. 'They found something dangerous?'

'I believe so. But it must be more than that. To return to the very same place from which they fled, after two long years, there could not have been *anywhere* in the unknown lands suitable for a new home. Nowhere safe enough, or perhaps nowhere that crops could be grown. Our predecessors were unwise to keep so many secrets from their kin, but the unknown lands may be unknown to us for good reason. I advise that you keep that in mind as our chief should life in this forest ever seem unbearable in future. As you said, it is up to us to decide which risks are worth taking.'

Omaraa said nothing back. She sat against the fruit tree and quietly contemplated his words, as was her nature.

No more words were shared between them but a fleeting *farewell*, before Poruus returned to his kin and prepared for another voyage.

*

Lia sat under the new growth of a blossom tree, watching the purpura pods above her slowly close for dayfall. She ate a sweet red fruit she picked from the queen's court. The taste was potent on her tongue, but not overbearing.

She never had such a time to enjoy the beauty of the purpura as she now did. She was disappointed that she could only do so now that their glow was dimming.

Her only interaction with them before this had been limited to cycles of fear. Candy had undergone her change and left her to sneak through Crescat alone, as a helpless target, all because of the purpura's light.

In truth, she initially went along with Candy's threats and left for the forest, with so little resistance, in part because of the beauty of the purpura's light calling her.

Lia saw them now in a new but familiar light. She wondered how it felt to live as a part of Mother Earth herself, as a mere flower growing by night and sleeping by day.

She wondered if *all* Hominum were fated to become one of the creatures of the forest themselves. She had some contempt nested deeply within her at the thought that a new life after death would mean her former life would be forgotten. Her memories of Kai would be forgotten. Even her love for Kai would be gone and they may never be together again after they pass.

It was a struggle to maintain anything purer than hatred for Mother

Earth anymore, after that kind of revelation.

Her mother. Her father. Even Miire Zin Fa; perhaps some figures from Lia's life had seen her from new eyes since they died yet had not known her. It was almost too much to bear, that this too was to be Lia's fate eventually.

And the fate of those who died during Susuuri's attack; Gal, Charaa…too many others. They too would be citizens by the Mother's will, and they died without ever knowing this truth. Lia could see them all again but would not know it.

Mothers are cruel, Lia thought. *Why do all mothers treat us so cruelly?*

Lia wiped any imagined tears from her eyes. 'I just needed time alone,' she said to the approaching steps rustling against the dead leaves. She could guess who they belonged to without seeing. She had to venture a long way from the queen's court to find a quiet place. With Omaraa Zan no doubt occupied, few others would venture so far to find her.

'Me too,' Zanuus Ka said. Lia heard the lie all too clearly. Her time in Candy's company had gifted her with an ear for lies and embellishments, it seemed.

Zanuus sat beside her and leaned against the same tree, fidgeting with a small red flower in his hands. 'I…thought you might have gone…' He trailed off, thinking better of it.

'That I would have gone with the others to find Kai,' Lia finished.

'…yes. I wouldn't have blamed you.'

'I wouldn't have blamed me either,' Lia said, quite honestly. Her fighting every urge to do just so had been one of her greatest trials. She wondered still where she found the will to restrain herself, as she still did. That had been one reason she sought isolation for a while, to keep this feeling for as long as she could.

'I'm not a hunter,' she said. 'I would have been no help had I gone. Only a hindrance and something else for the hunters to worry about.'

'I see,' Zanuus said.

Lia took her last bite of the sweet fruit. 'I trust your father, more than I would trust myself. So, I'll just wait for him to bring him home for me.'

Zanuus smiled, somewhat reservedly. 'Yeah. He's certainly dependable.'

'How do you feel now,' Lia asked, out of pure impulse. She had not voiced that question in so long that they felt foreign to her lips.

'About Mother Earth and the citizens,' Lia said. 'How do you feel about it all?'

Zanuus looked at the flower in his hand. 'I'm not sure yet,' he said. 'Everyone's quite distraught about it all. It's been hard to even talk to anyone for any time at all before they break into tears.'

'It's a lot to take. We lost our home and lost our kin. And we learned something so horrible. It's understandable that they would be distressed.'

'Is it? What has really caused this distress? When the queen told us how the Mother uses us, everyone was more distraught for that than our dead kin. But that is what we've prayed for since the first known generation, for every Hominum who dies. *We pray you grow well, instilled with our kin's spirit.* We asked for the Mother to use our spirit as she sees fit and that's what she's done.'

'It's *not* what we asked for,' Lia said. 'We asked for the land to grow and feed us. Not for us to become the very creatures that we hunted.'

Zanuus frowned. 'Just looking at this forest, that is exactly what we have been given.'

'But who would wish to lose all memories of their past life? To forget all those who they loved and start anew? And who prayed to be reborn as a citizen, hunted by their own tribe to be feasted on and built into tipis?'

'No one,' Zanuus said. 'But who, in their right mind would rather their eyes be closed forever?'

Lia's only answer was the anger in her which refused to wane, even in the face of Zanuus' calming manner. 'Maybe *I* would,' she said. 'Or maybe I would rather be given a choice. Who wouldn't want that?'

'Maybe,' Zanuus said. 'Death has never been a choice though. I...I think I'm glad to know there is a second life. It's more than I had before.'

Lia said nothing more. She sat in silence with Zanuus beside her, waiting for her anger to fade. It never did.

She quietly contemplated the new hazy future. She felt this anger would never truly wane and doubted that Mother Earth's embrace would ever invoke a sense of comfort again. She wondered if her mouth would be capable of singing the prayers which they had done her whole life, as the thought of praising such a mother made her sick.

Lia's future, and her kin's future, had never looked so hazy. And Lia had never felt so lost in an assured fate.

51

The third greatest failing of my predecessors was to create fragile order through the artificial spread of fear. For when such fear inevitably fades through a hard life faced and endured, so fades such order with it.

Ailen Zan Mo
Generation of Ailen the Kind
Sixth Recorded Generation

Citizen followed his nose toward the queen's beautiful and pure scent, though he needn't have. From the moment the vice curtly turned him away from the queen's empty throne, Citizen knew where she would be.

The silence truly was striking in this place, but it was more unnerving to Citizen's ears than it was comforting. Why anyone would care for such silence and seclusion was beyond him.

Citizen knew all too well the taste of isolation and knew it not as something one should voluntarily pursue. Eating, playing, talking; such things were not meant to be experienced without company. To come to this place, yearning for that lonely sensation by her own admission, it was yet another mysterious part of the queen's nature that Citizen could not hope to comprehend.

'Sit,' the queen said as Citizen approached. She watched the dawn sky, sat with her tail gently swaying.

Citizen did as he was bid. *Is this where she hibernates,* he wondered. *Maybe that's why she's here while the sun is almost up.*

'Was my inference too subtle for you rabbit,' she asked.

Citizen blinked. 'Sorry?'

The queen sighed. 'At least with the smoothskins, I can speak freely. I'm asking you if you misunderstood me the last time you were here. I thought I'd made it clear that you were not to come here again.'

Citizen gazed at his queen, who refused to return the courtesy. He knew his being here would anger her, but he had little choice. He could not live with himself, were he to keep his silence *now*. 'I'm sorry,' he said.

'Evidently, you're not. Or else, you would not be here. What do you want now?'

Citizen swallowed and took his long calming breath. 'I want to ask--'

'And the answer is no.'

Citizen blinked dumbly. 'But I didn't even ask--'

'I expected this from you, rabbit. I expected your guilt to bring you here for such a ridiculous request eventually. I saw it coming from when you sobbed before my throne and told me all about that little smoothskin. I afforded you curtesy with understanding, knowing how lonely it must have been for you being banished. I knew that that decision would come back to bite me and here you are, predictably making me regret my kindness.'

Citizen blinked again. 'I don't understand,' he said, only half honestly.

'No. Do you understand that? No, you may not follow the smoothskins to Susuuri. Not only do you have no place among our hunters, but I would never allow you to leave so close to sunrise. What difference do you think *you* would make there, rabbit? Do you think you would fare better than the bear or jaguar? Your request is ridiculous, and the answer is *no*. Go back to the burrow where you've hoarded your food supply and prepare for hibernation. I will do you one more courtesy and forget we ever had this conversation. Is there anything else?'

Citizen merely shook his head.

'Correct answer. Now, get out of my sight and put all thoughts of that smoothskin out of your tiny brain.'

Citizen did as he was bid, to a degree. He gladly left the queen to her peace. But he also did what he had already decided he would do, regardless of the queen's predictable answer.

His feet carried him towards the same dark place they had gone so many times before, this time with a foreign conviction. There was no hesitation or trepidation in his steps.

Citizen would soon leave the hyachin behind again, and perhaps earn the condemnation of his kin once more.

His little burrow would have to wait a while longer.

*

The walk through Crescat was long and arduous, filled with spectacle of the like that Poruus' eyes had never before been blessed with. He saw plumage that glowed even against the haze of the rising sun and wildly overgrown herbs with powerful aromas. He would happily study these upon his return from this venture.

Poruus had spent a great many nightfalls looking at the Ameyali Forest from behind the village walls, letting himself imagine what could have dwelt within. The glowing plumage he now saw was a little part of what he already envisioned.

It reaffirmed his belief regarding the Hominum's trepidation of this place, that their hesitation and caution had been counter-productive at best and detrimental at worst. *So many generations of potential research wasted on caution and unhealthy contentment.*

It was primarily why he insisted on accompanying the hunters on this expedition, against the wishes of his fellow elders. It was imperative to become well acquainted with the forest's makeup and potential, while it was still nightfall.

Poruus had developed one rather unpleasant but likely theory. The forest was instilled with the same energy that gave the animals their gift of speech, which is to say, the Hominum's life force. If the cat's words were true, Mother Earth took the life force of fallen Hominum upon their cremation and fed it to the creatures of the forest. This surely meant that it was their feeding on the forest's plantation and water that imbued them with this life force. And if so, all this plumage and water, everything he could see, was imbued with the life of his dead kin.

This is the return to the mother we sing for in our songs for nightfall. It's beautiful. And so tragic. We are born from a harsh mother.

He had thought better than to let this theory be too readily known. Many of his kin may have rathered starve than knowingly consume the life force of their descendants again. *Not all truths are best known. Perhaps this was the thinking that caused Inti to lead with such oppression and absolution. A dangerous philosophy to follow, but occasionally a necessity.*

The hyachin became less vibrate the further he walked, as he left most of the tree pods behind. Soon, the small army of lumen overhead became his main source of light.

'We are approaching the border,' the bear said. It was the first words anyone had spoken since they had departed. The Hominum hunters quietly followed the citizens' lead, with what was left of their weapons and shields in hand. 'And the smoothskin is not far.'

The atmosphere hung heavy. Both Hominum and citizen alike were there begrudgingly, chasing the shadow of a single boy who found danger willingly. Poruus understood their resentment but saw the potential in this expedition. It had far more significance than the rescue of one of their kin. It was also the first step in establishing a relationship they would soon have to foster with these creatures. It was the first opportunity to establish themselves as equals in this place, rather than inferiors in the queen's territory.

That standing *had* to be presently made known. Poruus did not relish the thought of his kin forever being subjected to any ruler, but particularly one with such a bizarre temperament.

However, the Hominum hunters were under strict instruction to return to the queen's court, should the voyage prove too dangerous. Poruus' threat to the queen had been genuine, yet he of course did not intend to allow his kin to die out over one expedition.

'What can we expect beyond this border,' one Hominum hunter said.

The jaguar cut him a vile look. 'Blood. Death. Preferably theirs, though unlikely.'

There was silence again, as the simple truth of its words burdened their steps. They silently concurred that any confrontation was unlikely to end favourably, yet guile would be difficult with the tebirii underground. Susuuri may have already known that they were approaching, as well as their numbers.

'Then, we must make the blood less likely to be our own,' Poruus said.

The bear glanced at him. 'How do you propose we do so?'

'Does Susuuri have any other means of knowing our location and numbers, aside from the tebirii?'

'Not to our knowledge.'

'That being the case, there is a clear weakness. The tebirii can only know our numbers so long as we walk on the ground, meaning we can approach Susuuri from the trees without their knowledge. Even if they were already aware of our numbers, they would not know the location of those who climb.'

'Some of us cannot climb trees,' the bear said.

'Indeed. So, some of us will not climb. Some will still approach by foot, acting as a diversion for the tebirii. As you cannot stay in Susuuri for long before your change, it would be better for you to stay on the ground where it will be easier to return to Crescat anyway.'

'And what of *their* citizens who can climb,' the jaguar said.

'I assume the creatures that can climb are not warriors. Monkeys, insects, lizards; they will not have the strength of the wolves we faced before, nor of any of you. However, the worst outcome is that they have scouts in the trees. Even then, we would still have a vantage point over their hunters too.'

The citizens shared the same vacant look. Poruus assumed they did not have the mental faculties to fully comprehend strategy, even at such a basic level. *I see now how a mere cat came to be the ruler over these powerful creatures. She certainly far surpasses all others in mental prowess.*

'A fine plan,' the bear said after a time.

'Not especially,' Poruus said. 'But it is the only one we have.'

There was only silence between them again as they left behind the hyachin's protection and willingly entered Susuuri's harsh embrace.

52

...and Waya's days were henceforth filled with sorrow. For all his arrogance and lofty ambition, the foolish wolf had only famine where there had been fruitage.
Fear where there had been comfort.
Pain where there had been shelter.
Death where there had been life.
From the day of the wolf's futile defiance, and indeed for time eternal, Waya would be known as the Guardian of Ashes.

Excerpt from *The Tale of Waya*
By Timor Ro
Hominum Tribe Writer, Generation of Inti
Fourth Recorded Generation

Kai covered his eyes from the sun, for the first time since the beginning of this long nightfall. The rain was beginning to subside. The tree's shadows were less looming, as the skies grew paler.

All this for me, he reflected. *They'd really come to Susuuri, just for* me. How foolish he had behaved, for so long.

The cat had the right of it. Had he stayed home as he was bid, there would be no slaughter to avert and no more lives at stake. And so foolish he was too to presume Lia, his sister of unwavering boldness and cunning, would ever be helpless without him. He couldn't stomach the thought of bringing himself before her again, after all the harm his stupidity had caused their kin. Yet, he would soon have no choice.

He now limped on his feet as fast as he was able, to prevent what he would be unable to bear above all else; bloodshed for his own sake. Kai was as directionless through the brightening forest as when he first entered its shadows, now with far less dignity and sureness of heart.

He huffed and breathlessly sang;

'Pearls in the snowflakes of nightfall.
Dayfall shines.
But by the reeds by the ashes of the daring
Are the brightest and truest of lights.'

A piece of his heartache selfishly faded away with each word. Lia and he never did figure out the melody, but the song always came effortlessly to his lips.

'When they tremble and stutter.
We hold our heads high.
And memories of the forgotten
Will fill the pages of time.'

Kai sighed, for his heart knew that his head had no business being held high anymore. Nor did his lips have any business singing the words so well, but the words still flowed easily from them on his way.

And the pages turn beyond
The hand's many ages.
Until the newborns' brave hearts
Break from their cages.'

Kai paused, finding a foreign yet familiar scent with the very next breath. It was a smell that hung heavily in the air like a mist. Through it, he finally saw his first glimpse of the hyachin's welcoming but dying purple light in the distance. Perhaps what he smelt was Crescat. Home. It had been so long that he had forgotten.

It was quiet, to Kai's relief. No citizens, none of his kin, no sounds of hostility. Just peaceful silence near the border. His own laboured voice and pained steps were all that he could hear.

Then we reeds will grow stronger
And taller than the weak.

And time will cheer--'

Kai was silenced at the sight of a part of the stench he'd found.

A colossal spider was before him, laid dead under the shade of the trees, drenched in its blue blood from the deep wound on his back.

Kai approached with shaking legs, unable to stop himself. Its stillness in death was terrifying and alluring.

The spider did not lay there alone. With it were wolves and monkeys and abandoned Hominum weapons. Spears were lodged into their corpses.

The smell now was hideous and undoubtedly that of freshly spilt blood; blood still oozing from their corpses and drying on the grounds where it had sprayed. Some of the bodies were disfigured beyond recognition. There were some trails of red blood leading towards Susuuri's shadows.

Here too was a jaguar, one he remembered from his time in Crescat's custody. Its fur was brandished with many bite marks. It had blue and red blood alike staining its own teeth.

Kai fell to his knees with the anguish of guilt.

*

Citizen hopped as quickly as his feet were able, which was not fast at all. He felt his very life essence leaving his body with every breath, as dawn's light seeped into his flesh. Every second now was an effort to stay himself. He longed for the comfort of his borrow to rest in.

The wholly abhorrent stench of blood was unmistakable and easy to follow. It was the smell Citizen suffered with every death of his kin. The taste and smell of their corpses always made Citizen sick. That time of feasting was the height of Citizen's loathing for the customs in this forest. He'd never had a taste for blood and meat.

This putrid aroma was therefore nested into Citizen's brain and impossible to misplace, but he'd never smelt such a mass of it. He could visualise the site from where it came and was terrifying.

But Citizen pushed on still, driven by Smoothie's scent emanating from it. He feared the very worst, for he also smelt an unfamiliar but equally putrid smell of death among that of his kin.

*

Kai looked to the skies again, to see his lone guide home spending the last of its light. It made way for a nearly complete dayfall sky, tainted with a patch of paling orange.

But between it and Mother Earth, something hung from the branches and swayed gently, with what was left of the winds of nightfall. So too were there others, three in total, hanging from their feet by a fine thread of webbing.

Their bodies and their faces had been left bare, pale and bloodied. Kai knew all their faces, but Poruus Zin Ka was the only one among them he could name.

Kai screamed, with all the power he could muster, yet not a sound left his lips. Blood had never looked so stark, nor had its smell been so suffocating.

The genius elder bled the worst of all, for all the bites and scratches in his flesh.

Why, was the only rational thought that passed through Kai's consciousness. It was the word his brain clung to, like a parasite to its host.

The world seemed to go dark to Kai's eyes. His every breath filled his ears as a hollow echo.

Why, why, Kai's mind repeated for some immeasurable time, slowly consuming his every thinking faculty.

*

Smoothie, Kai heard, or perhaps imagined. It was vivid enough in his mind to demand what was left of his awareness.

'Smoothie.' Kai *heard* it that time for sure. It was only through the word pairing with the darkness that he realised his eyes were closed.

He woke to find himself lying on his back, with a new and familiar face looking down at him.

'Citizen,' Kai said.

'You're alive,' the rabbit said, blinking away tears. 'It's me, Smoothie.'

'You found me.'

'You're hurt.'

Kai followed Citizen's gaze to his own body. It was covered in dark red blood and dirt.

He sat up, shaking the haze out of his head. He looked up again to his brethren hanging above them. Citizen followed his gaze. He seemed unmoved.

'But what happened here,' he said after a time, looking at the jaguar lying within his reach and the other citizens' mauled bodies. There was no measure of sorrow in his voice. 'No one brought them home to eat.'

'What happened,' Kai echoed, questioning himself. 'I don't know. They came here for me. My kin and the citizens. They came to help me and they…it's all my fault.'

'Yeah, they did,' Citizen said. 'But why is it your fault? It was the queen who told you to go to Susuuri, just so you'd be taken, you know? It's really *her* fault. I thought she had killed you.'

'No, *I* came to this forest myself. *I* came to Susuuri willingly. *I* let myself get captured and needed saving. So, they came here and died, because of me. Why…why did I even come here? After all this, Lia didn't even need saving.' Kai now shook as he spoke, the reality in his words sinking in. 'All I've done by coming here is cause everyone trouble. Now, they've been killed. How can I go back now? I don't deserve…I…I wish I never came here. I hate it.'

Citizen eyed Kai with the most curious of gazes, bewildered. '*I'm* glad you came, Smoothie,' was all he said.

Kai heard those simple words well. He finally let go and sobbed. He did not feel to, truly, but the pain had too strongly become of him to not be taken by this one moment of clarity. His face fell into his hands and he trembled.

Kai heard Citizen cry out too, in a quieter but equally hearty manner. Kai reached out in instinct and touched his soft fur.

Kai and his friend sobbed in a bizarre union, embracing the rare freedom of pure expression in each other's arms.

It felt amazing.

*

Citizen hung on Smoothie's back as he sauntered through the almost empty glow of the hyachin, feeling thoroughly deprived of energy. It was almost time for sleep, the time he ironically most despised. He'd rather choose his time of respite than have the sun force it upon him.

'Will you remember me,' Smoothie said. 'When you've changed again. Will you remember all this?'

'I don't know,' Citizen said, his voice feeble. It felt like he had few words left to give. 'I don't remember.'

Smoothie smiled, and something like a titter escaped from his teeth.

'What's funny,' Citizen asked, quite surprised.

'I don't know,' Smoothie said. 'Nothing.'

'You laughed for no reason?'

'Yeah. For no reason.'

Citizen was quiet again for a time.

Then he laughed too, dryly and with minimal zeal. It sounded more like a groan to him.

Smoothie stopped walking for that moment. 'What are you doing?'

'Laughing.' Citizen laughed again, with the same puny zeal.

Smoothie laughed too. His laugh brought Citizen to laughter again, imbued with any zeal he had left.

Their walk home became one of absurd laugher, ascending into screaming out all the breath in them. Then a little more laughter.

Their walk home was filled with absurd expressions of unity, until the silence and darkness fell upon Citizen, with the purpura finally beginning to close.

53

A fire draws near
And nothing to fear
A fine gift from the mother
To dance in good cheer

Excerpt from the *Song Greeting Dayfall*
Author Unknown

Lia knelt beside Ogmul, who lay on a bed of dead leaves under the shade of a naked tree. He glared at her with an atypical vacancy through his pain.

'Makes sense now why you'd want to come here so badly,' he said with some strain. '*Pretty and evil* as I thought.'

Lia frowned. 'How do you feel?'

'About how I look; crippled and broken. And fat.' He clutched at his ribs, which hid beneath a slightly meeker than usual belly. 'Look at this thing; filled to the brim with meat and marrow. I always brought home two meals after every hunt. Every damn time. Rabbits, tree rats, snakes; whatever was small enough to sneak under my linens and I gorged on it as a second breakfast. For every animal for the village, I'd take home one for my own fire and feast double, not even guilty for it. And now, I find out...what have I been eating this whole time? Dammit, I feel sick. *Who* have I been sneaking back through the walls to eat, to fatten this body of mine?'

Lia touched his arm. She had too much sympathy to be as appalled by his confession as she ought to be. Smaller portions for dayfall on his selfish account hardly seemed worth caring about now.

'It's what we prayed for,' was all she could think to say, half to see if the words bore more truth when spoken aloud. They didn't.

Ogmul scoffed, with a sound close to a sob. 'I'd pray for a lean body and a healthy head of hair, for all the good it would do me. Yet, we sing a song of nonsense, and we somehow get exactly what we ask for. What kind of mother is this?'

Lia had no response, no words of comfort. She could only allow her hand to find his. The gesture gave him enough cause to quieten down and eventually fall asleep.

Lia watched his worn face for a little while, distraught at the pain of a man she had always known as well hardened, yet pleased at the honesty of a man she had always known as stubbornly distant.

She eventually left him alone to his rest and to allow the herbs to take their effect.

The queen's court was laden with Hominum laying on their backs, injured or exhausted to varying extents. Some who had never held herbs now treated their kin, under the watch of Fanwei Zin Or.

Lin wondered whether Gal would have been proud of their unity or appalled at the *audacity*. Even Zanuus scarcely earned her trust in the craft, knowledgeable though he was.

He ran about now, from kin to kin, tirelessly and with unending urgency. Perhaps it was this type of zeal that inspired Gal to keep him under her tutelage, despite her relentless complaints.

Lia had to walk on before she fell too deeply into mourning with such thoughts. The rest of the court was quiet, but for the few creatures greeting the new day, who had not yet gone into hibernation.

Lia purposefully avoided the queen's throne, desiring nothing less than to think of her again. She vouched for distraction and explored her new home a little further.

The forest had become far more familiar in a very short time. Less of the bizarre glowing flowers and alien lights remained, replaced by comparatively dull plumage, to which she had long been accustomed. The new growth was touched by a new sun but was boring to behold. She sighed. *Boring,* she echoed, hearing Candy's voice rather than her own. *That stupid cat is still in my head, even now. I must let her be forgotten.*

Lia presently came upon another distraction; a subtle sound, which would be lost if the woods were not so quiet. She looked ahead beyond the trees and saw someone standing with their face in their hands. They were shaking.

'Omaraa,' Lia called out, recognising the long lock of grey hair on her back. Omaraa turned and faced Lia, with red eyes and streaks on her cheeks.

'Lia,' Omaraa said. 'I hoped to be alone here. I'm sorry that you would see me like this, child.'

Lia swallowed. 'What happened?'

Omaraa's tears still fell, though her voice was steady. She took a long while to respond.

She simply said; 'your brother is back in Crescat.'

Lia's relief was very short-lived, as her understanding of the weight of Omaraa's words brought about more anguish.

Kai made it back, but others didn't.

Lia's own tears began to fall. She fell into Omaraa's arms at her beckoning and they each wept on each other's shoulders into the quiet ether.

*

The queen walked through the familiar woods, once again, toward her court. She was seething, mostly at herself. To be pulled from her slumber so close to sunrise, for the smoothskin she had thought herself rid of, it was of her own doing.

She slumped onto her throne will all the energy of a half-dead flower. Sunrise was the time she despised the most for the energy it stole from her, but *this* one at the end of *this* nightfall was especially abhorrent. She hated how her home had changed so inversely from how she had envisioned it would.

She was greeted at her court by the insufferable chatter of the smoothskins tending to their infirm. Their stubbornness proved still to be a source of great irritation.

For this night, she had sacrificed. On this night, she had let her subjects bleed. On this night, she had been forced to embrace those she despised as though they were her own, in her own land. She was even forced now to share her citizens' food with them, on the strength of a baseless promise that they would help gather more for her kin while the sun was up.

Through the influence of this one nightfall, life was suddenly and wholly miserable. And as a confirmation of her torture not yet being done, she learned of the safe return of the small smoothskin. That he had survived at the cost of the demise of more of her subjects, as she had feared he would.

Her plan for the smoothskin to meet its death in Susuuri went unfulfilled, and her own kin were consequently taken from her. The one who was the arbitrator for these lamentations would soon be under her protection, feasting on her crops and guarded by her hyachin. And there was nothing at all to be done for it. The queen could only curse in her own bitter head at how cruelly the Mother willed her to be treated.

The queen looked to the skies, from where a lumen descended and landed on her shoulder. Its glow was dimming but its words were clear as ever.

The queen sighed. 'Fine,' she said. 'Now go and sleep.'

Her lumen flew off and carried out its order, as usual.

The queen waited, impatiently, for the creature to taint her caught. It wasn't long, as the boy was escorted at the heels of her vice and a party of lumen before her throne.

It looked utterly exhausted, covered in dirt and scratches. It carried the idiotic rabbit in his arms, who slept in undeserved peace.

'Was he harmed,' the queen said.

'No,' the vice started. 'He appears--'

'I was asking the boy.'

'No,' the boy said. 'He just fell asleep on our way here.'

'Then he's turned primitive already. The hyachin is weaker the further you are from this court. That's why my throne is here, under this colossal tree. The citizens furthest away from here change first when the sun rises. Most have had enough time to gather their food for hibernation before their change begins, but not the rabbit. Hence why I ordered him to stay in the court. Vice, take the rabbit to my burrow, and bring the smoothskin leader here.'

The vice shot the queen just the look of incredulity that she expected. 'Yes, queen,' it still said. 'Smoothskin, give me the rabbit.'

The bot laid the rabbit on the vice's back, who took him off into the trees. The queen was aware of the spite it would cause if her kin were to discover that *this* rabbit would be permitted to hibernate so close to her court. She disliked the notion that his disobedience would be rewarded, but there was little choice. No citizen could reach the rabbit's burrow now without turning primitive themselves.

'He helped me many times,' the boy said. 'I owe him a lot.'

'He helped you to his own detriment,' the queen hissed. 'Meaning his help only brought harm to himself. And his kin. Are you grateful for that too?'

'You could have stopped him.'

The queen's eyes narrowed, taken aback by the boy's sudden belligerence. 'Explain.'

He didn't hesitate. 'You have the lumen. You would have known that he left for Susuuri. You could have stopped him, but you didn't. If you wanted to keep him safe, you should have done so. But since you didn't, I think you just let him go, hoping that he would be hurt and not be able to get home. You abandoned him.'

The queen felt blood rise to her head. She grew dizzy with anger. 'You disgusting creature,' she retched out, jumping down from her throne. 'After all that you've done to your kin through your own stupidity, you dare to question *my* loyalty to my own? You dare call into question *my* actions?'

The boy appeared unphased. 'You sent me for the same reason,' he said. 'You sent me to die.'

'I gladly did, for my kin. And I would do it a thousand times, for my kin.' She didn't realise she was shouting until all the words had left her lips. The boy stood undaunted, even face to face with her. She grew even more incensed at his audacity.

'The rabbit risked his own life for me,' he said. 'And he abandoned me for his kin, even though he knew they hated him. You risked nothing but the lives of others. You just sat under that tree on that throne and told others to live or die instead.'

The queen glared dead into the boy's eyes with all the unbridled outrage she could muster. Yet, she had no words to respond with. She was, for the very first time, speechless. He looked back at her, utterly unmoved and without a hint of the fear he had the right to.

'My queen?' It was her vice's voice the broke the silence. He walked back into the court with the smoothskin leader, the one they called Houli, and the foul-mouthed smoothskin girl.

They too looked tired and skinnier than the queen remembered. She swallowed down her anger for the moment and went back to her throne to observe.

'Kai,' the leader said, with no hint of composure.

The boy didn't respond, locked as he was into the eyes of the girl; his *sister*. The queen admittedly watched this moment unfold with some interest. She wanted to see the conclusion to all the madness this nightfall with her own eyes.

They approached each other until they were standing face to face, trapped in a fleeting state of inaction.

They reached out to each other with open arms and held each other.

And then they fought. They threw fists and strangled each other, with tears falling onto their skin and roared without restraint.

The other smoothskins pulled them apart. They sobbed loudly and proudly at the centre of the queen's court, as their kin watched with wide eyes.

The queen looked on from her throne, with profound surprise that was foreign to her.

54

...the spilling of my kin's blood, the nature of the creatures who hunt in these lands; all these are memories I am blessed to have shrouded by darkness. But the sounds of their screams and lamentations, the smell of that spilt blood; those memories are vivid and shall never leave me.

Despite the lost freedom marked by our return to this place, I am grateful to be back where I will forever and happily call home. My whole life, I was bound by dark walls and was bade to wander lost within them. Now, I am joyfully bound by walls lovingly built by my kin's hands.

Excerpt from *Memoirs of Mora the Blind*
by Moro Ki
Generation of Osas
Second Recorded Generation

The hard and relentless downpour patted Susuuri's ground and the queen's body lying bloodied upon it. Her stomach had spilled out and her fur had been torn from her flesh.

The queen's cub looked upon her with disdain for the state she was now in. Her subjects were gathered around her and feasting on her. Wolves, monkeys, spiders, snakes; they all ate a small piece from the small corpse of their former ruler, even while her blood was still warm.

The cat looked on from high in the trees. My mother was killed, *she knew.* Everyone knows it. No one is stupid enough to think otherwise. And they all eat through the claw marks that killed her without hesitation because they're too stupid to care about mutiny. They did not even care to shed tears first. This is how Susuuri cares for its rulers. Mother was stupid to lead these fools for so long.

The cat almost retched for the stench of blood through the rain.

A wolf tore itself away from the queen's body and saw the cat in the trees, finally detecting her scent. Its eyes glowed in a dim red in Susuuri's shadows.

'Join us, kin,' it said, uninspired and without zeal. Its voice was plain and boring, like flavourless fruit. Others followed its gaze and waited expectantly.

The cat said nothing, unable to even voice her disdain for such an insult. You would have me eat my own mother, out of pointless tradition, before her killer has even been found. And you would call me kin while you do so. You vile creatures.

Her scorn must have been manifested through her gaze, as the citizens meekly returned to their feast without retort.

The cat fled to seek her usual comfort in solitude. She found a familiar patch. It was a place left mostly untouched and had long been overgrown by weeds and thorns. It was a fine place for hiding.

She laid beneath the tree's shelter and watched the downpour grow ever wilder.

My mother just died, *she reflected.* Yet I feel so little for her. I hardly care for her absence, yet I'm angry about how she is treated in death. This stupid place and its stupid customs have gotten to me, not permitting me even to grieve.

The cat lamented, for as long as she cared to, until she found a feeble escape in shallow dormancy.

Her dreams were even more bizarre and unfathomable than usual. She dreamt up songs about ridiculous longings for foreign lands. Before her were smoothskins melting away with the fire she spewed from her mouth and far-reaching trees set ablaze. She felt the heat of the fire against her ash ridden fur at the dream's conclusion and woke up short of breath.

She woke with the wind in her face and her feet off the ground. She hung from the teeth of a citizen, probably a wolf by how fast it ran and the agility with which it navigated the trees.

She sighed, annoyed by Susuuri's endless predictableness. This was expected, but this was so soon. Susuuri cannot stand to be without a ruler, even for so short a time. So weak.

'You need not carry me, you know,' the cat said. 'I'll follow you if you put me down. Promise.'

The wolf just grunted between its teeth in response. It ran on until they reached Susuuri's darkest patch; an opening surrounded by trimmed bushes and vines hanging from huge trees.

The cat's heart sank at the sight of it. She never came to this place if she could possibly avoid it. It was a place that perfectly encapsulated every aspect of her home which she despised. It enhanced her kin's stupidity without their knowing. She intended for this to be the very last time she saw this court, the place where her mother would sit every cycle.

Her kin watched her approach in the wolf's teeth, some with blood still on their mouths. She was sat before her kin, on the pile of stones they insisted on calling a throne.

The vice bowed its head to the cat, and the others silently followed. The cat was sickened already.

'My kin,' the vice said. 'I offer my deepest condolences for--'

'I refuse,' the cat said. The silence in the confusion that followed was pleasant to her ears. She smiled. 'I refuse this throne. I refuse this court. I refuse to lead you. I refuse to acknowledge you as my subjects. I refuse.'

The silence grew more satisfying. It marked the creatures' unexpected exodus from routine and tradition and predictably left them dumbfounded.

The vice slowly stepped toward her throne, until he looked up at her from her paws. 'You may not,' he said. 'The throne isn't so easily and carelessly denied, my queen.'

'It's not?' The cat smiled again. 'So, what's the point of being queen if I don't get to make the rules?'

The vice groaned, clearly not as disenchanted as his peers were. 'To guide your subjects,' he said. 'Susuuri needs a fine ruler to set it on a fine course. One not afraid of change, but one who also won't discard our roots.'

Her smile was wiped from her face. 'A fine ruler,' she echoed.

'Indeed,' the vice said. 'You'll make a fine ruler with your temperament. You're smart, cunning and unafraid to stand by your convictions in the face of scrutiny. You'll bring Susuuri the prosperity it deserves, with my guidance and some time.'

The cat glared at the tortoise before her with new intent. Susuuri needs a fine ruler, she echoed again in her mind. You've said this loudly and often, tortoise, and never in my mother's company. It may have been *you*. You would have my mother killed if you felt such a change necessary enough.

The court was silent once more, awaiting their new queen's retort. She said *nothing for a time, thoughtfully looking down at the vice of ancient times and learning from the core of his words.*

If you are willing to go so far for your own ideals…

The cat jumped down from the throne and faced the tortoise closely. He did not flinch.

'Fine,' the cat said. 'I accept the throne. Am I your queen now?'

The tortoise somehow looked surprised with his old and haggard face. 'Yes,' *he said, with some composure.* 'Yes, my queen. The throne is yours. Susuuri is yours and its citizens are yours to guide. Susuuri's shadows are yours to know and the tebirii's voices are for your ears alone. May the Mother bless you with a long reign.'

He bowed his treacherous head once more and his foolish peers did the same.

'Good,' the cat said. 'In that case, I order you to take this throne, and to rule in my stead.'

The reaction from the court was glorious. Her kin looked utterly lost and incredulous, using all their willpower to keep their silence.

'I was your queen for so short a time,' *the cat couldn't help but say.* 'It can't be that hard to lose your new queen already. Your mourning for the last one was so short-lived, after all.'

'My queen,' *the tortoise said.* 'This can't stand. A cat has sat on the throne since our inception. For me to dare to sit upon it, such a thing is unprecedented.'

The cat smiled again. She had an ear for the depth in one's voice and the truth behind their manner. Even in the tired voice of the tortoise, there were a great many layers to peel away and truths to learn, for those who bothered to listen.

You speak words you know you must say, without meaning any of them. You hide joy behind incredulity. Now I know, it *was* you who killed my mother. You must have wished more than anything that I would reject the throne, or you would have had me killed too, to leave the throne truly unclaimed.

'It's not unprecedented anymore,' *she said.* 'Because it just happened. May the Mother bless you with a long, long reign, my king.'

She left the court behind, in much higher spirits. Change, *she rejoiced.* Finally, some change. *And it was a change with the sweetest flavour, full of branching possibilities.*

Yet, as ever, no one else had the eyes to see it. All her foolish kin were good for was adherence. There was discontentment in every shadow of her home, yet no one with the heart to change the slow deaths they called their lives.

I'll show them, *she swore.* They'll have no choice but to see how pathetic they are.

She saw a selfish and hate-filled king's rule ahead, brought to an untimely end along with his ideals. Then the blindness of her kin would surely die with it too. Freedom *was what the cat longed for. Freedom for all she set her eyes on. Freedom from the monotonous and fragile order set by her own blood, who sat on that wretched throne.*

She longed for the end of the Susuuri she had always known.
And life had seen fit to gift her this one chance.

*

Candy dragged her paws as far as they would take her, slowly and with great strain. The sun felt hot on her back and sapped her of any strength she had left.

She had surely explored this part of the forest long ago but had probably not found anything worth remembering, since she had not bothered to return since.

This time around was the same, yet different. There were more trees with new growth, more rivers to tread, more dirt to cling to her fur. Yet, her journey this time was truly purposeless, with no expectation of what lay along the way, nor of what lay at the end. It was terrible and wonderful.

She fell onto her belly, lacking the strength to stay standing any longer. Her eyes were set on what must have been the end of the forest, beyond the last cluster of trees where she crawled.

All that kept her moving onward was pure will and the threat of peril. She was certain only that she could not be in this forest when her kin's hibernation ended.

An enemy of Crescat. An enemy of Susuuri. An enemy of the Hominum. This was no home for her anymore. *All of my own doing,* she reflected. *And I'm glad for it. Good riddance.*

She had long expected that her people would be rid of the absurd cycle of subjection to fear and fragile comfort and that she would be outcast for it. Yet, she had not expected this feeling to come of it. She felt free and only realised now how bounded she had been.

She finally left the last of Susuuri's trees behind her and crawled across the forest's border into a field of green and yellow, as far as her eyes could see.

The sun smiled on the horizon, with ghastly yellow teeth and orange ripples emanating from its body. The flowers danced to the song of its waking.

Candy's nightfall ended in exhaustion by the Mother's hand, yet joy in the fate she had laid out solely as her own.

There, she laid her head down. And she slept.

55

...and do not fear failure. Our predecessors failed many a time and still we remain. Be afraid only of failing without your knowledge.

Aileen the Kind said that one who is defined by perseverance will one day be defined by wisdom.

We are another link in a chain of perseverance and learning. We live so that our descendants will be wiser than us and those who preceded us.

Mayara Zan Fa
Generation of Mayara the Bold
Seventh Recorded Generation

Kai took another bite from the bizarre flower-like fruit in his hands. The hair on its flesh stroked his cheeks with each bite. Kai knew it to be the *polood* Citizen spoke so fondly of. It was actually quite dull tasting. He expected intense sweetness to erupt onto his tongue, as Citizen had described, but it never came. It was ultimately disappointing compared to the other fruits he had been treated to this nightfall. He chose to believe that he would taste the polood at its fullest the next nightfall when the hyachin was at its strongest again.

'Kai,' someone said. Kai ate in peace and quiet, until just then. He was now grateful to hear a voice, as he had suffered silence for long enough already.

He looked up at Omaraa Zan. She was puffy-eyed and uneasy on her legs. She walked to him through the trees like a woman double her age.

'I really am sorry,' she said.

'For what,' Kai asked between mouthfuls.

'For all that you have been through. It is not right for anyone to have gone through what you have, particularly someone so young. I should have done more to help you. I was insensitive to you on the day you left us, and I was foolish to underestimate your resolve. I'm sorry for failing you again, Kai.'

'You warned me not to leave,' Kai said. 'Everything that happened here was because I ignored you and all the elders. And now, I'm the reason that Poruus Zin and the hunters are dead. I'm the one who failed the tribe.'

Omaraa Zan appeared startled at his words. She took hold of his hands. 'Kai, you mustn't--'

'Please can I go out with the hunters at dayfall,' Kai quickly said.

It gave Omaraa Zan some pause. 'To Susurii? Why?'

'I want to help bring Poruus Zin and the others home to be burned. I know where they are, so I can help.'

'There's no need, Kai. The queen has already told us where to find their bodies.'

Kai looked down at his hands. The polood juices seeped through his fingers like blood. 'Please.'

Omaraa Zan didn't respond. She only nodded and let go of his hands. She slowly lowered herself to sit beside him, as he finished his polood and water.

'Are you angry at Lia,' she asked, after Kai's final mouthful.

'No.'

'Why not?'

That made him look up at her. It was so random that he didn't understand the question at first.

He thought for a moment. 'I did the same thing she did,' he said. 'I went to the forest too.'

Omaraa Zan softly touched his shoulder. 'Is that why you attacked her. Because you were angry at yourself?'

He didn't need to think about it this time. The chill he felt in his gut at her words was confirmation enough. He nodded.

'And you're confused that you reacted that way, aren't you? That you both did?'

He nodded.

'Can I tell you something, Kai? Just between us.'

He nodded, with a little more enthusiasm.

'I realised something this nightfall. We elders have rarely ever been tested. The generations before us built such a strict order that we needed only to follow their guidance and be a listening ear when needed. But we were called to action for the first time and, for the most part, I did not know what to do.

'I leaned heavily on the other elders to advise me, and especially Poruus Zin. He was *so* wise, Kai. And sensitive to those around him. Each time I felt like the burden of leadership was too much for me, he would help me carry it. Many of us died in that attack, yes. But, that any of us are alive now is thanks to his wisdom and his willingness to act when called upon.

'And now, he is gone. In this unprecedented time of change and uncertainty, we have lost him when he is needed the most. Perhaps I should be scared, but I am not. I have resolved to learn from his wisdom to keep on shepherding our kin, the best that I can. I have seen that sharing a burden means more than just asking for help. It means learning from the aid which you are given so that you can aid others in the same way.'

Kai nodded. The lesson hit him hard and firmly. 'I'll go and see her.'

Omaraa Zan gave him the warmest smile she could muster.

It was the first Hominum smile Kai had seen since nightfall began.

*

Zanuus sat against a tree with a closed purpura over his head.

Lia had found him in this broken state, and they had barely shared a word since. She waited for him to do something; to cry, to shout, to scream. Anything. But he just quietly stared at the half-eaten fruit by his feet.

Lia too had been distraught, of course, at Poruus Zin and the hunters' deaths. But she was not surprised. Her joy at Poruus Zin blackmailing the queen had blinded her to the reality of his proposal, but it soon became clear to her that he himself had been prepared for this outcome.

We would perish with him. That had been his answer when the queen questioned his resolve. Hindsight afforded Lia perspective, and she now regarded those words as an admission of his intentions.

To go into Susuuri, barely armed and knowing the citizens awaited his arrival, he could not have seen any other outcome but his death. He knew he was to die for a chance to bring Kai back and did so willingly.

That logic was how she planned to lessen the guilt her brother would surely be suffering. She bit her lip at the thought of him. *I'm such an idiot. What madness possessed me to attack him like that, after so long?*

But for Zanuus, she could not find any words worth saying. She had wisdom enough to listen more than she spoke.

'First Gal, now father,' Zanuus finally said. 'And so quickly, in so short a time. I don't think I've realised that they're gone yet.' He rubbed his head with his hands. 'They died for us. For the Hominum. Isn't that right?'

Lia nodded, not yet brave enough for words.

'But they shouldn't have had to,' Zanuus said. 'Why should they have died just so that the rest of us could live? Why should father have died so that Kai could live?'

Lia was taken aback by the shift in his tone. She breathed deeply before she responded. 'They shouldn't have,' she said, as softly as she could. 'But my brother isn't to blame.'

'I know that. Those *citizens* in Susuuri are to blame. It's *them* I hate. And now we must share the same forest with the creatures that killed them. I can't stand it.'

Lia couldn't stop herself before the words came falling out. 'Then *that's* why our kin have died.'

The words were not as harsh on her lips as she had feared they would be, and she surprised even herself with their soundness.

It gave Zanuus pause before he spoke again. 'That's like something father would say. Probably. I don't know. Maybe you're right. But I can't promise that I won't hate them after this, no matter what my father or anyone else would say.'

Lia nodded again, with sincere empathy. 'Not for a long time.'

Zanuus almost smiled. 'I admire your optimism,' he said. He stood and patted down his dirty breeches. 'I should head back. I guess I'm the tribe's chief herbalist now.'

'They would understand if you need time.'

'Gal would have disagreed. And I'd rather not have to *imagine* her moaning in my head, or I might just go insane.'

Zanuus left Lia sitting under the tree in admiration and contemplation. She admired Zanuus apparent new strength of mind, but she was also sad for it. Sad for his growth and her own, born out of necessity more than desire.

She had not cried at the news of her kin's death, nor even had Zanuus cried for his own father. Lia was yet to cry for Gal Ne, and the guilt she felt for Miire Zin was becoming a distant memory.

Death had long been paired with a sense of comfort to keep the Hominum's grief from overwhelming them. But, even with that comfort being stripped away and their concept of death being shattered, Lia kept her grief at bay with little effort.

Now that the future was filled with more uncertainty than the past ever had been, Lia feared for the growth that would undoubtedly be forced upon her and her kin in the times ahead.

*

Sweet solitude. The queen curled up tightly, embracing herself in her dark place of resting. *Finally, sweet silence.*

Her burrow donned the same aroma it did every sunrise, that of staling fruits and morning air.

Hibernation was what she called it, so as not to cause discontentment among her kin for hiding away in their most vulnerable state, while Susuuri tainted their land and its creatures sought them out. She happily sought out her hiding place, each and every sunrise, as a reward for her endless diligence at night. Crescat itself cared for her kin while the sun was up and did so well.

But she felt the times changing and felt that blissful routine being torn away from her. Those smoothskins were to be their new guardians by day, and she could not be more miserable for it. Perhaps they would prove more effective hunters and guardians in dayfall than in nightfall, or perhaps the events in this wretched nightfall only postponed their inevitable extinction. But oppression awaited the queen and her kin, whatever the outcome, by whoever proved themselves strongest. This was unprecedented, even with the Ameyali Forest's history of conflict.

I, the queen, allowed my land to be oppressed. I let my kin be bullied by inferior creatures who killed us at dayfall and let them even feast on the food in my land. Disgusting.

She could not stop reflecting on that little smoothskin's words, and they sickened her. *You just sit under that tree and tell others to die.* It sickened her mostly because she could not deny it. It defined her entire rule. She was powerless but for her wit; the same wit that had now led her kin into unparalleled disaster.

And yet, there was no alternative but to dance to the cruel song the Mother played to them. Her kin were bound to their oppressors by blood,

300

and life could not be worse for it.

It won't be forever, the queen affirmed, as she closed her eyes for her long slumber. *All this pain won't be forever.*

One day, we'll be prey to no one.

One day...

56

The pursuit of a dream births a great healing of dire wounds.
The realisation of a dream births a great wound in dire need of healing.
The absence of a dream births a great wound with the false face of a great healing.

Excerpt from The *Hominum Tribe Rebirth*
by Omaraa Zin Fa
Generation of Omaraa the Wise
Eighth Recorded Generation

It was finally dayfall. Pale morning light paved the queen's court in broken pieces. The pods on the trees were limp and a dull blend of green and purple. Birds sang songs of greeting to the Mother and were all that kept the court from deathly silence.

Lia was absorbed in momentary peace, staring at the queen's empty throne in empty contemplation. It was seamless and modest, integrated naturally into the crevice at the base of the immense tree. She thought it a bizarre concept for a shepherd's seat to hold any significance. To mark a natural place as one's own and to declare it a symbol of authority; it reeked of arrogance to her.

This whole court emitted an unnerving ambience alien to Lia. She thought of the labour of the citizens who kept the foliage trimmed and uniform, which would soon become overgrown and unkempt again anyway. She remembered how the birds drank the Hominum's' vomit, probably to keep the queen's court pristine. It was the same court they were now away from for their hibernation. She could not fathom the point of it all.

It all seemed such a waste of effort for a place that the Mother would inevitably blemish, again and again.

*

Kai walked toward the queen's court, feeling utterly restless. He couldn't put Citizen out of his head, now that his hibernation had begun. Citizen had been so proud of his burrow and the experience of their shred meal had been so memorable. Kai had no doubt he could find it again when he needed to. But he did not know where the queen's burrow was, where Citizen now hibernated.

Kai so badly wanted to enjoy his company again. He wanted to see his burrow and care for him after his change. But even if he could find him, it would be impossible with the elders' instruction to stay within the queen's court and surrounding woods. Kai resigned to waiting until the next nightfall to see his friend again.

But what he *wanted* more than anything was to enjoy *Lia's* company again. He had just not found the opportunity yet. It had only been a couple of cycles since they met again, and he had opted to wait until they were together naturally, rather than seeking her out.

Kai saw how hard Lia worked here, how she cared for the infirm and how she talked to those who were downhearted. He was happy she had been working so diligently and did not wish to deprive her of that on account of his own desires. He found himself chasing Lia's shadow again, ever as his aspiration yet never seeming within reach.

Kai entered the court again. It was quiet and quite the lonely place at dayfall. The throne was far less imposing without the queen on it and it was now a mere structure at the foot of the colossal tree.

Lia sat before it, alone. Kai's heart inexplicably raced at the sight of her again, and he *hated* it. This sensation was once only reserved for those he disliked, and for the elders during their hearings. He had preferred it that way. But this sensation was now unprejudiced and made no sense to him anymore.

He walked toward her despite it, his body refusing to bow to the hesitancy in his heart.

*

Lia heard Kai approach. She knew it was him before she saw him. No one else would approach her with such trepid steps, as though they were trying to go unnoticed. No one else had cause to treat her with such caution anymore.

This dynamic should have had no place between them. She had failed her brother by assuming everything would be as it was before the last nightfall. Or, perhaps she knew there would be changes but did not want to consider the nature of them. Either lack of discernment was a failure on her part.

Kai sat beside her. They both watched the same throne, hardly acknowledging each other. The quiet was not awkward, nor did it need breaking. It was a tone of silence unique to them, that they had embraced many a time, often while wrapped in their bedsheets.

The silence merely showed that there was nothing that needed to be said. Lia was glad to hear it again. *We still understand this, at least.*

Kai rested his head on Lia's shoulder. Lia rested her head on his. They were content with the silence lingering for a while longer.

*

Kai and Lia sat for a long while and were content to stay. Kai did not expect to be so glad to hear silence again. But he relished this time spent embracing it.

Yet, after this blissful passing moment, he was ultimately moved to break it.

'*And we will then fall in the waves of the seas,*' he said.

He could feel Lia raise her eyebrow. 'Fall in the waves of the seas,' she echoed.

'That could be the--'

'That's a terrible ending,' she said. 'Absolutely dreadful.'

'Why?'

'First of all, you've never seen the sea and you probably never will. So how would you know what falling in the sea would be like?'

'We've read about it, so we can just imagine what it's like. It's cold and strong, so it would make us feel weak if we fell in.'

'Okay, so now the song is saying that us falling in the waves of the sea and feeling weak would make snowflakes, ashes and reeds grow strong. It makes no sense. You just wanted something to rhyme with *pleas*, didn't you?'

Kai grinned. 'Can you think of something better?'

'I can because *anything* would be better than that.'

'Like what then?'

'Like anything,' Lia laughed. 'We should just do the whole song again, and have it make sense this time.'

Kai smiled and nodded. He was admittedly excited at the prospect.

He wondered what manner of new song the events of last nightfall would inspire them to create.

*

Lia enjoyed talking so freely. It was like all her worries had faded away and her anxieties were as simple as they once were. But she could not long ignore that which still hung heavy on her heart and what she longed to share with someone. The talk of songs only brought the anxiety back to the surface.

'So, did Omaraa tell you,' she asked, after an appropriate silence. 'About what happens to us after we die?'

'Yeah,' Kai said. 'She did.'

'Yeah,' Lia echoed, quite bewildered by his nonchalance. She waited patiently for him to elaborate.

He eventually did. 'Isn't it amazing?'

Lia was almost too surprised to speak. '*Amazing?* What do you mean amazing?'

Kai appeared surprised by her surprise. 'It means that we have two lives, right? And it means we can see each other again, even after we die. Why would that not be amazing?'

Lia scoffed. 'Do you realise what else it means? Whenever we've had meat for dinner, do you realise what we were doing? What Mother Earth had us doing without us knowing?'

'We were eating our dead. The citizens do the same thing to each other after they die.'

'But we *kill* them first. We were hunting our own kin, to feed our own kin. Don't you think that's cruel?'

'But we won't be killing them anymore. And we'll be living here now, so the citizens might want us to keep eating the dead like they do. That's the least we could do if they ask us. I don't think I'll mind.'

Lia frowned. She was as fascinated as she was dumbfounded by Kai's perspective. It was beyond what she would have expected him capable of. And he was right in some ways, Lia had to confess. She knew it unlikely that the taste of meat would ever become foreign, but she could not relinquish the contempt for that fact so easily.

'I don't like that we're being used,' she said, finally speaking with all the unaltered honesty she was able. 'I don't like that the Mother uses our lives however she wants to and that we're in her hands when we die. No matter what customs the citizens have, it's cruel. *She's* cruel, to not even let us die in peace.

'I don't want to pray to a mother like that anymore. I won't concern myself over her, or praise her, or thank her. She doesn't need me to do anything like that if she'll still use me after I die regardless.'

Kai looked Lia in the eyes as she spoke and hardly breathed as he listened. 'I think I understand,' he said. 'I don't know what I'll do yet. But I think maybe it's okay to have a second life.'

Lia sighed. 'We won't know each other in our second life. We probably won't even be related. We wouldn't know each other if we ever met again.'

'But we'll be alive. And we'll have been related in *this* life, at least. No matter what happens in the next one.'

Lia had to pause. Then she had to smile. 'You're right about that, at least.' She could barely recognise this brother of hers anymore. This, she now realised, was the biggest change she had failed to anticipate. *Can I even call you Orphan-Star anymore?*

'Also,' Kai said. 'It means I can meet father. And we can see mother again. And everyone else. Maybe we've seen some of them already and just didn't know it.'

Lia furrowed her brow, though still smiling. 'Why would you *ever* want to meet mother again?'

Kai thought for a while. 'I don't really know,' he eventually said. 'But I still would.'

Lia laughed, heartily and as honestly as she ever had.

'Me too,' she admitted, more to herself than to Kai. She herself understood her own reasons well enough. She would have wanted to show Sian Ro how she and Kai had survived and grown without her cruel influence. To show that even in the absence of her love and the absence of their tribe's help in their greatest time of need, they still grew strong enough to survive on their own, and brave enough to live life honest to their desires.

Lia Ro sat by her brother's side for a while longer, holding him in her arms before the empty throne. She felt a warm new sun on her skin again after her very longest night.

The burden of an uncertain dayfall was before them both, with many more beyond it. A day with no place to call home, no fantastical places to yearn for, and no unfulfilled dreams to chase.

Lia and Kai Ro felt, for the very first time, the bliss and pain of serenity.

And they each lamented the lost days when such bliss was their greatest adversary.

www.alexander-linton.com

Printed in Great Britain
by Amazon

19097401R00180